ROUGH & READY
COUNTRY

ROUGH & READY COUNTRY

BOOKS 13-15

COWBOY MOUNTAIN MAN / CURVY GIRL ROMANCES

ENGRID EAVES

JOIN THE ENGRID EAVES COMMUNITY!

ALPHA-**EMOTIONAL HEROES.**
HEADSTRONG, **CURVY GIRLS.**
SAVAGE ROMANCE.

GIVEAWAYS. FREEBIES.
NEW RELEASES. LATEST NEWS.

Subscribe to my newsletter today to never miss out on a
new steamy, small-town read.
SIGN UP FOR MY NEWSLETTER

LOVE AT FIRST SECRET

A COWBOY MOUNTAIN MAN / CURVY GIRL ROMANCE

TRIGGER WARNING

This book contains content/themes that may not be suitable for all readers, including discussion of human trafficking, brief descriptions of physical violence, and mention of childhood sexual abuse (off-page, non-graphic).

Please read at your own discretion.

PROLOGUE

h God, this is going to be so much tougher than I anticipated...

> Couldn't stop thinking about you all day.
> How are you, Tiger?

I take a deep breath, pushing thoughts of Axel St. Claire's perfection from my mind and failing ... *miserably*.

From his towering height of six foot three and his thick chestnut locks and full, well-trimmed beard to his kind, though rugged face, large indigo eyes, adorable smile with dimples, straight, proportionate nose, and irresistibly kissable lips... What's not to love?

Shit, I'm in over my head.

Even worse, he makes me feel safe and secure. Big, muscular build, rough, work-hardened hands, possessive, manly attitude, sexy as hell voice... And a gentle, caring energy that could forgive almost anything. *Almost*.

ASPEN

I'm fine. And you?

AXEL

Good. Busy with the latest batches of brews. These are shaping up to be as good as the last. I can't wait to give you the full tour and show you my facility. There are definitely taste testings of more than one kind in your future 💀

The last comment is my fault. All my fault.

I let things go too far during our last FaceTime call, and now Axel's the throb between my legs, too. Along with the kryptonite to my entrepreneurial, don't-need-a-man vibe. Time to rip off the Band-Aid before this gets any harder.

I flip back through our flirtatious-turned-downright smexy texts in recent days, fanning myself. Damn, this man can dirty-talk.

I'm not a relationship kind of girl, and I know this. But every couple of years, I get lonely and try another online dating site. I don't even know what I'm looking for at this point.

Mountain Mates, a site for women seeking sexy mountain men, appeared during my last lonely episode. Call it dangerous curiosity... Or an itch only an uber-masculine, rugged guy can scratch. Either way, the site introduced me to something I never saw coming: a man who could destroy me.

ASPEN

About coming to visit you. I'm no longer feeling it

AXEL

...

I stare at the three blinking dots for a long, tense moment. Suddenly, my phone vibrates. Looking at the number, I see it's from Axel.

How in the world will I have the strength to stick to my guns when I hear his deep, growly voice again?

"Hello, Axel."

"What's wrong?" His voice is rich, dark, and a little dejected.

"Nothing's wrong. I just ... I've had time to think, and although this has been fun and all, we should cut our losses before it goes any further, and we get any more invested."

Silence.

"Aren't you going to say anything?"

"I'm listening," he says gruffly.

I take a deep breath, racking my brain for more logical reasons we should never meet, even as my heart pitches a mutiny in my chest. "It's like I said when we first started talking. A SoCal gal who loves her big-city amenities and a Sierra Nevada mountain man really don't mix."

"We're like oil and water. But that's how you make a beautiful rainbow."

"Axel ..." I can't find the right words because I'm torn inside. I don't want to do this, but it's the only way. "We have different aspirations and goals in life, and we want different things from the world."

"No, we don't. Not in any unnavigable way, at least. You want to dominate the wedding planning ecosystem, and I want to top the craft beer market and own high-end West Coast gastropubs. Yes, we're different, but our ambitions complement each other."

"I don't want to live in a small town, and you don't want to live in a big city—"

"I don't want to live in Southern California," he clarifies.

"Well, I'm happy with my life and my place in the world, and I don't want things to change."

"What's got you so scared all of a sudden? Have I asked you to change? Or started making future plans? We kind of have to meet in person and go on a first date before all of that, don't you think?"

His points are sound, but I can't let them soften my resolve. Not since learning there are things about my past he could never be okay with. A man who can't forgive his mother for abandoning him as a boy and a former teen mom who gave her baby up for adoption? I can't think of a more ironic or lamentable mix. I also can't bring myself to tell him the truth and face his judgment. I care for him enough that his opinion matters to me. Better to leave things where they are, keep them from getting unnecessarily ugly.

Axel's voice cuts through my thoughts. "I know you're nervous about finally meeting, and I am, too. But it's going to be fucking amazing. The best time of your life. I promise."

I close my eyes, gathering my thoughts. "I'm sorry. This is not working for me anymore. I apologize for wasting your time, and I wish you the best in life."

"Seriously?" He chuckles deep in his throat like he can't quite believe what I'm saying.

Lowering my voice and lying back on my pristine white couch facing massive floor-to-ceiling condo windows overlooking the Pacific Ocean, I reply resolutely. "Yes, I'm serious. Are you going to be okay?"

"Yeah, sure." The nonchalant way he delivers the last answer stings more than it should. I sit up.

"Is it because I started asking too many questions?

Digging too deeply into your past?" His voice sounds raw, and it makes my heart throb.

"Look, we were both a little tipsy over the phone the last time we talked. We both pushed boundaries and asked more questions than we should have. Obviously, you have secrets you don't feel comfortable sharing with me, and I do, too. So, maybe things are better left this way."

He growls low in his throat, something I've noticed he does while in deep thought. "The secret part you're right about. But is it really so bad to have pasts we'd rather not revisit?"

Yes, it is. Because my past would come out at some point, somehow. And it would devastate me to see how it would change the way you look at me, how you feel about me.

That's what I want to say. It's what I need to say, but I can't find the courage.

Axel continues, "As for the rest of it, I personally enjoyed the boundaries we pushed. It was sexy as fuck." He refers to the sexting that turned into FaceTiming and a sweltering round of live-streamed mutual masturbation that still makes my cheeks glow. As if to prove his point, the phone rings with his FaceTime invitation. But I'm not falling for this twice.

"No, Axel, I don't want to FaceTime. I'm sorry to disappoint you. But our goals don't align, our lifestyles don't mesh, and I don't want this to get any more complicated. Besides, what successful, healthy relationship starts with two people unwilling to share their deepest, darkest secrets?"

"I knew that was it." He groans. "Fuck."

I purse my lips together, listening to him mutter under his breath and not feeling sorry for him. After all, leveling with me would be the obvious answer to our current dilemma. But then again, I could say the same thing to myself.

"Some things are better left buried. You can't let my past ruin our future."

"How could your past ruin our future? You won't even tell me about it," I reply in gentle, though firm, tones.

"The same's true for you…" The phone goes silent for so long I have to look at the screen to ensure he's still there. "Alright, then, nice talking to you or whatever polite bull-shit people say. Thanks for avoiding the whole 'it's not you, it's me.' That would've been … unpleasant as fuck. Have a good life."

He ends the call, and I breathe a sigh of relief that turns into a hitch in my throat and an unexpected, wrenching sob. Tears swirl as I quickly block his number. No good will come from future communication. *But why in the heck am I feeling so emotional?*

I glance around my coastal condominium, all white walls, minimal decor, gray and chrome accents, and pops of jewel-toned color—purple, electric blue, and emerald green. Could I really imagine giving this up for a rugged mountain man?

No, I can't. But for Axel St. Claire? Realization tightens my chest and thickens my throat. It doesn't help the steady flood of warm saltwater that moistens my cheeks or how I breathe like I'm having a panic attack. This is for the best. The way it has to be.

And yes, it did have something to do with what he said in our last conversation. Axel's words shuttle back through my mind like a freight train, laying waste to my emotions. *What kind of woman abandons her own flesh and blood? I could never respect or forgive her.*

The comments were directed at his mother. But he shut down when I pressed him for details, growing frustratingly reticent. I desperately needed clarification to better understand precisely how she abandoned him because there's a high likelihood I am *just like her*.

Burying my head in my hands, I give into the ancient pain, sobbing. I usually only allow myself to grieve this way once a year on my son's birthday. He's eight now, and his adopted mother has stayed in touch with me, keeping her word about sending me a card with a photo every year on his birthday.

I can't imagine the look on Axel's face if I ever told him the truth about the baby I had at seventeen and gave up for adoption.

My mind wanders back to the hospital and the smells of cleaning supplies as busy nurses bustled around my bed after my son, Luca's birth. For one moment, I allow myself to savor the memory of him pressed against my chest, his large, dark blue eyes scrutinizing my face closely, the picture of wonder and newness.

At that moment, I would have given up everything for him, throwing caution and logic to the wind and braving it as a single mom in a world that can be so uncaring. But before I could turn thought into action, his adopted parents came, spiriting him away.

It was the moment I sacrificed my heart for a better future, not only for myself, but also for Luca. I could never give him the life his adopted family has. And for me, it secured everything. A sure future that didn't involve getting disinherited by my father or having to deal with the baby's biological father, who remains the last man I ever want to see again.

It was the moment I grew up and quit dreaming about

the impossible ... about soft-hearted fantasies and things that can never, ever be, no matter how much I want them. Like Axel St. Claire.

CHAPTER
ONE

ASPEN

ONE MONTH LATER

"Thank you so much for meeting me," Stella says with pleading blue eyes as I find her at the Sunrise Cafe in Newport Beach and take a seat.

"Of course," I reply, reaching across the table to grip her hand. "The moment you texted, I knew I had to help out. Tell me what's going on."

The fifty-something wedding planner with salt-and-pepper hair in a stylish asymmetrical bob looks more tired and older than I've ever seen her. It scares me.

"So much," she says, shaking her head and looking down at the turquoise tablecloth decorated with a few white-painted seashells and starfish and a mini floral display in a small glass vase. "I don't even know where to start."

"You said your mother is unwell?" I prompt, shifting uneasily in my chair. A server approaches our table, dropping off two mimosas decorated with strawberries. I raise a questioning eyebrow.

"I took the liberty to order us both the endless mimosas. I hope that's okay?" she asks, wiping her free hand over her tear-stained cheeks.

"Of course, honey, whatever you need," I reply, throwing my current diet regimen and six-week glow-up challenge right out the window. At least for today. Sometimes, mimosas trump everything else. But it worries me that she's in this particular mood.

I observe Stella's face tenderly. She's the closest thing I have to a loving mom, having helped me through some of the worst times of my life. Without her, I would have no clue what it's like to have a caring parental figure. Without her, I'm not sure I'd even be sane.

"Mommy was diagnosed yesterday with late-term dementia and late-stage congestive heart failure. The diuretics they need to give her to take some stress off her heart are destroying her kidneys, so it's a careful balancing act that will only have one ultimate outcome. The doctors have given her weeks to live," Stella says, her face a study in anguish and disbelief. "I still can't wrap my head around it, especially with Dad terminally ill, too."

I press my lips firmly together, sympathy pouring from me. "That's a tough situation having both parents sick at the same time."

"Dying at the same time," she corrects. She looks away momentarily, squeezing my hand and fighting hard to maintain her composure. "I never thought it would end like this, and I can't continue pretending nothing's wrong..."

I wait for her to continue, but silence settles between us, broken only by the sounds of bustling servers and diners chatting at distant tables.

"I can't imagine," I add softly, and it couldn't be more

true. My father is a cold, cruel man. Among the vaunted one percent of this world, he has made money his sole desire and goal in life. The result? He's cycled through three wives and is currently on his fourth who's younger than my twenty-five by four years. He has no relationship to speak of with any of his seven children, including me, apart from holding our inheritances over our heads.

As for my mother, she left the picture when I was a small child. This wasn't by choice. It was a decision forced on her by Father during their divorce. But this knowledge didn't leave any less of a hole in my heart and my life. Although we've attempted to reconnect since I became an adult, the experience has been inordinately awkward and dissatisfying. In other words, I can't imagine being especially torn up about either of them passing away, although it's a terrible admission.

That said, if anything ever happened to Stella. Watching her attempt to collect herself, another wave of empathy rushes over me. I wouldn't be able to handle that at all. As uncharacteristic tears drip down my cheeks, we sit in a comfortable silence, the only way to confront life's worst situations. But at least we're sitting together. That's something that Stella taught me a long time ago.

Sniffling and wiping her cheeks some more, she finally straightens her back, looking at me and grabbing her mimosa glass. "Enough of this horrible sadness. I think we could both use a drink."

"Amen to that," I say, releasing her hand and grabbing my glass. We sadly clink our drinks together before each taking a sip. The bubbly, acidic, sweet beverage flows over my tongue, hitting the spot in ways no other drink could this morning.

"That's good," Stella says, breaking the first smile I've seen since arriving this morning. "Enough talk about my sad situation. Everyone has to lose their parents at some point."

I nod sympathetically. "Yes, but that's really tough to have it happen at the same time."

"Tough for me, sure. But there's something poetic and meaningful about them leaving this world together, like they came in. Did you know they were born in the same year?"

I shake my head. "No, I didn't."

"Yep. They grew up, attended school, and went to prom together, marrying at eighteen. By today's standards, they did everything wrong, and yet they remain the only reason I believe in soulmates despite my nonexistent love life."

I laugh. "You're far more idealistic than me."

"Aspen, twenty-five's far too young to be so jaded," she scolds tenderly.

I chuckle. "I've been jaded my whole life. It's a prerequisite of growing up an Everhart."

She nods empathetically. "Your father isn't the most understanding or affectionate man."

"No, and he's also the last person I want to talk about this morning."

Stella nods. "Change of subject, then. What about that mountain man you met on the dating website?"

I sigh, frowning. "I broke it off with him."

"So, meeting in person didn't go well?"

I shrug, not wanting to explain myself. "We would've never worked out. He turned out to be a lot more judgmental than I thought."

The look on my face must say it all because Stella leans over the table, adding, "Oh, sweetie, what happened?"

I squirm uncomfortably in my chair. "Everything was going fine, but then he got on the topic of his birth mother. Of how she abandoned him and that he could never forgive a woman like that, and well... As you already know better than anyone, it would never work."

Stella's face hardens, and she surmises, "So, you told him about what happened to you as a teen, and he wasn't understanding?"

I shrug.

She arches an eyebrow. "You didn't tell him?"

I shift uneasily. "If you had heard the vitriol pouring through the phone when he described his mother and how he could never forgive any woman who abandoned her child..." I shake my head, my stomach roiling as his voice washes back over me. "It was immediately obvious I wasn't the woman for him. Why waste more time and energy on something doomed from the get-go?"

"But you were so excited about him."

"Look, I refuse to put myself under another judgmental person's microscope. Believe me, I had to do enough of that as a pregnant sixteen-year-old with no resources, no hope, no future. I'll never regret what I did. It was the only way to give Luca the life and future that he deserves. So, that's that."

She nods, sniffling and leveling her steady blue gaze on me. "When are you going to forgive yourself, though?"

Her question comes out of left field, striking me as hard as a stray baseball. I shrug. "It's not about forgiving. It's about learning to live with the impossible because I have no other choice."

"The past is the past," she says, arching an eyebrow. "Have you considered moving forward with the mountain man and keeping this part of your life to yourself? Don't we honestly keep so much from our partners without even thinking about it?"

I lick my bottom lip pensively before biting it. "I could do that with any other man. But not the mountain man. I don't know how to explain it, but a relationship with him..." I look out the window across from our table, watching the expansive Pacific Ocean's waves crashing violently against the rough, rocky outcropping the restaurant is poised above. "He's not like other men. He would demand a level of intimacy I don't know if I'd ever feel comfortable with." I turn up the corners of my mouth, trying to lighten the mood. "I guess I did pick up on a few of Father's lessons."

"Like?" She scrunches her forehead.

"Keeping those closest to me at arm's length."

"That hasn't worked with me," Stella reminds.

I nod. "You're the one exception to that rule. Without you, I don't know how I'd be sane right now. Not with all of this."

"We're in the same boat," she replies fondly. "Have you heard more from Luca's mother?"

"Yes, and it's not good. His adopted dad recently passed away. He was much older than Nadine, so it wasn't a huge surprise. But due to a recent health scare, she's been more present in my life lately, bringing up all sorts of feelings that I think are better left where they lie."

"What kinds of feelings?" Stella asks, arching an eyebrow.

"Regret about everything that happened with Luca. Even though I know things couldn't have gone any differently."

She purses her lips. "That's what your father wanted you to believe."

I nod, crossing my arms over my chest. "But what was I to do at seventeen? Live on the streets, raising a newborn?"

Stella's eyes flood with empathy. "You did the best you could. You need to forgive yourself for the past," she repeats.

"The only thing I need to do is stop thinking about it."

She smiles warmly. "I'm here whenever you want to talk."

I may never. After all, my dad raised me to ignore any and all things involving emotions.

Stella says, "That's a lot under the circumstances. Are you sure you want to fill in for me this weekend? I can try to find someone else."

"No, I've got this wedding covered. I'll make it happen for you and your clients. Whatever it takes. After all, I'm the queen of powering through."

Concern floods her face, but one look at my stubborn expression, and she must understand I've made up my mind. Period.

"The clients are Ridge Dawson and Paige Laurier, and this is set to be the nuptials of the year. Like, make or break for Light and Love Wedding Planning. That's why you were the first and only person I called because I have no worries whatsoever about leaving this in your very capable hands. But this one has many moving parts, stuff we don't usually deal with..."

I sit up straighter, taking another sip of my mimosa. "Like?"

"For one, security must be top-notch. I didn't get all the details, but the couple has enemies who would like nothing better than to ruin their special day."

I sit back, knitting my brows. "Seriously?"

She nods emphatically. "It's the security level you'd

expect for celebrity nuptials, so you shouldn't feel completely out of your element. But be sure to review safety protocols carefully. And the entire event will be heavily photographed and videoed for the couples' reality TV show, *Honeymooning in the Wilds*. To complicate matters, the groom is one of fourteen foster brothers, and thirteen of them will be in attendance as groomsmen. In other words, prepare for a massive wedding party."

I nod, feeling a little overwhelmed about the camera crew and reality TV aspect of the wedding but relieved by everything else. I've done more than my fair share of massive SoCal weddings, so this should be a piece of cake in those regards.

"How did you get involved in a wedding so far from Newport Beach?"

"Paige is originally from Hollywood and appreciates Love and Light Planning's track record with celebrity nuptials."

I nod. "Well, we won't let her down."

"I've already shared my to-do lists and wedding bible for the event with you via Trello and Airtable. But let me know if you have any questions. I cannot thank you enough for dropping everything to do this."

"Of course. Thankfully, it works with my schedule, and I know you'd do the same for me. I have one question, though. How far is the event from Sacramento?"

Confusion flashes across Stella's face. "A good hour or more, depending on traffic."

My shoulders relax, and I sink into my chair, my one concern alleviated.

"Why?"

"Because the mountain man said he lives near Sacramento. Just wanted to make certain I wouldn't have to deal with him on top of everything else."

"Stranger things have probably happened," she replies, the world's weight still visually pressing her down. "But I can't imagine."

"Works for me," I say as the server appears ready to take our orders.

TWO

"Yes, the statute of limitations is ten years for child abuse cases that occurred before January 1, 2024—"

"Then, we're done here," I cut my foster brother, Flynn, off before he can finish his sentence. Jumping to my feet, I beeline for the door, feeling nauseous with a cold sweat on my forehead.

"Wait," he calls after me.

I stop in front of the door even though every part of my physical body longs to make a run for it. But I'm a grown man who can't act this way. So, instead, I keep my back toward him, asking gruffly, "What?"

"You weren't the only one abused in that way as a child. Bro, I've got your back, and I understand what you went through better than anybody."

I groan thankful things ended with Aspen like they did before our first meeting. God only knows how much more torn up I'd feel if there were even the slightest chance of her finding out about my traumatic past.

In raw tones, I ground out, "How long will I have to continue paying for what others did to me as a child? I'm done with this fucking up my life."

"I understand," Flynn says gruffly. "But you have valuable insight to provide in this case. No one is better acquainted with the darker side of the House of the Seven Prophets than you. And what you know about the interwoven network of individuals is invaluable. It could very well lead us to the top of the pyramid."

"No," I say firmly. "You have other witnesses. Besides, we're talking about stuff that happened over twenty years ago."

"Axel, what you have to say is relevant and admissible. It will provide jurors with a better understanding of the dynamics of abuse and the church and political hierarchy involved."

I wheel back around, crossing my arms. "At what cost? My dignity? My reputation? My fucking business and future? The guys I would be testifying against don't play fair, and they're all about the long game."

Flynn stands, rounding his desk and leaning against it with his arms crossed. He's got black skin with brown undertones, a perfectly carved face with an immaculate faded beard, and a lean, muscular build that attests to his self-discipline and love of horses and ranching activities. In fact, the man never starts his day without a pre-morning ride.

"What are you most concerned about?"

I run my tongue over my top row of teeth. *Where to begin?* "Let's see here," I fume. "I'm not especially pleased about my dirty laundry being aired for the whole world to see and talk about. Or what it will do to my reputation and my business. You know better than anyone how nasty the small-town rumor mill can be. And then there's the messy business of reliving the most traumatic and unspeakable moments from my childhood in front of virtual strangers. All while knowing that justice will never be served, despite what everyone says. Last but not least, there are the potential death threats and real risks associated with implicating people that far up the chain. After all, this goes well beyond the House of the Seven Prophets. I don't want to spend the rest of my fucking life in witness protection."

Flynn listens without speaking, his face impassive. At the end, he nods, pressing his lips firmly together. "You're stronger and braver than you know, and you'll get through this. Moreover, your testimony could help Holden."

"Maybe," I say testily. "Maybe not. He made the wrong kind of enemies."

"On account of you."

Those four words hang in the air, creating a tension thick enough to cut. Our foster brother, Holden, swore me to secrecy the night he was jumped by a group of dumbass fraternity brothers and nearly beaten to death. He only got the upper hand after pulling a knife and stabbing to death of one of the perps. Unbeknownst to Holden, the victim was the son of one of California's most powerful senators. I've never spoken about what happened at my older foster brother's urging, even though he's done years in the clink for it.

Now, I play a slippery game of figuring out what Holden may have finally broken down and told Flynn versus what Flynn may simply be surmising. I feel out of my element with my genius-level lawyer and brother. No matter what I say, my words are sure to cook me.

Narrowing my eyes, I ask, "What are you implying?"

"You and Holden have both left many unanswered questions over the years. Questions that have kept me from providing him with a better defense and the chance at parole. I'm tired of Holden paying for your silence."

"I am, too," I confess. I have been the entire time. "But it's not my secret to tell."

"Yes, it is."

I look down at my watch, exasperated. "Fuck, Flynn, you know how to monopolize a man's time. If you knew the number of things I have yet to do today to prepare for Ridge and Paige's wedding rehearsal." I shake my head, pacing back and forth in front of the door.

Flynn grimaces. "I know you don't want to hear this right now, but the truth will set you free."

"No, it won't," I snap. "But it will fuck up the life I've worked so hard to create despite everything I endured as a kid. And I want no part of that. My abusers have already stolen far too much from me."

Chief on the list of what I've lost thanks to my horrific childhood? Aspen Everhart. Sure, she broke it off with me before our first meeting, her nerves getting the better of her. But I knew her well enough that a few well-placed, comforting words would've reassured her and put our relationship back on track.

How could I do that, though? And why would I do that with the specter of the childhood abuse that nearly destroyed me hanging over my head again? I'd rather she remember me at my best, even if it means never meeting in person.

After all, I could never stand to have Aspen look at me differently, and she most definitely would if she knew everything that happened to me as a kid. A shiver runs down my spine. Some of my abusers are in their fucking graves. How is it possible they're reaching out from the Great Beyond and fucking with me some more?

"Are we done here? Because this is a very old, very tired conversation that'll never end how you think it should."

Flynn bites his bottom lip, shaking his head. "Goddamn it, you're stubborn," he rages. "Yeah, go do what you have to do to make Ridge and Paige's day special."

"Thank you," I say roughly, straightening and puffing my chest. *Keep it the fuck together, Axel.*

"But promise me, you'll give this serious consideration. Your testimony, especially about Mortimer Cady and his associates, could provide invaluable insights."

I pinch the bridge of my nose, closing my eyes for one long moment. *How in the hell could he expect me not to think about it?* It'll take me days, if not weeks, to stop having flashbacks and other PTSD-related symptoms.

Hell, I have them even when the last thing on my mind is my fucked up childhood in the House of the Seven Prophets cult. But I want this conversation to end, and I need to get out of his stuffy office for a breather. So, I say half-heartedly. "Yeah, I'll think about it. *After* the wedding."

"Fair enough."

An hour later, I sit at Sweet Rush Bakery with my sister-in-law, Cricket, who's in charge of the cake and other goodies for the wedding and Stacey and Jerry from the Silver Fork, catering the event. Stonie stands behind them with his arms folded. He has a bad lower back from years of hauling booze and moving beer kegs at his eponymous bar and grill, Stonie's. So, he prefers to stand for this tête-à-tête.

Cricket reads from a list for tonight's rehearsal dinner. "The rehearsal starts at four p.m. sharp, and the wedding planner will arrive at the ranch no later than three to go over everything. I spoke with her this morning as she was driving, so I'm assured we're on the same page."

Stacey chimes in, asking, "Is she nice?" She has long, hazelnut-hued locks, about the same color as Cricket's, and big, periwinkle blue eyes. But unlike Cricket's smoky, tiny voice, Stacey's is loud and proud.

Cricket shakes her head. "No, but very professional and business-like."

"So, is it a 'yes' or a 'no' when it comes to her micro-managing things?" Stacey asks, her face serious.

She and her husband, Jerry, recently opened a catering side hustle. Their restaurant, the Silver Fork, is renowned for its delish, high-quality cuisine, thanks to Jerry's exceptional culinary skills. But catering's still new for both of them, and I can tell by Stacey's grave face that she doesn't want to get anything wrong.

"Let's assume micromanager to be on the safe side," Cricket laughs.

My mind is a million miles away, and I can't hold one stray thought for long. There's only one wedding planner I have on my mind, and it's not Paige and Ridge's. I had trouble sleeping last night, thanks to my worries about having to testify and the disappointment of what happened with Aspen. I'm not in the mood to sit here any longer.

Interrupting, I ask gruffly, "No offense, but the booze is at the ranch, and Stonie and I have hashed out everything else for beverage service. If you'd like to add beer flights to happy hour, I'm game for that, too. Jerry and I can haul everything we'll need for that first thing in the morning. I'm also thoroughly familiar with all security protocols for this evening and tomorrow. So, mind if I duck out?"

Cricket's eyes widen. Looking over her checklist, she

licks her lips before saying, "Yes, to the beer flights. Jerry, are you good helping him with that tomorrow?"

Jerry nods, a big brute of a chef who looks more like a professional wrestler.

Cricket's eyes scan her list one more time. "In that case, I think everything involving you is covered. Thank you for stopping by, Axel."

"Sure thing. See you all later." I head for the exit.

Cricket calls after me, "Be at the ranch no later than three. Just in case."

I nod, blowing out through the bakery door to the clink of the bells strung on it. Outside, the town looks uncharacteristically quiet for a Friday afternoon. But considering Hollister's basically rolling up its sidewalks and closing most of the businesses for tomorrow's nuptials, I don't expect any less.

Back at my place, my mind races as I go through my regular weightlifting routine in my home gym. The wall is lined with mirrors to check in on my form, and I blast heavy metal, pounding out reps and increasing the weights to exhaust myself and sink into mindless abandon. Exercise and sex are two of the only activities that make my treacherous mind stop when I'm in this state.

After destroying my muscles, I climb into the shower and groan under the heat of the water. My body aches, and I likely overdid it. But I had to interrupt the dangerous cascade of thoughts running through my head.

Thoughts that haunt me from my childhood. Thoughts about Aspen and the in-person meeting that will never happen. It sucks because I really liked that woman, and we had far more in common than I ever would've guessed from her profile.

The worst part is knowing I saved everything up for

Aspen—emotionally, physically, and practically—beyond excited to finally meet her. Well, fuck it, a month of silence confirms I'm back to profound singleness and masturbation.

Masturbation ... not a bad idea. Maybe it'll take the edge off.

I spit into my palm, my fingers begrudgingly wrapping around my rod, knowing the fantasies about Aspen need to stop. But not today. Not now. I fist myself, biting my bottom lip and letting out a frustrated groan as I jerk my hand back and forth, beating myself off to every beautiful, dirty, dark, and twisted thought I've ever had about Aspen.

About her dark, mahogany hair feathered out on my pillows. About her juicy pink tongue, darting out to wet her lush lips as she pants and draws closer to her climax. My hand squeezes tighter, sliding back and forth to thoughts of her wet, hot pussy sucking me in, stealing my soul along with my heart. About how her lips would round on a little puff of satisfied air as I seize her hips demandingly, changing my angle and driving into her. Rubbing my head over her G-spot and stroking her deep and sensually until her hips buck up, and she screams my name, shuddering and gripping me as she comes undone. Only then, with her drenched channel milking the hell out of my dick, would I fill her to the brim with my hot seed.

I rest my free arm on the shower's glass door as my breathing reaches a fevered pace, buried in thoughts of Aspen's delectable softness. My balls pull up, and pain grips me for one excruciating moment before I dissolve into trembling pleasure, and cum creams the stall door.

"Fuck." I moan, leaning against the glass and trying to catch my breath. Of all the things my shitty-ass childhood has stolen from me, Aspen Everhart may ultimately be the most precious.

Instead of finding out for sure, she's now relegated to the what-if pile where all my greatest fantasies live. Still, never knowing and remaining dissatisfied is a whole hell of a lot better than her judging me for my past. I couldn't stand that.

CHAPTER
THREE

ASPEN

Okay, I was not expecting Hollister to be a town of two thousand people located this deep in the Sierra Nevada backcountry. Stella could've explained this quaint location to me a little better. But under the circumstances, I can't find fault with her. I make a mental note to call her after the rehearsal and dinner to touch base about the wedding and her parents.

My first meeting with Paige Laurier, formerly of Hollywood, and Ridge Dawson goes smashingly. The wedding venue, Ridge's foster dad's ranch, is breathtaking, affording incredible views of the natural scenery. And Paige and I instantly hit it off, two SoCal girls in a Hallmark movie.

Since meeting with Stella yesterday, I've had my nose in the trenches, pouring over her Airtable wedding bible for the event. Typically, I pride myself on memorizing the names of members of the wedding party and who they are in relation to the bride and groom. I haven't even had the chance to look at the Trello boards yet and doubt I'll get to them before the rehearsal. Fortunately, Ridge and Paige are so relaxed that they don't notice these minor discrepancies.

All I have to do is *not* see Sacramento's premier brew-master, even though his beer will fuel this wedding. It doesn't surprise me. Since the label began a handful of years ago, Rough & Ready Red has become the go-to, on-tap beverage of the West Coast, and one Axel told me months ago he's intent on expanding nationwide.

That said, there's no reason to think I'll see Axel around here anytime soon. After all, Sacramento's a long way off from Hollister and Rough & Ready Country. Why my brain continues to bombard me with thoughts of the rugged mountain man I corresponded with for a few months before breaking things off, I don't want to dwell on. What's done is done. End of story.

Pulling up to the adorable Victorian home-turned-bed and breakfast where I'll be staying, I straighten my spine, switching gears from road trip goddess to SoCal's hottest wedding planner. I remind myself that I'm at the top of my game and career for a reason. Despite its last-minute planner swap, security concerns, and TV-related complications, this wedding will soon be another set of lovely photos in my portfolio.

You're not here to make friends, fall in love with quaint small-town vibes, or pine away for a rugged mountain man. Time to get your head on straight and dive wholly and headlong into your professional duties.

Mrs. Chatterton, who I spoke to on the phone this morning to confirm my reservation, greets me. She's everything I imagined—elderly, polite, and forthright. She has red dyed hair that's grown out a few inches, revealing the white beneath, and she wears a cute little house dress. The type Lucille Ball sported in "I Love Lucy."

"Welcome to Hollister, Ms. Everhart," she says warmly, handing me the key to my room.

"Breakfast is from six to nine a.m. tomorrow, continental style with pastries from Sweet Rush Bakery and fresh coffee."

I immediately recognize the name. That's the bakery making Ridge and Paige's wedding cake. "Good to know."

Mrs. Chatterton nods, smiling broadly. "They are such a cute couple, and I'd like to think I had a little hand in their early relationship."

"Oh, really?" I ask, always ready to mine locals for a good story to share at the wedding.

"Yes. The honeymoon suite on the third floor had no small part in bringing them together. I'd like to think the flower petals on the bed did the trick. I hand-picked them from my own rose garden," she explains proudly with a wink.

I laugh ... awkwardly. *Small towns.* "Honeymoon suite? It sounds like they did things a little backward, then?"

She laughs. "Back in my day, it would've been downright scandalous. But who am I to judge? I've never seen a happier or more compatible couple. Ridge was always such a good boy. Did an immaculate job of taking care of the lawn as a young man. I'm elated to see him happy."

"What great stories you have about the couple. Will you be at the wedding tomorrow?"

She nods, looking a bit nervous. "Anybody who's anybody in Hollister will be there. Well, maybe except for the Amestoys."

I feel another deeper story here, falling for the bait. "Who are the Amestoys?"

"Basque sheepherders. They own the ranch adjoining Rough & Ready, and they've been locked in a grazing and land war with Ridge's foster dad for years now. It often comes to physical blows, something Ridge and Paige don't need at their wedding."

"So, the Amestoys are why people are on guard around here?"

"Oh, my no," Mrs. Chatterton laughs, shaking her head. "No, Ridge and Paige had a tangle with the House of the Seven Prophets, a cult with members spread across the West Coast. Rumors say the organization even has ties to Washington, D.C. Haven't you heard about it in the news?" She furrows her eyebrows, deepening the creases in her forehead.

"I don't have much time for TV, especially during prime wedding season."

"Well," she whispers, her eyes darting around, even though we're the only two people in the room. "You should look it up online or whatever you young people do and get caught up with the scandal. The 'church'"—she uses air quotes for the last word—"was involved in human trafficking and pedophilia. It's a horrible, sickening scandal, and one Paige and Ridge uncovered when they first met each other. Although the cult was infiltrated and the main participants have been taken into custody awaiting trial, retribution is still a primary concern. In fact, between you and me, I'm a bit concerned about attending the wedding."

A chill runs down my spine. "I guess I will have to do more research before the wedding. That said, I assure you every security precaution has been taken. You'll be absolutely, one hundred percent safe for tomorrow's big event."

Mrs. Chatterton's face relaxes. "I'm glad I talked to you, then. Because I hated the idea of missing out on Ridge's big day. He's one of the last foster brothers from Rough & Ready Ranch still unmarried."

"That changes tomorrow," I say with an enthusiastic

smile. "Now, if you'll excuse me, I have lots to do before tonight's rehearsal and dinner."

"Yes, of course," she replies. "If you need anything at all, don't hesitate to call me." She hands me one of her business cards stacked high on the reception counter.

"I appreciate it."

I find my room on the second floor, letting myself inside. The inn still uses metal keys. *Metal keys?* How quaint.

Unpack my suitcases, I fill the drawers of the Victorian suite with neatly folded stacks of lacy underwear and bras, camisoles, silky nightgowns, and all the things that make me feel sexy.

Next, I hang my sundresses and pantsuits in the armoire, along with a few light jackets, so that I'm ready for any and all potential weather. After all, it is an outdoor wedding at sixty-five hundred feet. Although the forecast looks fantastic for tomorrow, the weather can change on a dime in the Sierra Nevada I've been warned. Finally, I line the bottom of the armoire with my boots, high heels, and strappy sandals.

I've got half a day to kill before I'll be on duty at the wedding rehearsal. So, I unroll my yoga mat and slide into my exercise clothes, a pair of tight-fitting, calf-length black exercise pants and a matching black exercise top that fits like a glove and showcases the girls in wonderful ways that almost convince me I don't need a boob job.

The last thought references an insider joke between Stella and me. In the affluent SoCal wedding planning industry, we encounter countless women with obvious signs they've been under the knife. In fact, do men still like curvy bodies with flaws like cellulite, dimples, rolls, and boobs that barely fit B cups? I don't know. What does it matter anyway?

After the workout, I lie in savasana on my mat, enjoying the warm, radiant feeling that washes over me … until it hits me. I am absolutely, one hundred percent horny as fuck. I've been this way ever since arriving in Axel's neck of the woods.

What is wrong with me? I pad into the bathroom and turn the water on extra hot. I could use a nice long shower after spending more than seven hours on the road and working up a sweat with power yoga.

My thoughts turn to Axel again for like the millionth time. Despite ignoring it during the workout, my pussy throbs out its greedy demands. God, I need to get laid.

It's been more than two years, and although I laud technological advances like vibrators, they will never give me the same satisfaction as hot, pulsing cock.

I think back to Axel, second-guessing why I broke things off before our first meeting. The massive cock he beat while we FaceTimed would have done the trick and then some. Why didn't I let him scratch this needy itch?

Because I'm a masochist. It's obvious. And it sucks.

Getting in the shower does nothing for my need. I glance at my cell phone again, keeping track of the hour. I've got more than enough time to get myself off. It'll put me in a better mood at work anyway.

The hot water from the shower spills over my shoulders like a wet caress. *Wait, is the shower head detachable?* That would be a pleasant surprise. I mess with it for a moment. *No such luck.*

Instead, I drop my hands, sliding my fingers through my folds, amazed at how swollen and drenched they feel.

I'd love to blame this solely on hot-blooded womanly needs. But Axel fills my mind.

I close my eyes, relaxing my shoulders and focusing on the sensation of my fingers gliding through my pussy folds. If only they were Axel's. God, that rugged mountain man was gorgeous, and the way he dirty-talked me puts a thick lump of desire in my throat.

I let my mind wander, reliving the last conversation before the breakup.

Axel said, *"Yes, Tiger, I need that pussy in my mouth so bad. When I finally get a hold of you, I'm eating you out so fucking good. You won't be able to breathe. You won't be able to think. All you'll be able to do is mindlessly scream my name and grind those hips into my beard. I won't stop until every inch of my face is covered in that perfect honey of yours."*

My right middle finger slides back and forth over my clit, and my breath stutters in my throat as my left middle finger slides into my pussy. I pretend it's Axel's thick, work-hardened digits, my pussy instantly responding to the fantasy.

His promises wash back over me some more.

"I'm going to stroke that pussy slowly and sensually, adoring every damn inch of you. Taking nothing for granted. I won't stop until I fill every inch of your body with a bliss you'll never forget."

No wonder I broke things off with him. Although he didn't actually say it, he implied as much. Axel wanted to make me his. Claim me for good.

My finger slides over my clit, increasing the speed. I hold my other hand still, keeping my finger inside to gauge the increasing flutters and spasms of my pussy walls. As they increase, betraying my desperate need, I stroke my channel again, my pussy slicker and wetter. My right-hand fingers graze fast and repetitively over my swollen clit until I orgasm hard, feeling weak-kneed and shaky-legged, wishing Axel's strong, muscular arms supported me.

Fuck, I need that man so much. Would it really be so bad if I unblocked and texted him again? I could explain how things got hectic. That I felt nervous, stressed out, and fearful at the thought of meeting him. That I want to give things another try and am only an hour away.

Would it be so bad to maybe even say I need him? That I haven't been able to get him off my mind for the past month? That has to mean something, right?

Shaking my head and these rebel thoughts from my brain, I step out of the shower onto the fluffy pale pink shower mat. The entire suite is decorated in shades of uber-feminine rose pink with complementary floral patterns.

I dry myself with big, fluffy rose-colored towels before heading into the bedroom to slather on lotion and climb into my robe. I have some time to kill, so I grab my phone, unblocking Axel's number.

My finger hovers over the call button ... but I hesitate. After all, I broke up with him a whole month ago. What are the chances he would want to hear from me? And considering I've got a booty call on my mind, is reconnecting even fair? Besides, there's no way that gorgeous hunk of manhood is still single.

Throwing my phone across the bed to the opposite side to put some physical distance between me and temptation, I pull out my laptop and Google *Honeymooning in the Wilds* to catch up on past episodes and get a better feel for Ridge and Paige.

I also study favorite camera angles, the esthetic, and everything else that could help me gain an edge, crafting the perfect wedding for one of America's hottest reality TV couples.

My phone rings, and I scramble across the bed, staring at the screen. Nadine. My heart skips in my chest as I hesitantly take the call.

"I'm so glad you answered," she blurts out. I can tell she's been crying.

"Oh, my God, what's wrong?" Cold, hard fear grips me, even as I remind myself that Luca is no longer my son. Nevertheless, I will always be deeply, inexplicably marked by the need for him to have a happy, vibrant future.

"I'm not doing well ... *at all.*" She sobs. "Aspen, I don't know how else to spell this out for you, but I need you to really do some soul-searching."

"What do you mean?" I ask, knitting my brows.

"I need you to consider taking custody of Luca."

My heart stops, and I sit up straighter, my mind a swirl of thoughts, my body alive with too many emotions to quantify. "Nadine, what did the doctors tell you?"

"I'm standing outside my oncologist's office as we speak. He's given me less than three months to live. Which means Luca will have to go through the pain of being orphaned ... unless you would consider a reunification."

The selfish, career-driven part of me wants to lash out, tell her this is bad timing and that I'll call her back after I'm done planning the wedding event of the reality TV season. It's the response my father would give in all contexts, no hearts or fucks given. For him, the bottom line always be cold, hard cash, emotions be damned.

Instead, I take a deep breath, reminding myself I am not like my father, though I would like a hefty piece of his success someday. But people aren't merely objects to be used for my own gain. That's something my father's business partner, Chadwick Mayfair, Luca's father, would have done well to learn, too. "Nadine, I'm so sorry about your diagnosis. It breaks my heart."

Through sobs, she stumbles over her words. "I just need to know my little boy will be safe and happy no matter what."

"Of course," I say, trying to put myself in her shoes to understand her current despair and anxiety. But I can't because, honestly, I never allow myself to feel that deeply for anybody. It's a road to certain ruin.

"I'm in Northern California, planning a very important celebrity wedding, but what can I do to help? How can I make you feel better and more at peace before my return?"

"Will you consider reunification with Luca?"

I inhale sharply, surprised by how my breath shudders, dangerously close to tears. Running my hand over my face and feeling my heart unwind, I whisper, "I'll consider it."

"Thank you," she says from a place so heartfelt that I can feel the warmth coming through the phone. "I've got to go now. I can't stand out here like an idiot sobbing. But will you call me later, after you've done some thinking?"

"Okay." I would love to set her heart at ease, but this isn't the kind of decision that can be made in a heartbeat.

It was hard enough to shut off my heart eight years ago when Luca was born, and I had to stick to the plan, surrendering him to Curtis and Nadine. How do I find the strength to reopen those ancient wounds anew? And would it really be in Luca's best interests?

FOUR

AXEL

"Hey, bro, any way you can meet me at the ranch in a half hour or so? I know it's earlier than my wife originally told you, but we need help getting the wedding arch assembled, and the florist can only stay for another hour to complete all the decorating." My oldest brother Christian's on the line. He's married to Cricket, and they have triplets together—Cooper, Callie, and Cassidy. I hear baby noises in the background.

"Sure thing. Any tools or other things you need me to bring?"

"Nah, I think we've got it covered. But this arch is a royal pain in the ass, and I wasn't counting on the florist having to leave so soon."

"Alright, then. See you shortly."

I'm not surprised at the complexity of the wedding arch. It was some wooden monstrosity that my artist brother, Turner, was enlisted to create. It's supposed to look super rustic and cool, covered in flowers from what everyone's told me. But I've never been a fan of overly complicated shit. It's why I stick to making beer. Simple, straightforward, and delicious.

As I jump into my truck and head towards the ranch, my phone won't stop ringing. Clearly, crunch time has begun. I field a couple of calls from Stonie about beverage-related stuff before taking a call from Wolfe, who's ensuring security for the big day. There are so many moving parts to this whole thing that it makes my head spin.

Turning off four eighty-eight onto the large gravel road that leads to the main ranch house at Rough & Ready, I see my brother, Wolfe, and some of his crew of Army Rangers-turned-security guards at a checkpoint designated by a camo sun tent.

I roll down my window, eyeing my well-dressed brother in a black cowboy hat with black boots, dark wash Wranglers, and a long-sleeve, button-down, pin-striped black shirt.

"Could you possibly have gone for a hotter look?"

"Why, thank you, Axel. You're making me blush."

"I meant temperature-wise you, dumbass. Where are your AK-47s? I thought for sure you'd have the perimeter looking like Checkpoint Charlie."

He nods confidently. "We're going for the harmless, though deadly, look. Believe me, anyone who tries to sneak onto the ranch won't know what hit them."

Everything about his studied movements and well-chosen words tells me he and the Rangers have this place fully covered security-wise.

"Nice to enjoy the fruit of your labors and just be the brewmaster in the family." I laugh.

"Indeed. I guess somebody's got to focus on the enjoyment of the guests," Wolfe teases, tugging at the collar of his shirt.

"That's what I'm here for, and to keep you brutes happy. Should I send a keg out this way?"

"Fuck," Wolfe says, looking down and shaking his head. "You have no idea how good that sounds. But we've got to stay frosty. That said, you can leave a keg on the porch of my cabin when this is all over."

"Done," I answer, knowing full well he's only joking. His wife, Izzie, would flip out. They have a new baby and two older kids, so he basically needs to stay frosty all the time.

Wolfe waves me through with an amiable grin. I follow the long dirt driveway into an oblong valley hedged on all sides by the towering electric blue Sierra Nevada, white-dusted crests embellishing the highest elevations. The valley is golden and pastoral with fat, happy, black Angus cattle grazing in pastures cordoned off by ancient wood and barbed wire fences.

I pull up to the front of the house and park next to the line of trucks and Jeeps that congregate.

"Ready to decorate until your brain explodes?" Christian asks sarcastically as I jump out of the truck, heading across the expansive green towards him. Along the way, I pass row upon row of white chairs spread out in orderly lines.

A man follows Christian towards me, and I offer my hand as Christian introduces, "This is Martin, owner of New Leaf Florists."

"Nice to meet you."

"I appreciate your help," he prefaces. "This is my busiest time of year, so I've got a meeting to run to in a little under an hour. But as the wedding planner strongly suggested, I can come back after the meeting and will be here first thing in the morning for the finishing touches."

He shakes his head resignedly, whispering, "Micro-manager."

He's obviously been talking to Cricket and Stacey. "Let's get to it, then," I say, clapping my hands together. A pile of rustic, gnarled wood sits at the front of the aisle.

"What a puzzle," I observe.

Christian shakes his head. "You have no idea."

Logan adds, "Especially since dumbass here can't read his own assembly plans." He eyes Turner.

The clean-shaven, brown-haired custom homebuilder mutters, eyeing a pile of papers, "It's not that I can't read them. But I need to change something."

"Great, so we're proceeding blindly?" Christian groans.

"How do your construction crews put up with you, bro?"

Turner arches an eyebrow. "They're highly skilled workers who know what they're doing unlike this ragtag bunch of helpers."

A silky smooth, though cold, voice observes from behind us. "This won't be done before Martin has to leave."

"Thanks, Captain Obvious," I grumble under my breath, turning towards the oddly familiar sound. My eyes settle on a woman so captivating my heart stops, along with my ability to breathe.

Aspen Everhart. I would know her anywhere. But how? And why didn't anybody tell me? *Maybe because you stay so damn secretive that your brothers don't even know the name of the woman you were talking to on Mountain Mates.*

The beauty eyes sizes my brothers up, starting with Christian. Her eyes are large, expressive, and the mouthwatering color of toffee, and her dark brows are immaculately trimmed with high arches. Long, luscious mahogany locks flow down to her mid-back, thick and perfectly curled at the ends. She wears a black sundress that shows off her curvy, plus-sized figure to perfection beneath a light acid-wash denim jacket.

The finishing touches taunt me—arresting silver and turquoise jewelry that screams the American Southwest, tan hand-tooled leather boots, and a white Stetson cowboy hat that makes me swallow hard. She looks like she could be mine.

For fuck's sake!

Before I can wheel back around and avoid her snapping eyes, our gazes meet, and her face blanches before going red. Her lush berry-stained lips purse, and all I can do is count the ways I long to experience her with all five senses, starting with taste.

Christian steps forward. "Ms. Everhart, let me introduce you to my brothers and fellow groomsmen, Logan, Turner, and Axel."

Her eyes wash over each of our faces with a practiced care. She doesn't linger on mine any longer than the others, which makes me simultaneously breathe a sigh of relief and feel irrationally jealous. I don't know what the fuck I'm expecting. A desire overload grips my body, rivaling the jumble of thoughts in my head and the strange tangle of emotions twisting and knotting my insides.

When it comes my turn to shake her hand, she doesn't hesitate, and neither do I. Only after our flesh touches do I realize what a massive mistake I've made.

Electricity crackles the air around us as searing sparks shoot back and forth between every inch of our touching flesh. My heart gallops in my chest, a Mustang hellbent on avoiding a roundup, and I can't trust my voice. So, instead, I nod. Fortunately, Christian, Logan, and Turner remain oblivious because they can be terrible jokesters, especially at the expense at the few remaining single brothers.

When our hands let go, falling back at each of our sides, I feel like I've lost something precious, vitally important to my existence. How in the hell can that be, considering she broke up with me, making it clear she didn't even think a first meeting was worthwhile?

I scrutinize her curiously, licking my bottom lip and watching as her eyes devour the subtle gesture, sending heated waves in my direction. She looks downright ravenous, and her next words come out breathy and squeaky. "Martin, you'll need to return this evening as we discussed earlier. I won't rest easy until the arch is fully assembled and decorated."

Her strict posture and sophisticated bearing exude unshakable, emotionless professionalism. But the persistent glow of her full cheeks, how she twirls a strand of hair compulsively around her finger, and the nervous way she shifts her weight tell another story.

But, dude, why the fuck does it matter? She broke up with you. Let Aspen go before you make an utter and complete fool of yourself.

Fool me once, shame on you. Fool me twice, shame on me. It's a motto I would do well to live by under the circumstances. Instead, my thoughts smolder, randomly fixating on the flare of her nostrils and how she keeps subtly side-eyeing me, her eyelids fluttering as she appraises me when she thinks I'm not looking.

I haven't felt this awkward since high school, and my thoughts fittingly hang out at that maturity level, envisioning pulling her behind the barn for a stolen kiss. How would she react? If the thirsty way she continues to shoot side glances in my direction is any indicator, heated smooching would be the least of our problems.

I remind myself this is Ridge and Paige's wedding. It's not about me or Aspen. I need to get my shit together and keep it about the couple we're celebrating.

After all, pursuing Aspen Everhart is like horseback riding through a field of landmines. Nerve-wracking, painful, and potentially fatal. At least for my heart.

"Wait, do you two know each other?" Christian asks, bobbing his head back and forth between Aspen and me. I open my mouth to speak, not sure what will come out.

But Aspen beats me to it with a pained smile. "You definitely look familiar. We'll have to discuss how we know each other later. But right now, it's time to focus on giving Paige and Ridge the most picturesque, amazing wedding possible, which means finishing the arch. Martin, do you recommend stringing the fairy lights next or placing the floral arrangements first?"

Definitely look familiar? How many guys was she talking to on Mountain Mates?

I shake my head, pushing the last thought away. She never gave me any reason to believe I was one of many other men. She must be saying this to save face and remain professional. It's the only logical explanation. But, God, her cold voice and even colder words give my heart instant freezer burn.

Martin answers. "Flowers should come next."

Aspen nods confidently. "Good to know." She addresses Martin and Christian as if the rest of us don't exist. I assume it's because of Logan and Turner's physical proximity to me, the one she really wants to ignore. "It looks like these gentlemen still have a fair amount of work cut out for them, so I'll plan on seeing you here again after your meeting. I don't know how much you'll be able to get done prior to the rehearsal, but we'll only be using the space for an hour, and you can work during our practice if need be."

The florist nods. "Sounds good. In that case, I might as well split now."

Her face hardens. "Okay..." I can tell she's not happy and biting her tongue. "Will the placement of fairy lights in the barn upset what you're doing?"

Martin answers, "Shouldn't."

"Good. Then, I'll have some of the other groomsmen get on top of that."

Martin nods looking relieved as he heads towards his white, windowless florist van.

"Alright, then," Aspen says awkwardly, looking everywhere but at me. "I'll leave you to get back to business."

Christian nods, clenching his teeth until the muscle jumps in his jawline. "Are you putting Travis, Maksim, Zane, and the rest of our brothers on barn light duty?"

"That's my next stop," she says, her cheeks still burning and her motions flustered. She shoots one last, furtive glance in my direction, swirling with emotions too thick and bewildering for me to possibly read before heading back toward the house.

Removing my brown Stetson and running my fingers through my hair, I religiously watch her glide toward the house.

You definitely look familiar ...

Motherfucker!

But I can't deny she's walking poetry with a stunning hourglass figure that makes me as hungry as a kid after school waiting for his Happy Meal.

Christian whistles in that annoying older brother way that always warns me he's about to say something idiotic.

"Are you and the wedding planner done eye-fucking each other yet?"

"What?" I ask, doing an awful job of sounding nonchalant.

"Eye-fucking the wedding planner," he repeats, even as my gaze remains unrepentantly locked on the woman. As she climbs the stairs of the porch, she glances back over her shoulder unexpectedly, catching me in full drool mode. Her cheeks burn, and she lowers her head, rushing inside.

Turner chuckles. "Hey, I think Christian's on to something. Spill your guts, bro."

I shrug, annoyance rising. "It's none of your goddamned business."

Logan grumbles, "Never were good at hiding your feelings, Axel, although you've spent your whole life trying harder than anybody else."

"Nothing to hide," I say matter-of-factly, staring into three incredulous faces. "Besides, it's not like any of you have been especially forthcoming with your love lives. Hell, Christian, it took you nearly two decades to reunite with your high school sweetheart, Cricket, let alone tell us about it. And the first time we heard about your girl, Logan, you were announcing your engagement. Need I remind you, Turner, that you were the worst of the lot, calling us after you were officially married and raising five children to let us know you were no longer single."

"Things happened quickly between Jess and me," Logan counters. "Sorry I didn't call to let you know I was thinking about asking her to marry me. But I had my hands full saving her from a notorious serial killer."

"And y'all knew I had a thing for my neighbor, Lily," Turner pipes in. "Yeah, the marriage part came a little out of left field. But did it really?" Turner asks, cocking his head to the side and grinning.

Christian opens his mouth, but Logan and Turner cut him off simultaneously. "There's no excuse for you, big brother," Logan declares.

"You took the words right out of my mouth." Turner chuckles. "Fortunately, Cricket doesn't have a grudge-holding bone in her body, or you'd still be single, miserable, and pining away for your dispatcher-turned-baker."

Christian grumbles, "For the record, this conversation isn't about me. It's about Axel and how he knows the wedding planner."

Three pairs of eyes dissect me. I look down at my watch, determined to remain silent. "The rehearsal will start before we know it, so we better get this shit finished."

My brothers look mildly disappointed, but none can argue with my logic. As we dive into assembling the disparate pieces of wood, memories of Aspen wash over me. Keep this up, and I'll have to run home and jerk off before the rehearsal. It's fucking pathetic what the woman who rejected me does to my body.

CHAPTER
FIVE
ASPEN

I close the ranch house front door, leaning against it and panting. My hand comes up to my chest, resting on the place over my slamming heart.

Axel St. Claire. My God. I had no idea. He towers over all five foot-six inches of me, making me feel dainty and delicate. As a plus-sized woman, I'm not used to the addictive, feminine feeling or how it makes my insides quiver. But it's how his eyes boldly ravished me that has me unable to process thoughts or unpackage the emotions they inspired.

Did I really break up with that absolutely stunning, rugged specimen of masculinity before ever meeting him? I must have a cog loose in my head. I know I had reasons for what I did at the time. Hell, I made a list in true, neurotic fashion, like I do with every aspect of my life. Without lists, I would never make it as a wedding planner. But I can't muster one con against Axel at the moment, still drowning in the searing deluge of chemistry sizzling between us.

"Aspen, are you okay?" I hear from the landing of the stairs, looking up at Cricket.

I close my eyes for one regret-filled moment, wondering what I must look like standing here, completely gobsmacked by Axel, her brother-in-law. Inhaling sharply, I excuse, "Sorry, it's boiling out there. I thought for sure a visit to Northern California would provide a welcome respite from Orange County's temperatures. But wow!"

"Oh no," she says, rushing down the stairs towards me. "Have a seat on the couch, and I'll grab you a cold drink. Iced tea? Lemonade? Water?"

"Do you have Pellegrino or another sparkling water, by chance?"

"Sparkling water?" Her eyebrows climb into her hairline. "Sorry, but people don't really drink that stuff around here. I bet Stonie has some club soda, though. And there's always Axel's brews. Nothing cools me off better on a day like this. Well, before I was nursing triplets, that is."

I scrunch my nose. The last thing I need is some of Axel's brews. Seeing him nearly unhinged me. "Water is fine. Thank you."

"I have berry and mint-infused or cucumber melon. Which do you prefer?"

My head swims, struggling to answer the most basic questions. "The second one sounds lovely."

"Are you okay?" Another voice calls from the landing, followed by the thudding of feet. It's Birdie, another of the foster brother's wives, though I can't remember which one. She's our resident nurse for the event.

I open my mouth to speak, but Cricket thankfully beats me to it. "She got too hot outside talking to the guys about the arch."

"Really?" Birdie asks, leaning over to touch my forehead. "You feel cool as a cucumber to me." Her thick curtain of black hair flows like silk around her shoulders. The plump cowgirl looks gorgeous in a periwinkle floral sundress with capped sleeves and brown cowboy boots with floral pattern stitching.

Cricket hurries back into the living room, offering me a glass of water with pieces of cucumber and melon swirling between the ice cubes and a small kitchen towel moistened with cold water. She won't stop insisting until I begrudgingly place it on my forehead, despite Birdie's findings about my temperature.

The nurse frowns, eyeing me curiously. The sides of the glass already sweat, offering a welcome coolness to my hands. I excuse, bobbing my head between Birdie and Cricket, "I should've stood in the shade. That's all. It's been a long day. Doesn't help it started with a seven and half nearly eight-hour drive. I probably left my convertible's top down longer than I should have on the way up. I may be from SoCal, but that's still a lot of sunshine."

The front door squeaks open, and the handsome cowboy mountain man I need to avoid at all costs walks through it. He stops with a jerk of surprise at the sight of us at the couch.

"What's up?" Birdie asks, arching an eyebrow towards him.

He removes his hat, self-consciously looking down at the floor and running his big, strong hand through his thick, chestnut-colored hair. When he looks back up, his dark blue eyes settle on Birdie's, and my heart gives one last pathetic thump before passing out from excitement. The tantalizing odor of sandalwood and pine reach my nostrils. As if the composite of his looks and deep, rumbly voice weren't enough, he smells delectable.

"Just looking for another screwdriver. Christian thought it would be in the house toolkit in the washroom."

Suddenly, his eyes shoot towards me and the washcloth poised on my forehead. His brows knit as he murmurs hesitantly, "Are you okay?"

I nod, quirking my mouth. His eyes drop to my lips, and I try desperately to clear the thick lump lodged in my throat in case this interaction requires more speaking.

"She got overheated outside," Cricket explains, and he smirks, the cutest sight I've ever seen. It gives me the slightest glimpse into the adorable boy he once was, stealing my heart even more.

He shifts his weight, concern, and mirth, fighting for possession of his face. "She's not the only one." Directing his gaze at me, he winks, and I thank God I'm sitting down, immediately weak-kneed despite my lounging position.

"Maybe it's hotter outside than I think," Birdie says, looking out the window.

Replacing his hat, he nods towards the washroom. "Now, if you'll excuse me, I've got a flat head to find, so we can get this wedding show on the road. Ladies, Ms. Everhart." He says the last part tenderly before nodding and leaving the room.

Don't clutch your heart again, Aspen. Play it cool. You're a goddamned professional, not a pubescent teen with her first man crush.

But no amount of internal lecturing and berating could arrest the emotions this man incites. I'm a goner. I barely have a moment to admit this before he comes back through the living room, thankfully looking straight ahead.

My eyes shamelessly follow him, devouring his tight, round Wranglers-clad ass as he exits the house. Birdie and Cricket shoot quizzical glances at each other, and I realize I'm fanning myself.

Enough, Aspen! "Thank you. I feel better now," I declare

suddenly, jumping up and handing the towel back to Cricket. "Time to get back to work. Have you heard from the photographers, videographer, or the camera crew recently?"

Birdie and Cricket shake their heads. "Alright, then, I'm going to head back upstairs to Paige, and I'll see what I can do about getting them on the phone."

Birdie nods. "I'll be right behind you. I'm going to check on Wyatt and Billy."

I met Wyatt, Ridge's foster dad, and his best friend, Billy, earlier during my first visit with the couple.

Upstairs, I excuse myself into a guest bedroom to make calls, sitting down at a desk facing the window that I've been using as a mini-office ever since arriving at the ranch. I dial the first photography company, and my call goes to voicemail.

Next, I dial the videographer. She answers on the first ring. "Hi Trudy, Aspen here. I'm calling to confirm this afternoon's service. The rehearsal will start at four sharp. So, please check in with me on-site no later than three thirty. I would suggest factoring in extra time to pass through the security checkpoint that leads to the ranch."

"Security? Sorry, I'm still having trouble wrapping my head around all of this. We usually don't have anything this exciting going on around here. And I also have to admit, I don't video many wedding rehearsals, so I may need a little extra guidance from you regarding expectations."

"No worries. This is an exceptional event, and I'm more than happy to offer pointers once you arrive." As I speak to Trudy, I stand, pacing back and forth in front of the desk. My eyes keep fluttering towards the window and through the sheer white curtains to the green below where Axel and his brothers work on the arch. I stretch out an arm, teasing back the diaphanous curtains, careful to keep my head and body out of view.

The obstruction-free sight below takes my breath away. Axel's shirt is gone, and his muscles strain under the weight of the wood he braces for Turner to secure with screws. The heat of the day ensures his rippling, taut physique is moistened by glistening droplets of perspiration.

My mouth goes instantly dry, and my throat constricts. The juncture between my legs throbs, and I kick myself yet again for breaking things off with this man before they ever had the chance to get started. *What in the hell was I thinking?*

"Are you still there, Ms. Everhart?" Trudy repeats, pulling me back to the conversation.

"Oh, sorry, yes, I am. What were you saying again?" Even as I try to focus on the videographer's words, my eyes caress every inch of Axel's naked upper body, following the angular lines and planes of his suntanned core from his brown Stetson down to the teasing lines of his Adonis belt that disappear beneath the waistband of his criminally tight-fitting jeans.

My fingers and palms itch to touch him, just one time, to feel how rock-hard and solid he must be. My tongue begs to taste him, trace the planes of his musculature, and I would give nearly anything to make him sweat for me.

"Just confirming there are thirteen groomsmen and bridesmaids."

I try to process her words, but my mind is elsewhere. "Yes," I whisper. I sound like goddamned Marilyn Monroe as my eyes continue to ravage him from a distance, finding no satisfaction and only profound, soul-stirring hunger. *This* is not good.

"Perfect, I'll see you soon."

"Sounds good." I end the call feeling like the cat that swallowed the canary. Apparently, all professionalism went out the window the moment it opened up on views of the stunning cowboy who could have been mine. Regret and desire fight for purchase in my body, and I wonder how I'll get through the rehearsal and wedding tomorrow.

Come on, Aspen. You've had to do far more difficult things than this. Keep it the fuck together.

I pull up the camera crew's point of contact in my phone and dial it, my eyes still shamelessly poised on Axel.

"Scarlet, here."

"Hi, Scarlet, it's Aspen, the wedding planner filling in for Stella."

"Oh, yes, nice to hear from you. What's up?"

Axel's body strains as he braces the arch with the help of Logan, and Christian holds up a new piece that Turner secures with another screw. I've never seen such an intricate structure, but the thirsty part of me hopes it'll take all afternoon for them to build, the current show beyond tantalizing.

"What's up?" Scarlet repeats. "Are you there?"

I clear my throat guiltily. I need to look away, but I don't. "Yes, I'm calling to go over the schedule with you as well as address any questions or concerns you may have about today's filming and the order of events for tomorrow."

"Excellent."

Axel leans forward now, making the individual muscles along his ribcage pop. Mouthwatering.

"Shall we dive in?"

"Yes, please," I answer too quickly. *Dive into Axel's masculine goodness...*

"Alright, let's see here. Please hold for a moment while I pull everything up on my laptop."

"Of course," my voice squeaks. I step closer to the window, still hanging back but improving my view of the rugged mountain man. He's got the physique of Michelangelo's *David* only so much more enticing in flesh and blood rather than marble.

"Okay, today we're planning on a three p.m. arrival. That way, we can scope out the location and shoot some B-roll footage. Then, I have a start time of four for the actual rehearsal."

"Yes," I say, swallowing hard. "Do you need anything special from me?" My pulse pounds as I imagine asking Axel this same question.

"No, we want to keep things real, raw, and candid."

Real, raw, and candid. I can work with that. "Okay."

"Do you have any questions for me?" Scarlet asks.

"Umm." I glance at my laptop poised on the desk and open to today's Trello board. I narrow my gaze, scanning it. "Nothing I can think of at the moment, but I'll be in touch if anything comes to mind."

"Likewise. See you soon."

"Bye," I say, ending the call, my gaze still entirely absorbed by the window and the happenings going on below. Logan's got his shirt off now, too, and so does Christian, revealing a sexy smattering of tattoos on his chest and arms. But I only have eyes for Axel, the most tantalizing specimen of the bunch.

Suddenly, he straightens, looking up and catching my eye. With a sickening twist of my stomach, I realize I've inched so close to the window that I stand in full view of him. He smiles, waving, and I pull the curtain back over the window as a panicked little puff of air escapes me.

Shit, he caught me. I don't dare move the curtain again, peering through the white sheerness that blurs the men below into simple tan blobs. But I can see enough to know his head pans back to the window more than once as he removes his cowboy hat, running his fingers through his thick brown hair before replacing it.

CHAPTER
SIX
AXEL

"Looks like somebody's got an admirer," Logan grunts, his muscles straining as he holds the arch steady, and Turner secures another screw.

Christian and Turner both look up quizzically for a moment and then my eldest brother laughs. "It's not Cricket, and it's not Lily or Jess."

"Then, who the hell could it be?" I ask, scowling as I brace another heavy piece of wood for Turner.

"Why don't you find out?" Christian mutters impatiently.

"Me?" I straighten, looking up. My eyes go to the second story of the ranch house guest bedroom window, where Aspen raptly watches us. Or maybe me. The moment our eyes meet, I wave, and she steps back, letting the see-through white curtains cascade back over the window. Caught red-handed.

I chuckle.

"So, what's the deal between you two?" Turner mutters, holding screws between his lips.

"Apparently, she likes what she sees," I reply ambiguously, not ready to answer his question. Hell, I'm not even sure I'm capable of doing so right now.

"Quit being so vague," Christian scolds. "Where do you know each other from?"

"It's a long story," I reply, determined to tell them nothing.

"A one-night stand?" Logan asks, arching an eyebrow.

"Damn, I wish."

"I didn't see a ring on her finger, so what's stopping you?" he presses.

"Struggling with this fucking arch, for starters. Turner, are we almost done with this shit?" I ask, my shoulders burning as I continue to brace the same surprisingly heavy portion of the structure.

"Almost done," he says through clenched teeth.

"After that," I say. "I'll need a goddamned shower with how hot it is. I'm fucking drenched."

"You and me both," Christian growls.

Turner places another screw, stepping back and giving the structure a once-over. "All done."

We each let go of the portion we're holding hesitantly. Sure enough, it stays together and stands upright without any assistance. Sauntering backward a few steps, I can't help but marvel at the structure. Despite being a pain in the ass to put together, it looks surprisingly delicate and rustic now that it's completed.

"What do you think?" Turner asks triumphantly.

"Overkill," Christian mutters grumpily.

"Complicated to assemble," Logan grumbles.

Shifting my weight from one foot to the other, I put my hands on my hips, appraising it for a long moment. Once I feel three pairs of eyes on me, I add, "If you're looking to get some national attention for your work, Turner, this should do the trick."

He smiles broadly. "You think so?"

"Yes." I nod to emphasize my one-word answer. Side-eyeing him, I add, "I hope you're prepared to start manufacturing and shipping these nationwide because everyone's going to want one for their wedding after watching the TV show."

"Everyone may want one, but they'll have to pay a hefty price. After all, this is a one-of-kind design crafted from salvaged old barn wood."

"Well, it's cool."

Christian cocks his head to the side. "Do you really think Ridge and Paige are that famous?"

I shrug. "They're the only people I know who have their own reality TV show. Didn't Ridge confess the other day that they get millions of views per episode?"

Logan shakes his head. "I had trouble handling all the hubbub surrounding Jess after her rescue. I can't imagine recording my life and putting it out there for everyone to see."

I remove my hat, rubbing the back of my hand over my sweaty forehead. "It's ironic, considering how shy Ridge has always been." I sneak a glance back at the second-story window, disappointed to see the curtain drawn.

"Quiet maybe but never as secretive as you," Turner counters.

"True. Can you imagine a television program about me? It'd have like five words."

Christian chimes in. "More like a good dozen words if you're talking about beer."

I grin broadly. He has me figured out. Beer-making is my passion, and I can wax annoyingly long on the subject.

"So, if you hook up with the wedding planner, then all we have to do is find Bowie a woman, and we're all done," Logan mutters, staring out across the lawn where a towering black cowboy jumps out of his white F-250 dually. He saunters in our direction with a flashing smile on his face.

"If I'm relying on you guys to be my matchmakers, I'm in serious trouble. So is Bowie," I respond gruffly before stepping forward to hug my brother.

Bowie holds his palms up, stopping me in my tracks. "Keep your dirty-ass, sweaty chest away from my threads."

"What? You don't want to have to take a shower like the rest of us?" Logan growls, stepping forward and grabbing his hand. "Must be nice staying in an air-conditioned office all day and managing to show up right when you're no longer needed."

Bowie chuckles, shaking his head. "More like an air-conditioned car. Bounty hunters spend very little time in the office, no matter what you've seen on TV. As for showing up after the fact, it's the worst thing that can happen to a bounty hunter, so you'll have to chalk this up to an unhappy coincidence. What are y'all out here going on about anyway?"

"Trying to get you and Axel matched up with gals so that everyone's finally happy," Logan explains.

Bowie's eyebrows shoot up his forehead, and he looks at me awkwardly.

"Don't look at me. I'm shit when it comes to finding women."

Christian declares, "You all are. But with our combined matchmaking skills, we should have you past that by the end of the year."

"End of the year?" I repeat incredulously. "You do realize it's September already, right?"

Logan shrugs. "Yeah, and we've already got you lined up with the wedding planner if you don't fuck everything up, so then it's only a matter of finding a woman for Bowie. You think that's going to be tough with the way he works out and dresses?"

"I work out, too," I point out.

"Yeah, but you dress like a fucking bum, and you don't say enough to sustain a conversation, let alone a relationship. If you're lucky, though, Ms. Everhart will be okay doing the talking for both of you."

A bum? Appraising my boots, Wranglers, and dark gray plaid pearl snap shirt, I disagree. But today's outfit isn't what they're talking about.

During the summer, I dress functionally, preferring T-shirts to button-downs, ball caps to a Stetson, and leather sandals to boots. Sloppy by their standards. But for me, looking like fucking Roy Rogers is a weather-dependent proposition.

"You're kind of leaving out a brother," Bowie points out, and everyone stops, lapsing into momentary silence.

Christian finally says, "As far as I can tell, Holden and Delilah are still an item despite everything."

"We'll see," Bowie replies skeptically. "Prison changes a man, and it's rarely for the better. Dee's in love with the idea of who Holden was in the past. God only knows how he'll come out ... or when."

Another truck pulls up, and Flynn jumps out, striding around it to help his lovely Latina wife Jasmine out. He kisses her before she waves in our direction, heading up the porch into the house. Asante scrambles out of the back seat and straight for the ranch house.

Flynn watches his nephew streak past, shaking his head before sauntering towards us. He slaps the first brother he meets, Bowie, on the back, hugging him. Then, he offers us his hand politely, though obviously, as uninterested in getting sweat and dirt on him as Bowie.

"You showed up just in time, bro," Bowie says. "We were talking about one of your clients, Holden."

My throat tightens, and I suddenly feel guilty and anxious as Flynn's scrutinizing eyes go straight to me. "He's been in the clink for far too long, with so many unanswered questions. But when you go up against the family of one of the state's most powerful senators, what do you expect?"

Everyone shrugs, looking down sadly, but Flynn's eyes stay locked on me. "And then there's the matter of witnesses with obvious holes in their testimony. It was a perfect fucking storm that led to his conviction, but I haven't given up on him yet."

"I wouldn't expect any less from you," Bowie says.

Christian's eyes dart back and forth between Flynn's laser-focused gaze and my impassive face, and I can tell his mind works overtime. He's always been a perceptive man, and working as the Gold County Sheriff has helped him hone his gut instincts. His eyes narrow, curiosity etched on his face.

This is the last fucking thing I need right now, especially with Aspen here as the wedding planner. If there's anything I wanted to shield her from, it's my past. This concern was honestly the only thing that made our breakup palatable because I'd rather let her go than change her perception of me irrevocably.

Clearing my throat, I prompt, "We were talking about whether Dee and Holden are still an item and what we think will happen after he gets released."

Flynn presses his lips into a straight line. "She's been his lifeline for years now. I can't imagine anything will change."

Bowie chuckles. "That's where you and I differ, bro. I'd give them a thirty percent chance of sticking it out."

Flynn's face darkens, and his expression grows grave. "I disagree. If you can't count on your woman through the tough times, then what's the point?"

"Are you all going to stand there like a bunch of lazy assholes?" A deep voice calls from the barn. We turn, looking at Travis. He's a firefighter and member of the Rough & Ready Hotshots, which deploys to fight summer wildfires. Fortunately, he's home this weekend. I've heard rumblings that he wants to quit working as a hotshot to stay closer to his wife, Faith, and their growing family. Never did I foresee this adrenaline junkie going domestic, especially before me.

"What? You're not done stringing the fairy lights in the barn?" Christian calls in his direction.

"Hell, no," Travis replies, sounding exasperated.

"Sounds like it's light hanging time," Logan mutters, grabbing his shirt and heading towards the barn. The rest of us follow with me, consciously working to keep a healthy distance from Flynn. The last thing I need is more berating on his part to testify against the House of the Seven Prophets and clarify the record on Holden.

Yes, I feel like shit about the whole thing. And maybe I'm even a coward. But I'm certain my testimony won't change anything. That said, it could easily cost me everything.

Sighing deeply, I remind myself of my last phone conversation with Holden. He told me to keep my mouth shut regarding the official story of the night the senator's son was stabbed to death. That's all he's ever told me, and considering what he did for me, I have to respect his word and remain loyal to him, no matter what.

"Feels like forever since I was at the ranch," Bowie comments as we enter the barn, pausing to savor the coolness of its interior. Rows of round tables fill the airy space, glowing against the backdrop of the rugged wood floors and walls. Lights twinkle from the rafters, illuminating half of the barn and begging for more hands on deck.

"That's because it has been forever," Logan says. "Here's a quick catch-up on what you missed. Axel's sweet on the wedding planner, in case you didn't know. So, I'm about to write him off as taken. But what's your deal, Bowie? Any women on the horizon?"

"Women? Hell, yeah. Until I tell them about my job and its semi-nomadic nature. A bounty hunter sounds good and all until you have to live with the consequences of it day in and day out. Never found a girl willing to put up with it for long. But enough about me. What's the deal with Axel and the wedding planner?"

I shake my head, frowning.

"Good luck trying to pry it out of him," Christian barks in exasperation, side-eyeing me. "As always, he's got to be the secretive brother."

"Nothing to tell," I counter. "She's hot. I appreciate beauty. That's it."

"That doesn't explain why she keeps looking at you, though," Logan adds, and I shoot him an annoyed look.

"Yep, 'cause ain't nothing beautiful about you, Axel," Bowie adds with a chuckle.

"Something we can agree on," my brothers chime in.

"Who needs enemies when you have family?" I mutter

with a shake of my head. "I may not be pretty, but none of you will care once the Rough & Ready Red starts flowing."

"Except for me," Travis hollers from across the barn where he stands on an extra tall ladder. Maksim feeds strings of fairy lights to him. "It's still fire season, so I've got to stay in tiptop shape. Which means no beer."

I nod, chuckling under my breath. My foster brothers may be the biggest pains in the ass that I know, but they're still the best family a man could ever ask for.

A twinge of guilt hits me as I remember Holden isn't here to celebrate with us. He's missed every single family wedding, and it's not fair. But what can I do about it? Flynn's gaze catches mine, the corners of my mouth turning down as he hands me a string of lights, and I climb the ladder.

SEVEN

ASPEN

"Alright," I say projecting my voice. "You're going to line up behind Christian and Cricket in order, and when the music starts, you'll head out with your partner, walking, one step at a time, out to the green. Yes, it will feel excruciatingly slow, but step to the rhythm of the music. That way, the photographers and videographers will have plenty of opportunities to document everything. Are there any questions?"

My gaze settles briefly over various faces, inviting questions and looking too fast past Axel. I can't even with him. Especially not at work. Especially after he caught me visually devouring him through the window upstairs.

Christian stands at the front of the line with Cricket, the babies having been removed along with the smaller children to be watched by childcare staff enlisted for the event. The blond, tanned cowboy laughs, saying sarcastically, "No, ma'am. But then, this is far from our first rodeo."

Behind him, black-haired and bearded Logan, who works search and rescue, and his journalist wife, Jess, with a short, blonde bob, agree, nodding. Jess purses her lips, adding. "We're almost professionals at this point. There seems to be a wedding here every couple of months."

The wedding party nods in unison. I glance out the window at one of the members of the camera crew, a late teens or early twenties guy who has been given the duty of motioning when it's time to start sending couples out.

He gives me the hand motion for five more minutes. I look down at the Trello board on my phone, reminding myself that I should also hear the trio currently playing on the green go into Pachelbel's Canon in D when it's time to start.

"Alright, everyone, five minutes to go time. When it's your turn, you'll come and stand next to me, and I'll tap the bridesmaid's shoulder to head out."

My eyes return to the list on the board. It's the only safe place to have them with Axel in the room. I have to stay professional, no matter what. Yet, despite the internal pep talk, my eyes continue to flutter back towards him, getting lost in his stupidly handsome countenance. It's as if they have a mind of their own. My gaze darts back and forth to Steph's, the bridesmaid paired with him, and a tinge of jealousy sends stinging sparks into my chest.

Clearly, she's interested in the mountain man. The way she keeps side-eyeing him, finding reasons to touch his shoulder and upper arm, and leaning into him giggling. It makes me nauseous. And if that's not enough, she's got the kind of figure I could never compete with, rail thin with ample tits. They make my B cups feel sadly inadequate.

Despite the lovely woman on his arm, Axel's dark blue eyes unexpectedly find mine, and he licks his bottom lip sensually, incinerating me from the inside out. His hands are clasped in front of him, a sure sign he's been in a million weddings, and his face is contemplative. I would give anything, even my beloved TC2 Carice, to read his thoughts.

His unabashed gaze sends shivers of wild want shuttling up and down my spine to the juncture between my legs, where they settle in an agonizing, highly unprofessional, throbbing wetness. I can't help but think Steph's actually the last person on his mind. My heart slams uncooperatively against my ribs as my face burns despite every internal attempt to keep it together.

Get your mind off the brother of the groom, Aspen! This is Wedding 101 stuff. What in the hell is wrong with me? Remember, you are doing this for Stella. To maintain her awesome reputation. It's time to hyperfocus and ensure that no detail gets left to chance, hot cowboy mountain man or not.

Trudy, the videographer, stands next to me. Leaning forward, she questions. "You look downright glum all of a sudden. Are you okay?"

"Yes," I whisper, straightening my back and forcing a smile. "With the addition of so many camera people onsite, I guess I'm feeling an extra weight on my shoulders. Instead of merely planning an extra-large wedding, I'm also managing a film production."

She laughs, and I notice the intimidation etched in her face.

Turning to her, I observe, "I could ask you the same question. Are you okay?"

She chuckles. "Overwhelmed. This feels like a snowball rolling downhill and gaining momentum and girth with each pass. I've never been involved in an event this big before."

"I've done comparably large weddings, including Hollywood ones with lots of security. But never for a TV show. That said, I know what Stella would say if she were here right now. Act like this is every wedding, and do what you do best. Ridge and Paige hired you based on your previous work. Keep that in mind."

She smiles nervously. "That's what I keep reminding myself. How is Stella, by the way? I was sad to hear when she had to find a replacement, although you're absolutely amazing."

"Things are tough for her at the moment, with both parents ailing. But I'm happy that I can help. She's always been there for me."

"Well, you're doing a fantastic job despite all of the complications associated with this gig. And you look downright unfazed like you do this all the time."

I laugh. "Some people call it resting bitch face, and it's one of my secret superpowers."

Trudy giggles. "It's better than having a face that gives everything away. I'm blushing like it's 1990, and Johnny Depp just walked in the room."

"Don't tease," I say in silky tones, my eyes wandering back towards Axel again. Fortunately, he's busy talking to some of his sisters-in-law, and he doesn't notice the indiscretion.

But Trudy does, her head bobbing back and forth between me and him, and her face growing increasingly curious. She arches an eyebrow, and I look away, unwilling to explain.

Moments pass. Finally, she whispers, "Looks like you've caught the eye of one of the brothers." She nods towards Axel, who's back to studying me. "Lucky you."

I shrug, trying to play it off casually. "Maybe there's something on my face."

"Nope, not a stroke of blush or an eyelash out of place, and your lipstick's still fully intact. By the way, do you want to be in some of the film footage? Sorry to ask, but like I said, recording the rehearsal is a bit unusual for me, and I feel shaky about the accepted protocol."

I purse my lips together, glancing out the window for my signal. He shakes his head when I arch my eyebrows. I wonder what the delay is. Turning to Trudy, I say, "The first rule of wedding planning is that there is ultimately no protocol. Only what the bride and groom want."

"What if they can't agree?" she asks with a laugh.

"That's when we either invite immediate family in for a tiebreaker or we fall back on tradition."

"Have you ever had times when that didn't work?"

I repress a smirk. "In my nearly ten years of wedding planning, I've seen it all. And that's why we get paid the big bucks. Now, as for your question, I'm not completely sure how to answer it. You've stumped me, which rarely happens." I bite my lower lip. "What can it hurt to shoot a little footage of me directing everyone? For all we know, it might end up on television, with your permission, of course."

"Absolutely!" Trudy grins widely. "I would love to be TV famous."

"Me? Not so much." However, I've already resigned myself to that inevitability. Being in the wedding episode of *Honeymooning in the Wilds* will no doubt come with some very hefty perks for my personal branding. But I've never been comfortable with inhabiting the spotlight. Heck, it's one of the reasons why I became a wedding planner in the first place. To work behind the scenes.

"Okay, sounds good," Trudy beams.

The opening strains of Pachelbel's Canon in D reach my ears. It's not quite the same without the familiar cello line at the bottom, but Gregory, the violist, does his best to mimic the lower registers. Alex should be playing this, but that's one of the downsides of having the star classical musician of the quartet walking in the wedding. I look out the window, and the camera crew member gives me the thumbs up.

One by one, starting with Phil and Meredith, Paige's parental figures, and Ridge's foster dad, I send people out, reminding them in a whisper to walk slowly in rhythm to the music. Next, the officiant heads out, and Ridge follows behind. There is no official best man or maid of honor, so bridesmaids follow on the arms of the groomsmen.

Each couple stops in front of me as the previous couple walks out, and I do one last look-over to make sure their hands and arms are in the right places. I also make small talk with them to keep things light and fun.

My heart races the nearer Axel and Steph get. I avert my eyes, a mixture of jealousy and awkwardness overcoming me. While it doesn't appear, at least from my vantage point, like Axel and Steph are an item, the fact I'm even worrying about this variable annoys me. *I mean, make up your damn mind, Aspen!*

As if to prove I have no self-control whatsoever, my brain incessantly flashes back to previous conversations with the mountain man when we were still communicating through Mountain Mates. While we didn't know each other for that long, our conversations quickly went to a very desperate and carnal place, which makes my cheeks burn.

It's as if we both hurried over some of the most important parts of getting to know each other in our rush toward physical intimacy. For one, I didn't even know he had foster brothers or was a foster child, although there was a brief mention of siblings, a tough childhood, and his mother.

The lack of knowledge wasn't solely out of reticence

from him, although he's far from one to volunteer information. I never even asked, unwilling to speak about my own
family. *Asking about family is kind of basic dating etiquette,
Aspen. No wonder I'm still single.*

That said, it's interminably unpleasant to have to
explain to every man I date that my father is on his fourth
wife, I have seven much younger siblings, and my mom was
cut out of my life out of spite. Talk about dysfunctional.

When Axel and Steph stand directly in front of me, I
frown, perusing the way she grips his arm. Envy grips me as
I wonder if they're together, though it's none of my business. I should chitchat with them, but I can't bring
myself to.

To my surprise, however, Axel intercedes, asking cooly,
"Do we look all good to go, Aspen?"

Aspen. God, I love how the growly man says my name.
"Better than good," I reply before I can filter myself.

He winks again, sending my heart into freefall. The
cameraman calls through the door in a hissing whisper,
"What's the hold-up?"

Oh, shit. I tap Steph on the shoulder, despising the way
she brings her other hand up to grip Axel's arm more
tightly. "Only use one arm, please," I call after them in far
more impassioned tones than I need to, and Axel grins
broadly. God, this is awkward.

I look after them feeling like a voyeur as I appraise
Axel's broad shoulders and muscular back and ass. He's
gorgeous. Beyond gorgeous. Fortunately, he doesn't look
back, or he'd catch me with my jaw resting on the floor of
the ranch house.

Behind him stand the younger brothers and their
significant others, ending with the blond, bearded cowboy,
Maksim, and his wife, Alex. I go through the motions until

the classical cellist, with a wild mane of black curls and piercing, crystalline eyes stands beside me.

I squeeze her arm gently, gushing in warm tones. "You look gorgeous, Alex, and we're all clear on when you'll leave the wedding party and perform with the other musicians again?"

She gives me a thumbs-up, flashing a big smile. "I'm back to work starting with cocktail hour."

"After pictures," I remind.

She nods, smiling broadly like she does this all the time.

The camera crew member gestures, and I tap her shoulder, sending them out. Last but not least come the flower girl, Stasia, and the ring bearer, Asante. A gloomy teen, Asante wasn't especially interested in being the ring bearer, protesting that it's a job for little kids. Once I gave him a guesstimate of what the ring's actually worth, though, he turned around his thinking, admitting such a big responsibility shouldn't be left with one of the younger kids.

The handsome black boy stands stock straight with perfect posture, awaiting his turn. As I tap the shoulders of Stasia and then Asante, the wedding party portion of the rehearsal ends. Above me, I hear the rustle of fabric, looking up as Paige descends the stairs on Phil, her step-in dad's arm.

She wears an electric blue satin gown with a matching fascinator. "You look stunning," I whisper, stepping forward to adjust how her hair lays on her shoulders.

"Thank you," she says in giddy tones.

Phil pats her hand. "Ready to do this?"

"You mean practice?"

He nods.

I bustle back around to the front, straining my ears for

the break in the music and the start of Mozart's Wedding March. The opening strains ring out, and my signal waves.

"Alright, you two, time to shine."

I follow behind, watching them slowly walk towards the altar. Looking down at my phone, I prepare for the events to follow. Although we won't be going through everything today, I will give a little speech before the rehearsal dinner begins with a truncated form of what to expect for tomorrow.

It includes a performance in the middle of the ceremony by Ridge's foster brother Rock and his wife Effie, who do Civil Wars-style duets that send electricity crackling through the air. Following the ceremony, the string quartet will play for happy hour after Alex is done with group photos, and then, a DJ will entertain for dinner and part of the reception.

At some point, a local favorite, Bijou and her jazz trio, will take the stage for some live music, and the DJ will take a break, reprising his role well into the night when the festivities finally come to a close.

Something tells me the next two days will feel like a full week's worth of work or more. But the dollar signs at the end of the event make it all worth it. Now, all I have to do is avoid the kind of temptation that wears Wranglers and a Stetson.

EIGHT

AXEL

I spend the entire wedding rehearsal with my eyes locked on Aspen. She's so much more than I could ever imagine long-distance. Beautiful, radiant, sexy as hell, intelligent, authoritative, confident, and more focused on me than I can ignore. *Despite everything.*

The unforeseen, though not unwelcome, attention has my insides in knots. Her attraction to me is clear, unmistakable. So, why did she break things off? There has to be another man. I can't fathom what else it could be.

The conflict on her face vindicates me as she struggles to pull her eyes from my face, coming down the aisle to address the wedding party. She's a woman completely in her professional element, and it's tantalizing as fuck.

From her cowboy boots to her black, flowing sundress and tanned arms, which she revealed after removing her jacket, she's everything I want. And when she wears her white hat? It's all I can do not to pull her into my arms and taste her mouth. That said, she'd look far better wearing my brown Stetson and riding me buck naked.

Fuck, I can't think like this. My body shivers with longing. Never has a woman made me feel such visceral, soul-deep hunger. I fear and anticipate what will happen when I finally get her alone.

But I have to play it cool. After how things went down, the next move is clearly hers. *If there is a next move.*

After the rehearsal, we move quickly to dinner inside the decorated barn. We used the same space for Maksim and Alex's wedding, and it looks welcoming, with fairy lights decorating every corner and the circular tables decorated with white linens, thick black satin bows, and tables decked with splashy magenta peonies.

"Just like Christian said. Couldn't stop staring at the wedding planner," he says matter-of-fact, reminding me of what an ass I made of myself during the rehearsal. While I'd swear Aspen shares my feelings based on the way she returns my looks, she has yet to acknowledge my presence in any way apart from my role as a groomsman. Or even admit how she recognizes me.

"Was it that obvious?" I grimace.

Bowie laughs, shaking his head and revealing big, white, straight, teeth. "More than obvious. Sorry for returning to the same question you've been asked all afternoon, but how do you know each other?"

We take our seats at our place cards as serving staff bustles around. Country music croons in the background, thanks to my nephew, Asante, who volunteered to act as our DJ tonight. The professional guy couldn't make it until tomorrow, considering it's still prime wedding season. But so far, Asante's doing excellent.

Leaning toward Bowie, I explain, "Remember that woman I told you about who I met through Mountain Mates?"

"How can I forget? Hell, I'm thinking about creating a profile. Would you recommend it?"

The last time we discussed it, I was only beginning and didn't have much to say. My gaze follows Aspen around the room, and I've got plenty of opinions now. "I'd be lying if I said I didn't meet an amazing woman. But the whole long-distance thing seriously sucks. So, think through the filters you set, like how far you want to travel and all of that."

"Is that why you and the wedding planner aren't doing anything beyond staring like two lovesick fools at each other?" Bowie asks, amused.

I run my hand through my hair. "It's a long story. Too long for tonight."

"Huh. Well, are you going to make a move tonight?"

I shrug, keeping my cards close to my chest.

"Better figure it out, Axel, or you really will be the last single brother standing."

"It wouldn't surprise me," I reply, looking at the white tablecloth. "I'm not especially good at getting to know people."

"Or trusting them."

"That, too. But then, I haven't had a lot of reasons to trust humanity apart from Dad and you brothers. And women don't want the kind of baggage I have."

"No one has a right to judge you by what happened in your childhood," he says firmly, drawing a thin line with his lips. "It's ultimately none of their fucking business. They should focus on the man you are today. Period." His voice trails off for a moment as a server approaches us with salad plates. We both sit back, giving her access to the space in front of us. "Wait, is that the problem with the wedding planner? She can't hang with your personal history?"

"Dunno."

His eyes narrow. "You mean, you haven't told her yet?"

"I thought about it. But then she got cold feet and broke everything off with me before our first meeting. Maybe I'm not her type after all."

"The way she keeps eyeing you, I imagine you're more than her type. Maybe she's got secrets, too."

"She does."

"Sounds like an open, honest conversation is in order."

He has a point. But I counter in grumbly tones, "Yeah. But that breakup was pretty damn final. We haven't spoken in a month."

"Well, she seems to want to now," he observes, rubbing the back of his neck and nodding in her direction. Sure enough, her toffee-colored eyes are on me again. They flicker away the moment I notice, like a moth dancing around a flame, trying not to get burned.

"I guess we'll find out. But back to your predicament. I don't know if Mountain Mates women are more willing to put up with semi-nomadic bounty hunters than gals on other dating sites. I guess it would be worth a shot, though. Maybe what you need to find is a really hot criminal to pursue," I tease.

"Fuck, and then I can spend my time heartbroken about whether to turn her in. Hate to say it, but cashing in on a mark will always come before matters of the heart."

"You're cold-hearted, bro."

He moves his fork around on his plate, chasing a stray sprig of arugula hellbent on not getting speared. "Have to be in my line of work."

"Have to be on Mountain Mates, too. After all, there are a lot of matches to sort through."

"So, the wedding planner was at the top or the bottom of the pile?" he asks.

"She was the only woman I wanted to talk to," I confess, feeling like a fucking reject.

"Then, you better find a way to speak to her before this nuptial weekend is over. Promise me you will."

Aspen's eyes continue to sear me, her cheeks flushed. I lick my lips, equal parts ticked by his request and anxious to finally having a face-to-face conversation with her. "Alright, but if it's a total crash-and-burn session, you'll be the one picking me back up off the floor."

"Always, bro."

The rest of the evening is uneventful. After a delicious dinner and good conversation, we gather outside beneath a huge harvest moon to say our goodnights.

"Same place, different time," Ridge jokes as the family mill around, giving each other hugs.

It's the kind of warm outside that makes me want to sit on the porch and stare up at the stars for a while. Bowie finds me, hugging and reminding me, "You promised me you'd make a move. The clock's ticking."

I give him a firm nod, conflicted inside.

Flynn hugs me next, an uneasy silence between us. The other brothers and their significant others follow more jovially. I can't help but feel jealous at how they've all found love while I remain irretrievably single ... apart from a little eye fucking.

After everyone drives off, I unlock my pickup and rifle through the glove box for something I can't remember the last time I needed: a cigarette and my lighter.

I head out back where the chicken coop is and light up, walking a little way out to keep the smoke from Dad's window. I promised him I'd give up the habit, but these are special circumstances.

Every part of smoking, from holding the burning white

cylinder between my fingers to filling my lungs with the heated air and exhaling slowly and methodically, feels like a meditation. Holden's the one who introduced me to nicotine's nerve-calming effects, though I know it's shitty for my healthy. He always was the real black sheep of the family, though Rock tried hard to claim that title.

"Mind if I share?" a familiar voice lilts behind me.

"Sure," I say, tilting my head down to hide the bashful grin that instantly captures my lips as I hand Aspen the cigarette.

She takes a long drag, her pretty pink lips undoing me as I watch. She closes her eyes, and her shoulders relax ever so slightly. A thousand questions fill my head, but I say nothing, giving the mouthwatering wedding planner the moment she needs.

When her eyes flutter open again, I observe, "Tough day?"

"More than you could know," she says, hugging herself with her arms. "I didn't know you smoked."

"I don't," I reply too quickly, and she arches a curious eyebrow.

"I mean, I don't unless I'm feeling really anxious, which rarely happens these days."

"Same. It's a filthy habit," she says ironically, taking the cigarette when I offer it to her again, and our fingertips brush.

Electricity sizzles between us. I scrutinize her, noting how her nostrils flare, and she bites her bottom lip. Her eyes hold an invitation that my body longs to accept.

"We talked for a total of three months, and yet I still feel like I know so little about you," I say, leaning back against a fence post and crossing my arms. *Especially after the deaf-*

ening silence of last month. But I keep the last thought to myself.

"That's because you're incredibly reticent."

"So are you," I counter.

"What do you mean? I'm an excellent conversationalist," she replies, raising her chin.

"Yes, you are. You could talk my ear off without ever really telling me anything about yourself."

She shrugs. "You caught me."

"Maybe you didn't really want to get to know me?" I take another drag before handing her the cigarette. Her touch lingers over mine for a moment longer this time, incinerating me from the inside out. I clear my throat, trying not to sound raw-voiced and failing miserably. "I mean, isn't that why you canceled our first in-person date?"

She stares at me for a long moment, shifting her weight from one foot to the other. "It wasn't that I didn't want to get to know you. It's that I knew it could never work."

"And how could you know that, Aspen?"

"Just a feeling," she answers, looking down. Her voice tells me she's holding back. "I don't do illogical and impetuous any more. I used to, and I'm still paying for it. Maybe I always will be."

"Sounds dramatic," I remark, leaning in, using the cigarette as an excuse to invade her space. A tantalizing, delicate fragrance rewards me, honeysuckle and citrus. Something I could never learn about her from Mountain Mates or FaceTime. "Are you sure it's really that bad?"

She runs her bubblegum pink tongue over her top lip, her mouth open as she draws a couple of steps nearer. I'm so fucking confused at this point, unable to make heads or tails of her mixed signals. My heart slams around wildly in my chest, pulverizing itself on my ribs.

"Worse." The corners of her mouth turn down.

"We all have to pay for something in this life. Whether it's transgressions of our own making or the sins of others."

Aspen chuckles darkly, her light brown eyes vibrant with emotion. Knitting her brows, she whispers, "Or both."

She hands me the cigarette, our hands caressing blatantly. My pulse races, and I clench my teeth, grinding them together with the intensity of my longing.

"What are you thinking?" she asks breathlessly.

"You don't want to know," I answer darkly.

"I do, or I wouldn't ask."

A lopsided grin captures my mouth as I admit, "I was thinking what a pity it is we can't fuck without our hearts getting in the way ..."

She nods, looking down at the toes of her boots. "I was thinking the same thing. But I've never been able to separate sex and feelings that way—"

"Me, either." I drop the cigarette in the grass, snuffing it out beneath the toe of my boot.

"Hey, I wasn't done with—"

"Yes, you were," I growl, crossing the distance between us and pulling her into my arms. Her breath catches in her throat, and her eyes liquefy into amber pools as I inch closer, emboldened by her words and the feel of her fingers touching mine. Blinking slowly, she parts her inviting mouth, dropping her eyes to my lips.

NINE

ASPEN

Axel's face is less than an inch from mine, his smoky breath warming my cheek. He makes me feel things I shouldn't.

Animalistic things that could be my undoing because they have been before. But I tell myself I'm older and wiser now, better able to care for myself as I inhabit the frustrating space between us, begging him to kiss me.

"God, you're fucking beautiful in person," he says, an ache pulsing through his words. I tremble in his arms despite the heat of the night, my eyes fixed on his tempting mouth.

Suddenly, he steps back, letting me go. His face is conflicted as he looks up at the ranch house diagonal to us. "Take a walk with me?" He offers his hand, and I take it without thinking.

Axel leads me towards a gate we pass through. The night is still and quiet, punctuated solely by the crunch of our feet along the path and the roar of distant crickets absorbed in their riotous, late summer mating choirs.

Axel's large, thick fingers slide between mine, melting

me from the inside out as he glances back over his shoulder at me, his face determined. His stride shortens, and he murmurs, "Sorry if I'm walking too fast for you, but there's something I've wanted to show you ever since we first started talking."

"Okay," I whisper.

"Be careful with that dip in the path," he commands, slowing even more as he acclimates to holding my hand and walking next to me instead of in front of me.

We reach an ambling stream enveloped on both sides by tufts of golden marsh grass, the din of the insects deafening. He leaps it with ease, offering me his hand. I take it without hesitation, using his strength, rather than my momentum, to reach the other side. His mouth quirks, pleasure washing over his face as I realize how much this small surrender, this act of trust, means to him.

If he were any other man, I'd hesitate or refuse his help, determined not to rely on anyone. But Axel has always made me feel safe and understood. In person, this energy pervades his being, heightening my sense of peace and grounding. Like I don't have to put on acts or pretend to be something I'm not ... even though a strange gulf of mutual secrecy lingers between us.

The path steepens downhill, and we tentatively follow it out across a field of knee-high grass to two prominent boulders that look like they dropped from heaven during some primordial cataclysm. He leads us to them, leaning against one. I follow suit against the second, more distance between us than I want.

With hand gestures, Axel explains, "This whole valley was carved out by a glacier during the Ice Age. You can't see it in the dark, but the mountains on either side have steep sides with a U-shape down the middle."

"It's beautiful."

"I've seen way more beautiful," he sighs, eyeing me earnestly. "But this is one of my favorite spots by day, especially on horseback. Do you ride?"

"No, I've never been on a horse."

"You wear a hat like you do."

I chuckle. "I like to dress for the vibe of the place I'm visiting. This felt like the right outfit."

"You should learn to ride. You'd love it ... well, at least, I think you would based on previous conversations. But who knows?"

"Would you teach me?" I ask.

His eyes tick to mine, his gaze heated. "Of course."

I chuckle. "I had no clue you were a cowboy. I thought the whole point of Mountain Mates was to find mountain men. How did a cowboy sneak on there?"

He shrugs. "Every cowboy's a mountain man around here and vice versa. Always been like that."

"You never wore a cowboy hat in any of your photos or while we live-streamed, though."

He pauses, thinking for a moment. "I guess you're right. Never really thought about it. It wasn't intentional. Just a coincidence based on the photos I thought made me look okay. And I don't wear a hat indoors. It's impolite. But I must've done alright with images because you wanted to talk to me. At least for a while."

"About that," I say, looking down at the ground. "I may have jumped the gun on canceling our first date. But I got the feeling we weren't especially compatible."

He nods, frowning. "Do you still feel the same way in person?"

"We feel very compatible in person ... *at least to me.*"

"Me, too," he says gruffly and guarded.

The corners of my mouth turn up. "For the record, I had no clue I was going to see you at this event. While you mentioned having siblings, I didn't know you were a foster kid, let alone related to Ridge Dawson. Although I guess I should have figured it out after what you told me about your mother ..."

"Yeah, I don't open up to people easily, and I don't like saying too much about my past before people have a chance to know me. After all, the whole foster kid thing comes with countless assumptions. I wanted you to have a firm sense of who I am before diving into the unpleasant stuff."

"Makes sense. But you told me you lived near Sacramento, not Hollister. Why?"

He nods. "You're an Orange County girl. Would you have known where Hollister or even Ophir City are?"

I shake my head.

"Sometimes, its easier to tell people Sacramento."

"Makes sense." I level my gaze on him. "Anyway, I wanted you to know that I didn't come here purposely to see you."

"Is it usual for you to break a man's heart twice? Or is this a new record for you?" he asks with a teasing edge to his voice.

"Break your heart? I doubt that. Maybe bruise your ego a bit."

"I would be happy if you came here to see me."

"Despite everything?" I arch an eyebrow.

"Despite everything." He shifts the way he stands, crossing his arms over his chest. "So, bruised ego for sure. Along with some disappointment. I wanted to show you around my hometown, introduce you to my brothers, and let you get to know me and more about my life. If you remember, I was also very willing to head your direction and offered more than once. But you were hesitant to share your life in SoCal with me. Funny how fate still managed to get us together."

"Yes," I say, wetting my lips. "It seems like we were meant to meet no matter what." I pause for a moment, steeling myself for my next question. "What was the number one thing you looked forward to doing with me if I had stuck with the plan and visited?"

He shifts his weight, frowning. "Talk about a loaded question."

"Not loaded. You answer any way you like. I'm merely asking for the sake of curiosity and..."

"And?"

"And to know how hard I need to kick myself for getting cold feet."

He chuckles. "You don't need to kick yourself, Aspen. You weren't feeling it. Enough said."

I push off the boulder, pacing back and forth in front of him. The motion mirrors the fractious thoughts racing through my head. Suddenly, I stop. "You didn't answer my question."

"I know," he says in cool tones, looking out at the invisible point where the navy horizon meets the black tree line. "I was definitely looking forward to dancing with you. We don't have a lot of places to do that in Hollister apart from Stonie's. Have you been there yet?"

"No."

"I'd ask to take you now, but he's closed for the weekend for this wedding. Pretty much the whole damn town has shut down for it."

"We could dance here," I observe softly.

"And what would be the point?"

I stumble over my next words, ushering in an uncomfortable, expansive silence.

After a tense moment, Axel saunters in my direction, pulling his cell phone from his pocket and turning on country music, Morgan Wallen's *Spin You Around*.

He stops in front of me, offering his right hand. I take it, and he steps a hair closer, resting his left on the small of my back. The smell of his sandalwood and pine cologne fills my nostrils as a thousand little sparks shiver along the places where his flesh touches mine.

In breathy tones, I inquire, "Did you figure out what the point is?" My eyelids flutter as I stare into his stupidly handsome face, drowning in his indigo eyes.

"Yeah, to make you happy. I should quit worrying about anything else."

"Even though I've broken your heart twice now?" I ask in smooth tones, biting my bottom lip.

"You could kill me with that look, you know."

"What look?"

"That look with your big, brown doe eyes and your thick, full lashes fluttering up at me." He drops my right hand for a moment, stroking my cheek to push back a stray lock of hair. My face heats. "Biting your lush bottom lip and parting your mouth in a way that I can only read as welcoming ... *despite everything*."

I exhale all at once, feeling my pulse race. Cardiovascular overload is my new resting state around this man.

"With your nostrils flaring and your eyes dropping to my mouth, begging me to kiss you."

My gaze darts back to his face, my cheeks sizzling. "I never beg for anything, cowboy."

"That's a shame," he says darkly. "That means you've

never experienced anything worth begging for." His eyes sear me, his smile subtle though unmistakably naughty.

His words awaken my core, intensifying the throb between my legs as we sway to the music in the long country grass.

"Remember what you told me on the phone? That I made you feel seen, understood, and safe?"

"Wow, you still remember me saying that?" I ask.

"Of course, because I felt honored. You're not the kind of woman who says something like that lightly or insincerely."

"That's true."

"Which leads me to believe, with everything that happened next, that you didn't like feeling seen, understood, or safe with me."

Axel's not going to make this conversation easy.

"Do you know why feeling that way would make you panic?" He furrows his brows, knowing me better than I know myself.

Yes, I did panic, though I hate to admit it, even to myself. His intuitive ability to read me both fortifies the intimacy between us and annoys the hell out of me because the biggest lie I'm ultimately living is one I believe wholeheartedly. That I don't need any man.

I say, "What was happening between us felt too intimate. You know, like one or the other of us was going to get our feelings hurt, which is the last thing I wanted."

"Wait," he says, pausing mid-step to stare at me long and hard. "If you weren't looking for intimacy and getting close, then why were you on Mountain Mates?"

I shrug, the corners of my mouth turning down.

He waits patiently, drawing me out with his silence.

"I'm afraid you wouldn't understand. I've seen enough

of your family and how you interact to know you'd never get where I'm coming from."

"Try me," he grumbles.

"Okay." I take a long inhale, my mind racing as I struggle to know where to start. "It's not that I don't want intimacy and getting close to someone special. It's that I don't know how. My father is on his fourth marriage, which means my entire childhood was a revolving door of new stepmothers. The latest, interestingly enough, is a couple of years younger than me. I would be creeped out by it, except that I feel too sorry for her to entertain any other thoughts. She has no clue what she's gotten herself into. My biological mother was Father's first wife, and she was well-compensated to stay out of my life and childhood after the divorce. You know, minimize scandals and messy custody disputes. I've spoken with her a few times as an adult, but the gap between us culturally and historically is too big to bridge, in my opinion."

"What do you mean culturally?"

"My mom is Sylvia Gutierrez, a Mexican soap opera star. Pretty famous if you're into telenovelas. After Father and me, she became a serial monogamist, hiring surrogates to have my three younger brothers because she feared messing up her figure. She easily replaced me, just like Father with his six pain-in-the-butt younger children."

"Replaced you?"

"Maybe that sounds overly dramatic," I confess. "But that's how my parents made me feel. And I guarantee they're doing the same thing to my younger siblings. They don't like to get too close to anybody. Not their spouses, their children, their family and friends, nobody. I honestly think it's worked out much better for both of them because a healthy distance means fewer hurt feelings and misunderstandings."

"It also means less heartbreak, At least, theoretically," Axel adds.

"Exactly. But treating people like commodities and conveniences translates into a lifetime of loneliness. Sometimes, I get tired of the loneliness. But then, through dating, I remind myself why I can't fix it."

"But you don't treat people like commodities or conveniences, do you, Aspen?"

"Never," I reply, shaking my head. "Because I know how painful that is. Nevertheless, there's something broken in me ... that doesn't know how to trust and be intimate and do all the things normal people do. I shouldn't be telling you any of this. It makes me sound like a head case."

"Why shouldn't you?" he asks, narrowing his gaze. "I understand you better now, thanks to this one conversation, than three months of texting and talking ever did." He licks his bottom lip, setting my body on fire once more. As if it ever stopped sizzling and smoking between blazes. "Have you ever considered that maybe there is no healthy distance? At least with the right person?"

Our eyes lock, and I can't speak, letting the delicious suggestion unwind everything I've ever believed about love.

Still, dropping my defenses isn't an easy proposition. I shake my head. "Most men would say what I told you are red flags. That I have daddy issues."

"You do."

I shrug, "Which means most men don't want to touch me with a ten-foot pole." I eye him, scrutinizing has unreadable countenance.

"I don't want them touching you, either," he chuckles.

"Not with a ten-foot pole or anything else. If it were up to me, no man would ever touch you again."

"Sounds lonely."

"No way. I'd be the one exception, of course," he drawls with a lazy smile, his bedroom eyes searing into me.

"You would?" I whisper, staring up into his handsome, bearded face. "Despite everything that's happened between us?"

"I would," he sighs, leaning closer and holding me against his strong chest, more hugging than dancing as his phone falls silent. He nuzzles my neck, tenderly caressing my hair with his hands.

My body quakes, need rising. Brushing his lips over the shell of my ear, he whispers, "Look up."

I allow my gaze to wander heavenward, gasping at the sight overhead. The sky is a black velvet sheet inset with thousands, maybe millions, of tiny glittering diamonds.

"Bet you don't get views like this in SoCal."

"This is incredible. Magical." I'm awestruck by the sight and wrecked by our conversation.

"It is," he agrees quietly, his hands lightly roaming over my back and shoulders.

I strain to remember forever the stellar beauty of the sky above me and the feel of Axel's strong arms around me. The whole time I look up, he studies me, his eyes containing the same adoration I turn towards nature.

I don't know how much time passes, but this is exactly what I need. A chance to step outside of my petty existence and problems and surrender to something far bigger and more glorious than I can possibly comprehend.

Reluctantly, he suggests, "Do you want to head back? I'm not sure how long you want to stay out here with Paige and Ridge's wedding tomorrow."

His suggestion is logical and considerate, yet disappointment stings me. I wish he would kiss me. But I understand why he won't. And it's all my fault. There's so much I long to tell him. Instead, I shove my feelings down, burying them in the depths of my heart. "Thank you."

Letting go of me, he takes my hand, leading me back towards the ranch house. Our motions feel resigned, yet I can't find the courage to voice my need. It's uncharacteristic of me to be this quiet. By the time we reach my TC2 Carice, regret screams through me. *What might have happened between us if I hadn't ended things?*

Nodding at my convertible, he says, "You might want to put your top up before you go to bed. I saw overnight rain in the forecast."

"Thank you," I reply sadly. Not because he made the statement but because it gives me a taste of what it would be like to be cared for by this man. I want more. More than I'll ever get because of my stubborn, independent streak.

"What's on your mind?" he whispers, his eyes penetrating soul-deep. I can't hide from this man, and it both scares and thrills me.

TEN

AXEL

"What's on your mind?" I whisper.

Aspen looks down, licking her bottom lip. "I've missed talking with you, Axel."

The creases in my forehead deepen, and the blood roars through my veins. *Did I hear her right?* Shifting me weight, I say, "And I've missed you, too, Aspen, but …"

"But?"

"Fool me once, shame on you—"

"Fool me twice, shame on me," she finishes, trying to slip her hand from mine. I should let her, but I clutch her more fiercely, my heart throbbing. Her fingers squeeze mine, caressing and teasing my flesh. I need her … *desperately*. Though it makes no sense.

"I'm confused, Aspen. One minute, we're on the phone doing mind-blowing, naughty things together and making so many promises for our first meeting. The next, you're calling things off with air silence for a whole month. Likely forever … except you ended up here *by accident*."

"By fate," she whispers.

"Maybe. Do you really believe in that stuff?"

She shrugs.

"That's what I thought."

"What does that mean?"

I explain, "If you truly believed in fate, you wouldn't spend so much of your time meticulously planning out every detail of your life based on what you fear the future might hold."

Her eyes search mine, swirling with emotion. "Ouch."

"Ouch what?" I ask.

"Your words hit too close to the mark."

"I'm not trying to hurt you. I need to understand you and what happened to us. That's all."

She nods, looking down. "If I hadn't ended things, what else would we be doing right now, Axel? Besides dancing?"

"Well, I planned on showing you around the brewery and a beer flight so you could taste what I do for a living."

Her eyes flash to mine, a melancholy smile capturing her face. "That's right. I remember you talking about that."

"Yep..."

Inexplicably, I close the distance between us, pushing the hair off her face and snagging my finger under her chin to bring her gaze back to mine. Her toffee eyes swim with yearning as I drop my head inch by inch until my lips hover over hers.

What in the hell am I doing? My mind screams, but my body refuses to listen. I'm not thinking at all—only feeling. It draws me to her powerfully, like rapids to a waterfall's edge.

The breath strangles in her throat, a tiny whimper that ignites my blood. Before I can react, she leans up on her tiptoes, wrapping her arms around my neck and feathering her lips over mine. She tastes like smoke and regret and unquenchable need—everything I should avoid but crave no less. A growl rises from the depths of my chest, reverberating through my body like a warning before my lips respond hungrily, unhinged.

My hands thread into her hair, massaging her scalp and locking her against me as I invade her mouth ravenously. Her warm, velvety tongue urges me on, mating with mine as dangerous need mounts.

Throbbing, warm tension knots my lower core, demanding more. Aspen grips my neck desperately, pressing against my body with the same urgency devouring me whole. I need her more than I need air.

My hands descend ravenously, my mouth hungry and roaming along the length of her neck to her delicate décolletage, losing myself in the heady feel of her. Every sensual caress, every flesh-skimming breath, every brush of her lips incinerates me.

She grips my neck demandingly as my big, work-calloused hand slides to the tender flesh at the front of her neck, squeezing it possessively. My other hand descends lower, palming her lower back and then her ass as my hips thrust against her core.

But I can't make out like a horny teen in my Dad's front yard. Especially not in plain sight of his bedroom window.

I pull back reluctantly, not wanting to let go of Aspen. She tastes like a heaven I've never visited before. But the chemistry running between us risks deluging me. And I'd rather leave her on a high note, the hottest fucking kiss of my life, than let things sour between us again.

"I better get a move on," I pant, chest aching with longing. "Have a wonderful night, Aspen." I turn away, forcing myself to walk towards my truck. It takes every ounce of willpower. But if she's made up her mind this won't work, why prolong the pain?

"But, wait, Axel," she blusters. "Will we ever talk like this again?"

Wheeling back around, though still stepping in reverse closer to my truck, I don't mince words. "Probably not."

"Why?"

"Because I'm respecting your wishes ..."

Her big doe eyes plead with me, and she purses her lips, thawing my heart. "But what if my wishes have changed?"

Her words tug at my heart, but they're not enough. "Have they, though? Or are you caught up in the moment?"

"Would it be so bad to get caught up in the moment?" she asks, stepping towards me. "Stop worrying about the past or the future and enjoy the present? Without trying so hard to control it?"

I level my gaze on her. "You mean feel instead of think?"

She takes a few more steps towards me, and my pulse races, throbbing through my arteries and veins. "Exactly."

"Tell me about the last time you remember doing that, Aspen. Feeling instead of thinking."

"Apart from that kiss a few minutes ago and hanging out with you under the stars tonight? I can't ... though I do remember what made me decide to stop feeling in the first place."

"And what was that?" I ask.

She takes a deep breath. "When I was a little girl, my bio mother was allowed to see me once a year in December. I don't know why. But she always took me to the Newport Beach Christmas Boat Parade. We would stand on Balboa Island, eating Balboa Bars, and marveling at the beautifully decorated vessels. It was the only time I felt loved. I know that statement sounds dramatic, but if you knew my family, you'd understand. Anyway, those are some of the fondest, most amazing memories I have with her. They meant everything to me. But then, she got a new husband, and they focused on having more children, surrogacy, all of that. She got distracted, and before I knew it, she forgot all about boat parades and me. I still remember the last time I convinced myself she was coming to take me, though my father made it clear I was being foolish. I dressed up and waited in the sitting room for hours, my heart breaking. My father never comforted me. Neither did my stepmother. They left me sitting alone in a darkening room, learning never to count on anyone again … or to allow myself to feel."

I draw closer to her, the corners of my mouth turning down. "You're not that little girl anymore. You don't have to wait around for people who don't cherish you. You're a grown-ass woman, fierce as fuck and mesmerizing to behold. You can take what you want. And I'm pretty fucking sure you do that in every other area of your life … why not apply it to your heart, too?"

Her earthy eyes, with their thick fringe of lashes, search my face. "But if what I want doesn't work out?"

"It would suck, but we've already been there and done that … for a month. Tell me, how is our breakup going for you?"

She sniffles, admitting, "Shitty. I think about you every day. All the time." Burying her head in her hands, she adds, "God, I shouldn't admit this to you, but you might as well know. I got myself off earlier today thinking about you."

"Really?"

"Is that weird to admit?"

"Are you kidding me? It's fucking hot," I answer.

"What about you? How is it going for you?" she asks.

"The same," I admit.

"Even the masturbating?" she asks, a wicked grin lighting up her face.

"Especially the masturbating. Does that freak you out?"

"Not at all," she replies. "It's a turn-on to know you're thinking about me when you jerk off."

"Naughty girl," I growl.

"You have no idea," she flirts.

I would like to. But I keep this last thought to myself, still unsure of where this is going.

Silence fills the space around us as the air sizzles with unsatisfied longing.

"I shared with you, Axel. It's your turn this time. When's a time you remember feeling, not thinking?"

I don't want to delve too deeply into my past. It would bring up far more questions than I feel comfortable answering. But Aspen was forthright with me, and I need to offer her the same courtesy. Especially since I started this line of questioning.

"I can't think of a particular memory right off the bat. But I love fishing."

She chuckles.

"Yeah, I know it sounds stupid. But no other activity, well apart from exercise and sex"—I savor the way her cheeks burn at the last word—"lets me escape the thoughts I'd rather not have. It's kind of like a meditation for me. But one where I don't have to clear my mind..."

"I know exactly what you mean," she says softly. "Because your mind never really does clear, does it?"

"Nope, just fills with the wrong kind of memories." A dangerous thrill shivers through me. Inadvertently, I've steered the conversation exactly where I don't want it to go. If Aspen starts asking questions, I won't be able to answer them.

"Believe me, I understand …" Her face looks wistful as she says the last sentence, and I relax, blown away by the simple mercy of her words. Not curious. Not pushy. Simply choosing to inhabit the same space as me.

Silence overtakes us again.

"I remember why you called me Tiger," she says out of nowhere.

"And why was that, Aspen?"

"Because while I looked all fuzzy and cute, you were pretty sure I had a mean bite."

I chuckle. "Something I'm more sure of than ever. But you don't have things quite right. I *call* you Tiger because you look like an empress of the jungle, all slinky and regal and deadly as fuck. I'm pretty damn sure one of these days you'll eat me for breakfast, which brings me to another thing I wanted to do during our first weekend together. Cook you breakfast. I make a mean omelet and pretty amazing French toast and blueberry lemon muffins."

Her cheeks redden. "I remember you telling me that."

I stare at her, unmoving. Not certain what we're doing but unable to walk away.

"So, since it's a little late for breakfast, a beer flight, then? Am I following you back to your place?" she asks, wetting her lips.

I stare at her blankly for a long moment, my insides roiling. I should politely decline and steer clear of her the rest of the weekend. That would be the safest thing to do. Instead, I hear myself saying, almost as if someone else is speaking, "To my brewery and taproom. I'll give you the full tour and then the tasting I had planned for us."

She beams, and I know I've made the right decision. No matter what happens next. "I can't do a late night, by the way. You know, with the wedding and all."

I look down at my watch. "It's barely nine. I think we've got a little time to kill before you retire for the evening."

"Agreed."

"Besides, you can sleep in tomorrow morning, right? The ceremony isn't until four."

"There's no sleeping in on the big day," she corrects with a chuckle. Like what I suggested is downright silly. "Maybe for everyone else but not the wedding planner."

"Well, then, we better make the most of our time together," I say with a wink, turning and heading toward my truck.

CHAPTER
ELEVEN
ASPEN

I park next to Axel's big white truck in front of a massive warehouse-like building with a huge, elaborate, hand-painted sign that reads "St. Claire Brewery, Home of Rough & Ready Red."

"Wow, this is quite the facility," I exclaim awestruck as Axel rounds his truck.

He nods, walking towards the front entrance and pulling out his keys. "What do you know about the brewing process?" He asks over his shoulder as I take a few steps, caught in his undeniable gravitational pull.

"Not much apart from what you've already told me."

He holds the door open wide, nodding for me to pass through. As I enter, a sweet and earthy odor, almost like the smell of cookies, hits my nostrils. He turns on a row of switches, and the interior lights illuminate a large tasting room with at least ten booths and a rustic bar. Signs throughout and historic photos pay homage to the Sierra Nevada brewing tradition.

Axel stands next to me as my eyes crawl over the room, noting every detail of the cozy, dark wood interior with large ceiling fans overhead. The bar itself looks salvaged from a Victorian saloon, and I gravitate towards it, running my hand over the rich, dark wood.

"My brothers and I pulled that out of the International Saloon, Hollister's oldest bar, before the owners demolished it. That's the plot where Stonie's is now."

"It's stunning," I admire, looking at my reflection in the painted mirror behind the bar. The ancient glass bubbles and waves in spots, and a thin line of gold pin-striping edges it with fancy flourishes at each corner. "Too bad they tore down the original place."

"Yeah." He shrugs. "Locals protested at the time, but there wasn't much we could do about it. Stonie had nothing to do with it, of course. He ended up buying the property from the real estate developer after the fact and building his current facility. But the old place was held together by sawdust and a prayer, so it wasn't doing the community much good anyway."

Axel closes the distance between us. "May I take your jacket and hat?"

"Yes, please." His fingertips graze over my shoulders and décolletage as he removes the denim, and I exhale shakily. God, I want this man.

Removing my hat, I hand it to him, and he poises it next to his on the bar by the jacket. They look good together.

"I'm glad you were able to save this, though," I exclaim, still running my hands gently over the glossy wood surface.

"Do you want to have a seat and start with the tasting first? Or would you like a tour of the place?"

"What's the order you normally take visitors through the facility?" I ask.

"Usually, we start with the tour before they taste the fruits of our labor."

"Let's do that, then."

"Alright. Follow me." As we walk through the taproom and adjoining kitchen into the much larger, warehouse-sized building, Axel explains, "There are six major steps to the brewing process: malting, mashing, lautering, boiling, fermentation, and conditioning."

"Yikes, I hope there won't be a test on this later," I joke.

He stops, turning to look at me. "Only after you've sampled all six beers. You should be full of answers by, then."

"Is that what you say to all the girls you bring here?" I ask teasingly, arching my eyebrow.

"Only the pretty ones," he replies with a lopsided grin.

We stand in a massive white room by huge chrome containers with industrial-looking piping sprouting from them. "These are the fermenters," he explains, noticing where my eyes naturally gravitate, "But let's start in the cold storage area."

He shows me where the hops are stored, explaining the role of these plants in the brewing process and where the brewery sources its produce from. Next, he points out where finished brews are kept before they get shipped off-site for bottling and distribution.

"Eventually, we'd like to bring all of this back to the property, but as you'll see, we've kind of run out of room with the explosive popularity of Rough & Ready Red."

I nod, following him and hugging myself. He stops, eyeing me, "It's a little drafty in here. Do you need your jacket back?"

"No, I'm fine. Thank you. It feels nice compared to outside."

He nods. "Do you have any questions so far?"

My eyes gravitate back toward the massive, shiny,

chrome vats. "What were some of the biggest challenges you faced when constructing this facility?"

"Great question." He grunts. "Fitting all the right equipment into the space sometimes felt like a big, frustrating game of Tetris. Especially because I was also going for a specific look. But I think it turned out okay, although slightly more cluttered than I initially envisioned. And then there was getting the property utilities setup. I wanted a steam-heated brewhouse, which meant running gas lines and too many upgrades to count. Fortunately, the city was fairly cooperative about it because my foster dad's kind of the GOAT around here. Everyone loves him, and us foster brothers, by extension."

"It's incredible, Axel. I had no idea what kind of a facility this is."

"Yeah, I'd definitely like to go bigger, bring bottling and distribution onsite like I mentioned before. But even more than that, I'd like to branch out into my first gastropub. I've been dabbling with potential menus and working with a local architect to bring my dreams to life."

"And will the menu feature your own culinary creations?"

He shrugs. "Some. Others are a joint venture with Jerry Lee, you know, the guy who owns the Silver Fork and is assisting with the catering for his wife, Stacey, at the wedding. I'll show you a copy of what we have so far over your beer flight. Sorry I don't have any actual grub to offer you, but this is kind of unexpected, though pleasantly so."

"Was food something you were planning before I called things off, too?"

"Of course," he says with a nod, looking down. "I would never invite you to my facility without ensuring you leave with a full stomach. That said, I'm still stuffed from the wedding rehearsal dinner. But you didn't even eat. You must be starving."

"Believe me, I ate," I chuckle, enjoying the concern on his face more than I should. "Wedding planners learn quickly when and how to sneak a bite on the clock. It's one of my superpowers."

He chuckles. "In that case, let's finish our walk-through and then taste some beers." We stride down long rows of towering silver vessels, Axel explaining each step of the beer-making process in expert detail.

We peek into the malt storage area, and then he takes me up a flight of stairs to the second floor, where there's a large staff break room with arcade games, a long table with chairs, and bean bags on the floor in front of a big screen TV. "This may be a work environment, but we try to keep it light and have fun. After all, beer tastes better when it's made with love."

Why my cheeks burn at the last word. I don't know. But if Axel notices, he doesn't show it.

"And here's my office," he says, leading me into a large room with a huge, old claw-footed banker's desk, a comfortable, adjustable work chair, and more historic photos of the brewing process lining the walls.

"So, what made you so fascinated with beer?" I ask, awed by everything he's shown me.

"Beer," he says with a laugh. "Need I say more?"

"I remember you telling me that over text when we first started talking. But there has to be more to it than that."

"I've always been into things that make people happy and instill a sense of community. Whether that's great food, a comfortable place to gather, or delicious brews. And I have to admit the whole beer-making process is pretty fascinating. So is the history. You know it goes all the way back to the Sumerians?"

"I don't even know who the Sumerians are, although they sound familiar," I joke.

"Among the first significant agrarian civilizations in the Fertile Crescent. They grew massive amounts of grain annually, a significant portion fermented for beer."

"Seriously? That's dedication."

"That's having your priorities straight." He chuckles. "Any other questions, or are you ready to head back into the tasting room?"

"Yes, please. I can't wait to taste your brews."

"Good," he growls, his navy eyes darkening.

Ten minutes later, I stare at architectural plans, a gastropub menu, and a neat row of six tasting glasses lined up on a dark-stained oak tray. There's a little recess in the wood for each of the glasses, and the craftsmanship is stunning. The brews range from dark mahogany to light blonde, all with tall heads of white foam. "Wow, this is quite the presentation."

"Thank you," Axel says with a broad grin that shows off his dimpled, bearded cheeks to perfection. "Everything you see in front of you, apart from the glasses, was made by me, including the tray."

I arch my eyebrows. "I didn't know you did woodworking, too?"

"Just getting started. I don't have much time for it with all the beer brewing. This place definitely keeps me busy."

Diving into the plans, he speaks in impassioned tones, pointing out various elements and making my head spin with all the details. Next, he shows me the menu with downright delectable-sounding dishes.

Smiling, I admit, "I'm sold. When are you opening because I'm already hungry?"

He chuckles, running his fingers through his hair. "This is a way off for me, but as you can tell, when I get on this topic, I can't stop talking. It's uncharacteristic for me."

I nod, enjoying his sudden, passionate wordiness. "How many employees do you currently have?"

"Ten in the back and two to three up here when the taproom's open. We could honestly use a few more in the taproom, so I can focus on the business side of things rather than schmoozing with visitors all the time. But it is what it is."

"There never seems to be enough hands when you're running your own business," I say from a place of deep knowing. "So, is it etiquette that you stand behind the bar while I drink by myself? Or are you going to share this flight with me?"

Axel shifts his weight from one foot to the other pensively. "Are you sure you don't want light tapas to accompany your brews? I can offer some charcuterie?"

"No, thank you. But I would like your company," I answer sweetly.

He nods. Pulling out another wooden tray and glasses, he busily pours a second beer flight. I watch his muscular hands and forearms at work, veins and muscles rippling. How can every part of his body be so damn sexy?

He rounds the bar and sits next to me, facing me on the stool, which he dwarfs with his burly body. "It's too quiet in here. How about some music?"

I don't know if I can handle another country song after today's events. But I nod, also feeling the intense press of the overly quiet room.

He pulls out his phone and swipes into his screen before

the strains of indie rock fill my ears. My shoulders relax as I absorb the psychedelic, lo-fi folk strumming of alternative music. Phil Elverum's voice comes in, and I feel transported back to my teens when music was my only escape.

An uncontrollable smile lights up my face as I exclaim, "This is The Microphones, *Glow Part Two*."

Axel holds up his lightest glass of beer. "Indeed, it is. Cheers."

"I almost forgot about how eclectic your musical tastes are." I say, feeling irrationally giddy despite having yet to drink my beer.

He nods. "Very much like yours, if I remember correctly."

I nod.

"Music has always been my solace, though I don't play an instrument, and I can't sing to save my life. But it helps me redirect my thoughts when they go to the wrong places."

"Me, too," I say darkly. "That and the occasional cigarette when I'm feeling extra nervous." He opens his mouth to speak, but stops short. Silence overtakes the room again.

I raise my lightest glass, asking, "Is it customary to start with the blondest brew?"

He nods, and I take a sip, savoring how the refreshing beverage washes over my tongue, a complexity of delicious flavors.

My eyes go to his arm mere inches from mine, thirstily eyeing his ripped bicep and forearm. I'm close enough to feel the heat pouring off him along with heavy waves of crackling electricity. The angular planes of his muscles tempt me to touch him. But I refrain, self-control hanging by a few tattered threads. "So, what else do you have on your phone music-wise?"

He chuckles, lightly shoulder-bumping me. I notice with satisfaction that he doesn't fully lean away, allowing a thin sliver of our flesh to remain pressed together. My head spins at the chemistry simmering between us, my body wanting so much more from this man.

Swallowing loudly, I attempt to pay attention, despite the thrill of his touch, as he grumbles, "Everything from the Beatles to The Head and the Heart, the Lumineers, Led Zeppelin, Tame Impala, Prince, Nirvana, Jeff Buckley, Pink Floyd... In fact, that's what I really want to listen to with you. Will you indulge me?"

"What?"

"Pink Floyd's *Wish You Were Here*. You okay with that?"

"Of course. That's one of my all-time—"

"Favorite albums. I remember."

An unfamiliar sensation fills me, a sting at the back of my eyes warning me I'm dangerously close to tears. *What is this man doing to me?*

The loneliness and sadness of Pink Floyd's album, with its nostalgic impetus, grips me. Swallowing hard, I grab the next glass in the flight, taking a sip. The injustice of this ironic situation moves me.

How could I find a man more ill-equipped to handle the worst mistake of my past? I can't keep thinking about the bittersweetness of the current situation. I need a change of subject. Wiping my mouth with the napkin next to my flight, I say, "By the way, this is really, really good, Axel."

"Thank you. So, the blonde is like a Belgian, which makes for subtle citrus notes. Many of my customers swear by a slice of orange or lime garnishing the glass."

"I could see that. And this one," I say nodding towards the second beer in my hand. "Is really refreshing and light."

"Yeah, and it has a dry, slightly sweet finish with subtle fruit and malt flavors and only a little bitterness from the hops."

By the third glass in the flight, we're singing along to Pink Floyd, feeling like the two lonely souls mentioned in the song. I smile warmly at Axel, and yet there's a sadness around his eyes that he can't hide despite his own grin. Glancing at the mirror, I see it reflected in my own subdued gaze.

"You're a legitimately cool guy, Axel, and I'm really enjoying hanging out with you."

He shrugs, holding up the next glass. "With the medium brews, you'll notice a balancing act between lighter and darker elements. This first one is an amber ale with a richer, maltier flavor than the blondes. It also has toasted notes and hints of caramel, which are harmonized with a more predominant hops presence. At least, that's the goal." He licks his bottom lip sensually, and I feel all restraint and resistance crumbling.

Inhaling sharply to fortify myself, I take a sip, nodding my agreement. "I honestly never knew there was so much to beer."

"Yeah, most people don't, although the recent growth in microbreweries and craft breweries, like this place, has made an increasing number of people more receptive to the art of beer-making."

"Is that how you see yourself? An artist of brews?" I ask breathlessly as he leans closer, pressing his arm more firmly against mine. I reflexively bring my left hand to his bicep, letting my fingers dance over his firm muscles.

His eyes flood with a fondness I can't excuse away as

mere lust, and desire devours me whole. My body lights up, and the juncture between my legs tightens, moist and throbbing despite my attempts to stay logical and practical. All I can think about are his soft, kissable lips, and the way he set my soul ablaze in front of the ranch house.

I need a distraction. Like yesterday.

My hand goes to the next glass down, a redder color, and he explains, "Now, that's the brew that made me famous. By the way, I use that word very loosely. Rough & Ready Red. It's smooth and drinkable with hints of roasted malty sweetness and subtle hops."

"I wish I was more of a beer drinker," I confess, sipping from the next glass. "This is really tasty, though, and I like the complexity. It's nice on the tongue."

Axel grunts his approval, hunching over the bar and running his hand through his hair. "What if I told you I want more than tonight with you, Aspen?"

TWELVE

AXEL

What if I told you I want more than tonight with you, Aspen?

The words tumble out of my mouth in miserable tones. I sound downright morose despite trying to stay upbeat. But I need her so badly I can barely speak. It makes me feel pathetic and dumb. After all, she's already rejected me once. Why am I begging for another round of pain?

Aspen side-eyes me, pursing her lips. "There are things about me that I'm afraid would make you look at me differently if I told you." She shakes her head, studying the bar top. "I can't risk that with you."

She takes the words right out of my mouth. My stomach roils even as a weight lifts from my shoulders. We have so much unseen in common. Fate had to bring us together for a reason.

Angling my body towards her, I say, "It's the same for me. I'm not trying to hide shit from you, and I plan on being completely honest moving forward. But there's stuff in my past that I don't even want to think about, let alone discuss. And I'm also afraid of how your views of me might change if you knew."

Her face relaxes, her smile warming. It's the last expression I'd expect from any other woman. But Aspen is different. Attuned to me in ways I can't fully quantify or describe. "What if we quit worrying about things outside our control —the past, the future—and chose to savor this moment instead? Like you suggested earlier."

"Feel instead of think. Easier said than done but definitely worth the effort." I grab the Rough & Ready Red, drinking some more.

"One secret each. Is that really so bad?" her adorable little voice squeaks.

She's got me convinced. I open my mouth to speak, thinking better of it. Instead, my head descends, my pulse racing as the heat of our breath intermingles...

Tap, tap, tap, tap.

A percussive sound captures my ears, growing in intensity and frequency. "Shit," I exclaim, jumping to my feet. It's raining outside."

Aspen blinks slowly a couple of times before realization hits her. "Oh, no. My car!"

"Come on," I say gruffly, grabbing her hand and heading for the door. I ignore the flames licking back and forth between us, purpose in my gait.

Outside, we're met with a downpour. "Fuck!" I exclaim, kicking myself for forgetting about the top before we came inside. But my mind was a jumble of need for Aspen, unable to think about anything practical or purposeful. "You should stay inside. You'll get drenched out here!" I holler back towards Aspen.

"Too late," she retorts, racing towards her car with me at her heels. "It's a manual soft top," she explains, answering the question before I have a chance to ask it. "But I have to hop in and roll up the windows. I watch as she starts the engine and the windows rise. Then, she cuts the engine, jumping out.

We work together as quickly as we can to unfasten and unfold the top before securing it in place. Rain spatters my clothes, coming faster and faster until I have to shove my hand into my hair to get it out of my eyes.

"There, that should do it," she says triumphantly.

One look at her, and I laugh loudly. "You're drenched, Tiger."

I half expect her to freak out. After all, this isn't on Aspen's neatly organized plan of events. To my surprise, she looks down at her sundress, laughing.

"It feels amazing out here," she says, twirling around. "After so much heat, I love it."

I cross the distance between us, past words or thoughts, completely sucked into this unexpected moment. The warm rain feels refreshing on my skin, a wonderful break after the intensity of the afternoon sun and the incinerating need Aspen's presence excites.

She dances around, revealing an unguarded, free-spir-ited side that I've only gotten brief tastes of before. I can't get enough. Reaching out her arm to take my hand, I can't deny her.

Begrudgingly and despite my better judgment, I pull her into me. Unlike earlier, while stargazing, I don't start out with a careful distance between us. Instead, my left hand presses her into my firm arousal, making my inten-tions wordlessly clear. She freezes, staring at me as I hold my breath, uncertain of my next action.

Suddenly, frantically, her arms thread around my neck, her dainty fingers tangling in my hair. My pulse pounds as my lips inch towards hers, and I bring my other hand to her lower back, sliding both hands to grip her hips and grind her possessively against me.

Aspen's mouth crashes into mine, need overflowing in her passionate kiss. Her warm, velvety tongue slides into my mouth as she angles her head, deepening her claim. I'm beside myself with need and confusion, choosing instead to shut off my brain.

I devolve into a feeling creature driven by one impulse: to learn every inch of her body, every curve, every juncture. She strokes me with her tongue, inviting me into a different kind of dance, one that I wholeheartedly accept, mating with her tongue slowly and sensually as yearning sizzles through me.

Aspen Everhart is everything. Nothing else exists in this world but the feel of her warm flesh on mine and how her fingers thread through my hair, pulling me into the kind of kiss that has our teeth clanking together. My heart thunders behind my ribs as my hands squeeze her waist possessively, angling her hips into me.

"I need you, Axel," she stutters as the rain pours around us, awash in powerful passion and dangerous yearning. "Just this once."

She says it like a statement, but I already know it's a rule I'll never abide by. How can I when every cell of my body longs for a real, enduring connection with her?

Aspen pulls back, her breath catching in her throat. "Just this once?" she repeats, arching an eyebrow and staring pleadingly into my face.

There's nothing I can deny this woman. "Just this

once," I repeat, claiming her mouth fiercely even as my mind adds *until the next time.*

My lower core burns, tight, throbbing, and desperate to claim her. I walk her backwards, lifting her hands and pinning her against the side of my truck cab. I already know I'll never be able to get enough of her, and yet I have to try. "I need to fuck you and taste you and learn every damn inch of you," I growl.

She gasps, whimpering, "Yes, Axel. Please, yes."

"Tell me what you want," I grit out in lust-filled tones. I need to know she desires me the way I desire her.

"I want you to claim me," she confesses, grabbing my hand and sliding it under the wet sundress plastered to her leg.

"God," I groan, my body tight and angry with need as she shoves her hips towards me, and I firmly palm the outside of her upper thigh, running my thumb possessively over her soft, rain-soaked skin.

"Please," she repeats, covering my hand with hers and sliding it between her legs, revealing that her panties are more drenched than any other part of her. My cock jumps and my balls tighten at the tantalizing revelation, lower core aching with dangerous needs only Aspen can meet. But our first time can't be our last. I won't let it.

My fingers push her panties greedily to the side, sliding through her warm, slick folds as I let out a long, low moan. She's drenched perfection and so aroused she feels swollen against my fingertips.

"Not fuck you," I mutter darkly, leveling my gaze on hers. "Claim you?"

She nods, her head resting back as my thumb finds her clit, rubbing circles in the aroused nub. "Make me yours, cowboy."

I bury my head in her hair, sucking and teasing her neck with my teeth, lips, and tongue. "But don't give me a hickey."

"I'm going to leave my mark on you one way or the other," I counter in deep tones that make her sink into my embrace. My fingers slide through her pussy lips, and I penetrate her with my middle finger, never letting my eyes leave hers. She gasps as I locate the rough collection of nerves near the front, stroking her sensually and knowingly until the pressure and motion make her purr.

"Pull down your dress," I groan.

She complies without hesitation, captivating me with the way her dainty fingers move frantically and clumsily over the black fabric. Once it pools around her waist, I bury my head, taking one of her pebbled nipples in my mouth and playing with it through the fabric of her leopard-spotted satin bra.

"I'm sorry they're not bigger," she pants, momentarily pulling me out of my reverie.

"What are you talking about?" I ask, shocked by her insecurity. The otherwise cool, confident woman seems bulletproof. But then again, everyone has something that makes them feel self-conscious.

Determined to worship the hell out of her tits, I lick and tease her, sucking her in and out of my mouth until she arches back, letting out tiny whimpers of pleasure as my hot breath teases her. "They're fucking perfect, Aspen. Made for my mouth to adore."

She moans, grinding her hips against me. Her pussy tightens around my finger as I continue to stroke her, alternating one and two fingers on her G-spot and faster circular motions with my thumb over her clit. My breath races, and my pulse pounds as I draw her closer and closer to orgasm.

I won't stop until this woman is thoroughly pleased. Until I know I'm the man who made her that way.

Flashing headlights pass us, and I turn my back to the road, shielding her from exposure. "Oh my God," she exclaims guiltily, even as her pussy trembles and spasms around my fingers, her honey drenching my hand and palm.

"They didn't see a thing," I say between pants and kisses. And if they did? Well, fuck them. This is private property."

"Should we stop?" she asks, her voice thick and needy.

"I'm not stopping until you come for me, Tiger."

"Oh, Axel." She moans, her whole body melting against me as her pussy clenches and pulses around me, begging my rock-hard cock to possess her.

"Come for me," I growl deep in my throat, barely getting the last word out before her hips buck towards me, her body quivering as she drenches my hand in her hot cum. "Fuck, yes," I praise in dark tones.

Her head lolls back on my truck window as she attempts to catch her breath, and I weigh my next moves. "What else do you need from me, Aspen? Anything you want, I'll give to you."

Between frantic pants, her face rain-splattered, she says, "I need you balls deep inside of me."

"God, Tiger." I groan. "Like right here? Right now?"

"Yes. Now quit talking and fuck me, cowboy."

I love how confident this woman is. She knows exactly what she wants, and she's not afraid to demand it. It's the ultimate fucking turn-on. As if to punctuate her point, her fingers find my belt, pulling at the buckle. But first I need to hear her say it.

Bringing a possessive hand up to grip her neck, I

command, desire straining my voice, "Not cowboy. Axel. I need you to say my name."

"Axel," she pants.

"No, I need you to tell me what you want and use my name."

"Fuck me, Axel."

"Yes," I moan, in love with those words on her lips. I brush her hands aside, tenderly scolding, "Tiger, let me handle that." I can't wait any longer to feel her for the first time. Unbuttoning and unzipping my Wranglers, I pull the front down along with my boxer briefs, and the breath catches in her throat as she eyes my erection.

"My God, you're huge." She gasps, and my core tightens some more. I'm out of my head with need at this point, the buildup excruciating after so many months.

"I'm clean, and I have condoms—" I say, but her mouth crashes into mine.

"I'm on the pill, so we don't need those," she manages between hungry kisses.

"Raw, then?" I ask for clarification's sake.

"Raw as fuck," she answers, devouring my mouth.

Pulling her skirt up desperately and pushing her panties even more to the side, I slide the tip of my cock through her juicy goodness. I should ask her if she's worried about another car driving by or suggest going inside. But there's not a fucking thing on this planet that could pull me from this moment. Besides, this road gets very little traffic at night.

I invade her mouth possessively as my cock slides into her, inch by inch, taking my time and coming undone. This woman is my goddamn ruin, and I'm one hundred percent okay with it.

My eyes roll back in my head, a deep moan humming

through my chest as I savor every inch of her velvety goodness, my senses heightened by the coolness of the rain on our skin and the warmth of her honeyed channel sucking me in.

Her pussy grips me like she's been waiting for me. It's so fucking good. I strain to remain in control, every part of me longing to lose myself completely in her slick heat. The rain pitter-patters around us, our bodies as drenched and slippery as her heady arousal.

"God, Aspen," I groan. "Where in the fuck have you been all my life?" I ask, not expecting an answer. Grabbing her by each wrist, I press her against the truck as her legs grip my hips, and I thrust in and out of her like my life depends on it. Never have I needed a woman like this. Never have I felt more out of control or ravenous.

"Tell me what you need. I won't stop until I make you come again," I swear, slamming into her again, deepening my stroke with each pass as her flooded channel pulls me in. Her pebbled nipples tease my chest as water showers us. My lips steal the breath from her mouth. We kiss again, frantic, desperate, all rain and lust and depth-less hunger.

Soul-shattering tremors grip my body as I draw back again, pounding into her and bottoming out in her cum-drenched pussy. "God," I repeat, sounding strangely like a prayer as I take her again, bringing my hands back to her hips and gripping her jealously. Aspen's mine ... all fucking mine, whether she knows it or not.

Her arms cling desperately to my neck as she pulls herself up, crashing into my mouth until I can barely breathe and igniting the essence of my soul.

"Axel," Aspen pants, sliding up and down my rod, her face dissolving into pure pleasure. "You're going to make me come again."

"Come for me," I command, changing the grip on her hips to go deeper.

She screams my name into the blackness of the forest night, any fear of being discovered long gone. I stroke her long, hard, and mercilessly, the head of my cock stimulating her G-spot with each pass. Spitting into my hand, I lower it between our slamming bodies, slipping beneath her wet panties and rubbing her clit to push her over the edge.

"God, yes!" she screams, her channel convulsing and spasming around my throbbing cock until I can't take it anymore, biting my bottom lip and straining with my entire body to hold back for one or two seconds longer.

Her pussy grips me with powerful, surging throbs, milking my shaft, as I thrust into her again. Squeezing her hips as I explode inside her velvety warmth, I surrender everything I have and everything I am to her.

I don't know how long the silence extends between us, but I bury my head in the hair, wet and pooling, at the nape of her neck, panting and gathering myself. Enveloped in the smell of rain and the last remnants of her delicious honeysuckle and orange fragrance, I finally feel like I don't have to do life alone. Ever again.

"That was amazing, Axel," she pants, and the promise I made puts a frown on my face.

Just one time?

There's no fucking way.

Determined to nip that thought in the bud before it can become a serious issue between us, I bring my hands up to covetously grip her ass cheeks as I walk towards the brewery. Every sensation, every clench of her pussy makes me hard again.

Her eyes round, anticipation written in her face. "You're

insatiable," she says in breathy, wispy tones that let me know we have the same thing on our mind. Breaking her goddamn rule.

"With you? One hundred percent," I admit at the door to the brewery, which she opens for me, and I stride through the entrance. "And there's no fucking way we're stopping at one. I haven't even tasted you yet."

THIRTEEN

ASPEN

I haven't even tasted you yet.

My pussy clenches his cock at the words, and he smiles wickedly.

"You want it, too. I can feel it."

I can't deny it, trembling and aching around his firming rod again. He thrusts his hips naughtily towards me, mischief on his face, and I whimper, in love with how he fills me up.

"Yes, Axel. I want you," I confess, my pussy throbbing around him.

Reluctantly, he sets me down, muscles straining in stupidly handsome ways as he pulls a table out from the center of one booth and shoves the bench seats together. My eyes round with admiration at his strength and ingenuity.

Without missing a beat, he frantically tugs at my clothes. He's feral, and he makes me feel wanted, hungered for in the most primal, passionate ways. A sigh escapes me as he shimmies the wet dress over my hips, revealing my naked body except for the rain-soaked, leopard-spotted bra and matching, thoroughly drenched panties. The heavy fabric pools at my ankles. Wrapping his arms around me, he unfastens my bra with one efficient move, leaning down to suck me into his mouth.

My pussy clenches and tightens, ready for more action, my body tense with traitorous need.

"Your. Breasts. Are. Fucking. Perfect," he murmurs between mouthfuls of my cold tits. His warm lips lock around one nipple, sucking me hard and demanding a high-pitched cry as his hands slide between my legs, teasing and playing with me. My eyes roll back as my fingers thread into his hair, caressing his thick locks and pressing him desperately against my chest.

He growls, the naughty, deep vibrations shuttling through the breast he sucks and nips. His hands rove over my body, fighting with my sopping, clinging panties to pull them to the floor. My hands come up to shield my body as I stand completely naked before him.

"Stop trying to cover up. You're fucking beautiful. Every inch of you."

With cum dripping between my legs and rain sliding off my skin, I feel more than naked. I feel undone. "Aren't you going to undress?" I gasp as his mouth jumps to my other nipple, teasing and lapping me into oblivion.

"Undress me, then," he orders between pants as he sucks my breast, massaging my hips and waist and driving me closer and closer to the edge of ecstasy despite two orgasms outside.

My hands leave his hair, ripping frantically at his wet button-down shirt and Wranglers, which are still unfastened in the front, revealing his gorgeous manhood, already rock-hard.

His jeans and boxer briefs are nearly impossible to

remove. He has to pause, toeing off his boots and yanking at his socks. Then, he helps me pull the rain-soaked fabric until soppy piles lie around his bare feet.

I work his shirt over his broad, muscular shoulders, and he shrugs out of it. Stepping out of his pants, he grabs me around the waist, lifting me off the ground and pressing our bodies tightly together. The delicious feel of his rain-cooled skin and hot muscles beneath tantalizes me as he kisses and caresses me. Carefully, he deposits me, lying on my back, on the bench seats.

He drops to his knees in front of me, draping my legs one at a time over each shoulder. I raise my head, protesting, "But I haven't washed up or anything, Axel."

He grins a huge, dangerous smile, all big, white, straight teeth. "That's the point. I want to taste my cum on your pussy, Tiger. That way, I know you're mine." His voice trails off as his head descends, and his filthy words and desires sink in. This man really is wild. "Mine, mine, mine."

He unrepentantly licks and laps up my inner thighs, cleaning the cum from my legs as he closes the distance to my aching pussy. Sliding the warm velvet of his tongue through my drenched folds, he groans with desire at his first taste. I whimper, trembling and powerless to the delicious sensation. He leans in, demandingly slurping at my slit before focusing on my swollen nub. "Me on you is the best flavor ever," he declares passionately, sending our just-one-time rule up with the smoke of my need.

Lifting my hips, he slides my legs over his shoulders a little more, tilting my pelvis towards his face as he unhesitatingly dives into me, eating me out with enthusiasm. He's a beastly mess of growling licks as wet noises, and the smell of sex, fill the air. He adds fingers to the mix, stroking me with mind-numbing precision.

"Axel!" I scream, my heart racing. I feel out of my body, floating upwards towards the stars we stared at a couple of hours ago.

His beard tickles and teases the sensitive skin of my upper thighs as his tongue slides over my clit, circling, swirling, and sucking it into his mouth interspersed with teasing grazes of his teeth.

Axel strokes, caresses, and slides through my honeyed folds, bringing me to the knife's edge of orgasm again and again without letting me finish. My lower abdomen clenches and jumps in anticipation, and my channel throbs, swollen and painful. I'm mindless, thoughtless, regretless —unadulterated longing desperate for release.

My fingers dig into the soft upholstery of the bench seats as he alternates fingers with his large, thick tongue, fucking my channel as I spasm and buck. Never have I needed a man like this. Never have I given myself so completely, begging and pleading for the hot, messy satisfaction only he can bring.

He's tireless, merciless in his teasing possession of my body until I feel lightheaded like I'm floating away. He sucks my pussy lips in and out of his mouth, tracing his way back to my clit, lapping and flicking until I come undone.

My legs shake, and my core tightens past any point of return as a strangled cry leaves my lips. My pussy convulses and grips his fingers, my body surrendering completely to him. He talks me through it, adoring and worshipping me, drawing every ounce of pleasure from me, until I collapse panting, satiated, and drenched.

Sitting back on his heels, pride lights his face as I evaporate into the cushions, breathing hard. He climbs up onto the seats next to me, observing, "This is anything but comfortable. Why didn't you tell me, Tiger?"

"What?" I ask, reclining my head, my body soft and jointless.

"I want to make love to you," he says wistfully. "But there's no way in hell I'm pressing you into these cushions with my weight. You'll end up with bruises."

"Should we go somewhere else?" I ask, my logical brain protesting as my carnal flesh leads.

"Not yet," he says, tracing his pointer finger along my jawline before kissing my lips gently. I taste my musky flavor on his lips. "First, I need to feel you again—from the inside out."

I nod, astounded by my continued thirst for him despite tonight's lengthy foray into hedonism.

"Get on your knees, Tiger, with that sexy-as-fuck ass of yours in the air."

Shivers of anticipation tease my skin as I obey without question, rolling onto my hands and knees. My pussy controls me, throbbing and needy.

Kneeling behind me, he grips my hair possessively, wrapping it around his hand. "Tell me who this cunt belongs to," he orders, using his free hand to slide the head of his cock teasingly through my folds. My body responds, pushing back towards him, but he tsks his tongue, growling. "Aspen, tell me who you belong to."

My lower abs clench again, my channel tightening. If any other man talked to me this way, I'd slap him. I belong to no man. At least, there's no man who's ever been worthy of me ... until now. My body taut with need, I glance over my shoulder, meeting his hooded gaze. "You, Axel. I belong to you."

"Fuck, yes," he exclaims, a raw emotion in his voice that mirrors the ache in my chest. "Don't ever forget that." He uses his other hand to grip my hip, sliding slowly and sensually into me, taking his time inch by inch, as his long, thick rod fills me.

A strangled groan rumbles in his chest as he draws back, pounding me. I scream, arching back towards him, desperate for everything he can give me. He tugs my hair lightly but possessively, drawing my head back slightly as he slams forward, whispering in my ear, "This is how I want to breed you, Tiger."

Breed me? Any other man speaking this way to me would be an instant game-over. But the words do something so primitive to me, I can't describe. My pussy trembles and quakes around him, and I plead, "Fuck me. Breed me. Take whatever you need from me, Axel."

"Everything," he murmurs in deep tones, railing me at a punishing pace. A pace I urge on with every pant, whimper, and scream.

"Baby, I'm going to come so hard ... *again.*"

"Good girl." He groans. "And I'm going to fill you to the brim with my seed. There won't be a doubt in any man's mind who you belong to."

I arch back into him as he slams into me, exploding balls deep. His hot release fills me in waves as his large body trembles over mine. Wrapping an arm around me, he steadies me, shuddering as he continues to come undone inside of me, panting against the shell of my ear.

"Goddamn," he says, as his breathing slows, and he lets go of my hair, continuing to hold me. Pressing tender kisses against my neck and shoulder, he says tenderly, "I can't even fucking think right now. Are you okay?"

"There are no words," I whisper between ecstatic sighs.

He pulls out reluctantly, sitting back on the bench and dragging me into his arms. Cradling me and stroking my hair, he says quietly, "I can live with one secret. If you can live with one secret. For this, there's not much I wouldn't sacrifice."

I nod, tears brimming over my bottom lashes.

"Why are you crying?" he asks quietly, using his thumbs to push the water trails from my face.

"Because I've never felt this way about anyone before, and it scares the shit out of me. I'm afraid I'll mess things up by being me."

He strokes my cheek gently like I'm a precious treasure. "Shh... Some things are too good to mess up. We won't let that happen. Pinky promise?"

He holds out his big pinkie, and I giggle, staring at it. Locking mine with his, we make the promise. I sink into his warmth and strength, happier than I've felt in a long, long time. But a thousand voices conspire to tell me I've done everything wrong. Jeopardized my career and ambitions and trusted a man again.

"What's that look for?" he asks, furrowing his forehead.

The corners of my mouth turn up. "Just realizing I've thrown logic and reason completely out the window with you."

"Good riddance," he says with a grin. "Come on. Let's get cleaned up. I think I have some extra clothes upstairs you can wear. Do we need to swing by Hollister and the bed and breakfast for your stuff before heading to my cabin?"

I shake my head. I may have just caved in every possible way to this man, but there are boundaries I refuse to cross. Tomorrow belongs to Paige and Ridge, and, even more importantly, my mentor and maternal figure, Stella. Which means a good night's sleep and my wits about me tomorrow. "No, Axel, I can drive myself to the bed and breakfast. I need a good night's sleep. Remember?"

His arms loosen, the muscles in his shoulders and chest

rippling. There's an unbelieving look on his face, or maybe he's biting his tongue. The corners of his mouth turn down, and he raises an eyebrow. "But we're past that just-one-time bullshit, right?"

"Well, obviously," I chuckle, still trying to wrap my head around everything that happened and the way he blew my mind repeatedly.

"Good because that was too fucking amazing to ever walk away from."

"Agreed," I admit, my head spinning and my heart reeling. I'm not ready for the conversation I sense he wants to have. But I can tell he needs reassurances, and so I stroke his beard, staring into his eyes and saying, "That was amazing. Beyond amazing, and it absolutely has to happen again. But not before your brother's wedding."

His face and shoulders relax slightly, and he grins. Raising an eyebrow, he asks, "At least accept the offer of dry, clean clothes?"

"Yes, thank you."

"The bathroom's that way if you'd like to clean up, and I'll head upstairs to get you those for you." Without hesitation, he leans over, grabbing a pile of sopping wet fabric. "If you trust me to wash your stuff, I'll have it back to you tomorrow at the ceremony. They don't require any fancy schmancy soap or anything, right?"

I nod towards the brewery, saying, "If you can handle everything you showed me earlier, you've got my laundry figured out."

By the time I clean up, and he hands me an oversized khaki sweatshirt long enough to act as a dress, the downpour outside has stopped. He wears the matching bottoms, showing off his carved-to-perfection torso, and the faint tease of hair at the bottom of his abs, inviting me to greater pleasures. But I have to get it together. Act like the professional that I claim to be.

I slide back into my wet cowboy boots, a sloppy sound punctuating my new, ridiculous ensemble. Axel cocks his head to the side, staring at me for one long, simmering moment. "Not that you're asking, but you're stunning, Tiger. With or without makeup, hair wild and wet. I can't stop looking at you."

"Thank you." My eyes flutter momentarily to the mirror behind the bar, registering the disheveled mess that I actually am. And I almost call Axel a liar. But I can tell by the warmth overflowing in his eyes that this cowboy believes every word he says.

"I could drive you back to the bed and breakfast if you're not feeling the convertible tonight. I promise, I'll have it at the bed and breakfast first thing in the morning. Dried, clean, and ready for you to drive to the wedding ... and then back to California." The last five words come out strained, his voice grim.

"I won't be driving home until Monday, actually," I correct softly.

A happy smile captures his lips. "Even more reason to leave it with me, then."

"No, thank you."

He frowns. "In that case, I grabbed a few towels to help dry it out," he says, patting a stack I hadn't noticed before on the wood of the bar. He adds, "I pretty much figured that would be your answer, Aspen."

He leads me towards the door as if reading my mind, handing me my purse and cowboy hat on the way. "I feel so awkward in this. What in the world will Mrs. Chatterton think?"

"Since when did Aspen Everhart care about what other

people think?" He asks with a practiced coolness. He has a point. "Personally, I think you're hot as fuck in my clothes, beard burn and all."

My eyes round, and my hand comes to my chin, realizing it feels warm and tender. "Beard burn? God, no."

"I'm pretty sure it's between your legs, too, Tiger," he chuckles with a wink.

"No," I say, touching my face again. "You don't understand. This could be bad. Very bad."

"Isn't that what makeup's for?" He shrugs.

Men! I shake my head, not about to take my anger out on him for my indiscretion. Besides, I enjoyed the hell out of every moment of what happened, no room for regret left. Hopefully, I packed an overnight cream that will repair the angry skin.

He holds the door open for me to pass through, hovering behind me a few inches, the smell of his cologne filling my nostrils and reawakening all sorts of demanding needs in me. "At least, I didn't give you a visible hickey."

"Wait, you gave me a hickey, too?"

"Hickeys," he laughs. "Good luck finding them, though."

"You're incorrigible," I scold, and he chuckles some more.

"So, I've been told."

At my Carice, I hit the fob, and he opens the door, leaning in and using the stack of towels to sop up the dampness. I eye his ass hungrily, trying to decide if I prefer Wranglers or jogging pants. Both have their advantages.

Finally, he straightens, dropping the wet towels next to the car. I should get in. Instead, I stand awkwardly staring at him, torn over my next move.

Why didn't I keep my mouth shut and agree to go back to his place? What in the hell was I thinking?

Axel steps forward, lazily pulling me into his arms, his eyes overflowing with tenderness. "It's well past your bedtime and your better judgment, Tiger. You better get out of here before I think twice about letting you leave me."

His threat sounds amazing, but now I've got something else on my mind. Giving my poor cheeks and chin a chance to heal before tomorrow. My mind races. I've never been with a bearded man before. Will my skin ever toughen up?

"Oh," I exclaim, a tiny puff of air escaping my lips as he smacks my ass flirtatiously.

"Dream about me." He grins collecting the towels and sauntering back into the taproom.

CHAPTER
FOURTEEN
AXEL

I greet the day whistling and energized. I may not have slept much last night, but I slept hard, exhausted from mind-blowing lovemaking.

Fuck!

The sexy wedding planner is all I can think about. Before I even roll out of bed, I text her:

AXEL

Good morning, Tiger

ASPEN

Morning baby

How'd you sleep?

Didn't

Shit, I'm sorry. Are you okay?

Yeah, don't worry about me. How'd you sleep?

Like a baby

I hate you

No, you don't

You're right. I hate not sleeping

Understandable

How's your face?

And your thighs?

You're in so much trouble later

Good. I like trouble

The official story is heat rash, okay?

Is it that bad?

I dial her, needing to hear her voice and to apologize for the beard burn. But she doesn't accept. Instead, she texts back:

ASPEN

Last comment's a joke. But I'm in wedding planning mode now, which means no room for a devil on my shoulder. We'll talk after

AXEL

As in don't distract me?

Exactly

Good luck today, and your ass is mine tonight just so we're clear

No, actually, yours is mine

Damn, I like it when you talk to me like that

Back to work

My doorbell rings downstairs, and I curse under my breath, "Who the hell can it be at this time on a Saturday morning?"

Jumping into a pair of jogging pants, I run downstairs, open the door, and stare at Jerry Lee, owner of the Silver Fork and the uglier half of today's catering team. I'm about to ask why he's here when it hits me. Yesterday, I offered beer flights during Happy Hour. Shit. I shrug, playing it cool. "Hey, man, sorry I'm running a little behind. I was just getting ready. Come on in."

"No worries," the big, tattooed chef grumbles, coming inside. "Thought I'd take the morning lull before the wedding to help out with those extra kegs and shit."

"Thanks. I appreciate it. We'll also need to load up glasses and trays." We recently moved into the new brewery and taproom facility, which means plenty of unpacking remains. Never thought it would prove so convenient.

"Sounds good, man."

"Let me grab a shirt and my keys, and we'll get this show on the road."

Jerry nods, taking a seat on one of my big, beige couches.

"There's a Keurig in the kitchen, so help yourself. And I've got cream and stuff in the fridge."

"Thanks, but I'm good. I always wake up at four a.m. It's a habit from so many years of cooking ... and prison."

I nod, feeling awkward. Jerry used to never talk about the time he did in the clink. But ever since returning to Hollister and marrying Stacey, he's become far more forthright about his past.

It makes sense now why he's such a good friend to my brother, Holden. Corresponding with him and often visiting him in prison.

Without another word, I climb the stairs in twos, grabbing the first shirt I find. At the front door, I snag my keys and lock up before we head to the brewery. Backing our trucks up to the back entrance, we open our tailgates and make quick work of finding and loading the right kegs and boxes.

For some reason, curiosity holds me in its grip, and I ask as we work, "How did Stacey take it when you first came clean about being a felon?" The sunshiny waitress-turned-caterer never struck me as the type to go for a man with so many flaws.

He shrugs, swiping a hand through his hair as we load another keg. "She was pissed at first. Mostly because I hadn't leveled with her sooner, and it didn't help that she's from a law enforcement family. So, there was the challenge of proving myself to her dad and brothers. Which, believe me, was the hardest thing I've ever done. Hell, I have a fucking bullet scar to show for it."

"Wait, one of her brothers shot you?"

"Nah," he says with a chuckle. "It was one of my cousins, and it's a long fucking story we better save for another day."

"Stop by the brewery anytime you'd like a free flight or drinks."

"Thanks, brother," he says.

"Speaking of brothers," I say darkly. "How was Holden the last time you saw him?"

"Hanging in there." His face goes grim at the answer. "I know he'd appreciate more visits from you. For whatever reason, he's always been more concerned about you than the other brothers." He clenches his jaw with the last state-ment, his eyes narrowing. I wonder what Holden may have divulged to him over the two years they've known each other.

"Yeah." I shrug. "I was what you could call highly self-destructive, so he had plenty to worry about with me. I learned far too young the value of delinquency to get what I wanted. And it didn't stop once I came to live in Rough & Ready Country. For whatever reason, Holden wanted to protect me. He wanted me to turn out better than him. Maybe because I learned a lot of my petty crimes from him in the first place." Theft, drug dealing, fighting. Holden was a terrible influence on me until he started trying to save me.

Jerry nods, understanding in his face. "Tough to change patterns when you've grown up a certain way. And if you went through half of what Holden went through, there's that, too."

I scrunch my nose, snorting and looking down at the ground. "Yeah. You know what I wonder sometimes?"

"What?"

"How long will I have to keep on paying for the sins of others?"

"Which led to sins of your own." He chuckles. "That's the million-dollar question. Let me know when you figure that out."

"Seems like you've figured it out," I challenge, eyeing him.

He stops for a moment, really thinking through my words. "I guess I have. But only because I quit running from my past and faced it head-on, no matter the outcome."

"Helps that you have a loyal girl by your side."

"Yeah, but I would've never known she was so loyal if I hadn't gone out on a limb and told her my deepest, darkest secrets, knowing full well there was a good chance I could lose her."

His words stun me. They couldn't be simpler, more obvious, or more daunting. "Not every woman's like Stacey, though," I counter.

"You're preaching to the choir on that one. That said, how are you going to find out without laying yourself bare and making yourself vulnerable?" He chuckles. "Fuck, this is way too deep a conversation before lunch. How's your love life anyway? Any luck in the female department?"

"Maybe."

"I saw you making eyes at the wedding planner yesterday. Anything going on there?"

I can't fight the huge smile that illuminates my face. "She's amazing."

He raises his eyebrows. "I'll take that as a 'yes.'"

"Now, I've just got to figure out how to keep her."

"Whoa, hold on a second. This sounds serious."

My smile grows. "Yeah, man, it is."

"Well, congratulations."

"Save that for when I'm sure she's mine," I counter.

"Well, in that case, best of luck to you, Axel."

I nod, counting the kegs and boxes one last time to confirm we're done. I've got to get myself together and quit acting like a lovesick teen. "Good talk, man. Call if you think of anything else we need to do before heading out to the ranch for the big event."

"Will do. See you in a few."

After Jerry leaves, I return to the cabin, loading up everything I can think of for the wedding, including my change of clothes before the ceremony. Despite the rain last night, it's shaping up to be another hotter-than-hell day, so I switch into shorts and a tank. I blend a protein powder shake, adding handfuls of blueberries, fresh spinach, raw almonds, and ice before blending it to the perfect consistency. Then, I find a seat on my patio, enjoying the cooling beverage and getting lost in thought.

Jerry's words run back through my head, flooding me with a mixture of regret, guilt, shame, and doubt. What he said about Holden couldn't have been more spot-on. But then, I've been avoiding my brother far more than I should, largely because I feel like total shit when I see him.

Holden would have never been involved in the altercation that sent him to prison if it weren't for me. He followed me to the scene of the crime that night, trying to prevent a drug deal his gut told him would go bad.

It sure did. In the worst possible way.

Not for me, but for him. I fled the scene when I saw Holden, later finding out he was confronted by the senator's son and his friends in the parking lot. They jumped him, beating the shit out of him, and determined to steal the drugs that they couldn't find on him, mistaking him for me. This only made them more violent and vicious in their assault. The only way Holden got the upper hand was with a knife he always carried in one of his boots.

Although my testimony about that night would have never been enough to result in a different jury verdict, maybe I should have been more forthright. But Holden knew another drug charge would get me kicked off the ranch. And maybe he also knew the guilt of living with what happened would finally provide the impetus for me to turn my life around. But what a fucking price to pay.

Holden always told me his heroic actions that night were a double-edged sword. Yeah, a jury might appreciate his attempt to look out for me. But they might also see his arrival as premeditated, knowing trouble lurked and bringing a knife to the fight. Either way, he traded his life for mine because he already had a rap sheet a mile long.

How the fuck could I ever possibly repay him? Let alone look him in the eyes?

My phone rings, and I look down seeing unknown digits from Los Angeles.

"Hello," I answer hesitantly.

"Axel, it's Steph," a giggly, sunshiny voice says.

"Oh, hey, Steph, what's up?" My brows furrow as I try to figure out how Paige's friend and bridesmaid got my number.

"You're probably wondering how I got your number," she says as though reading my mind. "Mrs. Chatterton at the bed and breakfast gave it to me because I'm hoping to get a ride from you."

"Oh, sure," I say, anxious for another chance to see Aspen. Even if it's only for a moment or two. I know I should leave her alone, that she's in work mode. But fuck, I can't stay away. "Have you asked around to see if anyone else needs a ride?"

"No, but I can. Thank you!"

There's only one woman I want her to ask. The only one who will refuse.

"Of course. But I hope you're okay with getting out to the ranch early today because I need to be available to help out with last-minute needs and projects."

"Yes, that's fine. It'll mean more time hanging out with Paige on her big day. Tell me a time, and I'll be ready."

"Thirty minutes from now?"

"Okay. I'll keep an eye out for you."

"Bye," I grumble.

"Bye-bye, cutie pie."

CHAPTER

FIFTEEN

ASPEN

Tossing and turning all night was miserable. Fortunately, I packed the heavy-duty makeup for dark circles and, apparently beard burn, too.

I'm a notoriously bad sleeper outside of my own bed, especially after having sex in the rain with a mountain man who sets my blood on fire with every look, every word, every small gesture. Even the way he licks his lips or eyes me ravenously from a distance.

Somewhere around three-thirty this morning, I figured out I did everything wrong by refusing the invitation back to his place.

Yes, it would have doubled down on my transgression. Yes, it would have placed me in the camp of the impetuous and foolhardy once more. But I'd wager my father's inheritance that I would have slept better curled up on Axel's warm, furry chest.

Suddenly, it hits me. I've been here before. The regret of saying 'no' to Axel when I should have said 'yes.' Through both incidents, my inner voice has remained the same, urging me to trust this man, to surrender to him, and to free myself from the chains of my past. It's such a departure from how I've lived my life up to this point. And it's also assuming he never finds out about my past.

But I can't worry about that now. Glancing at my watch, I realize breakfast is almost over. I only have a few more minutes to help myself to coffee and pastries. Normally, this would not be an urgent need. Cricket's Sweet Rush Bakery is across the street along with The Human Being, a coffee shop countless people have recommended.

Everything remains frustratingly closed, thanks to today's wedding. Heck, even Mrs. Chatterton warned me she'll be attending, so fresh linens and other room service needs will be unavailable after four.

Grabbing my room key, I rush downstairs, striding across the receiving room towards the breakfast buffet.

"Good morning, dear," Mrs. Chatterton hollers in chipper tones. I nod in her direction, not ready to make polite conversation.

Bursting into the great room where a spread of delectable pastries tempts along with the coveted caffeinated and decaffeinated thermal carafes, I come to a sudden, awkward standstill. Directly in front of me, Steph and Axel sit at a table together, eating breakfast.

My jaw drops, toying with sprinting from the room before they look my way. But before I can act, their heads turn, both appraising me quizzically.

Axel stiffens awkwardly, holding a delicate white porcelain cup of coffee in his large hands. Rough, strong, amazing hands whose pleasures I know all too well.

I blink slowly and hard, trying to comprehend what I'm seeing. Envy as green as the forests enveloping Hollister overtakes me, and a deep, simmering anger springs up inside me, irrational, silly, but powerful.

Steph smiles at me enthusiastically, a veritable spread of goodies in front of her. I'd like to smack that perky grin off her face. "Oh, it's the wedding planner!" She squeals in her best Valley Girl voice.

I fight the urge to facepalm.

Axel's eyes search my face, his expression searing and instantly taking me back to last night. A broad smiles captures his face, and his cheeks warm as he jumps to his feet, leaving his Stetson on the table next to Steph and excusing himself.

The blonde grimaces, watching him approach me, her face reddening. I can't help but grin. "Do you want to sit with us?" she asks in a taunting tone. The kind men never seem to pick up on but women recognize a mile off.

I glare at her, reminding myself that, technically, I can't slap her. It wouldn't be professional under the circumstances. Especially since she's a member of the bridal party.

Besides Axel is mine. All mine.

Smiling as broadly as I can muster, I mimic Steph's stupid-ass blonde voice in sing-song tones, "Oh, my God! Yes, I am the wedding planner, and no, I don't have time for a sit-down breakfast. But thank you."

Axel hesitates in front of me for one long moment, scrutinizing my face. I shake my head, letting him know this is not the time or place, though I'd love to wipe the smirk off Steph's obnoxious face. Our relationship must stay professional, at least until this wedding's over.

Heading towards the coffee, he grabs one of the paper to-go cups, saying over his shoulder, "If I remember correctly, you told me you're a black coffee kind of girl for the first cup and then one cream, one sugar for the second?"

I'm keenly aware that Steph can hear our conversation as she squirms uncomfortably in her chair. I watch as the handsome cowboy fills two paper cups, placing one cream and one sugar in the second before topping each with a plastic lid.

My heart warms as I draw closer to him, touching his thick bicep and crooning, "Thank you."

"Steph called, needing a ride to the wedding."

"Of course," I reply, frowning. Is the man completely oblivious to how she's been flirting with him since they first met at the wedding?

"I can give you one, too?" he asks hopefully.

I shake my head, still too envy-green to say more.

Drawing closer to me, he says in low tones, "I have to admit. Steph's request served another purpose. I wanted to see you again before you're back on professional duty today."

"Then, you should have knocked on my door. Not sat down for breakfast with ..." I can't even finish my sentence, ignoring the fact that Axel doesn't even know what room I'm staying in.

He freezes, staring at me. Slowly, an extravagant smile captures his lips. "Wait, are you jealous?"

"Me? Jealous? Never!"

"Yes, you are," he counters, drawing so close to me that I can feel the heat pouring from his body. His sandalwood and pine cologne envelopes me, and my thoughts wander back to the sinful pleasures of last night in the rain and inside the taproom. "Might I remind you that if it were up to me, you'd be eating breakfast in bed, cooked by your soon-to-be favorite chef?"

My pussy throbs at the visual. I'm going to have to change my panties before the wedding, thanks to this mouthwatering man.

I open my mouth to counter him, but he winks,

shooting a dimpled grin in my direction. "As last night attested, you have absolutely nothing to worry about. Hope I did okay on your coffee. I'll catch you later at the wedding. Steph, you ready to go?"

"Oh, yes," the blonde says, eyeing Axel possessively, and I'm back in pissed-off mode despite his words. Standing up quickly and leaving a half-full plate, she shuffles towards us to the slap of her flip-flops.

Grabbing Axel's arm and grinning at me, she says, "We'll see you at the ranch."

Axel looks uncomfortable, pulling his arm away from Steph's. Glancing at me, he adds, "The breakfast offer stands tomorrow, too." He saunters out, grabbing his hat at the table with Steph red-faced, shuffling frantically behind.

What in the hell was with the uncontrollable jealousy, Aspen? Talk about unprofessional ... downright unhinged. You're representing Stella. This is not about you.

Grabbing two small croissants, I balance each atop one of the precious to-go coffees Axel made me and tentatively take the stairs back to my room. At the door, I poise the drinks and pastries carefully in one hand while unlocking the door with the other before entering.

On the other side, I barely have the chance to set my breakfast on the table before my phone vibrates. I already have the sound turned off to ensure nothing interrupts the coming wedding ceremony.

I answer without checking the number. "Aspen here."

"Aspen," a raw voice says. It's Nadine. "I'm sorry to bother you again, but I thought you were going to call me back last night. I know you're busy with weddings, but I wanted to know if you've had time to think through the possibility of reunification with Luca? I don't mean to pressure you on this decision, but I can't think of anybody else I would trust more with him, and it only makes sense to reunite him with his biological mother. Especially now that you've got the career and financial means to support him."

I exhale long and loud. *This* is the last thing I need at the moment. But I remind myself this woman is a recent widow with a terminal cancer diagnosis. I can't begin to imagine the terror and panic she must feel. Still, I can't lie about my deep-seated doubts. "But I'm a virtual stranger to Luca."

"Curtis and I have always been very forthright about who his biological mother is. He's familiar with your photographs, what you do for a living, all of it, Aspen..." Her voice shakes, and she breathes hard as if she's trying to master her emotions. "I'm sorry if this is wrong on my part, but it would make everything so much easier if I knew my baby was going to be with someone who loves and cares for him. And if you're considering this, I'd like to start meeting in person, getting him used to you ... before ..." Her voice cracks.

"I don't know if I can be the person you and Luca need," I reply, struggling through the words and feeling my heart break.

"The teenage mother who refused to part with Luca in the hospital loved him more than anything. It was written all over her face. It was in every tear she cried. I was never certain if what Curtis and I did was the right thing that day, taking your baby from you, though your father and step-mother insisted. Maybe this is fate's way of course correcting."

Her words pierce me. "No, Nadine. Everything happened for a reason. You and Curtis have been a blessing in Luca's life and in mine, by extension." Tears pour down my cheeks, smearing my recently applied mascara. I swallow the lump in my throat, trying not to sob. I don't normally react this emotionally, especially about things I've spent years hardening my heart to.

Maybe it's the lack of sleep. Maybe it's the charged dealings I had with Axel last night and this morning. All I know is I want nothing more than to curl up in a ball and sob.

"Thank you for your kind words, Aspen."

"I can't imagine what you're going through. But the timing on this call couldn't be worse. I'm about to leave for one of the biggest weddings in reality TV, and I need to be fully focused."

"I'm sorry." She sniffles, her voice breaking. "But the one thing I'm out of is time."

Her words are the slap in the face I need. I think about Stella and how she took me under her wing professionally and personally as a young woman. Without her help and insistence that I could make something of myself in the wedding planning world, I would likely be another affected SoCal heir, groveling at my father's throne for whatever inheritance he decided to toss my way.

"Maybe if I got a nanny to help out," I say, thinking out loud. "But he would have to understand there will be ground rules upfront. I can't stand a messy house or a bratty kid who talks back."

Nadine laughs thinly. "There are few givens in this life. But Luca will most definitely mess up your house and talk back at times. I can assure you, though, that he will pay those minor infractions back a hundredfold with kisses, hugs, hand-holding, and the devotion that only a son can give his mother. He will become your everything, even if you don't believe it's possible."

He already was my everything, the first and only time I got to hold him. I swipe my hands over my cheeks, straining not to lose it completely. "I'm so sorry I can't be more present for this conversation, and I'm sorry I didn't get back to you last night. But as soon as I return to Newport Beach on Monday, we'll set up a time to meet. Okay?"

My insides tremble. Although I've kept up-to-date about Luca's life and welfare since the adoption, I have avoided meeting him in person, fearful I could never recover from the heartache. And certain I would never be able to let my son, my flesh and blood, go twice, no matter how unreasonable. So, even the promise of meeting feels life-altering.

"Thank you," she sobs.

My phone beeps with another call. "I have to go now, Nadine, but I promise to seriously consider this. And I'll be more considerate of your time in the future, getting back to you with a definitive response next week."

"Okay, you better go. I don't want to keep you any longer. Bye."

"Please take care of yourself. Bye, Nadine."

I click over, seeing my mentor's number. This is a call I can't avoid. "Hello, Stella."

"Hi, babe. Wait, what's wrong? You sound like you're crying."

"I am," I confess, sobbing at the sound of her maternal voice.

"Oh, Aspen, what is it?"

I shake my head, trying to put into words the emotions swirling around inside. "I just got off the phone with Nadine."

"Oh no. What's going on?"

"She's been diagnosed with terminal cancer, and doctors have only given her months to live."

"Oh, that's horrible," Stella says.

"Yeah." I shake my head, still trying to wrap my head around everything. Talking business feels better than talking emotions. So, I say, "Let me catch you up on the wedding. I've double-checked all of your lists and my additional ones, and you can trust that nothing has been left to chance."

"I would expect no less from you. That's why you were the only wedding planner I would trust to fill my spot."

"I promise I won't let you down."

"I so wish I could be there with you."

"Me, too. How are your parents?"

She dives into a lengthy answer, and I listen carefully, asking questions and helping her process things the way she does for me. I sip the black coffee and tear at the buttery croissant as she talks, trying to keep my mind from wandering to Axel and failing miserably ... again. Always.

"Just don't fall in love with a cowboy or a mountain man while you're partying it up in Rough & Ready," Stella adds with a chuckle, grabbing my attention. The segue into unexpected territory tells me I'm not paying nearly enough attention to the conversation.

I chuckle, caught red-handed.

"So, how's Luca handling everything with Nadine? I feel so badly for him."

"I don't know." I sigh. "All I know is she's got it in her mind that I'm the only person who should take custody of him. Even though I know nothing about kids. Even though he and I are more or less strangers—"

"Babe," Stella interrupts. "You have to do this."

I blink hard a few times, trying to process her words. It's the last response I expect from her. "I don't have to do anything."

"Let me rephrase that," she says firmly. "You've been

running from this ever since he was born. I know you've never forgiven yourself for what happened or how your father forced you to give Luca away. And I know you still have so much healing to do after how Chadwick Mayfair assaulted you."

I groan, unwilling to dig up secrets better left in the past.

"What he did to you was wrong, and he was never made to pay for it as your father's business associate. Instead, you were gaslighted, belittled, abused, and forced to give away the only good thing that came out of so much bad. But now you have a chance to heal old wounds and make things right."

"Yes, I was underage," I counter. "But I gave Chadwick the wrong signals. Hell, I had a crush on him."

"A school girl crush. He took advantage of your feelings," she counters.

"It doesn't matter," I say, though I know Stella is right. "Enough about that man. It's Luca I want to talk about. He deserves so much better than I an possibly give him."

"How can you say that, Aspen? You're not a scared seventeen-year-old anymore. You have the career, finances, and assets to make this work. And I know how much you love him, whether you're willing to admit it or not."

"Some things are better left unsaid." *Unfelt, too*. Dangerously close to breaking down completely, I straighten my back, squaring my shoulders and taking a deep breath. "I am my father's daughter. I should choose business over love. Never let feelings get in the way."

Stella croons, "That isn't true, babe, and you know it. You don't have to be like your father to secure success. You have grown into the most amazing, beautiful, wonderful woman. I couldn't be prouder of you. And you've done it despite tremendous odds. You've got this, too, Aspen."

Tears pour down my cheeks. "Thank you, Stella," I whisper. "I know you have a lot going on in your life right now with your parents. The last thing you need is to worry about me."

"Babe, you're my daughter. I will always, always, always worry about you, and I'll also do whatever it takes to be there for you and Luca. You don't have to do this alone."

I wipe more tears from my cheeks, swallowing hard. "So, I haven't even made my decision, and you're already calling grandmother duty?"

"You've already made your decision, Aspen. Now, it's time to find out why."

CHAPTER

SIXTEEN

AXEL

C alls blow up my phone with endless requests in the hours preceding Ridge and Paige's wedding. Giving Steph a ride proves to be the easiest of those, though it gave me, by far, the most interesting results of the day and plenty to think about.

God, I love Aspen jealous. She's all I want. All can think about. Nice to know she can't stand the sight of me with another woman. My mind wanders back again and again to last night, and not just the naughty parts. I remember our conversation, her witty observations, her fantastic musical taste, sharing beer flights, and singing along to *Wish You Were Here*.

She feels like something I've never really known before. At least not deep down in the marrow of my bones—home. And I don't know what to do with this realization.

Thankfully, endless errands and projects keep me busy right up until the moment Aspen rounds up the groomsmen to get dressed and ready. Grasping her arm as I pass, I draw closer, caressing her with my thumb and leaning down to whisper in her ear, "You look stunning. I can't keep my eyes off you. Is there anything I can help with? Are you good?"

The uber-independent woman smiles warmly, and I notice her usual walls don't come up at the suggestion she might need help. Instead, she bites her juicy bottom lip pensively, asking, "I think I've got it all. Have I missed anything?"

My eyes dart around the room as pride wells inside. She chose vulnerability with me over the cool facade she projects to the world. I say far more tenderly than my question deserves, "Have you double-checked all those fancy lists of yours, Tiger?"

"Yes," she says breathlessly, her large toffee eyes drawing comfort from mine. It's the single most intimate exchange between us to date, and that's saying a lot. My throat tightens, my need for her so far beyond anything mere physicality could quench.

She says, "I think this is shaping up to be another cigarette-smoking night. Find me after the wedding?"

A lopsided grin captures my face. "That's a filthy habit, you know."

She nods, smiling until it reaches her eyes. Her long, thick lashes flutter, and it's all I can do not to pull her into my arms in front of the world.

"As for a cigarette, only if you're serious about breakfast with me tomorrow morning?" My brows furrow, my heart laid out before her.

"Breakfast and you are all I want."

Thank God. My eyes dart to her berry-stained lips, but I see the sudden warning in her eyes. "You have no idea how much I want to kiss you right now," I confess. "But you don't seem like a smeared lipstick, smooching-on-the-job kind of girl, so how about a rain check?"

Her face beams. "Only if it's like last night's rain check, cowboy."

"God, yes," I murmur, my eyes dancing over her suddenly glowing cheeks.

"Now, go get dressed before I have to dress you myself," she scolds.

"Damn, Tiger." I groan, my soul aching at the suggestion. "You know how to make a man's mind wander." I climb the stairs two at a time, my heart racing at the promises awaiting later.

After dressing and taking our places downstairs in line with the bridesmaids, I only have eyes for Aspen. I want to make it clear through my body language, where I place my attention, where my eyes stray, that she's all I want. Not Steph. Not any other woman in the room or the state of California, the United States, or the rest of the goddamned world. Aspen's got my complete and total focus, and by the way her cheeks flush, she gets the message.

As Steph and I stand in front of her, preparing to head out, I feel a little nervous, the hubbub outside and all the cameras finally hitting me. Unlike the rehearsal, when she barely acknowledged me, Aspen faces me, straightening my tie and adjusting my collar. Then, she combs her fingers through my beard.

The gesture is unabashedly possessive and makes me growl with pleasure. Arching an eyebrow, I scowl. "I thought I did a decent job upstairs. No?"

"No," she says firmly, but it comes out more like a seductive purr.

"So, I don't clean up well?" I flirt.

She leans back, assessing me for a long, delicious moment. "Quite nicely, actually, although I prefer you in the rain or the taproom."

My blood ignites at her words. But before I can respond, she steps back, winking at me as she taps Steph's shoulder. The blonde grabs my arm begrudgingly, staring off to the side. I don't mean to give her the cold shoulder, but she has to understand my heart belongs to someone else.

Paige and Ridge's wedding is heartfelt and moving. I don't know how they manage to remain so authentic despite the cameras enveloping them on all sides. But they've been through so much together, hardship forging a soul-deep bond, that little stuff like that no longer seems to matter. It's the kind of connection I want with Aspen.

Our eyes meet a couple of times during the exchange of vows. However, the gorgeous wedding planner remains hyper-focused on the ceremony, as professional as it gets, her cheeks only slightly warming as she returns my unrestrained gaze. Is this what it's like to finally find the one? I swear she's thinking the same thing as her unguarded eyes flood with passion.

Justice Powell finally declares, "You may kiss the bride."

The crowd of hundreds breaks into applause as Ridge dips Paige back. Cheers break out even as the hairs on the back of my neck stand up.

"May I introduce to you Mr. and Mrs. Ridge Dawson."

At a distance, I see movement along the tree line, and a couple of Wolfe's Army Ranger buddies appear. They have someone on the ground in handcuffs.

Fortunately, the rest of the wedding party and guests don't seem to notice, except for Bowie and Wolfe. My eagle-eyed brothers' gazes fixate on the scene as my eyes tick towards Aspen. She paces a distance away, alternating texting on her phone and staring towards the scene.

Wolfe pulls out his phone, telling Izzie to head inside

the barn and keep the kids close as he dials his phone, pressing it to his ear. "What happened?" he grunts.

As Paige and Ridge exit and the cheering and applause continue, Bowie and Wolfe take off across the field. When they pass Aspen, she reminds them in strained tones, "Please remember, photos are next."

"This has to come first," Wolfe mutters, striding past with Bowie. Looking back, I see Christian following a distance behind, his face stony and unreadable.

I beeline for Aspen, grabbing her upper arm and noticing the sudden paleness of her face. She explains, "The guards have detained at least five people attempting to infiltrate the property. All at different points where security was most vulnerable. As if they had the whole place scoped out in advance."

Her voice trembles, and I long to pull her into my arms and comfort her. But her stiff posture and closed-off face remind me to keep things professional.

Are the apprehended individuals the culprits? Or a distraction for something else? The thought puts a shiver down my spine.

"What should I do?" she asks, big brown eyes pleading. "I've done celebrity weddings with security before. But nothing like this. With such high stakes."

"Let's stick to your original plan until we know more about what's going on. I imagine you have camera crews to redirect and crowds to control? Shit like that?"

"Yes," she whispers, her bottom lip trembling.

"Don't worry, Aspen. My brother Wolfe and his crew are the best. They've got this handled." Even as I say the words, I feel uneasy at how close at least one of the perps got to the ceremony.

Aspen nods, wringing her hands tightly in front of her. She looks bewildered.

"Hey," I reassure her. "I'm not letting you out of my sight. So, give me whatever wedding planning jobs you need to because I'm keeping you safe tonight." *And forever if I have my way.*

"Thank you," she says in a wispy voice. "Can you stay in touch with Wolfe and let me know if there's anything else I need to be concerned with?"

I nod, staring into her lovely eyes and fighting with every ounce of my self-control not to pull her into my arms and comfort her. But my hand comes up, palming her cheek as I urge, "Take a deep breath."

The corners of her mouth turn up, and she complies.

"And another," I say, fighting hard not to rest my forehead on hers. "You've got this, Tiger."

"Thank you," she whispers, capturing my hand with her own and squeezing it tightly.

AXEL

Any updates on the security breach?

WOLFE

We apprehended five members of the House of the Seven Prophets

THE NAME of that cult constricts my chest, and I break out in a cold sweat. I grew up in that piece of shit excuse for spirituality, enduring constant abuse, thanks to my spineless, gutless, brainwashed mother.

AXEL

I hate those fuckers

WOLFE

The feeling is mutual

I imagine

Not your imagination. A couple of them mentioned you, Birdie, and Faith in their rants as much as Paige and Ridge. They had some very choice words for you

Let me guess... Backsliders, heathens, sons and daughters of perdition, apostates?

How'd you guess?

They love defaming those who've left the church or testified against them

Hold up. I'm sending you pictures of the perps

Why?

I feel nauseous even thinking about looking at their images.

WOLFE

If any of them hurt you, let me know, and it's handled

The photos come through, and I stare at five faces gaunt from malnutrition and hollow-eyed from years of abuse.

AXEL

None of them hurt me, though I see a few familiar faces

WOLFE

Good. You're our first witness, then

Witness to what? I didn't see anything that transpired apart from some of your guys wrestling a figure to the ground

Character witness

For fuck's sake. Will my past ever stop sucking me under at every turn? Jerry's words from earlier hit me again. Instead of running from my past, I need to confront it. It starts with acting from what's right rather than a place of fear.

AXEL

If you need me to, I can testify

WOLFE

Good

Are there any other security issues we need to be aware of?

Not at the moment

And you're certain the people you apprehended were the actual culprits and not a distraction?

That'd be a helluva lot of explosives and firearms to carry around for mere distractions

Explosives and firearms? Are you shitting me?

Sadly, no. We'll discuss later. Please tell your girlfriend that we'll be back in ten for wedding photos

Girlfriend?

Come on, man. Everyone sees how you two
keep drooling all over each other

The evening turns thankfully uneventful after the arrests, though a certain unease hangs in the air. God only knows what those assholes had planned for the ceremony. One thing's for sure. They hold grudges. Very long grudges.

Tonight would've been a coup of unparalleled proportions for them had they been able to exact revenge on Ridge, Paige, and all those who helped crack open one of the biggest human trafficking scandals on the West Coast.

Paige spearheaded the effort, a reality TV producer who profiled the church, finding far more than she bargained for as interviewees turned into whistleblowers, recounting horrific abuses, criminal activity, and a cult with a stranglehold on its brainwashed followers.

But she did something even more deadly. She discovered ties to major politicians and cartels, stumbling across a scandal of epic proportions. And when Ridge and our foster brothers rode to her aid, they sucked our whole family into the danger. That said, Dad first made his stand against the cult long ago, whether he knew it or not, when he took a chance on me.

Birdie, Faith, and I, all raised in the church, would've have been icing on the cake. The only thing the House of the Seven Prophets hates more than whistleblowers are apostates.

"You look like you have a lot on your mind," Aspen says, brushing her fingers playfully over the lapel of my dress coat. She knits her forehead. "Is there more you haven't told me?" She refers to my communications with Wolfe.

"I've told you everything you need to know to get through this event with a smile on your face. Tonight, you'll get the rest. But suffice it to say, all known threats have been neutralized."

She exhales sharply, relief washing over her face.

"And in case nobody's told you yet, this wedding's perfect. Exactly what Ridge and Paige wanted. You've outdone yourself and somehow managed to look hotter than fuck the entire time."

She laughs, standing on the edge of the dance floor in a sexy short-sleeved black floral dress with a flirtatious keyhole cut out teasing her lovely cleavage and a slit up her left leg to her mid-thigh. Strappy, black sandals match her Chanel purse, and her lustrous mahogany locks flow over her shoulders.

I don't know where I want to start first, massaging and teasing her feet with my fingers and tongue, burying my head in the keyhole above her tits, or sliding my hand up the slit of her skirt to the place where I'm pretty sure heaven begins.

"You should go out there. Don't stand here on account of me. Especially when there are so many bachelorettes that keep making eyes at you."

"Only if wedding planners are allowed to dance?" I arch an eyebrow.

"I wish," she says, face flushing.

"No worries. We'll make up for it later."

"I'm going to hold you to that promise, cowboy."

"Please do, and any others I have yet to make."

The rest of the night goes by in a blur. Ridge and Paige find Aspen at the end, hugging and thanking her profusely before handing her the final check for the evening. I watch a couple of steps away, trying to respect her professionalism as she and Paige chat.

"Why don't you two get a room?" Ridge teases, patting me on the shoulder.

I choose to ignore his question. "How does it feel to be a married man?" I question, raising my fists and shadow boxing with him.

"Best feeling of my entire life," my brother replies without hesitation. Ridge always was a romantic at heart. Growing serious, he adds, "Without Wolfe and the rest of the crew, sounds like it might have never happened."

I nod. "You made enemies in high places," I observe solemnly.

"The same enemies you made by surviving."

"By being born," I correct in dark tones.

"Be careful, brother," Ridge says, running his hand through his hair. "Things are bound to stay dangerous as the trial proceeds."

"Yep," I say, looking down at my hands. "And I'm still afraid you don't fully grasp what kind of enemy you've awakened. The House of the Seven Prophets is only part of it. One of many crime factions fighting it out for dominance and money. The religious wackos, the politicians and their relatives, the cartels."

"Lots of fucking trouble for our teeny ass hometown."

"Trouble that's always been there," I reply firmly. "In plain sight. Just nobody wanted to look."

"Or talk, for that matter," Ridge adds, eyeing me knowingly.

"That's about to change, for better or worse," I say with a firm nod.

SEVENTEEN

"Time for that cigarette?" Axel asks, fingers entwined with mine as we head towards our vehicles, leaving the disassembling wedding behind.

I inhale long and loud before exhaling and letting my shoulders relax. "You want the truth?"

"I do."

"What I really want is your cock."

The unexpected words put a huge grin on his face. "That's what I was hoping you'd say."

"Was it really?" I ask playfully, scrunching my nose.

"Well, now that you've said it, it sure as hell is. I'm going to rock your fucking world and make you forget about everything."

"I don't even want to remember my own name when you're finished, Axel," I say seductively, leaning in.

"Done." He wraps his arm around me.

"Of course, we'll need to stop by the bed and breakfast and get my belongings. And I'll need to follow you home with my car—"

"Starting another list so soon? Why don't you let me figure out the logistics?" he teases in growly tones.

My body tenses, unused to letting someone else take charge. It feels equally scary and liberating to be this vulnerable with another human being. Instead of running from the uncomfortable experience, I decide to embrace it. See what happens. "Yes, please. I'm done thinking."

Axel's face beams, and he stands a little straighter, puffing out his muscular chest. I'm trusting him to be my man, to care for me, and to look out for my best interests. It's the ultimate gift I can give him as a highly capable, professional woman. I can tell that he innately understands this.

"If I get all cheesy with you, are you going to hold it against me?" he asks, side-eyeing me. I lean closer, intrigued by his lead-in.

"I think a little cheesiness is allowed at this point in our relationship. I mean, you did rail me in the rain and then ruin me for any other man in the taproom," I remind him with a giggle.

"Don't even talk about other men," he grumbles.

"I'm teasing, baby. Besides, how else can I convey that thought?"

"Point taken," he says as we stop in front of our vehicles. He turns, wrapping his big, strong arms around my waist and drawing me closer. "When I'm with you, I feel like I'm home. For the first time in my life, I realize that concept was never a place at all but a person. *My* person. You."

Tears fill my eyes at his words as I stare up into his sincere gaze. Coming from someone with Axel's background as a foster kid, I know the words have extra import.

Though I don't have all the logistics worked out.

Though I don't even know how I'll tell him about Luca and what happened to me as a teen, I bring my hands up to his bearded cheeks, running my fingers through his silky, soft facial hair and saying, "You will always have a home with me."

He leans in, seizing my mouth gently but firmly. A warning light goes off in my head. *What if the remaining members of the wedding party see us? Could it cause trouble for Stella?* But his lips graze over mine expertly, demanding my relaxation and surrender as I let him take over.

When he pulls back, we're both breathing harder, and he says with a lopsided grin. "Yep, way better than a cigarette."

I smile, adding, "Though no less filthy."

"Just you wait," he promises in dark tones, opening his truck and boosting me into the seat. He leans over me, buckling me in, his hands moving slowly and sensually over my flesh.

I want to ask about my car, so used to taking charge. But I tell my brain to shut up, take a breather, and let this man lead. He rounds the truck, removing his jacket and throwing it in the extended cab. Loosening his tie and removing it, he adds it to the pile behind his seat, unbuttoning his shirt at the neck. Exhaling, he says, "That's better. It's so fucking hot again tonight. I wonder if it'll rain."

"If it does, I'm ready," I observe, eyeing my Carice with its top up and windows closed as he backs up, and we drive away.

"I'm ready, too," he says with a naughty grin, reaching over the console to grab my hand and bring it to his mouth. He kisses my fingers tenderly, one at a time, as I use my free hand to change the dials on the satellite radio until I settle on Marvin Gaye's "Let's Get It On."

Axel stares at the console in amazement.

"What?" I ask.

"Just surprised yet again by your excellent taste in music."

I shrug. "So, you think you could deal with my musical tastes for a while then?"

"Maybe forever," he says, glancing in my direction to gauge my reaction.

I squeeze his hand, my heart racing and my stomach roiling. I know what I want without hesitation, but it comes with the scariest thing I may ever do. Share my deepest, darkest secret with Axel. "You know how we agreed last night to let each other have a pass on one big secret?"

He nods.

"That's no longer going to work. We need to have a conversation when we get back to your place. There are some things I want to tell you. "

"Likewise," he says quietly. "You need to know everything."

At the bed and breakfast, Axel and I make quick work of packing my bags. Mrs. Chatterton is AWOL, thanks to the wedding. But she has my card number and can run my payment. I leave my key in the drop box, and we head outside.

Menacing voices boom the moment we walk through the inn's main entrance, startling me.

"We saw everything."

"You filthy whore!"

I barely have a moment to think before something hard pelts my back, and then another and another. I look down, shocked to see rocks hitting the pavement.

"You were fornicating in the dark in front of the brewhouse," one masculine voice yells.

Another screams, "I drove by and saw it all."

More chime in. "Whore! Prostitute! You're going to burn in hell for all eternity along with your backsliding, demon-possessed lover!"

Axel drops my luggage without hesitation, running towards a small crowd of men in black suits that instantly disperses. He seizes the oldest by the collar, shoving him against the side of the bed and breakfast. The man has a long, thin, unkempt beard, thin, angular face, and beady dark eyes.

"You want to cast the first stone, motherfucker!" Axel screams in a voice I've never heard before. One that makes my body tremble and my blood go cold in my veins. "How about we talk about burning in hell, Malachi? Does it start with brainwashing? Or abusing little boys the same way we were abused? Is that it? Unthinkingly leading the same fucking life that destroyed you as a child?"

Axel grips his collar with one large hand, screaming in the man's red face. Pulling him away from the wall an inch or so, he slams him back into it repeatedly, the sickening sound of the man's head hitting the hard surface.

"Is that how the fuck you get to heaven? By human trafficking and treating people worse than the shit you scrape off the bottom of your shoes? Because that sounds like fucking hell to me, right where all you goddamned pious motherfuckers belong!"

I cover my mouth with my hand, blinking hard. Never have I seen such rage before.

Axel slams him against the wall again, shoving his forearm up under his neck as the man sputters and gasps before going silent, his face turning from red to a sickening shade of purple. I run forward, gripping Axel's flexing bicep and begging, "Please stop. Please."

It's like Axel can't hear me. His face transformed by unadulterated fury.

"Please," I plead again, gripping his arm with one hand and shoulder with the other.

Suddenly, he relaxes a little, and the man gasps, his breath gurgling in his throat.

"Call the sheriff," Axel orders in dark tones. "Before I rip this motherfucker apart with my bare hands."

My fingers shake as I search for the number. A tense moment passes until Axel calls out numbers to me. I stop Googling the Gold County Sheriff's Department and dial, getting a familiar male voice.

"Sheriff Christian here."

"Christian," I pant, sounding like I've just run a marathon. "It's Aspen. Can you come to the Hollister Bed and Breakfast right away? Axel and I got attacked."

"Fuck. Are you okay?"

"Yes, but please hurry before something worse happens."

"I'll be right there."

Axel lets go of the man, patting him down for weapons. He finds a knife in one boot and a firearm strapped to his back. A shiver runs down my spine as Axel orders him to sit on the curb. "Another word out of you, and the curb will be the last fucking thing you ever taste," he promises, his voice ferocious.

Time passes in a flash. I stand shivering despite the heat of the night while Axel paces in front of the man.

Suddenly, headlights flash, and Christian's pickup pulls into the lot. Jumping out, he laments, shaking his head, "What a fucking night. Bowie got ambushed by some of these motherfuckers, too. Only there was a woman lying in wait who helped him during the attack. Have you checked this guy for weapons?"

"Yeah, and I found this," Axel answers, pulling the knife from his pocket and the firearm from the back of his waistband. "Is Bowie okay?"

"Fine," Christian mutters, grabbing the man roughly by the upper arm and handcuffing his hands behind his back. The blond sheriff leads Malachi to the back of his truck, dropping the tailgate and shoving him in.

I stare wide-eyed and unblinking as he closes the tailgate. Christian frowns. "Upholstery's too good to let this lowlife mess up."

Axel hands the weapons to his brother, and he places them in the glove compartment of his truck, locking it.

"And the woman?" Axel calls as his brother works.

"Yeah, as far as I know."

"Do we know who she is?" Axel asks.

Christian returns to stand by us, scowling, "Bowie says he'll get to the bottom of it before he lets her out of his sight."

"I don't doubt he will. As for Aspen, if she has even one bruise on her body..." Axel growls, banging on the side of the pickup bed. "I'll be the last thing you ever see, shitface."

I shudder, terrified at how Christian will respond. He may be Axel's foster brother, but he's also the duly elected sheriff.

"That's right, asshole," Christian hollers, and my jaw drops. "I may be the law-abiding sheriff of this town, but I'm sorely understaffed and undermanned, which means homicide investigations of pedophile human traffickers are at the bottom of my fucking priority list."

The specter of how justice gets served in Hollister both

shocks and comforts me as my head bobs back and forth between Axel and Christian. "Axel, Aspen," he nods. "I can take it from here. Try to have a decent rest of your night, and stay frosty. No telling what else these motherfuckers have planned. "

Axel grunts, "If they're sending Malachi and teenagers to do their bidding, they're desperate. Feels kind of like the last gasping breaths of this fucking cult."

Christian nods, clenching his teeth. "Let's hope so. That said, cornered animals are the deadliest."

Axel nods, his muscles rippling with anticipation. "I'm ready and willing to smash plenty more heads, so bring it."

It's a side I've never seen of Axel before. But Christian doesn't look remotely shocked. Instead, he says, "Keep your head on a swivel."

"Will do, bro."

We drive in silence. I can feel the rage pouring off Axel. It fuels the countless questions bouncing around in my head. We turn off four eighty-eight onto a dirt road, seeing a lone man with a gun up ahead. Terror grips me for one frantic moment until I realize it's one of Wolfe's Ranger buddies.

Axel stops, rolling down his window. "Rutger."

The blond man nods, drawling, "Figure we'd provide a little extra security for you tonight. Did you hear Bijou perform at the wedding?"

"Yes," Axel grunts. "Your wife is an amazing singer."

"Yeah, she's a little bent I missed it and that I'm out tonight. But we're not taking any chances." He cocks his head to the side slightly, eyeing me. "Ms. Everhart." He nods. "You couldn't be safer with Axel. Alright, y'all, have a good night."

Axel nods.

He follows the gravel road, parking in front of his cabin. We sit in silence, unmoving for a long, tense moment, the slight coolness of our open windows stirring the air around us. Axel grips the steering wheel until it creaks and groans, the muscles in his body straining. The places where stones pelted me earlier already feel tender, and I fear the reprisal to come when Axel finds marks.

Opening his glove box, I find a half-empty pack of cigarettes with a green lighter stuck inside. They look ancient ... like he bought them years ago.

My hands shake as I try to light the cigarette I place between my lips. Finally, Axel lets go of the steering wheel, turning to help me. I put the pack and lighter on the dash, leaning back into the seat and taking a slow drag. I offer him the cigarette, and he takes it as we sit in an expansive silence.

Finally, he relaxes, leaning into his seat and eyeing me, his face somber. "I guess it's time for that truth-telling we discussed ..."

EIGHTEEN

A long pause follows, and we pass the cigarette between us, the only sound air through the filter and our soft exhales. A slight cooling breeze rolls through the truck cab, humid with the promise of future rain.

Axel says in raw tones, "I was raised in the House of the Seven Prophets alongside kids like Malachi. When I was probably four or five, my uncle sexually abused me for the first time. I tried to tell my mother, but she didn't give a fuck. She punished me for 'wicked lies.' Accused me of being demon-possessed. Soon, I was being passed around by the elders along with kids like Malachi. It was fucking disgusting. Still makes me nauseous and my skin crawl."

His hands shake as he talks, though his voice remains oddly steely. "About the age of eight, I acted out for the first time. Beating the shit out of one of the other church boys. Beating him to the point the sheriff's department got involved, and I was temporarily removed from my home into a juvenile detention facility. It was a revelation for me.

Act up enough, and I could escape the filthy things that happened behind closed doors ..."

I reach over the console, placing a comforting hand on his bicep, and he looks surprised, relaxing almost imperceptibly.

"After that, it was one string of delinquencies after another to stay out of the grips of the church, though my fucking mother fought tooth and nail to keep me. I bounced from her home to the detention center to too many foster homes to count, encountering more abuse in one placement. It brought out a side of me, Aspen. A side I don't even want you to know about. I nearly killed the motherfucker." He pauses, hanging his head.

A cold shiver runs through me at Axel's recollections of being a foster kid. Suddenly, it hits me. If I don't step up for Luca, despite my fears and reservations, he could end up a foster child, too. The nauseating thought solidifies what I know I must do, whether I feel equipped or not. But what will this decision mean for Axel and me?

Axel continues gruffly, "I was on a sure path to prison. In and out of homes, shelters, living on the streets, all of it. Human refuse, condemned by the entire world by my early teens. But then, Wyatt, my foster dad, offered to take me in. At first, I treated everyone like shit, suspicious of their kind gestures and helpful moves. I knew nothing but abuse, pain, and exploitation. But eventually, my dad and brothers got through to me, teaching me what family is. Showing me through consistent daily actions that some people I could trust."

"And so that's how your mother abandoned you? By refusing to help you when you were being abused?" Everything makes so much more sense now.

"Yes," he says in broken tones. "She was my fucking

mother, and she let every man in that church lay his grubby hands on me. What kind of woman does that?"

"I don't know," I answer, fighting the sob that grips my voice.

I offer him the cigarette again, and he waves it away. "No, I'm good." I crinkle it between my fingers, snuffing it out before tossing it through the window.

"One of my foster brothers, Holden, was a terrible influence on me. The worst. He introduced me to smoking, drinking, drugs, all of it. But then, at some point, he had a come to Jesus moment and started trying to save me instead. One night, he got wind I was going to be involved in a drug deal. His gut told him it wouldn't go well, and so he showed up at the scene. As soon as I saw him, I fled, afraid of being caught. One more drug charge, and I'd have to leave Rough & Ready Ranch for good. Holden was right, though. He got jumped by the guys meeting me, and they nearly beat him to death. Fortunately, he always carried a knife, which allowed him to gain the upper hand. But it came at the expense of one of his attacker's lives and Holden's freedom. He's been in the state pen for a decade now because of it, swearing me to secrecy. In fact, you're the only person I've ever told this to. Holden feared my testimony could screw him over even harder by making his arrival on the scene armed look premeditated. I've lived with the guilt of not coming clean ever since, but I have to abide by my brother's word. Don't I?" He side-eyes me, his face conflicted.

My head spins at his revelations. I feel out of my depth when it comes to legal matters. After a moment's thought, I answer, "If it were up to me, I would consult a lawyer. That way, you can always fall back on attorney-client privilege. And at least you'll know for sure."

Axel rubs his temple with his left hand, saying gruffly, "You're right." We sit in silence for a long moment. Finally, he breaks it, saying, "If this changes how you see me, I understand. It's a lot to learn about a man. I spent years of my life in therapy working through the abuse, and I can answer any questions you have about what happened and how it continues to impact me."

Pushing back the console separating us, I slide closer, snuggling against his chest and feeling his body shudder as he holds back a sob. "Thank you for trusting me to confide in. It doesn't change anything between us, Axel. In fact, it makes me love you even more," I confess, saying more than I probably should but somehow feeling it's right.

He palms my cheek, turning my head up towards his and sinking into me for the most tender kiss I've ever experienced. It's a kiss of the soul, shivering through me with a heady intimacy I didn't know was possible. True, complete, total connection.

I inhale, confessing, "I was abused as a kid, too, though much older than you." It's the first time I've ever acknowledged this out loud, and a massive weight lifts that I didn't even know I've been carrying all these years. "I always told people I consented, though I couldn't legally at sixteen. I felt like it was all my fault. Like I led Chadwick Mayfair on. He said as much afterward. That I had tempted him by flaunting around the house when he would stop by for work meetings."

"Work meetings?" Axel grunts. "How old was he?"

"Forty-two. My father's business partner. I admit I was bowled over by the man. He came across as warm, handsome, and charming. He showed me the attention I craved from my father ... until I found out why." I sniffle, fighting through a sob to steel my voice.

Axel wraps his arms around me, stroking my hair and whispering comforting words as I pause, collecting myself.

Channeling the rage still screaming inside, I say, "One night, he showed up at the house for a meeting, and my father wasn't there. I think the meeting was just an excuse ..." My voice shakes as painful memories flood my brain. "He transformed into a monster. Something I had never seen before. The charm, the caring, the attention all evaporated, replaced by a man who wouldn't take 'no' for an answer. I was a virgin, and I don't know what came over me. I froze, petrified. I couldn't move, speak, anything. I laid there, and he did what he did. He hurt me ... *badly*. Took what he wanted and blamed it on me. Said me not fighting proved I asked for it. And I believed him."

Axel's fists clench, and his jaw tightens. I caress his bicep, trying to calm him once more. "That went on for a couple of months. My grades dropped in school. I was a total mess, and when I tried to ask my father for help, to explain what happened, he blamed me. Said it was all my fault. That my false accusations would fuck up his finances and business dealings, and God knows we couldn't let that happen. *That* was the only unforgivable thing in my family. Afterwards, I promised myself I would never trust another man. Fortunately, Father sent me away to boarding school, which was the escape I needed ... until I found out I was pregnant."

A sharp exhale pierces the air, and I wonder if this is the moment when Axel starts hating me for what I've done. Guilt oozes through me, inky and ugly. But I have to finish what I've started.

"I delivered Luca eight months later. A beautiful baby boy. The most beautiful baby I have ever seen, and they let me hold him on my chest for like an hour, I think. Maybe less. I'll never forget that moment, all of the love I've ever felt pouring into that little baby and then somehow back into me. But then, they took him and my heart with him. And that was it. After you told me that your mother abandoned you as a child and that you could never forgive a woman like that, I called off our first meeting. I was sure you were describing me ..." I can no longer fight the sob that racks my whole body, still half-expecting Axel to hate me. Apart from Stella, all I've ever known is rejection, especially when I'm at my most vulnerable with my shields down.

"No, no, no," Axel whispers, pulling me into his lap and wrapping his arms more tightly around me. "You're not like my mother. Not in any way—"

I continue through sobs, "I knew Luca's adopted parents could give him the life I never could. But I haven't gone a day in my life without thinking about him, even though I've gone to great lengths to stay away. I knew I couldn't bear the pain of seeing him again ... of having to say goodbye all over. So, I chose the coward's way out. But I can't do that anymore."

"You weren't a coward, Aspen. You were giving your son a chance at a good life. That takes courage and selflessness, the kind I wish my mother had when I was a child."

I wrap my arms covetously around his neck, tangling my fingers in his hair and beard and reveling in the feel of his strong heartbeat. I crave closeness with him, total intimacy, like last night. I need him inside of me, a part of my body and my soul. But first, he has to know what he's getting into if he chooses me.

Inhaling slowly, I add, "Luca's adopted dad died a couple of months ago, and his mom, Nadine, was just diagnosed with terminal cancer. She's asking me to take custody of him."

Axel's big hands massage my shoulders and slide into my hair, sending luscious shivers of want through my core. "And how do you feel about that?"

I bite my bottom lip. "At first, I was terrified at the prospect. Of reopening that painful wound. Of whether I'd make a decent mom and am even up for the challenge. I don't have much to go on when it comes to parental figures and how functional families work, apart from my mentor and unofficial adopted mom, Stella. But the more I think about it, the more sure I become that reuniting with Luca is the right decision, even if it means major sacrifices and stepping outside of my comfort zone."

"This goes without saying," Axel says gently, showering my forehead and cheeks in kisses. "But I'll be there with you every step of the way if that's what you want."

I nod. "Thank you, baby. It's what I want more than anything. But first, I need some time to get to know my son —" My voice cracks over the last word, and I sniffle, attempting to wrap my head around the months to come.

"Of course. Whatever you and Luca need, I'll be there for you. Always."

"And I'll be there for you, Axel. No matter what, because you're my home now, too."

Silence fills the cab for a long moment as we kiss, dissolving into each other as the windows fog, and our hearts race. Axel's hands rove over my body, filling me with the most delicious sensations of love, tenderness, and anticipation. Finally, he confesses, "There are so many ways I feared you would respond to my past, but this was never one of my hopes. Even in my wildest dreams."

"You didn't do anything wrong, Axel. And you have nothing to hide or be ashamed of. But the people who hurt you do." As I say the words, I realize they're meant for me, too. A great weight lifts as I think about Chadwick Mayfair, realizing what happened was no fault of my own.

"If I ever meet your father, there's a very high likelihood, I'll knock him out. Be forewarned, Aspen. And as for Chadwick Mayfair?"

His body tightens, and I lean up, feathering his face in kisses until he relaxes again. "No, Axel. Please don't. I want you more than I want revenge," I whisper.

He strokes my cheek, nodding resignedly. "Nobody will ever harm you again. That's all I can promise. Now, what can I do to make you feel better? A foot massage? An ice-cold beer? A hot bubble bath? Some good music?"

Staring into his indigo eyes, overflowing with love for me, I say, "I want you to make love to me, Axel."

"That's the easiest request you've ever made," he answers softly, palming my cheek. "Because there's something you said earlier that I need to respond to."

I arch an eyebrow.

"I love you, too, Aspen."

CHAPTER
NINETEEN

AXEL

"Can I get you something to eat or drink?" I ask, standing in the doorway to my cabin, holding her luggage.

"No," Aspen says breathlessly, wrapping her arms around my neck and straining on her tiptoes to kiss me. "I want to feel you, Axel. That's all."

I drop the luggage, thankful I kicked the front door shut as I entered because I can't entertain another thought after that softly spoken demand. Wrapping my arms around her waist, I lift her off the ground as her lips cover mine, her wicked pink tongue darting into my mouth and setting my heart on fire with her ravenous stroke.

"Please, baby," she says between kisses. "I need you so much."

I thought we'd at least make it upstairs to my bedroom, but I'm not about to make my girl beg. At least not this time. Instead, I carry her to one of my long beige couches, setting her down on the cushions. Her eyes flutter towards my fireplace, and I know what she wants.

I work quickly to get a blaze going, the warmth of the

golden flames and the crackling of the fire mesmerizing. Especially the way its rays illuminate Aspen's face as she looks at me with those huge brown eyes eyes that could make me do anything for her.

I feel her in my chest, a raw ache of pain and pleasure, in my core, which tightens and thirsts for her, and down to the depths of my soul, in places I didn't even know existed. Propping big, fluffy pillows on the ground along with faux fur blankets, I make a cozy spot for us to stretch out and undo each other one delicious kiss, caress, and lick at a time.

I take her hand, leading her to the pillows and blankets where we stand, soaking in each other's presence for a long, beautiful moment. I rest my forehead on hers, allowing her aura to envelop me—soft, feminine, and radiant. Dropping my head slowly, I savor the distance to her mouth, the welcoming look on her face, the way she closes her eyes as my lips feather over hers, my breath warming her mouth.

Although we're both still fully clothed, I feel naked in front of her for the first time. She knows everything about me, my deepest, darkest secrets, and she still wants me. The intimacy of that knowing makes this feel like the first time I've ever been with anyone. As if the Universe is giving me a chance to rewrite everything I know about love and sex with this woman.

Her breath catches in her throat as I adore her face in whisper-soft kisses, awakening a great throbbing need between us that defies time and bodies, the physical in all its forms. It's as if our souls are touching, our spirits mingling.

My lips claim hers with more authority a sigh parts her lips, and I sweep into her mouth possessively. She's mine. All mine. And I won't let any man ever hurt her again.

Our hands remain at our sides, a sliver of distance between our bodies as my fingers find hers, slowly stroking and caressing hers, enjoying every reverberation of want shuttling between our flesh until our fingers tangle fiercely, making love with our hands.

"You're my everything," I whisper between kisses as our hands part, my arms slipping around her waist and pulling her demandingly against my arousal. Hers slide around my neck and her fingers into my hair, sending pleasurable chills into my scalp and down the length of my neck. "All I've ever wanted. More than I could have ever dreamed up or imagined."

I inch back, staring into her flushed face. Aspen's eyes flutter open, tears pooling. "And you're all I've ever wanted. My only regret is we couldn't have found each other sooner," she whispers. "Or even just known about each other's existences and that we would meet some day. It would have made everything leading up to this point so much more bearable."

I feel her words in every cell of my being. But who are we to question fate? Instead, I say, "We're here now. That's all that matters."

She nods, tears pouring over her lower lids. She raises a hand, palming my cheek. "You have no idea how much I've needed you, Axel. All these years of playing the tough, heartless career woman, who doesn't need anyone."

"I do know," I counter, feeling a sting at the back of my eyes. "Because I've needed you all that time, too."

Her mouth crashes into mine, her hands coming up frantically to my shirt. Sliding her hands between us, her fingers trip over the buttons, pulling and tugging until they come loose, more out of coercion than skill. My hands slide up the slit in her floral sundress as she gasps, urging me on.

My body burns, sparks flying, as my hands slide to her hips, grabbing them possessively and arching them against my rock-hard cock.

"Oh, God, Axel." She pants. "I need you inside me so much."

My thumb slides beneath the edge of her lacy, silky panties, and she groans, her head lolling back as I slide through her folds. "You're drenched, Tiger."

She nods. "Yes, I need you so much, it hurts."

I shrug out of my shirt, locked in anticipation's vice grip, as Aspen's fingers drop to my pants, working frantically to unbutton and unzip them. The whir of the zipper makes my cock jump, and my balls tingle, ready to slide into her deliciously wet, tight channel.

My thumb explores her juicy pussy, already swelling and gripping me. I slide upwards, finding her clit and circling it with my thumb as my other hand finds her need. My thick middle finger penetrates her, and she cries out, her breath coming in little pants.

While the last few frayed threads of my self-control remain intact, I withdraw from her, needing to get her more comfortable. "Get on the floor," I order authoritatively, and her eyes darken, her eyes dilating. Aspen may lead in all other areas of her life, but clearly, she wants me holding the reins in the bedroom.

She drops to her knees, reclining back against the cushions. Her eyes swirl with longing as I scramble out of my dress pants and socks, and she unrepentantly stares at my tented boxer briefs. Pride fills me at her admiration, that I can be enough for this magnificent woman. Pulling my briefs down until they pool on the floor, I step out of them, closing the distance between us.

Kneeling on the floor, I straddle her legs, making quick

work of the rest of her clothes, unwrapping her like a precious gift. One that's all tanned, heated skin, racing pulse, and burgeoning need. I can smell her desire for me as I shoulder between her legs demandingly.

She opens her mouth to speak, but a strangled gasp comes out instead as I bury my head in her pussy, savoring her musky smell, her animal need for me. I circle her pearl with my tongue, sucking her into my mouth.

"Yes, Axel!" she screams as I tease and toy with her, taking my time.

I confess between licks, "I am so addicted to your pussy. It is the favorite fucking flavor I didn't even know I needed. And I love how you keep it shaved—the prettiest shade of brown, swollen, and so goddamned sexy covered in your shiny cream."

I dip my head again, swiping my tongue along her slit and sucking her lips in and out of my mouth. She trembles, her thighs and abdomen flexing, her hips straying towards my mouth. Her hands tangle in my hair, pressing me urgently against her pussy.

Sliding my middle finger along her slit, I savor how she whimpers, confessing where to touch her and begging me to take her over the edge. I slide my finger back and forth, penetrating her more deeply with each pass until I'm two knuckles deep, her honey dripping into my palm. I stroke her knowingly, authoritatively, finding the perfect pressure and position to take her there.

After what she told me about her past. About how she was abused and exploited by her father's partner, all I can think about is restoring her sexual agency. About pleasing her in ways she didn't even know were possible. About inspiring the kind of orgasm that makes her squirt and sob and dissolve into the cushions and blankets, a satisfied heap of quivering pleasure.

"Yes, Axel, please don't stop," she begs, her hands sliding down my neck to my shoulders and back. Her nails dig into my flesh as she draws closer, angling her hips towards my seeking mouth as my fingers stroke her, stretching out her pleasure.

"Yes, yes, yes!" she screams, giving her entire body to me as she comes so hard that her lower ab muscles jump, and her pussy grips me hard, sucking my fingers deeper with each spasm. She drenches my face, writhing under me and letting out a great gasping sob. I work her through it, lapping and stroking her until her body trembles beneath me, and she begs between gasps of air, "Please, I need a moment."

Sitting up, I swipe a hand over my beard, amazed by how her body reacts to me. Never have I had a more responsive lover or one I'm more attuned to. It's almost like I read her mind through my fingertips, lips, and tongue, adjusting to draw the rawest, most feral pleasures from this otherwise buttoned-down, self-controlled woman.

Covering her face with both hands, she sobs, "That was the best ever. God, Axel, what are you doing to me?"

I crawl up next to her, both vindicated and a bit concerned by her tears. If she's crying from pleasure and losing control, fantastic. But if it's something else, I need to address it immediately. Either way, she needs comforting—thorough, tender aftercare.

"Are you okay?" I ask, lying on my side next to her and propping my head up on my hand.

She peeks at me between her fingers, her face still awash in bliss. "You make me feel..." She sobs.

I wrap an arm around her gently, running my fingertips

up and down the sexy hollow of her back, round ass, and delectable, thick thighs.

"Everything," she sobs.

"Aspen," I whisper. "Is feeling everything okay?"

She nods emphatically, slowly lowering her hands to reveal tear-soaked cheeks. "Yes, but I can't hide any parts of myself from you. I can't even maintain my self-control around you."

Palming her cheek, I use my thumb to wipe the tears. "You make me feel the same way, Tiger, and it's scary. Or at least new and uncomfortable. But I swear to you I will never do anything to purposely hurt you or take advantage of this intimacy."

Through more tears, she leans forward to gently kiss me. I hold her, crooning comforting words until her tears turn into giggles, and her hands start exploring my body again, making her desire known.

"How about that ice-cold beer now?" I ask, and she heartily nods.

I pad back into the living room a few minutes later, holding two uncapped bottles and devouring Aspen with my eyes. She lies back, relaxed and confident, her dark hair feathered out on the pillows. The empress of my living room, her legs unapologetically spread, she slides her fingers through her folds, igniting my blood. Never have I been with a more sexually confident woman, and I fucking love it as I drop to my knees next to her, enjoying the show.

She leans forward, bringing her cream-slick fingers to my mouth, and I lick them clean one by one, sucking, teasing, and nipping them before she grabs a beer, sitting cross-legged next to me. "Clearly, you're not afraid of a woman who knows what she wants," she says, raising her bottle and taking a sip.

"You figured that out last night, Tiger."

"I did. And I have the distinct impression that you and I are going to spontaneously combust one of these days. The chemistry between us is too overwhelming, too insatiable."

"If I could go up in smoke fucking you, I'd consent in a heartbeat."

She giggles, bringing her bottle up. I raise mine, clinking them together. Purposely, I let mine lean forward a little too much, sending a chilly mouthful of beer onto her tits.

"Oh," she exclaims at the cold liquid.

"Oops," I flirt, leaning forward to lick her tits clean, sucking and nipping with glee.

Without hesitation, her bottle tips towards me, and a little beer trickles down my abs, causing an immediate tightening in my core. Her eyes follow the droplets, daring them to slide past my Adonis belt to my cock and balls. "Oops," she says. "Lie back and get comfortable, Axel. I want to taste you before I feel you."

My throat tightens, and my pulse pounds. "Yes, ma'am." I lower myself back, bottle resting on the floor next to me with one hand steadying it.

Her tongue slides up my thighs, wresting a surprised cry from me. "Is this okay?" she asks, and I know she's worried about what I do and don't like touch-wise after our earlier confession.

"As long as my eyes stay on you, Tiger, it's all good. The best."

She nods. "Tell me if there's anything you don't like."

"Always. And the same goes for y—" Her tongue swipes up the base of my cock, and my eyes roll back in my head. "God," I manage as the tip of her tongue thrums up and down the bottom side of my rod from base to tip and back again.

My body sinks into the cushions. My thighs and abs taut. After pleasuring her and the feel of her hot, velvety tongue on my dick, I'm ready to explode. "You're going to kill me, Aspen," I moan.

"No, I'm going to make you lose control. Like you do to me," she replies in cheeky, sexy tones.

I groan as her tongue laps at my head, swirling and circling before her lips tighten around me. Sucking and twisting her tongue around my rod, she lowers her head until I'm buried in her mouth, my tip pressed suggestively against the back of her throat.

Pulling back, she pants, "I don't know if this is the right time for this information. But I don't have a gag reflex."

"Oh, God," I cry as she covers me with her hot mouth again, bobbing back and forth and playing with the depth and speed as her tongue kneads and twists me into oblivion. I am so fucking close to coming that my fingers dig into the cushions and floor, and I grip my beer so tightly I'm damn sure it's going to shatter.

She swallows my head, taking me down her throat, and I see stars, lightheaded and taut in every place that need holds me. My balls pull up as she swallows, bathing my head in mindless, wordless, unnamable pleasure.

My hips thrust up, a scream strangling my throat as my mind explodes, my body following behind. She takes everything I have to give, sucking and swallowing again and again, holding my throbbing rod in her mouth until I've spent my cum. I shudder as she pulls back, every sensation lighting up my nervous system.

Looking up at Aspen, I gasp, a stupid grin seizing my

face, "That's the closest I've ever come to blacking out from pleasure."

"Oh my God," she gasps, staring wide-eyed at me. "Are you okay?"

I chuckle at her shocked expression. "Better than okay. That was fucking mind-blowing. Now, get over here so we can cuddle, enjoy our beers, and get a second wind for that lovemaking you requested earlier."

We sip our beers silently, staring into the fire, and I don't know how I'll ever let Aspen go back to Newport Beach. But there will plenty of time to worry about that later. Stroking her arm with my fingertips, I say, "We've talked a lot about the bad stuff that's happened to us. But what about our dreams and aspirations for the future?" I raise my head, gazing at her peaceful, satisfied face.

Her tongue darts out, wetting her bottom lip as she palms my chest, her fingertips swirling and playing with my hair. "Well, we talked about our career goals before on Mountain Mates. How I want to be one of the nation's top wedding planners and how you want to dominate West Coast brews and gastropubs."

"Yeah, but what about outside of work? If you could have anything you want?"

"Between us or just in general?" she asks, kissing my chest.

"What you wanted before you ever met me."

"I thought it was my coastal condo in Newport Beach and my career. But maybe what I've really wanted all along is a family."

"Me, too," I confess.

Aspen asks, "How about you? What's something you want?"

I finish my beer, pushing it to the side and propping my

head up with my free arm. "Besides you," I say nipping flirtatiously at her mouth. "And us, as I think you've already figured out. I've always wanted a really good, top-of-the-line bay boat for fishing. I know it sounds weird for a land-locked mountain man. But there are plenty of lakes around here where I'd like to go fishing in something other than my ratty-ass, hand-me-down, metal rowboat. And no offense or objectification implied, but I'd love to see you slathered in sunscreen or tanning oil or whatever you use, sunning yourself on my deck. That's not so easy with my current boating situation."

Aspen chuckles, her voice oozing mirth. "I would love to indulge your boating dreams and create some sexy new memories together. You know, Newport Beach is very welcoming to boats," she hints, raising an eyebrow.

"I suppose so, although there's a big difference between lake boating and facing off against the Pacific Ocean. I might need some lessons before that."

"You have a point," she chuckles.

"That said, we do need to get a date on the books some time soon in your neck of the woods. After all, inquiring minds want to know what Balboa Bars are."

"Oh, yes," she's agrees enthusiastically.

"Well? Are you going to explain them to me?"

"It's better to taste one than explain it. What's some time soon look like to you?"

"Next weekend?" I arch an eyebrow, already feeling the bittersweet tug of knowing she has to go home on Monday.

"Really? So soon?"

"It won't be soon enough, Tiger."

She nods. "You're right. How in the hell am I going to say goodbye to you Monday?"

"By knowing you'll see me in a few days."

"Next weekend, then," she smiles from ear to ear.

"By the way, I meant to tell you this before, but I think it's hot as fuck that you're Latina. Just like everything else about you."

"Thank you," she croons. "I don't know much about the culture, though. My father wanted to keep me away from it, I think. He considered my mom's Mexican family beneath him."

"From everything you've told me about your father, I really hate that guy. Having you was his only redeeming feature." And as for Chadwick Mayfair, he's the one favor I'll call into Wolfe.

"It's okay. That's how I feel about my father, too. He's not even worth the wasted breath," I say, turning to lie on top of Axel, kissing his chest and curling my fingers in his hair. "Instead, why don't you show me how sexy as fuck I am."

EPILOGUE

ASPEN

When I say goodbye to Axel on Monday morning, I feel it in the same place where letting go of Luca hit me. The very center of my heart.

We part after an amazing breakfast with countless promises pledged and the agreement that once each of us sorts out the immediate problems and challenges we face, we'll take the next step together.

As much as I need him to walk with me every step of the way as I get to know Luca, it's not fair to my son. Luca needs time to get to know me while leaving plenty of space to mourn his adopted parents before I introduce a new variable into the mix. Still, Axel remains the lifeline I need, texting and calling me day and night and always available no matter what I need when I need it.

The drive between Newport Beach and Hollister becomes well-paved with our tire treads anytime we can sneak in a getaway weekend. As the months pass, and Nadine's condition weakens, I increasingly become Luca's primary caregiver, enlisting a nanny to help with daily activities and responsibilities like shuttling him to and from school.

Three months later—one month after Nadine's passing —I sit at breakfast with Stella, Luca by my side, coloring the kid's menu provided by the restaurant as we catch up.

Moments of this journey have been inordinately painful and challenging. But Luca and I visit a therapist together weekly, and my son is starting to adjust to his new life and schedule. Curtis and Nadine lived in Santa Barbara, so changing schools was one of many shakeups in Luca's life. But his resilience has amazed me.

I listen sympathetically as Stella describes the equally difficult past month she's experienced. She describes her mother's funeral and the great outpouring of condolences and gifts. Her father passed a few weeks later, both a painful double wound and a relief for the pair always fated to be together.

"But enough about me," she says, shaking her head and eating her last bite of quiche before washing it down with coffee. "How's my grandson doing?"

Luca beams, his black, wavy hair disheveled and wild, his face expressive and filled with the indomitable glee of being a child despite everything he's endured. "Better, Grandma," he says with a big toothy grin that reveals missing teeth. "But Mama's missing her friend."

While he has always referred to Nadine as Mom, ever since reconnecting and reuniting with me, he has been in a slow transition from calling me Aspen to calling me Mama. It warms my heart in ways I can't express.

But his words surprise me now. "Mama missing a friend? What do you mean?" My eyes dart to Stella's before we both look at Luca.

His grin widens as he mischievously says, "Axel, the

cowboy. He and Mama talk all the time. They're like Rapunzel and Flynn. I think she'd be happier if Flynn came to stay, or maybe we went to live with him in the forest?" He scrunches his nose at the suggestion, laughing.

"Sorry," I say to Stella without skipping a beat. "But his favorite movie is *Tangled*, if you haven't already guessed. And he's also a little romantic at heart."

Stella's face warms. "And he wants his Mama to be happy."

I nod, finally understanding what Nadine meant about the rewards of motherhood. Is my condo as neat as before? Hell no. Is my time my own? Or even my worries? No. But nothing can replace the little moments throughout the day as my relationship with Luca continues to deepen.

"Speaking of your friend ... You know, I never did tell you about the complaint I got after the wedding you did in Hollister."

"The complaint?" My stomach drops, considering all that nearly went wrong that night.

Stella chuckles. "Apparently, there was a certain blonde bridesmaid who felt the special attention the wedding planner afforded one groomsman was excessive."

I laugh, taken aback by the revelation. "Are you serious? Why didn't you tell me about this sooner?"

"Because I know what a perfectionist you are, Aspen, and how much it would have bothered you."

"True. So, what did you tell her?"

"Duly noted and to mind her own business. Love is love. Even when it blooms in unexpected places. I think my grandson's right, though. My daughter would feel much happier this holiday season with a certain cowboy mountain man under her tree."

"I wish," I say, staring off into space.

"Well, what's the hold-up?"

I shrug. "Axel's been so busy over the past few months. He recently finished testifying in a human trafficking court case that's garnered national attention."

"Yes, I've seen some of the news coverage. He's a brave man."

He is, and I've been there every step of the way to support him. Even though the truth has been liberating for Axel, it has been hard-won at the expense of reopening incredibly painful wounds. I wet my lips, continuing, "So, he's still catching up on everything he had to forgo during the trial. And he's been involved in his brother Holden's parole case. It looks like they might finally have what they need to exonerate him."

Stella nods knowingly. "The wrongly convicted brother, right?"

I nod. "On top of that, Axel's brewery business continues to explode, and he's scoping out potential spots for a second location along with his first gastropub."

"Wow, busy man," she remarks with a knowing smile.

"What's that look for?"

"Nothing," she says with a grin. "And how has the trial gone? Did they get the verdict Axel and his associates hoped for?"

"Thankfully, yes. Full convictions for all charged and maximum sentences. This case has sent shockwaves through the nation about human trafficking, pedophilia, kidnapping, and those involved in some of the highest places in government. It's a huge win for those fighting to end modern-day slavery."

"Wow, that's incredible. So, Axel's a hero on top of it all?"

My face beams. "On top of it all."

"All the human trafficking talk reminds of the strange news about your father's former associate." Stella frowns, whispering. "Not that it should surprise me." Her voice contains an edge of rage.

I nod, unwilling to discuss the matter in greater detail in front of Luca. All he knows is that his biological father is dead. The truth is far more salacious, however. According to the official story, Chadwick Mayfair died of a heart attack in a brothel in Thailand with an underage prostitute. Apparently, his transgressions finally caught up with him in the end.

We sit in silence for a long moment.

Finally, Stella forces a smile. "Back to more pleasant topics. Maybe I need to get a Mountain Mates account. Find my own Sierra Nevada mountain man," she says with a chuckle.

"Maybe you should."

We both laugh, before the waitress comes back around, and we fight over the bill. I manage to get it, determined to pay today.

Resigned, Stella says, "Alright, Grandson, are you ready to go Christmas shopping for Mama?"

"Yes." Luca grins, jumping up from his seat. I grab his to-go box and mine, standing up and rounding the table to hug them both. "Let me know when I should pick him up."

Stella nods, her eyes matching the smile on her face. "How about we meet you at Balboa Island later tonight for the Christmas Boat Parade? By Sugar 'n Spice at six?"

"Wait, are you spoiling my kid with a Balboa Bar, too?"

"Yes," Stella says unrepentantly. "And you too, when we see you later."

"Deal!"

"Boat parade?" Luca exclaims. "Balboa Bars?

Seven hours later, Stella, Luca, and I scope out the perfect spots to watch the Newport Beach Christmas Boat Parade, diving into our messy, delectable, crunchy Balboa Bars. Sugar 'n Spice claims to have been making them since the 1940s, although nearby Dad's says they are the progenitors of the bar starting in the 1960s. The vanilla ice cream bars dipped in chocolate and then covered in our favorite toppings are downright sinful and very messy. Stella gets crushed Oreo sprinkles while I go with crushed peanuts, and Luca gets M&Ms.

After devouring our bars, we stand together near the water, awaiting the decorated boats, almost like a family. I fight back tears, wishing Axel were here to complete it. Pulling out my phone, I text:

ASPEN

Wish you were here

He doesn't respond right away, which I find odd. But it is the holiday season, and he did warn me he would be much busier in December. Instead of worrying about it, I put my phone back in my purse and pull my jacket more tightly around me. Although the weather remains balmy and temperate year-round, evenings get chilly.

As late afternoon descends into the gloaming, the crowd continues to gather, excited voices filling the air.

"It finally feels like Christmas," I say, smiling at Stella and Luca. Luca's face is a mess of chocolate and ice cream, and I search in my brown leather Coach handbag for one of its new and most useful additions, wet wipes. Pulling one out, I scrub his face as he scowls and complains.

Stella laughs. "Just you wait, Aspen. It's really going to feel Christmasy soon."

As twilight ushers in distant stars and memories of stellar gazing with Axel, the parade begins. Stella, Luca, and I transform into a jumble of 'ohs,' 'ahs,' and pointing as we marvel at increasingly spectacular boats decorated with Christmas lights. As Santas float by along with reindeer, elves, decorated trees, and everything else festive and merry, we choose our favorites, marveling at the sights.

One, in particular, catches my eye. A large fishing boat decorated with light displays shaped like stars, gold rings, and glowing mistletoe. "Wow, they really outdid themselves!" I exclaim, eyeing the flashy boat.

Stella chuckles, raising her cell phone to get pictures.

Luca asks, "Do you like it? Grandma and I—"

"Shh," Stella says gently but firmly. "Remember?"

Luca slaps his hand over his mouth, and I knit my brows. But before I can ask any more questions, the boat catches my eye again.

I turn to Stella, asking, "Should we move? It looks like that boat's headed straight for us."

She shrugs, and Luca giggles, covering his mouth with his other hand, too. "What?" I ask, noticing the sneaky smiles back and forth between the two of them.

The boat docks next to us, and the wording on the side arrests my eyes: The Tiger. Looking up, I'm unable to register the sight inside. Instead of a Santa, Elf, or Grinch, I find a cowboy mountain man decked out in a brown Stetson, red and black flannel, button-down shirt, tight-fitting Wranglers, and black leather boots. Axel secures the boat with a rope, grinning at my shock.

"Need a lift?" he calls in our direction, and I'm speechless, tears springing to my eyes.

Stella answers, "Yes, we'd love to be in the parade. Come on, everyone."

"Yes!" Luca screams, raising his hands with excitement.

I hang back, watching as Axel helps Luca and Stella into the elegant fishing boat, admiring what a beautiful family they make. I've been nervous about Axel and Luca finally meeting, though they've spoken over the phone. Now, I wonder why I was so concerned.

Luca high-fives the cowboy, and Axel kneels down, laughing and joking with him. Reaching inside a drawer, he pulls out a second, smaller brown cowboy hat, and Luca squeals with delight, putting it on his head.

Axel furrows his brows, cocking his head and stroking his beard as he assesses the boy, tipping the front of the hat slightly downward before saying, "Perfect! You're a real buckaroo now!"

"Mama, did you hear that?" Luca screams, looking back at me. "Axel says I'm a real cowboy!"

"That said, you need to wear this on the boat, too," Axel urges, grabbing a child-sized life vest from the same drawer. The man thought of everything. He helps the boy into it, securing and adjusting the straps for a perfect fit.

"Now, don't go thinking just because you have this on, you can go for a swim, okay? Stay away from the edges of the boat because this water's colder than ice, and there are a lot of boats out here tonight."

Luca nods, his face growing serious as he absorbs Axel's words, holding his shoulders a little straighter to mimic the cowboy.

Axel straightens, his eyes washing over me warmly as he strides towards the edge of the boat, offering me his hand. After I board, he pulls me into his arms, planting a chaste kiss on my lips.

Luca laughs and says to Stella, "Grandma, see what I mean? They're like Rapunzel and Flynn."

Stella laughs, leaning down to hug the boy. Her eyes catch my quizzical expression, and she shrugs. "Axel's been planning today for a couple of months, and Luca and I helped a little today with decorations and logistics."

"Thank you again, ma'am," Axel says, leaning forward to hug me again.

"But how did you two connect?" I ask, shaking my head.

"Ridge and Paige," Axel chuckles.

Of course. As the original wedding planner for the Dawsons' wedding, Stella talked extensively with Axel's family. "When I heard your mountain man was one of Ridge's brothers, I knew you'd found a keeper," she smiles broadly. "That family's filled with good men, starting with Wyatt."

"Very appreciated, Ms. Stella," Axel nods. Untying the rope, the boat drifts away from the dock. He tangles his fingers with mine, leading me over to the captain's chair. "What do you think of this baby? Will it do as a family boat?"

His brow arches as he stares down at me, the depth of love immeasurable. The word "family" sounds amazing on his lips.

"Yes, it's perfect. The boat. The decorations. Having you here with us all together like a family."

He wraps his arms around me from behind, snuggling me close. Nuzzling my neck, he says, "Merry Christmas, Tiger."

"Merry Christmas, baby. I can't believe you named your vessel after me."

"Why not? You're the inspiration for this purchase," he confesses, burying his head in my hair. "I envision you right over there, your hair fanning out around you as you soak up the sun's rays, and I fish until you tempt me into other more interesting activities."

"It sounds amazing," I say, breathlessly.

Luca runs up beside us to tug on Axel's shirt. "Axel, have you shown her the gift yet?"

Stella shakes her head, laughing.

"Gift?" Axel says questioningly. "Hmm... Let's see here."

He shoves his hands in his pockets, and I excuse him, saying, "Baby, you've already done far more than enough. I don't need any gifts on top of this."

He continues searching, patting down his shirt pockets, and now I'm curious what's going on. Suddenly, he pulls something out of his front shirt pocket, holding it up behind my head for Luca to see. "You mean this?"

"Yes!" the boy cries, clapping his hands together.

Against the shell of my ear, Axel whispers, "I would do this on one knee, but I don't want us to crash into the other boats, and I'm not certain of your navigational skills yet. So, please excuse the slight departure from tradition."

Bringing his arm around me, he holds up a large diamond engagement ring on a rose-gold band. The solitaire sparkles in the Christmas lights decorating the boat as I cover my mouth, gasping.

Whispering next to my ear so only he and I can hear, he asks, "Aspen Everhart, you've already got polished, perfect wedding planner mastered, amazing mother clinched, beloved daughter down pat, and all the wild tiger I could ever want behind-closed-doors. But I need, with every beat of my heart and every breath that I take, to call you my wife, too. Will you do me the honor of marrying me?"

I can't even speak, emotion thickening my throat as tears pour down my cheeks, and I nod enthusiastically.

"Thank God," he says, slipping the ring onto my hand. I hold it up, admiring the beautiful diamond.

Luca and Stella eye us keenly, and Axel points to my hand, calling out above the sea breeze, "She said 'yes!'"

They both cheer, doing an improvised happy dance together.

"I know you're particular about your jewelry, so level with me if you don't love this. I had Stella and Luca help me pick it out. We've been talking back and forth online and over the phone. So, I hope it's okay."

"It's amazing. Beyond perfect!" I shake my head, turning to slide my arms around his neck and capture his lips for a kiss overflowing with the passion and hope emblazoned in his engagement ring.

Wrapped in Axel's arms, sailing in the Newport Beach Christmas Parade, I feel like the most loved woman on the planet. It's almost too good to bear. But it also feels like something I could get used to, even come to rely on. And for once, that thought doesn't scare me.

"I can't believe you all," I say, looking at Stella and Luca, who beam. Stella has her phone up, capturing the moment in photos and videos, and it couldn't be more perfect, surrounded by the people who truly love me. *Forever.*

LOOKING for more from Aspen and Axel as they build a family together with Luca and Stella? Read an exclusive bonus scene here: https://www.engrideaves.com/freebies/

INTRIGUED by Bowie's mystery woman in *Love at First Revenge*? Get the full scoop on this steamy, action-packed romantic suspense thriller here: https://www.engrideaves.com/love-at-first-revenge/

READY TO DEVOUR Stacey and Jerry's off-limits workplace romance? The kitchen isn't the only place cooking in this steamy, naughty Christmas romance. One-click *Mountain Man Santa*: https://www.engrideaves.com/naughty-spice-christmas/

YEARNING for more about Ridge and Paige, as well as Axel's other foster brothers? Check out the fast-paced, spicy Rough & Ready Country series, jam-packed with steamy cowboy mountain man and curvy girl love. Explore the series free in KU: https://amzn.to/43zZCzO

BONUS SCENE

ASPEN

FIVE MONTHS LATER

I awaken slowly, wrapped in the warmth and security of Axel's arms. His firm, muscular body is relaxed behind me still lost in sleep. I snuggle back into him, enjoying the feel of his heat and safety.

A low growl rumbles through his chest as he pulls me closer, whispering, "Morning, Tiger, how'd you sleep?"

"Okay, once I finally found a position that didn't make my back hurt."

"Did the body pillow help?" my cowboy mountain man asks lazily behind me, bringing his hand to palm my growing stomach. I'm five months pregnant with our first baby, and I had no idea how amazing it could be to have the man I love ready to support me every step of the way.

"Yes, it did, baby. Thank you for finding that for me."

Axel yawns next to the shell of my ear before covering it in feather-light kisses. "I saw it on one of those pregnancy forums where women talk about what's helping. Glad it's working."

I can't help but chuckle at the thought of my big, burly cowboy searching pregnancy forums to find the right gear. I snuggle into his arousal, sighing at the feel of his thick, hard rod.

"What are you laughing at?" he grumbles, grinding against me as he continues waking up, stretching next to me.

"I'm laughing at the thought of you doing all of this baby research for me."

"Last time I checked, I'm the one who fucked the hell out of you and got you pregnant in the first place. Aren't I?" he whispers naughtily against my ear. "So, I figure it's my job to keep you comfortable, rested, well-fed, and satiated." His hands drop to my waist, angling me suggestively back towards him.

A knot of desire lodges in my throat at his words and actions. He has done all of these things since we officially moved in together after the Newport Beach Christmas Boat Parade, making his ample, gorgeous cabin in Rough & Ready Country Luca's and my new home. "And how do you plan on satiating me this morning, cowboy?"

He chuckles in low tones, spitting on his hand and sliding it between my thighs to find my clit. He swirls the greedy nub expertly. My pussy tightens and throbs with instant, overpowering need. We sleep naked, wrapped in the delicious warmth of each other's flesh. This time, when my ass grazes him, he slides into me, lazily moaning.

"Is the door locked?" I ask, the golden light of early morning reminding me that Luca could burst into our bedroom at any moment. Axel and I have worked hard to get him to knock, but he still only remembers about fifty percent of the time.

"Yes, and Luca's not up yet."

We have a nanny who helps out during the week, but Hazel doesn't work weekends. I don't want to leave Luca alone too long, although the kid is an expert at self-entertaining between bins of Legos, his wooden train set, and the stack of storybooks lining the shelves in his room.

Axel's answer makes me melt, surrendering to the sensual warmth of my husband. We married in an intimate elopement in February, which means we're still on our honeymoon as far as I'm concerned. Of course, that honeymoon will extend for the rest of our lives if Axel has his way. The man makes it his life's mission to spoil and care for me in every way.

Groaning against my shoulder, he drives into me, continuing to work my clit as I arch back into him. "God, your cunt feels so good. Every time with you feels like our first time."

I can't help but giggle, the motion making him more frenzied as he pounds into me.

"Except without the rain and the cars," I murmur.

"One of these days, we're going to have to reenact that scene, Tiger. It was hot as fuck."

"Yes," I whimper, both an agreement to his statement and a response to the way his slick finger swirls around my pearl at the perfect pressure and pace to make me quiver and clench him. As my pussy throbs and swells around him, fluttering and drawing toward a big, extravagant orgasm, he drives deeper, squeezing my hips and demanding my pleasure.

"Fuck, yes," he praises through fast-paced breaths. Pulling his hand from my pussy, he licks it ravenously. "Damn, I love it when you squirt. You taste so fucking good."

I can't even respond, my eyes rolling back in my head as

he slams into me once more, flooding my pussy with warm waves of cum. Afterward, we lie tangled together, catching our breath. I finger his wedding band, bringing his hand to my mouth and kissing it.

"Best morning sex ever and best husband ever," I finally manage between pants.

"That's what you always say," he grumbles, nuzzling my neck and feathering it with his lips.

"Because it's always true," I whisper, emotion coloring my voice.

"Hey, are you okay?" he asks, squeezing me tightly.

"Yes," I struggle, trying not to sob. "I've just never been so happy as I am with you. I didn't even know this life was possible."

We've discussed this before. The differences between my first pregnancy as a teen—a wholly ostracizing, lonely experience with no one to lean on or confide in—and now. Axel has been there every step of the way, attentive, loving, and totally devoted.

"You never have to do anything alone again," he reminds tenderly, lifting himself slightly to look down at my face. I turn toward him, and he palms my rounded stomach, affection washing over his gaze. The baby jumps in my stomach, and he laughs. The feeling is still so new to him, and I can see the unadulterated joy it brings him.

"Thank you," he says in raw tones.

"For what, baby?"

"For giving me the home and family I've always want-ed." Tears fill his eyes, reflecting the ones pooling on my bottom lashes.

"I could say the same thing to you, cowboy."

He leans down, kissing me tenderly and bringing a

hand up to stroke the tears from my cheek. "Why don't you sleep in a little bit. Mornings seem to be working better for you these days, anyway."

"But what about my work and Luca and—"

"It's Sunday, so your work can wait. As for Luca? I've got it. Try being lazy for once, Tiger. Your body's already doing enough work growing a mini mountain boy or girl."

I chuckle, nodding as he reluctantly gets out of bed, returning a few moments later with a warm washcloth to clean me. As my ears settle into the sounds of him dressing for the day, I nod off.

I don't know how much time passes, but when I wake, I feel relaxed and comfortable, ready for a new day.

We don't know the gender of our baby. We decided to make it a surprise, but considering how free I've been of morning sickness and nausea, just like with Luca, my guess is we're having a boy. If we do, his name will by Leonard. And if the baby's a girl, we plan on calling her Leonora, which means I've settled on Leo for now.

I sit up in bed, stroking my stomach and stretching. "Alright, Leo, time to quit being lazy." I rub my stomach, feeling the baby kicking and marveling at this new life.

Then, I take a hot shower, allowing my muscles to relax. I blow-dry my hair, apply makeup, and get dressed before heading downstairs. I hear soft voices below as delicious cooking smells greet my nose.

"Happy Mother's Day!" voices ring out as I enter the kitchen, absorbing the scene in front of me. Axel and Luca are hard at work on batch after batch of his delectable blueberry lemon muffins, and Stella works on non-alcoholic mimosas made with sparkling water and garnished with strawberries.

"Oh my goodness!" I exclaim, tears filling my eyes as they stop what they're doing, rounding the counter to hug me.

Axel hangs back, letting Luca and Stella embrace me first. Luca holds up a drawing to me with a family of four stick figures. He's got lines with names scrolled next to them for Axel, Stella, himself, and me. Another line points to a circle over my belly that says Leo.

"This is amazing," I admire, looking at the drawing.

"Happy Mother's Day, Mama," the black-haired boy screams as tears spill over my cheeks, and I lean down to hug him.

Stella follows, embracing me tightly before stepping back to place a hand on my stomach. She wasn't around for the first pregnancy. I met her a couple of months after giving Luca away. "The baby's been busy growing, I see."

"Yes, ma'am," Axel beams. "You figure he or she has a lot more to do if they're going to be anywhere near the size of their daddy."

Everyone laughs, stepping back to make room for Axel. Pulling me into his big, strong arms and making me feel pleasantly dwarfed as usual, he whispers, "Happy Mother's Day, wife!" Removing something from the pocket of his apron, he hands it to me.

"What's this?" I ask, my forehead knitting as I open the long, thin black velvet box to reveal a gold charm bracelet.

Pointing to the charms, Axel says, "I chose to go with the first letters of our names for the bracelet. But if you want charms instead, we can shop the jewelry store together." I look down at the A, two Ls, and S, a physical remembrance of my amazing family."

Now, I'm ugly crying, sobbing as I say, "Thank you so much. This is amazing. I love it."

Axel pulls me tightly against his chest, letting me wet his shirt and regroup for a moment. "No, thank you, Aspen, for forgetting to put up the top of your Carice ... and for taking a chance on this Sierra Nevada wild man."

"Always and forever," I whisper, leaning up on my tiptoes to kiss my husband.

LOVE AT FIRST REVENGE

A COWBOY BOUNTY HUNTER / CURVY GIRL ROMANCE

TRIGGER WARNING

This book contains content/themes that may not be
suitable for all readers, including discussion of human
trafficking, physical violence, and gun violence.

Please read at your own discretion.

CHAPTER
ONE

BOWIE

'm being followed ...

I'm being followed ... The thought inches through my mind, inky and grim. I scan the rearview mirror and the two white trucks behind me. Suddenly, the sickening screech of tires brings my eyes back onto the deserted two-lane road from Rough & Ready Ranch's main house to my secluded cabin.

I slam on my brakes, rubber grinding into pavement as my truck stutters to an unexpected halt. Jumping and bucking toward the truck in front of it, it stops mere inches before a crash. They've jammed their ride sideways, blocking the entire roadway.

It's an ambush ...

I flex my shoulders, the familiar tightness of my double holster reminding me I'm prepared for whatever the fuck this is.

My stomach churns, eyes flickering back and forth between the pickup in front of me, blocking my passage, and the two behind me.

Followed from my brother Ridge's wedding. I have to assume these are the same motherfucking clowns who infiltrated the event. I drop a pin in the group text I keep with my foster brothers. They'll know what to do ... *if they aren't in similar situations.*

A long-bearded man dressed in a bland black and white suit knocks on the window. I roll it down an inch, asking, "Friend, what's the deal?" The word "friend" comes out tense and stern.

His face twitches. "Nothing personal."

Leveling my gaze on him, I clench my teeth until my jaw muscles jump. "You've got that right." I survey the growing group of men, piling out of vehicles. I should've never let myself get in this situation. Rubbing my hand over my face, I weigh my options.

The click of a hammer trains my eyes back on the man on the other side of my driver's side window. "Step out of the vehicle. We don't want any trouble from you."

The corners of my mouth tip down. *The hell they don't.*

Members of the House of the Seven Prophets, this archaic religious cult has ruled Rough & Ready Country since early pioneer days. They've always been secretive, shady as hell. But since Ridge's new wife, Paige, first exposed a nasty pedophile and human trafficking scandal in the church, their ranks have thirsted for my family's blood.

"You won't get anything but trouble from me," I mutter through clenched teeth.

"What'd you say, boy?" the guy with the gun asks.

Boy. One wrong move out of this bearded asshole, and he's dead, though he doesn't know it yet. I have no patience for racist assholes, especially ones incriminated in human trafficking.

"I said, I wonder how many of you and your *boys* have warrants out for abusing children?" I grumble, anger welling inside. The fucker better shoot me in the head now because if he doesn't, it'll be the last mistake he ever makes.

"Out of the car now, dumbass." He spits.

I oblige, hoping at least a couple of my brothers are on their way. But they better fucking hurry. I'm outnumbered ten to one.

I step out of my truck slowly. Survival depends on stalling. That said, a part of me wants to stay in the vehicle. Drive through as many of these child abusers as possible. Go out in a blaze of glory ... or better yet, revenge.

"Hands up." A wizened older man with a beard growls, stepping closer. "Patrick, pat him down for weapons."

The man with the gun trained on me visibly shakes. He must be Patrick because he steps forward hesitantly, his brows furrowing and his lips tipping down at the ends. He's clearly not accustomed to things going kinetic. I can use that to my advantage.

I comply with my palms facing the men, my mind working out the details of what comes next. My best bet remains acting quickly and unexpectedly. Patrick grimaces as he stretches out his arms to pat me down, still with his firearm in hand.

"Mind not pointing that at me?" I ask, taken aback by the man's inexperience. He's clearly never done anything like this before.

The old growly guy says, "Hand me your weapon." Patrick complies, his face relaxing slightly as he steps away from me. Fear glazing his eyes. "If you accidentally shoot him, where's the fun in that? What say we lynch him, drag him behind one of the trucks, or burn him alive? That'll set a much better example."

"Example of what?" I counter, laser-focusing my gaze on the old man giving the order. "Seems like y'all should be the ones having the example set with what you do to vulnerable children and women."

"Did I ask for your opinion?" the old man growls. Angry spittle flies from the corners of his mouth.

"Just stating the obvious," I answer in steely tones.

Patrick's about twenty years younger than the guy with the bad suggestions, putting him around forty-something. He asks the old man, voice shaking, "Are you out of your mind? You want to get slapped with a hate crime?"

He and the older man resemble one another. I'd wager they're related. But then most of the people in this cult are. After all, you can only get so many freaks to drink the Kool-Aid.

"Every crime's a hate crime," the old man responds. "Are you planning on getting caught or something?"

Patrick's cheeks darken, and he shakes his head. But everything about his tentative body language indicates he's not sold on the current plan.

"You're both fixing to get caught by coming after me," I interject.

The old man shakes his head. "Keep your mouth shut. We're not talking to you."

"Well, you should be because your current plan's shit."

Patrick looks intrigued by my words, like he wants to take heed of them. But the older man's face fills with disgust.

"Not only am I a fugitive recovery agent, which means harming me is akin to harming a law enforcement agent. But need I remind you my brother's the sheriff of Gold County? There's no way in hell you'll get away with any of this."

"Shut your mouth," the old man barks. "Patrick, get back to patting him down.

"Yes, Uriah."

The old man's face tightens as Patrick steps forward, wilting the closer he draws to me. I don't know what this pat down will entail, but the fucker's only getting a hold of my weapons over *his* dead body.

Patrick's touch is too light, and he moves hesitantly. I've checked marks for weapons hundreds of times. This guy doesn't know what he's doing.

I need to buy time until one of my brothers arrives. In an easy drawl, body language relaxed and confident, I say, "This is all a simple misunderstanding. Let me go now, and that'll be the end of it."

"No," Uriah barks from behind me.

"But he really doesn't have—" Patrick stops mid-sentence as his hands scrape across one of the guns in my shoulder holster. Our eyes meet, the tension in the air thick enough to cut.

I rush the man, taking him down in one clean move. To the side, Uriah opens fire, but thankfully, his aim is godaw-ful. I tackle him next, driving him to the ground in one efficient move. Like back in my football playing days. Wresting the gun from his hand, I turn it back on the old man and his younger lookalike.

"On your knees," I order. Uriah obeys without hesitation, his face tight.

All eyes are on me. A quick rustle of fabric whispers through the crowd, and I've got more gun barrels pointed at me than I care to count. *Where in the fuck are my brothers?*

I eye the men tensely as the reality of my current, hope-less situation sinks in. Instead of facing off against a mark working my job as a bounty hunter, I'm about to make a last stand against a religious cult. Never saw the trajectory of my life headed this direction, but then who can rightly predict the future?

Patrick rolls on the ground, holding his head. He hit it when I slammed him to the ground. I wonder if he's genuinely injured or putting off the inevitable consequences of fucking up as a member of this group.

"Drop the weapon!" a man hollers behind me.

I don't comply.

I may have eight firearms trained on me. But as tense seconds pass, I realize many of the men holding them look no more comfortable than Patrick did. It figures, considering most of the elite members involved in criminal activities and working with cartels have already been arrested.

Uriah looks past me, urging someone behind me to act. Nothing happens.

"You may have me outgunned," I say matter-of-factly. "But your men seem reluctant to act, old timer."

"Let the cowboy go, Uriah. Our fight isn't with him." It's the same voice that ordered me to drop my weapon and then did nothing about my non-compliance.

"The hell it isn't. It's with his whole family." Uriah retorts.

I chuckle deep in my throat. "Believe me, you're not ready to face off against my whole family."

"Don't be so sure about that," Uriah says, narrowing his eyes and frowning. "You may get a bullet or two off." He rubs his palm over his forehead, looking down to the side. "Hell, you may even kill me. But one against ten are bad odds, boy. And if you hurt me, my men will make sure you feel it a hundredfold. They'll skin you alive."

"You've got farmers out here, Uriah. Not warriors. I figure, you're the only one I need to take down to disperse this crowd. And last time I checked, the odds are eight with you and your man, Patrick, down. Closer to five if you count the inexperience of this ragtag group."

"Get up," the old man orders, his scathing eyes cutting into Patrick's pathetic form. The younger man continues rocking on the ground, feigning injury.

"What happened?" I ask. "All your good men already incarcerated?"

"I could ask you the same question. Where in the hell are your brothers? I thought you prided yourselves on being such a loyal crew—"

Bam.

Uriah stops mid-sentence, grabbing his neck reflexively. Scarlet smears his hand. He transforms from curious to shocked in an instant. Someone just grazed him. His face freezes, shock etched in his expression as he drops to the ground in front of me with a newfound urgency.

Gunfire explodes around me, and I crouch on the ground, trying to get a better sense of what's going on. But the guns of the men from the House of the Seven Prophets aren't trained at me. Instead, they point towards the trucks that followed me into this trap and a new car I haven't seen before—a sleek, silver Mercedes-Benz AMG GT.

I admire it for one solitary second before a pepper of gunfire splits the air. The car takes the brunt, bullets shattering the front windshield, driver's side window, and punching holes in the exterior. I hope whoever was inside escaped. Otherwise, they're dead.

Flattening beneath my truck, I use it as cover, targeting those in my view. My only thought? Whittling this gunfight down to manageable odds. I have to assume whoever started it is on my side. Or at least ambivalent about my death, unlike these bearded sons-of-bitches.

CHAPTER
TWO

JI-SU

The blockade ahead is anything but official ...

Turning off the headlights of my car, I inch closer to the scene, quietly parking and exiting my vehicle. A group of white, bearded males surrounds a handsome Black cowboy. They're far too busy with him to notice me.

I skulk behind the metal frame of my car to appraise the commotion. A few eavesdropped phrases convey the injustice unfolding.

Sinister words reach my ears, ugly ones meant to instill fear in the gorgeous man I assume they've ambushed. *Shooting, lynching, dragging, fire ...*

Over my dead body.

I can't watch a man get gunned down, or worse. Though this is far from my fight, I can't stomach the horror of it.

Sneaking closer, I realize this fight serves dual purposes. Allowing me to target some of the men indirectly involved in the murder of my younger sister, Ae-cha. The murder that destroyed my life and shattered my family ...

228

I recognize Uriah Matthews, an elder from the House of the Seven Prophets. The rest of the assembled men are unknown to me. Many look too young and inexperienced for this dispute. But I imagine the cult's running out of guns, so many of their elite members and leaders arrested thanks to the investigative television journalism of Paige Dawson.

What Paige uncovered is just the beginning, though. The tip of the iceberg.

What I have will lay waste to the goddamned state. Because members of the House of the Seven Prophets are mere pawns, small-time players in one of the most significant corruption scandals ever to hit California. *Money laundering, fraudulent campaign donations, human trafficking, drug smuggling, murder …*

I get Matthews in my sight. I've trained for this for months. Unlike the many gunmen surrounding their black and white clad elder, my hands don't shake.

I pinch the trigger with a steady ease. I always hoped that when things got real, I would be this calm. Yet, the reality of it still amazes me. The practiced action of a warrior rather than a scared, helpless whistleblower on the run.

I can't fathom how profoundly the last six months have redefined my identity. Impacted my actions. Influenced how I lead my life.

Six months ago, I never would have intervened in this situation. Would I have called the police? Certainly. But not stuck my neck out, sneaking in the dark toward a potential gunfight, firearm in hand.

I've always heard it said that you never hear the bullet that's meant for you. It feels much the same for the shot I fire. I don't hear it at all. In fact, I would doubt I fired it except for the kick of the recoil and the blaze of return gunfire that follows.

I sprint in the dark back to my vehicle, dropping to the ground behind it. I may have training. Nevertheless, I've bitten off more than I can chew.

I underestimated Matthews's guns, assuming they'd be so scared shitless after watching their fearless leader fall. I thought they'd turn tail and run. I couldn't have been more wrong.

Of course, my aim might have also been off. I'm far from an expert marksman. Poorly lit conditions don't help, either.

Fear oozes through my veins, sticky and cold. My flesh trembles to the marrow of my bones. But, no, I can't give in to these feelings. These men have made my existence a living hell for the past six months.

It ends here. It ends now.

In a break from gunfire, I peer beneath my vehicle, getting another clean shot off. A man drops to the ground, but I don't know if he's injured or taking cover. I see another man drop when gunfire sounds, confirming the Black cowboy's still alive and able to shoot.

A hail of percussive pops sounds again, and I pray for my life as bullets whiz past me. I'm pinned down, locked in the fog of the action until the distant sound of a siren captures my ears.

Dammit! I should applaud the arrival of law enforcement. But I don't trust anyone. Especially not state officials.

After all, the evidence I have from Ae-cha implicates everybody, law enforcement included. I have to get out of here, and I have to do it fast. Thankfully, the sirens stir panic in the remaining members of the House of the Seven Prophets.

A cacophony of screams breaks out. "Come on. Let's go. Now." Then, truck engines roar and tires squeal. I hope the cowboy's alright, but I'm out of time and options.

Jumping to my feet, I scan the scene. No more gunmen. I race to the driver's side of my vehicle, noting the shattered windshield and window.

I open the door, hesitating for one second about what to cover my hand with to scoop the glass sparkling in my seat away. It shines like diamonds against the black leather.

"And where do you think you're going?" a deep voice asks behind me.

I jump, turning and coming face to face with the cowboy. My breath hitches, and my throat constricts. The man towers above me, well over six feet tall. His dark eyes blaze with a searing fury. His clean-shaven, angular face exudes a kind of masculine strength that would put me at ease under any other circumstances.

But I can't let him impede me. I have to make my exit before it's too late.

"I have to go," I say, scrambling to get in.

"Oh, no, you don't," he counters, grabbing my wrist. His hot touch sizzles, sparks lighting up in equal proportion to the goosebumps rising on my flesh.

For one naughty second, I wonder what his bare skin pressed against mine would feel like. *Unadulterated bliss.* My breath comes out in an extravagant sigh, cheeks burning and heart racing. Still, I have to go ... now. Irrational sexual attraction or not.

"Please," I plead, eyes shooting to his face. His return gaze is bare, naked before me. I have the impression I'm looking straight into his soul. It's the most uncomfortable, gratifying, intimate moment I've ever experienced.

But it can't be happening. Not here. Not under these circumstances.

"I have to go," I repeat firmly, trying to pull my wrist free of his grip. But it's no use. The man's so much stronger than me, I might as well be a mosquito flapping my wings in his direction.

"Not until you answer some questions," he orders, his voice dark, rich, and gravelly.

"You don't understand. I'm not safe here—"

"You're safe with me," he reassures, furrowing his brows.

I shake my head, fear welling as the sirens draw closer. "No, law enforcement's in on this. If they get me into custody, I'm a goner. I'll end up like my sister."

The creases in his forehead deepen, and his face hardens. "I don't know what you've been through, ma'am. But my brother's the sheriff of this town, which means I can personally vouch for your safety."

He says it like it means something. Still, I flutter against his hold, panic-stricken. "I don't know you from Adam. Why should I trust you?"

"Because you saved my life. You may not want to believe this, but you're safe now. You're with good people who won't let anything happen to you."

I shake my head, straining against the futility of breaking his iron-strong grip. One look at my car, riddled with bullet holes and leaking fluid, tells me I won't get far. But I've been on the run for so long, I don't know any other way.

"Please," I roar, sounding more like a terrified animal than a human being.

"Woman," he says, voice steely. "Nothing will happen to you as long as you're with me." His words instill a calm and peace so deeply rooted, I feel it in my soul. "What's your name?"

My body trembles as the sirens close the distance, and an unmarked truck, followed by a sheriff's deputy vehicle, pulls up.

"It would be better for you not to know who I am. If you care about your life," I answer flatly as cowboy boots hammer across pavement.

"It's about time," the cowboy calls out, his grip on my wrist unyielding.

A blond, clean-shaven man with the posture of a military veteran and two sheriff's deputies approach. The blond mutters something under his breath to the officers following him, and they dive into documenting and securing the scene.

He stares at my destroyed vehicle long and hard, putting his hands on his hips. He wears a suit like he's come from a wedding. It matches the outfit of the cowboy next to me. Both wear white Stetsons.

"Brother?" I hiss, utterly betrayed and eyeing the man still holding me.

"Foster brother," he corrects, and my shoulders relax slightly. Though the past six months have taught me to trust no one, this man exudes a steady strength that puts my body wordlessly at ease.

The blond man removes his hat, shaking his head. "A lot of bullet holes for one car. What in the hell happened here, Bowie?"

"Still trying to sort that out, Bro."

The new arrival eyes me and my captured wrist, his brows furrowing. "And this is?"

I frown.

The one called Bowie eyes me, finally dropping my wrist. "Your name?"

"Cynthia Lee." It's the alias I've used on the run, so I answer with practiced ease.

But Bowie looks dissatisfied, cocking his head to the side and narrowing his eyes. His gaze invades me, possesses me.

Shivers of heat shuttle up and down my core. Usually, I'd appreciate this man's intense stare. Maybe even swoon under its heat. But the last thing I need is scrutiny ... or the army of butterflies fluttering around in my stomach.

"Your *real* name," he murmurs dark and dangerous.

I raise my chin imperiously, prepared to repeat my lie. But it's no use. The man sees right through me. Dropping my shoulders and shaking my head, I cave. "You can call me Ji."

"Ji what?" The blond scowls, unappreciative of the earlier alias.

I take a deep breath, whispering, "Ji-su Park. But I really shouldn't be here. I need to go."

"I'm Bowie Reeves," the man I saved introduces.

I nod.

"This your car?" the blond asks, frowning.

I nod again.

"Doesn't look like you'll be going far."

I want to say sarcastically, "Thanks, Captain Obvious." Instead, I bite my bottom lip.

"I was followed by members of the House of the Seven Prophets," Bowie explains. "I realized it too late. I drove right into a blockade with ten to one odds and murder on their mind. I can provide descriptions and a couple of names. They wanted to make an example of me, do something to get back at the family for opposing them. But Ji-su showed up in the nick of time."

"My name's Christian McLeod." The blond offers his hand, and I hesitantly take it. "I'm the sheriff of Gold County and Bowie's brother. Anyone who makes a stand for this guy, especially against the House of the Seven Prophets, is a friend of mine."

"And anyone who fights this kind of corruption is a friend of mine," I say with a firm nod. "But I can't stay here. I have to go."

"What are you running from?" Bowie asks gravely, his rich voice sending shivers up and down my spine.

I cross my arms over my chest because he finally lets go of my wrist. "Everything."

"But why?"

I shake my head. "It's tough to explain. The less you know, the better."

Christian eyes me skeptically. "And yet you happened to be here at the right time to save my brother?"

I shrug, uncertain what he's getting at.

His gaze narrows, and he sighs. "Well, I'm going to need statements from both of you."

"No," escapes my mouth before I can think. Both men appraise me quietly.

"I saw nothing. I did nothing. End of story. Additional questions will require my attorney's presence."

I'm a seasoned paralegal, and I know my rights inside and out. I refuse to endure questioning of any sort without proper representation. But I can't be taken into custody, either. It would be the final nail in my coffin.

A buzzing sound sends the sheriff fumbling for his phone. Putting it against his ear, he grunts, his face hardening. "Fuck, are you okay?"

Silence.

Christian says, "I'll be right there." Shoving his phone back in his pocket, he turns to Bowie. "Bro, there's some trouble brewing with Axel and Aspen, the wedding planner. I'm headed back into Hollister." He eyes me, conflicted.

As if reading his mind, Bowie says, "We're good here. I'll make sure our visitor is available for questioning with her attorney when the time's right."

"But my lawyer could take days to get here. He's an older man driving from San Francisco ..."

"Then, he can join us via conference call. Or our lawyer brother, Flynn, can act in his stead," Bowie concludes as if it's already decided.

Christian agrees, "I appreciate it. Better than locking her up."

Bowie nods, and I furrow my brows.

What exactly would the sheriff charge me with? Helping a man being accosted by the side of the road? Of course, the discharge of firearms does complicate the situation, especially if my aim proved better than it appears. But still ...

"I have rights, you know. You can't hold me for no reason—"

"I can, ma'am," Bowie says matter-of-factly. "We can either do this the nice way or the hard way. Up to you."

"I'm calling my—"

"The hard way?" he asks, raising his eyebrows.

"Holding me against my will is kidnapping," I hiss.

"The sheriff of Gold County needs to interview you. Until that happens, you're with me. Period."

"What kind of legal system is this?" I ask in disbelief.

Christian shakes his head, frowning. "You're in Rough & Ready Country now, ma'am, and we do things differently.

Especially when it comes to matters that impact our immediate family. I'll catch up with you two later. But in the meantime, try not to make Bowie's life difficult. He's one of the best bounty hunters in the nation. You may think you can run and hide from him, but it won't go well."

"Bounty hunter? But I'm no criminal, and I've never skipped out on bail."

"How do I know any of this is true until we vet you more thoroughly and question you on the events of the evening?" Christian hollers as he sprints back to his truck, climbing in. "Good luck. Bowie. I'll touch base with you later."

Bowie nods. "Keep me posted on what's going on with Axel and Aspen, too."

"Will do," the sheriff confirms, tipping his hat and speeding away.

THREE

As soon as Christian's truck vanishes, the Asian beauty streaks from her bullet-ridden vehicle towards the forest. I don't try to pursue her. She won't get far in the Sierra Nevada backcountry.

Especially not wearing skintight jeans that showcase her scintillating curves, high-heel black leather boots that end below her knee, and a lacy, floral, short-sleeved shirt that I long to bury my head beneath.

Her glossy, raven-hued hair cascading to her waist won't help with nature survival, either. But it sure would feel good wrapped around my large, work-hardened hands. And her honey and lavender fragrance? I can't even ...

Mouthwatering as fuck. Goddamn.

I put my hands on my hips, appreciating every inch of the woman, from her frantic dash to the woods to her return to the car. Staring ruefully at the glass-filled seat, she grimaces, mind grinding out potential next steps.

"Come on." I gesture towards my vehicle. "The sheriff's department needs to impound your ride."

The sheriff's deputies standing next to me mirror my body language and expression, mildly amused by the woman's impossible attempts to escape. But my stomach churns, wondering what has rendered a woman who appears highly capable and intelligent so scared and desperate.

"Impound?" she asks, pressing her deliciously full pink lips into a thin, hard line. "No, I can't do this. I can't be here."

"You're safe, Ji, whether you believe it yet or not. Time to come with me and let these deputies do their job," I coax, trying hard not to caress her with my eyes. But she's so damn beautiful, I can't help myself.

"But where will I go? What will I do?" she asks, eyes blazing.

"Until you decide to start talking, you can stay at my cabin."

"Your cabin?" she lets out a sharp sigh, panic seizing her eyes.

"You heard my brother. You're wanted for questioning. And since you're not giving off the most cooperative vibes, you require babysitting."

"Not babysitting," she spits out as if it's the most dishonorable thing she's ever heard. But there's an edge of fear behind her expression that alludes to the volumes she doesn't speak. "Abduction."

I shrug. "You can leave as soon as you talk. The duration of that process is entirely up to you. But we're not taking any chances when it comes to the safety of our family and our town."

"I helped you. I'm not a threat."

"Maybe not. But you know far more than you're telling,"

I reply, eyes washing over her in greedy waves. I suddenly feel very much like my groomsman brother, Axel, who spent this evening eye fucking the wedding planner, Aspen, during the ceremony and reception.

My brother Ridge and his bride Paige married today, and all thirteen of us brothers acted as groomsmen. All but Holden, who remains in prison for a crime he didn't commit.

His woman, Dee, came to the wedding, perpetually standing by her man, though they've spent years apart. Either Dee's the most loyal lady on the planet, or there's something so durable between them I can't fathom it. No matter what, as a single man with no prospects, it makes me jealous.

Ji-su bobs her head around as if she's looking for additional options. But without a working car, she's at a standstill. And I'm getting impatient.

I hedge off further escape attempts, observing, "You have nowhere to go. Might as well cooperate."

"That's right," the sheriff's deputy closest to us seconds.

"But I can't stay with you," she cries, the passion in her voice sudden and overwhelming.

"I'm not giving you a choice."

"You don't get it!" she howls. "You keeping me will not only put me in danger, but you, too. You don't know what you're doing."

I level my gaze on her, brows furrowing. Everything from her tense face to her panic-stricken eyes and the way she forms her words tells me she's terrified. *But of what?*

"Ji, I can protect you."

She starts to shake her head, face dissolving into terror. I raise a hand, gaining her attention.

"No one will harm you on my watch," I declare, chest rumbling. She stops, expression suspended in surprise, eyes searching my face for reassurance. What she finds must satisfy her because her face looks less pinched, and her shoulders drop slightly.

She opens her mouth, and I wait as she searches for words. "I want to believe you."

"Believe me."

Conflict washes over her face, and Ji's eyes redden. She looks like she could burst into tears. But she doesn't. Instead, her pink tongue darts out to lick her thick bottom lip, and my pulse races. I don't know what it is about this woman that makes me feel unhinged, animalistic, and fixated on protecting her. But my eyes follow her tongue, obsessing over her taste and feel.

What in the hell is wrong with you, Bowie? Get your mind out of the gutter.

To distract myself, I focus on the crime scene. The sheriff's deputies work to secure things, noting the bullet casings, skid marks, and tire tracks attesting to what occurred. They take photographs and document every square inch of the pavement as a few unlucky cars line up behind the caution tape, waiting for the road to reopen.

"Did you shoot anyone?" one deputy questions me.

"Not sure. Everything happened so quickly. There wasn't a moment to think. But they all appeared to leave on their own two feet. That said, it would be interesting to see if anyone visits the ER with a gunshot wound tonight."

The deputies nod, returning to their work.

Looking at Ji-su, I ask, "Now, are we going to do this the easy or hard way?" I cock my head to the side, echoing my earlier sentiment.

Her nostrils flare, her black eyes snapping. "The hard way," she spits, her chin trembling.

Her words take me aback. I thought for a moment I was getting through to her.

"For the record," she adds. "You can't hold me, and everything about this attempted incarceration is a violation of my rights. You haven't even read me my Miranda rights."

"Either you come with me or go into sheriff's custody," I remind, eyes narrowing. "You want me to handcuff you or something?" The last question comes out dark, rich, and far too seductive for a crime scene being worked by deputies.

"Yes, and you better keep me that way because the first chance I get, you'll never see me again," she promises.

Before I think better of it, I ground out in simmering tones, "Well, that would be a shame, seeing as I only just found you."

"You didn't find me. I found you," she corrects, crossing her arms over her chest.

Yep, nothing about this is going to be easy.

I grab her upper arm loosely. She tries to pull away.

"Woman," I mutter. "Don't fight me. I'm serious about taking you back to my place until you behave for questioning."

"Well, then I'll be there forever," she threatens tersely.

"Forever's fine by me," I counter, a strange warmth filling my chest.

"If you want to help me," she says breathlessly, her large, dark doe eyes pleading. "You'll let me go and report me dead."

"What?" I ask, floored by her words.

"Let me go, and report me as dead."

I scrunch my face. "But you just talked to the sheriff of

Gold County, and you've got two deputies staring at you. *You* are very much alive."

"Please. He's your brother. You have some pull with him, and he obviously has pull with his deputies."

I shake my head, trying to wrap my head around her proposal.

"If you do this for me, I'll come with you ... without a fight."

It's hardly a bargaining chip, but I'm too intrigued by her request and the pleading look in her eyes to turn away.

"And what does being dead get you?" I ask, furrowing my brows.

"A respite," she whispers, her voice shaking. "You can handcuff me, impound my car. Fine. But please, at least consider my request. It's the only way I have an out in any of this."

"So, you need to vanish?"

"More than vanish. I need to die," she says with a quiet gravity that both intrigues and moves me.

I can't imagine what would bring a rational person to this conclusion. "Are you getting abused by a husband or a boyfriend? Or is it some issue with the law?"

She firmly shakes her head.

What in the hell could have a grown-ass, confident, mouth-watering woman riled up like this? I stare at her, willing her to start talking.

Ji-su returns the gaze stubbornly, refusing to look away or speak.

"I can't make you any promises. After all, I highly doubt Christian would risk his career or his reputation for something like this. But I can ask that he and his deputies keep everything on the down low, at least for the moment."

Her face is stony—impassive and unreadable. But as my

eyes drill into her cool expression, I note how her mouth quirks slightly to one side, and she blinks more rapidly.

"That means," I continue. "I'm going to need you to tell me exactly what's going on, and what brought you to Rough & Ready Country in the first place. Something tells me none of this is mere coincidence."

"Not in the least," she confirms, her face ambivalent.

I frown. "I'm going to need more than that."

"Think of it like witness protection ..."

I cock my head to the side. "What exactly are you tied up in?"

She presses her lips together, eyes round and begging for help despite the over-the-top independent act. "Something big ... something that goes as high as it can go. I'm a whistleblower."

A whistleblower? There it is ...

I nod, feeling ambivalent about the whole thing. "Before you step in my truck, know that all I can offer you is a safe place to stay. As for the rest of your request ... Quite frankly, there have already been far too many eyes on you in this town. And you're going to have to get real talkative real quick with Christian and me to change our minds."

After handcuffing her and placing her in the extended cab of my truck, I check in with the officers arranging a tow for her vehicle to the impounding yard.

Retrieving the key fob from the car's center console, I unlock the trunk, pulling out a purple suitcase that I assume holds her belongings, throwing it into the back of my truck bed.

Then, I get Chris on the phone again.

"Bowie," he grumbles.

"Everything okay with Axel and Aspen?"

"They got accosted by members of the church like you.

Only they chose to use stones instead of bullets, thankfully."

"Are they okay?"

"Shook up is all. How about you and the girl?"

I walk a distance away so the deputies can't hear me. "We need to keep everything under very tight wraps for the moment. She's dead as far as the media's concerned."

"She's what?"

"Dead."

The silence on the phone communicates volumes more than words ever could. Finally, he says, "A no comment from the sheriff's office is the best I can give you for the moment."

I grunt. "Something along the lines of an anonymous good Samaritan helped at the scene should handle it. At least for the moment. Think you can get your deputies behind this?"

"I can tell them to keep their fucking mouths shut until we have a better sense of what's going on ..."

"Thank you, Bro."

"Don't thank me yet. You owe me big time."

Christian's traditional role as the bossy older brother never sits very far beneath the surface.

I chuckle. "I figured you'd say as much."

"I'll check in with you as soon as I get shit sorted with Axel and Aspen."

"Sounds good."

After the call and saying goodbye to the sheriff's deputies, relaying a bit of the message to come from Christian to keep this close to their chests, I return to Ji-su, handcuffed in the back of my truck and frowning.

Opening the door, I say, "You know, you'd be much

more comfortable seated next to me, riding along as a passenger rather than as a detainee."

She shakes her head, the cut of her clenched jaw firm and unyielding. Her large, ebony eyes plead with me. In breathless tones, she whispers, "Did the sheriff agree?"

I put my hands on my hips, replying in muted tones, "The best he can do is a no comment until we have more time to discuss the trouble you seem to be neck-deep in."

"And the deputies?"

"They'll stay quiet. The one we need to speak to is my brother, Wolfe. I'll contact him when we get back to my place. But I imagine he and his crew are very busy tonight."

"Why Wolfe?" she asks, arching an eyebrow.

"I'll explain at my place." I don't want to get into it with her yet. But my brother Wolfe is a former Army Ranger-turned-undercover agent. He and his team of ex-military men hunt down human trafficking syndicates across the nation. Sometimes around the world. This translates into extra layers of security at the ranch and the help and resources this woman needs. "Now, you riding up front with me or staying back here handcuffed."

"If you remove these handcuffs, I'll run. End of story," she replies, eyes blazing with a challenge I'd like to taste.

I chuckle. "You're stubborn. Aren't you?"

"More stubborn than you can ever know," she answers emphatically.

"Good. I like stubborn." Without another word, I unlock the handcuffs, removing them from her wrists. Then, I hold the door open for her, offering my hand to help her down.

Surprise washes over her face.

"I'll take my chances on you running, Ji. Something tells me you won't."

"And why is that?"

"I just know," I reply firmly. Call it gut instinct. Call it the warmth seeping from my heart through my chest. All I know, on some wordless, inexplicable level, is that fate brought me Ji-su. Put her in my orbit for a reason, and destiny won't be easily denied. "Any woman who's got my six rides beside me."

Our eyes lock, and her hand finds mine. Sparks dance up and down my flesh at her touch.

I nod somberly, not sure what's going on between us but feeling the full conviction of it to my very core as she steps down. She drops my hand when her feet hit the ground. I instantly miss the dainty feel of her fingers in mine.

I'd kill to feel that again. Why she makes me so irrational, I don't know. But I need her in a place buried deep in my soul. I'm afraid once this seed of feeling takes root, I'll never be able to let her go. Maybe it's already too late.

I close the passenger door behind her once she's seated, heading for the driver's side. She could run. This would be the instant to do it. But instead, she relaxes into the cushions. I start the engine and back up carefully before continuing down the road where the ambush occurred.

"You like music?" I ask, side-eyeing her.

"This is no time for music," she whispers.

"Why the hell not? Looks like you could use something to take your nerves down a notch." I turn on the satellite radio, Teddy Swims's "Lose Control" softly accompanying our ride. The lyrics mirror my current mood with this mysterious beauty around.

Her lashes flutter, and my heart pounds against the back of my ribs. Honey and lavender fill my nostrils, heady, intoxicating. My mouth waters, desperate for a taste. I don't know what this woman does to me, but I sure as hell know what I want to do to her.

She says firmly, "If you end up dead for this, don't blame me. I tried to warn you."

"And why would I end up dead?" I drawl lazily, taking extra time with my words to set her at ease.

"Because the people after me would eat the people who were after you for breakfast. Any day of the week."

"Huh," I answer, mind puzzling over her words. "Sounds like you really need my protection, then."

"I don't need anyone's protection," she says too quickly.

"Everyone needs someone who's got their six."

"Like I had yours tonight?"

"Exactly," I reply. "There's no place safer in this town than my family's ranch, which is where we're headed. It's a veritable compound at this point. What with all the trouble we've had recently with the House of the Seven Prophets and other people."

"Other people?" she repeats.

"Yeah."

"Aren't you going to elaborate?"

"It's simple." I level my gaze on hers as I turn toward the far side of Rough & Ready Ranch. "You trust me. I trust you. You talk. I talk."

Maybe.

She snorts, shaking her head.

At the entrance to the ranch, I pull up to the makeshift post-wedding security guard for the evening, Rutger, one of Wolfe's buddies. A blond cowboy from the Texas Hill Country, he does occasional fugitive recovery work, though our paths have never crossed professionally.

Rolling down my window, I say, "Wild night. All good here?"

"Sure thing," he drawls. His eyes migrate to the passenger seat. "And who is this?"

"We're keeping that on the down low."

"As in I didn't see her?"

"As in she doesn't exist," I state resolutely.

The woman slightly relaxes next to me, her energy less frantic. I bask in the shift, determined to make her feel safer than she has in six months. *Happier, too, if I have my way.*

"Christian asked me to hold her for questioning. He's helping Axel and Aspen in Hollister. So, discretion is key."

"Understood."

Rutger removes his cowboy hat, wiping his palm across his forehead. "Heard you had trouble tonight? A veritable Wild West shootout."

I nod. "If it weren't for this lady, I'm not sure what would've happened to me. But I'll spare you the details until I can set up a meeting with Wolfe."

Rutger nods. "Boss man's busy tonight, as you can imagine. But if I talk to him before you do, I'll let him know."

I nod. "Thank you."

"Boss man?" Ji-su questions as we drive slowly down the long dirt road to my cabin.

Her voice is whispery soft and silky. I imagine what she'd sound like panting, begging me to take her. The thought rushes through me, a shiver of desire. I side-eye the beauty, catching her hungry eyes devouring me.

I don't even know if Ji-su is a friend or foe. All I know is I'll never let anyone scare or harm her again.

"You're safe with me, Ji-su," I repeat because she needs to hear it. "Probably the safest you've been in a while with the way you keep talking. You might as well relax and enjoy the experience."

Her eyes flash with fire. I suppose it's anger, but it feels more like longing. She should look away. But she doesn't, challenging me in ways I'm not sure she's ready for. Her dark gaze drips with lust.

My cock strains against the zipper of my dress pants. Goddamn, this is going to be a long night. But it'll be worth it to know she's safe and secure for the first time in six months ...

That is, if I can trust what she's telling me.

CHAPTER
FOUR

JI-SU

"**Y**ou said you want to be dead, Ji-su. Why?"

I swallow hard, not ready for this question. But the handsome stranger's eyes dig into me. He won't settle for anything less than the truth. *The truth.* Never has something felt so heavy to carry.

I shake my head. "Like I said earlier, the less you know, the better. The people who want me dead don't discriminate."

"Let's start there, then. Who wants you dead?"

I chuckle, shaking my head again. "Who doesn't?"

"We're going to have to work on the specificity of your answers, Ji. If you want my help and the help of my brothers, we need facts. The truth. You said you were a whistle-blower. Tell me more."

"Okay," I whisper, clenching my jaw. "I have incriminating evidence against one of the most powerful senators in the State of California."

Bowie eyes me quietly. "What kind of evidence?"

"The kind that can bring the entire house of cards

down," I say in steely tones. "The words may sound dramatic ... exaggerated. But they're the honest to God truth."

"Tell me more."

I look around the cab of his truck. "When's the last time you did a sweep for bugs?" I expect him to look surprised by the question.

Instead, he says matter-of-factly, "I implement tracking device and monitoring searches of my vehicle and home weekly. Sometimes daily, depending on who I'm tracking. Never can be too careful as a fugitive recovery agent or bounty hunter, as some people call us. Lucky for you, I did one this morning."

"As a bounty hunter, do you deal with cartels? Violent gangs? Organized crime?"

"Sometimes."

I clear my throat, heart racing at the thought of confiding in this man. The mere fact that he regularly sweeps his vehicle, though, is a good start.

"Your cell phone?" I ask.

He pulls it out of his pocket and hands it to me without hesitation. I press the power button until the screen goes black, handing it back to him.

"I'm a paralegal for an attorney in San Francisco. We work on environmental law cases. Things of that nature ..."

"And that's how you got tangled up in whatever this is?"

"No." My voice trails off. "That happened because of my sister, Ae-cha."

"Your sister?"

"She preferred to go by Annie Park because most people couldn't pronounce her name right. I don't know if you've heard about the case at all?"

Annie Park? Why does the name sound so familiar?

Suddenly, it hits me. "The woman who drove over the levee into Lake Torrent?"

"Yes," I answer, working hard to steel my voice.

"I'm sorry. It was tragic."

Passion fills me as I counter, "It was murder."

His brows scrunch, and he rubs his hand over his stubbled chin. The scratchy sound is so damn masculine. It puts a thick knot in my throat and a throb at the top of my legs.

Stop thinking like this, Ji. Especially when talking about your beloved sister.

But it's just been so long since I could trust a man, let alone think about surrendering to one ...

"*She* didn't drive into the lake. But they made it look like she did. Ae-cha was not suicidal. Not at all."

The man's eyes fill with empathy. In soft tones, he says, "But sometimes your siblings don't tell you everything. She may have had a lot going on that she didn't want to divulge to you or anyone else who might have talked her out of it—"

"No!" I exclaim firmly. "She didn't kill herself. She would've never done that. But she did have access to something that could get her killed."

"What kind of something?"

It's the question I don't want to answer but know I must. "She worked in politics, mapping out districts, poll results, that type of thing. She was a cartographer and geographer by trade. But she stumbled into something she never should have seen ..."

He stares straight ahead, driving slowly along the rough dirt road we follow. "And?"

"She uncovered evidence of election fraud on a level so

massive it's tough to fathom. Fraud fueled by human and drug trafficking."

His face says it all—a mixture of surprise and skepticism.

"What Ae-cha uncovered proved so complicated that she started mapping it out. But I don't think she ever truly understood the breadth and depth of what was going on. She started linking organizations on every level involved in human trafficking and drug smuggling. I've continued her work, preserving the external hard drives where she stored corroborating evidence and adding to them, compiling the evidence for a grand jury investigation. But no lawyer wants to touch it with a ten-foot pole ... not even the lawyer I worked for. So, I took over myself, writing the whole story, researching legal angles and case law, piecing disparate documents together into something that's so incriminating and so dangerous ..." I sigh, shaking my head. "I've worked tirelessly day and night while on the run. There's still so much to do, but I won't stop until the many trails Ae-cha uncovered and I connected lead to solid convictions. Honestly, though, there's still so much to sift through. So many angles to research and explore further. I would need a team of lawyers and investigators working for years to complete what my sister and I have started."

"And you have these hard drives?"

His question is fair enough, but it still sends a cold chill down my spine. After half a year on the run with people willing to kill me to get a hold of this information, trust doesn't come naturally or easily.

"I have everything ... in an undisclosed location with a killswitch," I answer firmly, though quietly. "As well as up here," I say, tapping my finger against my temple.

"Smart woman," the rugged cowboy murmurs, eyeing

me warmly. The chemistry swirling around the truck cab is electric, incandescent. Goosebumps line the flesh of my arms, and a delicious warmth radiates from my heart.

I don't know how to explain it, but this man's energy reassures and relaxes me. It also inflames and awakens desires I haven't let myself consider for who knows how long ... *maybe ever*. It's simultaneously terrifying and gratifying.

"I've had to be smart to survive." I say the words slowly, registering their weight with my verbal emphasis. I don't even want to think back on all I've endured. "But I imagine your line of work means staring down death regularly, too ..."

"Yes and no," he answers. "This job will always come with a certain level of inherent risk. But I'm also a careful man, Ji. So, no, I don't stare down death often." He says it like there's so much more he wants to tell me but doesn't. "So, election fraud, human trafficking, drugs. All tied up with a nice, big governmental bow?"

"Yes, because the money from these illegal activities was then funneled through real estate and not-for-profit businesses back into political campaigns via PACs. In other words, I've pieced together a direct link from California elected officials to lower-level players. Like the House of the Seven Prophets and cartels who operate in the area at the Three Nations Reservation and other places."

He removes his cowboy hat, rubbing his forehead and temples. "My brothers have helped shut down much of the human trafficking in this area, along with my new sister-in-law, Paige."

Paige Laurier. I'm floored at the coincidence. His new sister-in-law? She's who I'm here for.

I open my mouth to say as much but press my lips

tightly together at the last second. No telling how he'd feel about me endangering her and his family by bringing them into my trouble. Instead, I return to his last statement. "You can shut it down locally. But Ae-cha's evidence shows it goes much higher than Sacramento. All the way to D.C. Something I've since been unraveling."

Bowie glances at me, his face a mixture of curiosity and disbelief. "Which means exponentially heightened danger for you. Why aren't you in witness protection?"

"Because that's a federal program, and this is still considered a state matter."

"You're telling me a state as big as California can't provide you any protection?"

"Not against its most powerful senator," I answer resignedly.

"And that's why you need to vanish? Or die?"

"Like my sister. Without a trace ... Until I've got it all connected, sorted out, thoroughly researched."

"But what if nobody wants to hear what you've uncovered?"

His question hits at the heart of my greatest fear.

I shrug. "All I can do is bide my time. Hope that there will come a day when all of this darkness can be revealed."

"But what if that never happens? You plan on staying dead the rest of your life? In hiding and running for your life?"

I shiver at the thought. "I can't worry about the future when the present feels so overwhelming ..." Silence fills the space between us, palpable and painful. All I can do is continue hoping and acting in good faith. "But you can help me now, right? I mean, this is technically the middle of nowhere," I say hopefully, peering into the black of night on the other side of the vehicle's window.

"Staging your own death means no going outside. No potential of getting photographed by surveillance devices. Whether it's shoplifting cameras at the grocery store or CCTV systems at gas stations."

"Unless I'm in disguise."

"Maybe. But facial recognition software is getting better by the day. So, I wouldn't necessarily count on that, either."

I look down at my hands, confessing, "Believe me, I'm fully versed on disappearing. Nothing would change for me, lifestyle-wise."

"That's no kind of existence."

"No," I agree. "But I *am* still alive. That's more than Ae-cha can say."

"And when will this nightmare come to an end for you?"

"I don't know ..." I've asked myself this question too many times to count. "Maybe when the whole house of cards falls. If it ever falls."

"Which senator?" he asks.

"Moreau."

"No surprise there," the cowboy remarks with a dark chuckle.

"Why?"

"My foster brother, Holden, has spent a decade in prison, thanks to that man. His son, Gregory Moreau, and a bunch of his frat brothers jumped Holden outside a bar, nearly beating him to death. In self-defense, my brother pulled a knife and stabbed one man, inadvertently nicking his femoral artery in the process. Gregory bled out and died at the scene."

Pain drips from Bowie's voice, though he relays the story with a steely calm. I know about this case. I've researched Senator Moreau and his family thoroughly.

"He's still in prison. Despite having good time credits and a spotless record behind bars. Every time he goes up for parole, the senator's powerful friends and family come out of the woodwork to ensure he stays incarcerated."

Reaching across the console of his truck, I surprise myself, grabbing his hand. Though I'm far from an affectionate person, especially with strangers, something about Bowie makes touching a prerequisite to sharing the same air space. "So, we've both lost a sibling to Senator Moreau, then."

He nods, pulling up to a stunning A-frame cabin with massive floor-to-ceiling windows that I can only imagine afford incredible views of the surrounding forest by day. He parks out front, sitting in the cab without moving, his eyes flickering to my hand holding his.

"You've lost a lot more than me, though," he says quietly. Sparks shuttle between our flesh, lighting up my core with a nameless, all-powerful need.

"Tell me more about your new sister-in-law, Paige, the investigative reality TV producer who broke the scandal in the church."

The cowboy's eyes melt into mine. I don't know what's happening between us. But the sliver of skin touching as we continue to hold hands feels life-changing, like a revelation I'll never be able to come back from. His nostrils flare, and his eyes dilate until they look like two rounds of obsidian.

Does he feel what I'm feeling?

"She's who I came to see," I confess, blindsiding myself.

What in the hell are you doing, Ji?

A part of me immediately regrets the forthrightness, tempted to slap a hand over my mouth to stop further talking. But a much larger part adores the growing intimacy between me and this man, like I don't want anything between us. Not one deception, misunderstanding, or unspoken word.

"Then, you'll be here for a while," he says in rich tones, dark and sweet like molasses. "Because they just left on their honeymoon, and they've made certain they're unreachable."

Good. I want to be here for a while. I press my lips firmly together to keep from voicing my thoughts, though holding back is nearly impossible with this man.

"Why do I feel like I know you from somewhere?" His gaze levels on mine, drilling into me, digging down to the essence of my soul.

I swallow loudly, hearing my breath come faster. "I don't know. But I feel it, too."

"You do?" he drawls.

"Yes," I answer more breathlessly than I mean to.

Bowie nods, staring at me long and hard. Finally, he starts to move, his hand loosening its grip on mine.

"Before we go inside," I say in rushed tones. "There's something I need to tell you."

He arches an eyebrow, eyes digging beneath my flesh.

"I'm sorry, so very sorry for dragging you into the middle of this."

"Don't be," he says firmly.

"You would do better to drive me back to my car and leave me. Seriously."

"Too late for that. I'm invested in you and your future now. I've got to keep you safe."

"But how are you going to keep yourself safe?"

"Don't worry about me, Hummingbird," he says with a wink, letting go of my hand and opening the door of his truck. He jumps out.

I follow suit, meeting him on the other side of my open door with his arms crossed and a frown on his face.

"What?" I ask, surprised by his expression.

"Get back in the vehicle so that we can get something straight," he orders.

"Back in the vehicle?" I sigh, brows scrunching.

"Yep, back in the vehicle," he says, nodding toward the passenger seat.

I comply, uncertain what's going on. He closes the door, eyeing me for a moment before opening it and offering me his hand.

"Are you serious?"

"Serious as sin," he murmurs as I place my hand atop his. The sparks start again, incinerating and scintillating, shooting up and down my wrist and arm.

"You'll never open another door with me around. Got it?"

"Got it," I answer, working hard to suppress the giggle that suddenly overtakes me. It's been a long time since I felt amused.

"What are you laughing at?"

I shake my head. "Just thinking about my sudden change of fortune. For so long, I haven't been able to trust a living soul. And now I'm suddenly with a cowboy hellbent on spoiling me."

"How do you know you can trust me?" He asks the one question I don't have an answer for, though I know to my soul's essence, for some inexplicable reason, that I can.

I shrug. "Just a gut feeling. Believe me, it hasn't happened in six months, so I'm not going to second-guess it."

His warm gaze washes over me. "Your gut's right."

The words are sparing, but they slam into me like a freight train. My pulse quickens, and my respiration increases as he leads me toward his cabin. Things will never be the same once I cross over the threshold. God, I wish I understood why.

FIVE

BOWIE

"Hummingbird?" she asks once we're on the other side of my cabin door.

I nod, resting my hands on my hips, appraising her in the dark of the living room. "Yep, Hummingbird. You got a problem with that nickname?"

"No, but it does make me curious. Why that name?"

"Because you're small-boned, delicate, and you make these fast little bird-like movements. Graceful, yet a little frenetic."

"Frenetic," she says, wrapping her arms around herself for a hug. It takes every ounce of self-will not to step forward and pull her into my arms. Though I fight it, I long to touch her, keep her close. "Small-boned?" she adds, laughing. "Hardly."

"What do you mean?"

"I'm a big girl if you haven't noticed. Lots of junk in the trunk."

"You mean your curves?"

She nods, incredulity written in her face.

"Believe me, I've noticed them," I reply in flirtatious tones.

"And?"

"And I appreciate them more than you can ever know," I confess, my cheeks warming. "But compared to me, you're still delicate as fuck ... little and fine-boned, whether you like it or not."

I shut the door behind us, reaching for the light switches on the wall and illuminating the place. A puff of air escapes her mouth as she looks around, dark eyes large as two saucer plates.

"This place is stunning ..."

"Thank you," I say, removing my Stetson and hanging it by the door. I toe off my cowboy boots as she watches me, placing them on the welcome mat by the front door.

She unzips and removes her black riding boots, striding forward to place them next to mine before hesitating. Her head bobs between the large exterior windows and me. "I don't want anyone to see my shoes ..."

"Anybody that sets foot on Rough & Ready Ranch without permission'll be incarcerated or dead before they register their mistake. I haven't filled you in on my family yet. But you'll soon realize there's no safer place for you to be than here. So, set your shoes where you like, and don't let fear rule you anymore."

Ji-su's dark almond-shaped eyes soften, and her round face relaxes ever so slightly. She looks beautiful like this, expression open and welcoming, shoulders dropping and melting into the safety I can provide her. I wonder how long it's been since she last let her guard down.

"Well, I guess if Paige is safe here, then I am, too."

"Exactly."

She sets her boots down, turning and wrapping her

arms back around herself. Her head lifts as she takes in the second floor above us, her eyes traveling to the very top of the vaulted Great Room ceiling. "This place ..."

"Glad you like it. I designed and built it myself with some help from my brothers, especially Turner. He's a custom homebuilder."

"And who decorated?" she asks, a sudden tightness in her voice. "This definitely bears the touch of a woman."

I chuckle, falling in love with her mahogany eyes, blazing with jealousy. It complements the thick electricity darting back and forth between us. "My sisters-in-law helped out some. Before all of my brothers started getting hitched, this place had like two chairs and one couch. It wasn't the most comfortable. But it didn't matter since I don't spend a lot of time here, you know. Thanks to work."

"That's right," she says, eyes shooting to the ground and voice tensing. "You must travel a lot for work."

"I do. But the job's on a case-by-case basis. And I've been working my ass off non-stop for longer than I care to admit. So, I can back off the gas a bit, especially until we figure out what's going on with you."

"I don't want to mess up your life or work schedule ..."

"You could never mess up anything as far as I'm concerned."

My words hang in the air for a long moment.

"I still don't get it," she says, quirking her mouth.

"Get what?"

"Get why you'd stick your neck out for me like this."

"And I don't get why you drove into the middle of a gunfight to save me."

She shakes her head. "I hate injustice. That's all."

"Me, too. Can I show you around?" I ask with a sweep of my hand. "That way, you can make yourself comfortable."

She nods, and I give her the full tour. Afterwards, she follows me into the kitchen, asking, "So, if you get a nickname for me. Do I get one for you?"

I shrug, turning the lights on as she examines the airy white room with big windows. "You keep this place spotless," she notes, running her finger along the white and gray marble countertop.

"Because I never cook."

"That's the secret to your interior perfection?"

"Yep, not living in a house will ensure it looks good at all times."

"But you must dust. I don't see a drop anywhere."

"I have a maid who stops by to tidy up—Lucretia. I imagine you'll meet her at some point."

She shifts her weight, returning my gaze nervously. "I hate to ask this. But while I'm here, could you keep her and other guests away as much as possible? It's for their safety as much as my own."

"The people pursuing you really have you terrified, don't they?"

"Because they're terrifying people. Although I'm tired of living in fear. I hope Paige can help."

"Before we bring any more of my family into this, we need to sort out your safety. She and Ridge have already been through enough ... like you."

"Like me." Ji-su's brows knit. The corners of her mouth turn up slightly. "You're a good brother. You put family first. That's rare these days."

I shrug. "What's the point of having family if you don't prioritize them?"

"True. But it's something I don't think a lot of people get."

"Maybe not."

"Lancelot," she says out of nowhere.

"Lancelot? What does that mean?"

"That's your new nickname. If you're okay with that?"

"And why 'Lancelot?'" I ask, crossing my arms over my chest and widening the spread of my stance.

"Because 'Black Superman' is already taken, thanks to the Rock. But, no, I like 'Lancelot' because that's what you are to me. My knight in shining armor."

"Though you saved me, Ji?"

"Something tells me you'd return the favor in a heartbeat ..."

"Without hesitation. Lancelot it is then."

"And you alluded to something earlier. About your brothers and me being here. That there's no safer place for me. What did you mean?"

"I spent much of the day standing thanks to Paige and Ridge's wedding. Mind if we take a seat and talk? I could get a fire going and pour us some wine. Unless you're more of a beer girl?"

She laughs. "That sounds amazing. I'm a total wine snob."

I hesitate. "Uh oh. Doubt I have anything that good."

"Whatever you have will be fine. Anything to take the edge off."

"Make yourself at home. I'll be right back."

I disappear into the kitchen, returning with two glasses of wine. Ji-su lounges on my oversized white couch, snuggled into the emerald green pillows like she belongs. Her presence feels amazing, pre-ordained. I don't know how else to describe it.

I'd love to head out back to the jacuzzi with her for a soak and to stare up at the stars. I wonder if the luggage she pulled out of her Mercedes includes a bathing suit.

But after all she's been through, I don't want to come off as a creep. Instead, I hand her a glass, poise one on top of the coffee table, and then beeline for the hearth to get a fire going. Only after the logs crackle and flames lick the air escaping through the chimney do I take my seat next to her, grabbing my glass.

"You know, this isn't half bad," she remarks, holding up her wine.

"Not half bad? In other words, you'll be hand-selecting wines for us in the future?" As soon as the words leave my mouth, I realize how presumptuous they sound.

Apart from a slight darkening of her cheeks, she doesn't seem to mind. "If that's what you envision as my role here, I'll take it."

"Well, it's not all I envision. But it's a decent enough start, right?"

"Oh, yeah? What else do you have in mind?" she asks, a flirtatious note in her voice.

"That's probably a conversation for another time or, at a bare minimum, another glass of wine," I tease.

"One glass should be more than enough for me."

"So, you're a lightweight, then?" I ask.

Her luscious mouth serves up the first full smile I've seen from her. Radiant, warm, exuberant. It feels like the place I always want to be with her.

But a frown immediately chases it, betraying the strain and stress she's lived under for far too long. "I used to love wine tastings and a glass or two with dinner. But after constantly looking over my shoulder ... Hell, in some cases, not even being able to sleep, drinking has been the last thing on my roster."

"So, you haven't been able to stop running this whole time?"

She shakes her head. "Not for one minute. And the couple of times I was tempted to relax, almost as if by fate's irony, something would happen to show me just how misdirected that momentary hope was."

"Like what kinds of things?"

"A near-miss with someone sent to hurt me or worse. An attempted kidnapping or menacing encounter. My car brakes, at one point, were tampered with. Thankfully, I only drive manual, and I'm skilled with my e-brake."

I appraise the brave woman next to me, still trying to figure her out and imagining all she's endured. The loneliness would be hardest for me, though I work a job that comes with a lot of downtime and a nomadic lifestyle.

"You're tough as nails."

"I have to be," she says, the firm set of her mouth communicating more than her words.

"Yes, you do. If everything you've told me is as you say."

"You don't believe me?" she asks, sitting straighter.

"You've given me no reason to doubt you. But it's still a lot to comprehend. You keep saying 'they' when you talk about the people after you. But who are 'they'?"

"Good question," she says, wetting her lips and knitting her brows. "The people surrounding and supporting Senator Moreau at the highest level. You don't get into a place with that kind of power without having deep ties to organized crime, syndicates, churches involved in nefarious activities. Think of 'they' as one big pipeline of influence, power, and wealth ... all fueled by criminality. And all ready to defend to the death the racket they have going. That's why they want me gone."

The mention of people who might want to kill her immediately raises my hackles. I'll kill any motherfucker who comes near her. But if she's not certain who her enemies are … Well, that complicates matters.

"I get it. But beyond this general sense of who's pursuing you, do you have more specifics? Identities? Descriptions? Affiliations?"

"Yes, I've got a long list of perps that they've either sent or might send after me."

"I want to see who those men and women are. Familiarize myself with them to better keep you safe. Hell, Ji, I want to hunt as many of them down as possible, ensure your security."

Her eyes flicker to mine. "Revenge," she says quietly. "We haven't even talked about that yet. It's what I want, too. What drives me. To avenge the murder of Ae-cha if it's the last thing I do."

Her quiet voice simmers with rage. We've finally hit at the heart of what's going on. *This* is the motivation driving her. "You said you're here to see Paige, but by the tone of your voice, I'd say you're here for retaliation."

She presses her lips firmly together. "If Paige can help me tie up the loose ends surrounding my sister's murder … further corroborate who I think offed her and link them back to Moreau? Then, know I'll act on it."

I shake my head, unconvinced. "You can't target Senator Moreau. Not in an overtly violent manner, at least."

"Consequences may come later. But I can't worry about that." Ji-su returns my gaze unblinkingly, her face unreadable, her eyes dark and frigid. "I won't stop until I restore my family's honor and my sister's dignity. She did *not* drive off the levee. She did *not* kill herself. If I'm the right-hand of Karma, so be it."

CHAPTER
SIX

JI-SU

Leveling his gaze on me, Bowie says, "I know what you think you want is revenge, Ji. And there might be a time and a place for that. But you can't let it devour you, destroy your whole life."

"No, what destroyed my life was Ae-cha's murder. Everything since has been a natural consequence." I shake my head, tired of this subject—my principal obsession for the past six months. It feels like beating a dead horse. "But enough about the past. For one night, I want to let go. Forget about everything."

Snuggling imperceptibly closer to him, I'm drawn to the gravity of his presence. His strength, his animal magnetism, the smell of his spicy sandalwood cologne. My eyes drop to his work-hardened hands, musing at the contrast between the delicate glass and his large, thick fingers. They could be put to much better use …

"Forget about everything? How do you propose doing that?" Bowie asks darkly.

I smile, inhaling slowly. "Change of subject. Tell me about yourself," I urge softly. I want to know everything about this man. What motivates him. Why he lives in this small town. How he became a cowboy or if he always was. How he ended up with foster brothers.

He shrugs. "Where do you want me to start?"

"Anywhere. I can't imagine any of it's boring."

He chuckles. "Nope, not especially. So, you've already figured out I was a foster kid, and you met one of my brothers, Christian. He's the oldest."

"How many foster brothers do you have in total?"

"Fourteen."

I arch my eyebrows. "That's a big family."

"Yes, it is. And one I'd sacrifice my life for without hesitation. They're closer to me than any blood ever could be. And my foster dad, Wyatt, taught me everything I know about being a man and a decent human being. I shudder to think how I would've turned out without him."

"Is he the reason you're a cowboy?" I ask, nodding towards the white Stetson poised on a hook by the front door.

"Yep. Taught me how to ride, rope, wrestle, all of it. And every year, we still go on a cattle drive, though Dad hangs back with my sister-in-law, Birdie, now that he's older. She's his home healthcare nurse. You know much about cowboying?"

I giggle at the absurdity of the question. "Only what I've seen on *Yellowstone*."

"I figured as much. You've got city girl written all over you," he murmurs, echoing my body language and drawing a little closer to me in return.

It doesn't feel like two strangers inching nearer. It feels like two inevitable forces finally coming back together after too long apart. I don't know how else to describe it, the revelation both thrilling and terrifying because I would never want to hurt this man. And I come with so much baggage ...

"What's that distant look in your eyes?" he asks. "That hint of sadness."

I shake my head, forcing the corners of my mouth up. "Just thinking I wish I'd met you sooner. Before I got tangled up in all of this. I don't want you to pay the price for my problems."

"Your problems are my problems now, Ji."

"Why would you say something like that to a virtual stranger?"

"Because it just is. I can't explain why. And you're no longer a stranger as far as I'm concerned."

"Agreed." I look down at my hands timidly for a moment, another realization walloping me. I don't want to do this alone anymore. And I don't want to die a virgin, never having experienced the completion of the pull I feel with this man. This need that goes beyond words or thoughts, that wrecks me to the foundations of my being.

"You feel it, too, then?" I ask, eyes flickering to his ebony ones.

"I do, though don't ask me to figure it out—"

"Because it's beyond words."

Bowie nods slowly.

"What else do I need to know about you and your family?" I ask, so overwhelmed by the electricity zinging between us that I can barely think.

"Not much to tell." He chuckles, chest rumbling with the rich, deep sound.

"How did you end up in foster care?"

He shrugs. "Poverty, abuse, the usual."

"How do you mean?"

"I'm one of at least twelve kids, most half-siblings. Hell,

I still can't keep all my mom's baby daddies straight. And the only thing she went through faster than men was work, which often put us out on the streets or living in squalor." His hand comes up, reflexively rubbing a scar along his jawline that I haven't noticed before.

"What do you mean by squalor?" I ask, stomach roiling.

"You know how the news sometimes reports on 'nightmare homes?' Places with atrocious living conditions? Kids neglected … that kind of shit. Well, that's what I came out of."

A shiver travels the length of my spine as my heart opens to this man, amazed by his transformation in adulthood, despite his upbringing. "Do you mean like children in dog cages or something?" My brows knit, body tensing in anticipation of his confession.

"Nothing like that. Hell, she encouraged us to run away if we could make it on our own because she had her hands more than full trying to keep us all alive and fed. But filth, neglect, inadequate parental supervision, lack of clothing, food, and medical care in a timely fashion. Those types of things." He rubs the scar again, and my stomach twists and knots trying to put myself in his shoes.

"The scar on your cheek? Is that from your childhood?"

He nods. "Yeah, I cut my face trying to climb over a broken fence. Fucked myself up good. Broke my arm, too. Should've gone to the hospital right away. But that wasn't a possibility for us kids back then."

"Thankfully, the school nurse stepped in, and then the authorities. They removed me and my siblings from her custody."

"I'm sorry," I say tenderly.

"I'm not. Best thing that ever happened to me."

"But your brothers and sisters. Have you stayed in touch with them? Do you ever miss them?"

"*My* brothers live in Rough & Ready Country, except for Holden. Bond is thicker than blood, and I'm bonded to my foster dad and brothers something fierce. As for my biological family? We couldn't be more different. I've apprehended more than one sibling who skipped bail."

"Seriously?" My voice is laced with a horror I can't conceal. "I can't wrap my head around that. In Korean culture, family is everything."

"So, you're Korean, then?"

I nod. "Do you know anything about the culture?"

"Only that the food's good, and the most beautiful women in the world come from there."

"Oh, really?" I laugh, surprised by the declaration.

"Yeah, really," he answers, simmering eyes ravishing me. "Just for the record, family's everything to me, too, Ji. It was just a matter of finding that family. Once I sorted that out, most of the heartbreak and trauma of my upbringing vanished. It's the same with my brothers. No one understands what I went through as a kid better than they do. Hell, some, like Axel and Flynn, endured way worse than I ever did. They inspired me a lot ... to let the past go and move on. I may not have had any control over where I came from, but I have absolute control over where I'm headed."

"So, family is important to you, then?"

"The most important thing. It's why I want so badly to start my own ... with the right girl."

My cheeks darken as he levels his searing gaze on me. Shivers of desire shuttle up and down my spine, settling in the juncture between my legs. The throb is downright criminal.

I swallow loudly. "And what does the right girl look like?"

He chuckles. "Five foot four. Long, straight ebony locks. Black almond-shaped eyes, a round, expressive face, sculpted pink lips that make my heart race—"

"Five foot five actually."

"Noted," he says with a wink. "Confident as hell and with those curves you mentioned earlier. Though I know I could improve on them."

"Improve on them?" I ask, scrunching my nose and cocking my head to the side.

"Yes, Hummingbird. They'd look far better with my big, rough hands on them."

His forward words take me aback. "Wow," I exclaim. "So, now we're onto the pickup line portion of our conversation?" My voice seductively dances over the last question.

"Every good man dissolves into pickup lines with the right woman."

"Right woman?" I giggle. "You're repeating yourself."

He ignores my last statement, continuing, "Because our minds turn into Swiss cheese. A bunch of holes and no substance."

"With the *right* girl?"

"I always did hope to find a girl who has my six," he flirts.

"Always. Do or die. That's my motto ... *with the right guy.*"

"So, how do I convince you I'm the right guy?" he asks, eyes sparkling.

"You're gorgeous, strong, powerful. Everything I could ever want in a man," I admit, eyes dropping to my hands.

"Why did you look down when you said that?"

"Because your heated gaze feels like it's melting me," I confess.

"It is heating your cheeks pretty good," he observes, reaching up to brush a thumb gently over my face. He snags my chin, drawing my gaze back to his. "You shy is adorable, don't get me wrong. And I imagine it's rare with that fierce tigress inside of you, just beneath the surface. But I still prefer you looking directly at me," he murmurs, the muscle in his jaw bouncing.

"Fierce tigress? And why isn't that my nickname?"

"Could be if you want. But I prefer Hummingbird because you've got a fragile, graceful side you hide from the world that I'd like to see more of."

"If I hide it from the world, then how can you see it?" I ask, lifting my chin.

"Because sometimes you meet a person whose soul you can see straight into. Don't know why. Don't know how. But that's how it is with you."

"I know exactly what you mean," I whisper. "But why now? Under these circumstances?"

"Because the Universe gives you what you need when you need it," he answers, tenderness flooding his features and overflowing in his eyes.

His words are innocent enough, yet they wreck me. After six long months of terror, hiding, and the heartbreak accompanying my sister's death, I can't fathom the idea that the Universe might still be on my side. That it might gift me someone who sees me. Who gets me. Looking away, I bite my lower lip, suppressing a sob.

"You okay?"

Quickly swiping the backs of my hands over my eyes, I say, "Yeah, just tough to think the Universe is siding with me at this point."

"You're still alive," he points out.

"Sometimes that feels like more of a curse than a blessing," I confess without thinking.

"Let's see what we can do to change that." His warm eyes continue to wash over me.

"What are you? Some kind of optimist? Always seeing the glass as half full? Even when it's empty?"

"I've had to be," he answers. "Because I was born in what you might call a broken cup. The only good around me was what I imagined in my own head ... for a long time."

"How old were you when you went into foster care?" I ask, chiding myself for complaining when this man has endured so much.

"Nine."

"And what birth order were you?" I ask, trying to imagine the boy version of Bowie. He must've been adorable.

"Smack dab in the middle."

"I'm a middle child, too. Ae-cha was the oldest, and I have a younger brother named Steve."

"Steve?" The cowboy laughs, shaking his head.

"My parents are both big fans of Steve McQueen. After they came to America, they learned English by watching his movies."

Bowie grins, showing off big, white, straight teeth. "So like *The Magnificent Seven?*"

"Absolutely ... *The Great Escape*, *The Towering Inferno*, *The Thomas Crowne Affair*. I could go on and on."

"Can I assume they like cowboys, then?" Bowie asks.

"Does it matter?"

"Might at some point." He flashes a lopsided grin that could make me agree to anything.

"Whether they like cowboys is immaterial, considering

I'm twenty-eight. I make my own decisions ... despite being from a very traditional Asian family."

"I'm thirty-eight. Is that too old for you?"

"You're getting mighty forward with those questions, Cowboy."

"I just like to know where I stand when I'm in the same room with a beautiful woman."

"Is that a compliment?" I ask, soaking in the heat from his eyes.

"You're stunning. But you still haven't answered my question. What are your thoughts on a ten-year age gap?"

"Sounds delicious to me."

"Delicious?" His eyes sparkle with curiosity.

"A mature man? Who knows what he wants from life and isn't looking for a perpetual babysitter or sugar mama? Sounds like a dream."

"Sounds like you haven't had the best dating experiences," he observes.

"Suffice it to say the only plus side of going into hiding was no longer having to date ..."

Until now.

He nods. "So, back to your family. You're the rebel, then?"

I nod. "Guilty as charged. My parents were always so busy pressuring Ae-cha into being the perfect eldest child and then Steve into being the male heir that they kind of forgot about me."

"Doesn't sound like it was a bad thing, though?"

"No, for me, middle child syndrome worked out pretty well. How about for you?"

Bowie shrugs. "I try not to think much about the clusterfuck that was my bio mom's household—"

"Sorry, I should have clarified. I mean, once you came here."

His face relaxes. "There was no getting lost in the crowd. Dad put us all through our paces, churning out one good cowboy after another. Let's see here. We ended up with a PBR World Champion, Zane. An award-winning rescue rider, Hawk. And a bunch of buckaroos who can ride fast and rope decently, though I'd say Maksim and Logan both lack talent in the saddle. And who knows about Holden after years incarcerated ..."

"Some prisons hold rodeos for inmates, don't they?" I heard of one once, but I can't remember where.

"Texas used to, and I believe Angola in Louisiana still does. But no such luck for Holden in the California penal system."

"I can't think of anything wilder than competing in a rodeo."

Bowie chuckles. "I've competed in many. So, they're not too wild in my way of thinking. More like fun."

"What was your event?"

"Mostly steer wrestling. I'm no flashy rider like Zane, Hawk, or Christian, though."

"Steer wrestling?"

"Chasing a steer from horseback before dismounting and wrestling it to the ground by its horns."

"So, exactly what it sounds like."

He nods.

"You're used to dealing with stubborn in that case?"

"Yes, ma'am." He smirks.

"Good. It'll come in handy with me."

"Already has."

CHAPTER
SEVEN

BOWIE

P uffing out her cheeks, Ji says, "Already has?"

"Don't forget. There was a time tonight when you were handcuffed in the back of my truck."

"I was looking out for your safety. Even now, the best thing I could do for you is run."

"Nope," I counter, shaking my head. "Don't even think about it. You and I were meant to meet. End of story. Quit overthinking it."

"But I don't want you to suffer for me."

"Keep talking like that, and I'll handcuff you to the headboard tonight," I growl.

Her eyebrows shoot into her forehead, and a naughty smile lights up her face. "Which headboard?"

I unsuccessfully try to suppress the smirk her playful question elicits. "That's up to you, Hummingbird."

Her cheeks stain as I appraise her. On the one hand, she says plenty of flirtatious things. On the other hand, timid reactions like this make me wonder just how innocent she is.

"So, what else do you want to know about me?" I ask, trying not to devour her with my eyes. It isn't easy, considering everything about her personality and appearance lights my body on fire.

"What do you like to do in the evenings? You know, to unwind?"

Talk about a loaded question. My thoughts dive straight to the bottom of the gutter, delectable images of her legs spread with my head between them filling my mind before I can even string two words together.

Fuck, I want this woman.

But I would never take advantage of someone in need of help and a place to hang her hat until things blow over. That said, it's going to be a long-ass stretch together, with me constantly wondering how she tastes and what she sounds like when she comes.

I run my hand across my faded cut, answering quickly, "I have a jacuzzi in the backyard. It's perfect for stargazing and drinking wine this time of year."

"Is that what you do with all the women you invite over?"

"All the women? Are you jealous, Hummingbird?"

Her achingly sculpted lips turn up at the corners, forming a cat-got-her-tongue smile. "Honestly? Yes. I can only imagine the kind of line you get at this place ..."

"A line of women?" I chuckle.

"Yes."

"You make it sound like the mall on Black Friday. But I assure you, things never get that busy around here. Honestly, it's been ages since I had a steady woman. How about you? When's the last time you babysat one of those immature boys you mentioned earlier?"

"You don't really want to talk about them, do you?" she asks, scrunching her nose.

"No," I say, shifting closer to her so that our knees touch. The innocent move sends a flurry of fiery sparks up my thigh and into my lower core, where a slow, steady pressure continues to build. The kind only one sort of release will satisfy.

"Back to the jacuzzi. Sounds divine. Can we migrate in that direction for a little stargazing?"

I nod. "I'll grab a couple of towels and the bottle of wine if you don't mind taking the glasses? Can I interest you in anything to eat?"

"No, thank you," she answers, eyes black with desire.

"I put your luggage in the guest bedroom," I add, nodding in that direction. "If you want to get your bathing suit."

"If?" She laughs.

As soon as the words leave my mouth, I realize my mistake. Shaking my head, I apologize. "Sorry. I don't know why I said it that way ..."

"Question is, was that a Freudian slip or something else?"

I shrug. "Honestly, I didn't think too much into it before I spoke."

"Is that usual for you?" she asks.

"What? Speaking without thinking?"

She nods, licking her luscious bottom lip and lighting my soul on fire. The thirst I feel for her is unquenchable. Never has a woman made me feel such extreme passion. I need her like I need air, though I still have so much to learn about her.

"No, not usually. I tend to be a man of few words. But you kind of muddle my brain. Make me say stupid shit."

"You're blaming what you say on me, now?"

There I go again, caught in another word soup. "I guess I am. I sound like a royal tool, don't I?"

"How about we go back to where we left off in the conversation?"

"And where was that?" I ask.

"Discussing if we're getting bathing suits or not." Her eyes have a naughty glint in them, which I definitely want to see more of.

"I can go either way. How about you?"

"You know, earlier you asked me if I was the rebel in my family, and I said I was. But it occurs to me that I've led quite a tame life for a rebel. You know, generally playing by the book. Doing things on the up and up, following the rules."

I like where this is going. "What's the fun in that?"

"Good question," Ji says, that dangerous sparkle still illuminating her eyes. "What would you say to skinny dipping?"

"Yes, please, and thank you," I answer, feeling like this is a trick question.

"Then, that's what we'll do. Just this once."

"Just this once." There are a lot of places I'd like to apply that logic. "Let me grab a couple of towels, and we can head out back," I say, working hard to steel my voice. But my heart pounds against my ribs like a bass drum at a band concert.

When I enter the kitchen again, two big, fluffy white towels in hand, Ji stands by the door. She holds both glasses, staring up at me with those large, dark doe eyes that are my kryptonite.

Snagging the bottle, I ask. "You second-guessing your-self yet?" I don't want to push her into anything she isn't wholly committed to. I know how adrenaline and near-death experiences can fuck with somebody's mind, make them want things they regret later.

"Not in the least," she answers, eyes unrepentantly devouring me. I would almost feel objectified if I didn't want her so badly that my skin sizzles. I unlock and open the slider, inviting her to go first and following her out into the cool evening air.

Ji-su's pupils dilate as the ghostly light of the full moon washes over her face. I jealously observe how it pools around her mouth, radiating from her face. She looks sensual and otherworldly. I would give my right arm to be one of those pale, rogue rays, dancing over her features and caressing her flawless skin.

Suddenly, her eyes dart from side to side, surveying her surroundings. Fear tightens her features.

My eyes follow hers, scanning the darkened forest before returning to her mouthwatering face. "What's wrong?"

She shakes her head, looking down, the corners of her mouth dropping. "Old habits die hard."

"You've got nothing to worry about, Hummingbird. We're in the middle of nowhere. Smack dab in the center of ten acres that abut my family's ranch on one side and the Amestoy property on the other. And the Amestoy property is even more secluded and wild than the ranch. I'd pity the idiot who trespassed on their property. Those Basque bastards don't ask questions, and they don't play nice."

"I'm sorry," she says, forcing a smile. "I've just lived in fear for so long, it's hard to do things any other way."

"Don't apologize, Hummingbird. I can't imagine what you've been through. Though I want to hear anything you feel like telling me in the jacuzzi." I set down the towels and the bottle of wine. "Let me get everything going."

Ji perches the wine glasses in two drink holders, watching me work. I can feel her eyes searing the back of me, admiring my frame and ass. Pride wells inside, savoring the feeling of being wanted by someone I'm ready to devour.

When I turn around, the glow of her cheeks confirms my suspicions. It takes every ounce of willpower not to gather her in my arms and kiss her breathless. But this night is all about moving at her pace, letting her dictate how things unfold. My sole job is to set her at ease and satisfy her in every way she'll let me.

After the water bubbles and churns, I offer, "I can get you a T-shirt if you'd prefer to go in dressed?"

My hummingbird shakes her head, and I appreciate how her eyes darken and her pupils dilate. Her nostrils flare, and shivers of need rocket through me, inspired by the sizzle in Ji's simmering gaze.

"I know this sounds crazy, and maybe it is," she explains. "But I want to do something naughty. Wholly out of character and unprecedented. Something dangerous and wild. Something that I can think about for the rest of my life ..." She looks sadly to the side like she wants to say more. Instead, she presses her lips tightly together.

"Something unforgettable?"

"Exactly," she says, wetting her lips with her tongue. My eyes follow the move, incinerating at the visual.

"I can make sure you never forget me," I say confidently. "Take off your shirt."

"You first," she challenges, craning her head to look up at me. She stands a good foot shorter than I do, enhancing her curvy, petite frame.

Without hesitation, I shrug out of my dress coat and unfasten my button-down dress shirt, removing both and leaving them in a pile on the wooden deck by the hot tub. I don't wear an undershirt due to the heat of the summer day. Just my shoulder holster with two loaded firearms.

Her eyes inch over my naked chest until I expect to see smoke rising from my flesh as I remove the pieces, setting the holster atop the deck pointed away from us. I keep the weapons within grabbing distance ... *just in case.*

Ji's gaze drops lower to the unfortunate tent in the front of my black dress pants. I would turn away and adjust myself. Take a few deep, cleansing breaths and jog around the damn cabin if she acted disturbed by the sight. Instead, she laps me up hungrily.

Busted.

Her dark eyes meet mine, and she knows I know. Her next move will tell me everything.

"Your turn," I say, throat tightening. I'm surprised I can make a sound at all, let alone talk.

Her face darkens, gaze swirling with yearning. I half expect her to come up with an excuse, find a reason not to remove her shirt. Maybe we've taken this game farther than we should have ...

To my surprise, she slips her floral print top over her head, revealing a lacy lavender bra and ample tits, nipples pebbled through the thin material. I long to suck them one by one into my mouth, swirl my tongue around her areola, awaken her animal need for me.

Her torso curves in all the right spots, and she's got soft rolls that my mouth waters to cover in ardent kisses and worshipful swipes of my tongue. Her body is perfect. Soft, full, alluring. Low-slung on her hips is a holster that looks like a black lace corset. It's sexy as fuck. She removes it and her gun, placing them next to mine.

"Gorgeous and armed," I whisper, eyes dancing over her, enjoying the interplay of lunar light on her warm flesh. A bittersweet notion clobbers me hard. I don't just *want* Ji-su Park. I *want to keep her.* Claim her as mine, and everything that comes with her. "Fuck me."

I say the last two words like an exclamation, but her mind takes them another way. "If you insist." Despite the bold words, her voice trembles as she steps forward, palming my chest. "You're so hard and muscular. Rugged and strong. Everything I'm not."

"You're those things, too, Ji. In your own gorgeous way."

"But I'm fat," she laments, eyes scanning my face for a reaction. "Especially by Korean standards. I'm sorry I haven't taken better care of myself."

"What?" I exclaim, horrified by her words, heart stinging at the sentiment behind them. "You're fucking perfect, every inch of you."

"But my rolls and lumps, extra inches and cellulite, which you haven't seen—"

"Stop it right there," I retort testily. "I don't ever want to hear you talk about yourself that way again. "You. Are. Perfection. My dream girl."

"You're just—"

"Ji, I'm serious. It fucking hurts me when you say those things about yourself. Please promise you'll stop it with the negative self-talk." My eyes drill into hers pleadingly. Every nasty thing she says about herself feels like a knife to the chest. "I'm here to protect you, worship you, make you love your fucking body. Whatever you need from me. But I won't put up with self-hatred ... *ever.*"

"I'm sor—"

I lean into her, wrapping my arms around her waist and drawing her tightly against my core as I capture her mouth passionately. If I can't make her understand how fucking sexy she is, then I'll show her with every cell in my body, every part of who I am.

She moans against my mouth, lips parting. I don't hesitate, sliding into her. She feels like warm, wet silk, and she tastes like sin. I stroke my tongue against hers, initiating a dark, primal rhythm she mirrors ardently.

A growl rips from my chest, famished and demanding, as I change the angle of my head, thrusting deeper. I pull her so tightly against me that there isn't a sliver of air between our needy bodies. Her hips arch towards me, echoing the thrusts of our tongues and undoing my self-control one knot at a time. My cock feels hard as granite and ready to explode. I need her so much I can barely think.

We both pull back, gulping for air, inches apart. It's not close enough. It never could be. I need to get inside this woman, leave a part of myself with her forever. The pull of her gravity is unbreakable and tantalizing.

"Is it supposed to feel this good?" she asks breathlessly, and I wonder through the foggy haze of want how innocent this girl really is.

"No, it's not supposed to," I whisper, eyes fixated on her mouth and ready to dive back into her intoxicating flavor and feel. "This is too good …" I don't know how else to describe it.

"Dangerous," she adds, her eyes on my lips, too.

Sunk beneath waves of desire, I strain for air. Only the oxygen I need is buried in the heat of her kiss, a desire so basic and primal that I don't know how I'll ever exist without this woman again.

"It's like my soul is kissing yours, not just my mouth," she whispers. With any other woman, this kind of confession would give me pause, make me wonder what she's after.

But with Ji-su, it's the best and only articulation for a feeling without expression or precedent. I already ache for her, knowing I'll be hopelessly hungry forever after that first taste.

CHAPTER
EIGHT
JI-SU

My hands go to Bowie's dress pants, fumbling with the button and zipper. His arousal strains against the crotch, making my task nearly impossible. But I need more of this man. It's not just desire, it's an imperative.

His big hands go to my pants, unbuttoning, unzipping, and pulling them down so that they pool around my ankles. His fingers tangle in the waistband of my lacy lavender panties, and I thank the Universe I managed to wear matching underwear today, though the briefs are still control-top and not especially sexy.

But he doesn't notice, fingers sliding greedily down to the wet spot at my crotch. I don't know what's worse, wearing granny panties or feeling so out of control when it comes to how my body reacts to him.

I've masturbated enough times to expect moisture when I'm aroused. But is my pussy supposed to get *this* drenched?

As if reading my mind, he groans sensually, thumb sliding along my slick seam. "God, you're so wet for me, Ji."

He slides my underwear over my hips, sending them to the deck beside my jeans. I toe off my socks, naked before him. Worshipful eyes caress my skin, memorizing every inch. "I love how your body responds to me."

"I love how my body responds to you, too," I confess, hips straining towards his thick, rough fingers as they invade and claim me. "Mmm," I moan, feeling all self-control unravel at his expert touch. He hasn't even penetrated me with a finger. Yet, I'm ready to explode, body floating upwards and head in the stars glittering above us.

"I want to make you feel better than you ever have before, Hummingbird. I want to make you fly ... *if you trust me*."

"First, you have to catch me," I say between fast-paced breaths, kicking my feet out of my pants and underwear and darting for the water.

I climb into the jacuzzi, glancing over my shoulder as the towering, muscular cowboy struggles out of his pants, boxer briefs, and socks before sauntering in my direction. His cock is massive, so straight, thick, and taut.

Angry veins line the shaft. The smooth, bulbous tip makes my mouth water. I wonder what it would feel like sliding between my lips, possessing my mouth to the back of my throat, pushing deeper with each thrust until his hot cum fills my mouth.

Never have I fantasized about a man like this before. Never has my pussy throbbed out more demanding need. His sensual promises thrum through my head.

I want to make you feel better than you ever have before. I want to make you fly.

A thick knot of desire strangles my throat as I watch him sink into the water, his abdominal muscles tensing at the temperature change.

"So, what do I get when I catch you?" he asks seductively.

"Everything," I whisper, pulse pounding. "Whatever you want."

"Everything is what I want with you," he declares, grabbing my wine glass and handing it to me before he takes his. "But first, welcome to Rough & Ready Country." He takes a sip of his wine, looking up.

Annoyance grips me. We were in the middle of something. What could be good enough to interrupt it?

But when my eyes follow his heavenward, a strangled cry escapes my lips. The sky is black velvet covered in millions of glittering diamonds. An infinity of sparkling lights. Never has a sight more stunned or dwarfed me. I'm small, inconsequential beneath the glorious sweep of nature.

"Oh, Bowie, it's beautiful," I whisper, voice trembling. As my eyes adjust to the lack of light, I note lines and trails, the makings of constellations. Time stands still beneath this veil of glimmering beauty, and the rightness of the Universe, its power and majesty engulf me—living, breathing, timeless.

"No, what's beautiful is you."

Our eyes lock. Everything feels ordered as if it were supposed to happen this way. But it confuses the hell out of me.

How does this fit into my plan to seek vengeance?

"What's that look for?" the cowboy asks, setting down his wine glass. I do the same.

I shake my head, eyes dropping to the white bubbling cauldron of the hot tub. "Just trying to figure out what's going on. Why I found you now ... under these circumstances."

"Because for some things, two are better than one," he answers in silky tones, drawing closer.

"Like what things?"

"Like loving," he answers, wrapping his arms around me as he draws me into his lap, straddling him. My legs instinctively wrap around his waist, his rock-hard rod pressed tightly against my inner thigh.

"Just this once," I say, trying to convince myself this won't hurt anything.

"Just this once," he echoes, his voice rumbling through me at this close proximity. "But never enough."

My voice catches in my throat. "I'm clean," I say, trying to keep my head on straight, operate from something approaching logic. "But I'm not on birth control, and ..."

"And?"

"And I'm a virgin," I confess, appraising his face and reaction.

"A virgin? Are you saving yourself for marriage?" he asks, his face ambivalent.

I shake my head. "Just the right man at the right time. But then, all of this happened."

"And is that what I am to you? The right man at the right time?"

"More than that," I whisper.

"How more?"

"Like everything I could ever want," I admit, wrapping my arms around his neck. "If circumstances were different."

"They are different now," he counters, leveling his gaze on me. "You can stay here, safe with me. I won't let anything happen to you—ever. You'll be mine, and I'll be yours. Simple."

"Simple." I chuckle, trying not to dissolve into tears. The way he says it makes so much sense and sounds so impossible. What I want and what I need collide in the stillness of the moment, leaving a bittersweet cloud in their wake. "You make it sound so easy."

"It is easy."

If I could let go of my need for revenge. *If* the people after me didn't have a long memory. I look down, shaking my head.

"What's standing in our way?"

"Like I warned you when we first met, knowing me is dangerous."

"I like dangerous," he says, big hands gripping my ass.

"But if anything ever happened to you ..." I bite my bottom lip, trying to sort out the sting at the back of my eyes. I've known this man for less than one day. Why do I care so much about his welfare?

He snags my chin with his damp, spa-warmed pointer finger, lifting my face until our eyes meet. "Life is filled with uncertainty, Ji. You know that better than anybody. But you and I exploring why destiny brought us together isn't dangerous. It's natural. What we're meant to do. And whether you're ready to admit it or not, I believe the Universe brought us together for a reason. To be each other's strength and comfort, each other's home."

"But I can't have those things," I whisper. "Don't you see? There is no resting spot for me. Only places that feel safe until they don't."

"This is different," the handsome cowboy argues. "Because I'm carving that spot out for you with my own two hands, and I'm going to keep it safe. Protected. Until you learn again what it's like to live with peace."

"There can't be peace as long as I need revenge," I whisper.

His hand palms my cheek, turning my face back

towards his. "Then, we'll be each other's revenge, too." The gravity of his face proves he's not just saying the words.

My body burns, pussy throbbing and slick, as his rock-hard shaft digs into my thigh. I yearn for him to quiet my mind with his massive cock. Fill me and take away my loneliness, even if it's only temporary.

I need a heated memory to carry with me until my dying day. And I need to not die a virgin, without ever having shared my love with a good man, the kind of man worth total devotion.

He covers the distance between us, his mouth nipping playfully at my lips. "Stop it with the frowns, Hummingbird. You look so serious. I need you to relax, smile more."

My lips part, and he takes my invitation, possessing my mouth once more. Delectable shivers dance up and down my core as my arms tighten around his neck, and my tongue matches the scorching pace of his, mating with him, showing him what I need.

"You taste like everything that's missing from my life," he confesses between gulps of air and skilled kisses. "Laughter and seduction, beauty and sophistication, family and love."

"Love?" I sigh.

"Yes, Ji. Whether you want to hear that or not."

"Right when I convince myself just once won't hurt a thing, you come back with a statement like that." I pant, eyes catching his.

"I can't help it. You make me feel things I've never felt before. I can't lie about it or ignore it."

My hands slide down his back, caressing every inch of him, both devouring and adoring him. I learn him by touch, taking in every sizzling inch of his topography. Every hard angle and muscle, every dip and bulge. My hands descend, grabbing his ass and drawing him hard against me.

"Take me, Cowboy. Ride and wreck me. No mercy."

He chuckles, hands coming up to my tits. His thumbs find my nipples, rubbing over the pebbled surfaces and drawing a languid exhale from me. "No mercy," he whispers. "And nobody but me. First and last, you understand?"

"First and last lover?" My voice hitches.

"Yes," he declares, head descending to suck a brown nipple into his mouth. "First and last forever. No mercy. No quarter."

"And babies, lots of babies," I whimper before I catch myself. The melancholy confession hangs in the air, a relic of a future that feels out of reach in my present circumstance.

He pulls back a little, appraising my expression. *Have I finally scared him?* Against my will, my chin and bottom lip tremble, my face grave.

"Lots of babies, Ji. A big family we make together," he whispers, big hands roaming over my soft flesh, massaging and kneading me.

"I want the thought of it. To forget about everything else for one excruciatingly beautiful moment," I confess. "Though you should use a condom because ..." My voice fades on a tremble.

"Because?" he prompts.

"There can be no future with me."

He stops, pulling his mouth from my nipple with a tug that makes my head loll back and a sigh escape my lips. "You've let the enemy in your head, Hummingbird. That's the first and most important defeat. If they've got you mentally, they've got all they need."

"But—"

"There are no buts about it. You're doing half the work for them, vocalizing their desires, running away, letting them dictate your future ... even how long it will be. Of all the things I've thought of you since our first meeting, someone who's given up hasn't been one of them."

He says it ruefully, anger etched in his countenance. I feel instantly ashamed of myself. My eyes search his pleadingly. "I need you to fight, Ji. For us. For a future together."

My eyes lock with his. Grabbing me around the waist, he pulls me from the water, setting my ass on the edge of the jacuzzi. Only my feet dangle in the swirling water.

"Spread your legs," he commands darkly.

"Why?" I whisper, voice tight with a swirling mixture of apprehension and anticipation.

"Because it's time to take what's mine, Hummingbird. And to show you *we're* worth fighting for ... *worth living for, too*."

NINE

BOWIE

I angle her body so she leans back on her elbows. Starting at her ankles, I feather her flesh with slow, sultry kisses. My lips trace their way up her legs one at a time, finding a sensitive spot behind her left knee that makes her giggle. Her body melts as I continue up her inner thighs, alternating sides and chasing kisses with swipes of my tongue. Languid sighs part her lips and awaken a need so feral, I don't know how long I can hold back.

Goosebumps cover her flesh, heightened as I blow on her skin, hot breath blazing a trail to her pleasure center. I'm hungry for my first taste, ready to eat this stunning woman out. The pull to claim her is unbearable, but first, I must make her feel everything.

I moan, tasting the salt on her skin as my mouth glides higher, riding her soft, round thighs. "You're perfection," I whisper. "So goddamned stunning. You set my blood on fire."

Her eyes roll back as her head falls. "Yes," she whispers. Her voice sparkles with yearning.

My big hands stroke her outer thighs, lighting up her

body and preparing her for more. Her hips arch towards me, straining for satisfaction. I will blow her fucking mind, make her so addicted to me she has to live … has to stay with me to get her next ecstatic fix.

I internally swear to plunge her over the edge, make her mind stop unceasingly fixating on the past and what-ifs. My tongue will turn her into a mindless, writhing ball of pleasure. No matter what it takes.

My right hand slides through the ebony hair of her pussy, spreading her lips and savoring the way her already swollen clit pokes out, begging for attention. Her labia are brown and gorgeous, shiny and creamy with her arousal.

I sink into her for the first time, swiping my tongue up her slick, aroused slit. A heady sigh parts my lips as I taste her honey for the first time, instantly in love with her musky, tangy flavor.

She's all I need, the taste of her juices like a custom flavor made exclusively for me. To think she's saved this pussy for me puts a thick knot of desire in my throat. "We're going to have babies together, Ji. Lots of them. Beautiful babies that look like their mama," I murmur against her clit, wresting desire from her lips, unintelligible but perfectly communicated. "I'm going to fill you with my seed. Fill you with our future so that there's no more room for surrender or fear. You'll be my woman, and I'll be your man, keeping you safe and protecting you always."

"I want to believe you." She sighs, hips bucking toward my mouth. I swirl her clit for the first time, sucking it between my teeth and flicking it with my tongue. "Yes," she yelps, urging me on.

"Then, believe me." I growl, lifting my head and catching her eyes. "Believe in our future, Hummingbird."

"Yes," she moans as my tongue slides up and down her

folds, sucking her pussy lips in and out of my mouth. Her body shivers beneath me, her pussy drenched with desire as I slide my pointer finger into her, sinking knuckle-deep.

Ji feels like heaven and everything I've ever wanted. The way she grips me, tight and hot, is almost more than I can bear. I can't wait to slide my dick into her flooded channel, work her G-spot, and make her claw my back and scream my name.

I want her most primal marks on me. Her wild screams of ecstasy reverberating in my ears.

"Have you ever made yourself come before, Hummingbird?"

"Once or twice. With my fingers."

"Well, I won't stop until you drench my face," I whisper, fucking her with my tongue.

"Oh, God, Bowie," she exhales urgency in her voice.

My tongue slides up her length, circling her clit as my finger penetrates her channel. Then, a second. She squirms at the stretch, mercilessly gripping my fingers. But I need her to relax, get ready for me because I won't stop until she's riding my cock, tits bouncing in my face.

"I will make you feel this good every day," I promise, sucking her clit until her lower half strains toward me. I take mental notes on what she hungers for, learning how I'll please the hell out of her daily. I slurp her, sucking up her goodness, in love with the way her swollen clit sticks up, demanding its pleasure.

My fingers curl back towards me, hitting the rough spot at the front of her pussy repeatedly. Every stroke draws more juices. I marvel at her slickness, arousal sliding down my fingers and pooling in my palm as the motion elicits wet, naughty noises.

Suddenly, in the midst of overflowing ecstasy, I sense a disconnect. Looking up, I notice her eyes are open again, scanning the horizon. She bites her thick bottom lip, the gears of her mind turning so loudly I swear I can almost hear them. Her mind and worries have brought her out of the moment. But I won't rest until I take her there.

Talking her through it, I urge, "Eyes on me, Ji."

Her dark orbs flicker to mine, her pupils so large and dilated, the brown warmth has receded into the ebony edges.

"You and me and this moment are all that exist," I whisper, lapping ravenously at her pearl. "All you feel is the stroke of my finger, the warmth of my tongue mastering your clit, pleasing the hell out of you. That's all that exists is this pleasure and your amazing fucking body."

My hummingbird nods, face serious, newly determined to take what's hers. I won't let her settle for anything less. Stroking her gently but firmly, I bring her back to the moment, talking her through it as I draw her closer and closer to the precipice.

"I'm going to make you fly, Hummingbird. And then, you're going to drench my face and my hand," I order.

She whimpers, hips bucking towards me. I double down on her clit, tongue sliding over her nub, giving her the friction she craves until her hands grip my head, urgently pressing me against her pussy. I hum low in my throat, vibrations racing through her heightened sensitivity. Then, I pull back slightly, blowing on her as my fingers continue curling inside, dragging her need from her, forcing her to surrender to bliss.

"Oh, God, Bowie," she gasps, pussy grinding into my face. "I'm about to—"

Her velvety wetness flutters and spasms as she comes undone around me, milking my fingers and gushing her warm release. I lap up everything she has to give greedily, not willing to waste one drop of her precious honey. My fingers work her through it, my voice crooning between swipes of my tongue until she melts against the hot tub, surrendering fully to the experience.

Fat tears streak down her cheeks as her eyes absorb me. Warmth and tenderness pulse behind them, stealing my breath.

"Why are you crying?" I ask, licking her from my fingers before bringing my hands up to palm her cheeks, swiping away the droplets.

"Because you're the first respite I've had in so long. I don't ever want this to end."

She keeps saying shit like this, alluding to the end of us. As far as I'm concerned, we've only just begun. I can't entertain anything less than a lifetime with her, no matter her present circumstances.

"Listen to me, Ji-su," I say sternly. Frustration fills me. "You're safe with me, and you don't ever have to leave. Understand? We'll find a way to make this work. All I'm asking from you is a little faith."

"Okay." She nods. "I'll work on faith. But I have to warn you, I've always been very analytical-minded. If I can't work out how and when something's going to happen, I have trouble believing in it at all."

"I doubt you worked out how and when we would meet. Did you?"

"The thought never crossed my mind until I pulled up to the blockade in the road and heard those men harassing you."

"And yet despite not even knowing I existed, the Universe still ensured our worlds collided," I remind.

"Yes," she concedes faintly. "You're the best thing that's ever happened to me."

"And you're the best thing that's ever happened to me. I refuse to squander this opportunity because of fear or anxiety about the future. Come live in the present with me instead."

"But living like that isn't what's kept me alive all this time," she counters.

"True, but things are different now."

"Okay, but if the opportunity arises. If I have the chance to seek revenge, I will. You have to understand that."

"I do understand that," I answer. "And I promise to be there every step of the way because we're a team now, Ji."

She nods.

Smiling warmly, I pull her back into the jacuzzi so that she straddles my lap. "In other words, you're mine now, Ji."

Tears pool in her eyes as she smiles, radiant and genuine. "And you belong to me, too."

I slowly nod. "I'm clean, and I've got condoms."

"No condom," she says. "I want you raw, unprotected."

I cock my head, eyeing her in silent disbelief. "For a woman hellbent on fatalism and the belief she doesn't have a future, that's too big a mindset shift to ignore."

She licks her lips sensually.

"Why the change of heart?"

"Because I can't bear the thought of anything between us ... ever."

"And if I put a baby in you, are you going to be pissed at me later?" I ask, head reeling at her request.

"No," she says, feathering my face with her lips. "The thought of you breeding me makes me so wet. I can't even

..." She pants out the last sentence, grabbing my hand, slipping it between her legs, and grinding against me. "I don't know what you do to me, Bowie. I've never wanted to have babies with any man. But damn, I need your seed in me."

Blood rushes to my cock at her words. I never knew talk of breeding could make me so damn hard. "Say it, Ji," I order between clenched teeth. "Tell me what you want."

"I want you to fill me with your cum."

"Until it's dripping down your thighs? Is that what you're after?"

She slides back and forth against my hand, desperate for friction. "Yes, Cowboy. It's what I need more than anything."

Her words unravel my last threads of self-control. I'm desperate to fulfill her darkest fantasies.

"The first time is going to hurt," I say, bringing my hand up to stroke her cheek. "But I'll talk you through it. Okay?"

She nods.

"If you're sure this is really what you want?"

"Yes, Bowie."

"And this cabin and this mountain, too? Because I refuse to mince words. You let me make you my woman, and I'm keeping you here with me. Understood?"

"Understood."

"No more giving up. No more giving in. No more hiding."

"Never again."

"Ride or die," I add, sliding my thumb over her swollen nub.

She repeats it like a vow. "Ride or die." Her eyes flood with steely determination and unwavering loyalty.

The words put fire in my blood. I grab my cock, sliding the tip through her slippery folds, need burning me from the inside out. Sliding the tip into her, I marvel at the warm tightness, knowing I'll fight for every fucking inch, and it'll be worth it.

I grip her hip with one hand, pulling her demandingly over me, encouraging her to sheath my length at her pace. My other hand finds her pearl, circling and rubbing it, teasing it into a hard nub under my thumb until her breath comes faster.

"That's it, Hummingbird. You're taking me so good," I encourage, sliding her down over me a little further. The squeeze is painful but tantalizing. As she gives herself to me, opens up, it's like a fucking addiction. I'd walk through fire for the fix only this woman can bring. "Your pussy was made for me."

"Yes," she gasps, pushing her hips down further over me and grimacing.

"Fuck, woman. The way you grip me is everything."

My head descends to her tits, sucking and teasing her, nipping and drawing out her pleasure. Simultaneously, I work her clit, sliding her up and down over me, pressing deeper with each thrust and encouraging her as I take her to the edge of pleasure and pain again and again.

"This pussy's all mine."

"Yes, Bowie. Fuck." She moans.

"You're going to learn to ride me so good, Ji. And I'm going to learn how to please the hell out of you."

"You already do." She gasps.

"It's only going to get better. I promise, Hummingbird."

My thumb slides demandingly over her hard, swollen nub, increasing my pace as I feel her walls fluttering around me. With my other hand, I grip her waist, pulling her down over me with increasing urgency. "Relax," I urge her. "And give me everything. I won't stop until all of you is mine."

"Yes." She sighs, melting around me.

I drive into her as her orgasm unfolds, and her hot, flooded channel milks my cock. I demand everything, laying claim to her body, possessing her soul. Seating myself completely, I scream her name, and she claws my back, urging me over the edge. The familiar pressure at the base of my spine grips me, balls clenching and pulling up as I explode into her, filling her with warm waves of cum.

I rest my forehead on hers as we both collect our breaths, faces flushed and bodies relaxed and sated. "I know you don't want to hear this. But you are my every-thing, Ji-su. So, from now on, I'm going to need your most dangerous pursuit to be me and you ... *us*. Revenge'll have to come second."

Her black eyes examine me, ambivalence shrouding them. Her palms come up to my cheeks, and she leans in, planting the most tender kiss on my lips.

"No," she pants, voice passion-filled. "As much as I want to forget about the past, focus on our future, I can't rest until justice is served. It has to happen *first* ... before I can truly allow myself to rest or be happy."

I knew she'd say this. The thought of her ever being in harm's way kills me, though I can't claim I don't under-stand her need. Ji and I are more alike than I care to admit.

"If I were in your shoes, I wouldn't stop until the people who did this were six feet under. An eye for an eye ..." I pause for a moment, still processing everything she's told me tonight. "Senator Moreau may not have killed my brother, but he stole his life. Holden deserves vindication and retaliation, too."

"Yes," she whispers solemnly, tilting her head back slightly to lap me up with her eyes. "What are you saying, Bowie?"

"We live together. We fight together. We restore peace and order together ..."

Her eyes fill with tears as she processes my words.

"And we burn down the fucking world if we have to," I add.

Pressing her lips resolutely together, she adds, "*Together.*"

CHAPTER
TEN
JI-SU

"Are you sleeping at all?" a voice grumbles next to my ear as Bowie nuzzles my neck, pulling me more tightly against him.

I don't know how many hours have passed with me staring up at the ceiling of his blackened bedroom, savoring his warmth and closeness and ruminating over next steps. "Trying to, but ..."

"But your mind's racing a hundred miles per hour ..."

I nod, and he pulls me closer. "What are you thinking about, Hummingbird?"

I work to keep my voice steady. "How I can rest knowing my sister's killer is still out there ... I can't tell you how many sleepless nights this thought has given me."

"Sleep comes before revenge. You won't be any good to either of us exhausted." He has a point, though I still feel guilty, basking in the warmth and security of this man's embrace while my sister lies unavenged in her grave.

"I know. Easier said than done, though."

"We'll get to the bottom of what happened to your sister, and we'll make every one of those sons-of-bitches pay for hurting you and forcing you into hiding. But now, you've got to rest, Ji."

I nod, seeing the logic in his words but unable to put it into practice. I shift in his arms.

"Tell me about Ae-cha," he says softly, large arms shielding me from the world and making me feel safe as he tugs me closer. "I've heard all about the vengeance you seek. But what about the woman? What was she like?"

It's been so long since I let myself think about her that I don't know where to begin. My breath hitches, and my eyes smart as I speak. "She was beautiful and gutsy. Always stood up for what was right and defended those who were vulnerable, beaten down by life. As a kid, she went toe-to-toe with bullies on the playground despite being half their size. As an adult, she thought she was fighting the good fight ... until the end."

Bowie nods against my shoulder, drawing me out with quiet patience.

"She loved Strawberry Now and Laters, Frank Ocean, Marvel movies, and pugs. Though she only had a pet goldfish, Mr. Sammy, when she passed away. Her apartment manager didn't allow dogs." Thinking about the vibrant woman I loved rather than the crime that took her from me feels good. It lightens the weight of carrying her memory, and it makes me miss her fiercely.

"And Mr Sammy?" the cowboy asks drowsily.

"Safe with my parents." I wipe my eyes with the back of my hand, and Bowie nuzzles against my neck, kissing my cheek. Who knew such a big, gruff cowboy could be so tender?

"Good."

"Ae-cha loved pineapple on her pizza, which I thought was a sin. She always had my back, and she was the kind of person you could bring any troubles to, and she'd be ready with a huge hug, a shoulder to cry on, and a glass of wine. Our *Yellowstone* marathons were legendary, and she would be green with envy, knowing I found a cowboy of my own."

He chuckles deep in his throat.

"But she'd also be endlessly happy for me ... Tell me about Holden."

Bowie clears his throat, rubbing his hand over his face. "Holden was the first of my foster brothers to talk to me and play with me when I arrived at the ranch. He was always outgoing and kind like that. He cared too much about other people, I think. Kind of like Ae-cha. Always wanting to right the wrongs of the world. Always getting in trouble despite everything. Hanging with the wrong crowd, getting into smoking and drugs young. Resistant to discipline and the cowboy lifestyle—what my Dad was trying to do for us. But ironically, I also think he's the most like Wyatt, caring and generous to a fault."

"He sounds like a good man."

"He is," Bowie sighs. "And the thought of him locked up for self-defense fucking kills me, Ji. It has kept me awake more nights than I care to admit. I want my brother back ... the kid who thought if he left trails of Reese's Pieces, he could summon E.T. The teen who collected vintage comic books like they were going out of style and listened obsessively to Portishead and Bjork when everyone out here was country as hell. But he was a troubled man. Even before the incident that changed everything. I visit him regularly in prison, and I wonder how thoroughly it has altered him. What he'll be like when he's out. And whether he and Dee, the woman who's been his lifeline for all these years, will be able to make their relationship work."

"With a brother like you, he's already got a head start at

a new life," she observes, voice trailing off. We lie together silently for a long time. I close my eyes, but I can't sleep. *Who am I fooling?* He shifts next to me, pulling me closer.

"I'm sorry I'm keeping you up," I whisper.

"Not your fault." Bowie's big, rough hand caresses my body slowly, sliding up my torso to my tits. His thumb teases and squeezes my nipples, twisting and pinching them until I whimper. "I should've done my job better."

"And what's that?" I giggle, still trying to wrap my head around my change of fortunes. Being here, safe with this man, wrapped in a tenderness I've never experienced before, instead of running for my life, always looking over my shoulder.

"To tire you out," he murmurs, feathering his lips over my neck and decolletage. The breath catches in my throat, my pulse racing.

"Tomorrow," he says gruffly. "We'll go see my brother, Wolfe, and his Army Ranger crew. They've been busting shit like this longer than anybody else I know. They'll be able to help."

He leans over me, finding a nipple and sucking it into his mouth as I moan with pleasure. His hand drops between my legs, finding my clit and circling the still-sensitive nub. My hips arch towards him, greedy for his touch despite the many pleasures of the night.

"You need me, don't you, Hummingbird?" he asks darkly, fingers sliding through my arousal and awakening my hunger.

"More than anything," I admit, breath hitching in my throat as his touch turns more insistent. He slides a finger into my channel, curving it back towards him, finding the perfect pressure and spot to drive me over the edge ... to beautifully wreck me again. "Is that a problem?"

"Not at all because you make me fucking insatiable," he answers, climbing down my body until his face is centered between my legs. His first swipe of my clit with his tongue puts stars behind my eyes. I'm still so swollen and sensitive from earlier that every move heightens my pleasure, magnifying it. "And your flavor and feel? Let's just say I could eat you out all night and never get enough."

"Those are big promises—"

His mouth interrupts my train of thought as he sucks my pussy lips into his mouth, undoing me sliver by sliver until I grind mindlessly into him, enjoying the hell out of this cowboy's face.

"Yes, Bowie. Please don't stop," I beg, holding the back of his head with my hands, pressing him into me like a lifeline. I let my eyes roll back in my head, thoughts finally halting. I'm already so close, I feel myself floating upwards, my whole body trembling with anticipation.

My orgasm destroys me, lower ab muscles and thighs clenching and need burning through me as I drench him again. *Will it always be this good?* I scream his name, melting into a pile of happy satisfaction, half expecting him to roll back over and go to sleep.

Instead, he commands, "Ass in the air. I need to breed you again." His voice has a tantalizing, dangerous edge to it that sends shivers of need sizzling through me. And the verb "breed" makes my pussy throb avariciously.

If any other man talked to me this way, I'd slap him. My feminist streak coming out. But I'm ravenous for his touch. Never has complying felt so good, so fucking basic to my existence.

I roll over and climb onto all fours, anticipation tightening my throat and hitching my breath. Looking over my shoulder, I admire his rugged masculinity for one timeless moment before he drags me greedily backwards, pressing me hard against him. His thick, hot arousal digs into my thigh, demanding my pleasure.

Bending down, he bites my ass cheek teasingly. I moan at the surprise move. He smacks me lightly and playfully, and God help me, I love it. Tremors of lust dance across my flesh, begging for more.

"Oh." I moan, savoring the delicious stings left by his mouth and hand.

"You like that?" he asks, voice thick and raw.

"God, yes," I confess.

He smacks me again. A little harder this time, and I moan, clit throbbing and pussy clenching. "That's my good girl," he praises, coming up behind me and teasing my folds with the head of his smooth, hot cock. "I need your pussy so much, Ji."

I whimper, body pulsing with anticipation.

"Unless you're too sore for this?" he asks, craning his head towards me.

In truth, I probably am. But the painful need for him outweighs all other concerns. "No, Bowie. I need you to fuck me. Make me forget everything but the feel of your cock undoing me."

"Greedy little hummingbird," he tsks, gliding into me slowly, taking his time. From tip to balls, he strokes me again and again, drawing out at the end and exaggerating the wet, juicy noises we make each time we slap back together. "Fuck, I'm going to live in this pussy of yours, Ji. It's so damn good."

"And your cock feels like heaven, the way you drive into me ..." My swollen pussy magnifies every sensation, every inch. I push my ass back into him, taking everything he has to give and enjoying the hell out of his girth. He's so big it makes me wince as my body reshapes to accommodate him.

His breath races, and he spits into his hand. My core tightens, knowing what's coming next. Finding my clit, his slick fingers circle and work my nub, lighting me up until my pussy greedily gobbles his cock, moments from coming hard.

"The way you tighten around me and suck me in, Hummingbird. There are no words for how fucking amazing you make me feel." He grunts out the words through clenched teeth, concentrating hard on holding back. "What do you need from me?"

"Everything," I whisper. "Please, Cowboy, fill me with your hot cum."

"Fuck, you've got a dirty mouth." His other hand finds my tit, clutching it and rolling my nipple between his pointer finger and thumb. "I won't give you any of my cum until you get off again for me, Ji. I want you too tired to think."

He grabs my hips with both hands, altering the angle so that each time he pumps into me, the head of his cock slams into my G-spot. My mind swims, unable to hold rational thought.

I dissolve around him, pure animal need as I scream his name, fisting the bed sheets and spasming around his full-ness. With another thrust of his hips, he fills me, waves of hot release matching the shudder of his body as he collapses on top of me.

After our breathing slows, he jumps out of bed, saun-tering into the bathroom and returning with a warm wash-cloth to clean me. Never have I imagined having such an attentive lover. Or such a drop-dead gorgeous one.

Yawning, he says, "Let's give this sleep thing another try, Hummingbird."

I open my mouth to speak, three words on the tip of my tongue that I've never said to any man before. Never even wanted to.

I love you.

I could say them now and mean it wholeheartedly, unreservedly. The thought is mindblowing. Especially since I didn't know he even existed twenty-four hours ago.

My hand comes up, stroking his stubbled cheek, and he wraps his arms jealously around me, relaxing at my touch. The big beast of a man instantly goes from dangerous to cuddly. I love having this kind of power over him.

I love *him*. But I keep the sentiment to myself, not wanting to ruin this perfect moment. I hope I don't regret it later.

Bowie holds me possessively against his chest, kissing my cheek and slowly nodding back off. I follow behind, finally sinking into a restfulness I haven't experienced since before my sister's passing.

ELEVEN

JI-SU

Buzz. Buzz. A vibration fills the room, and my groggy mind strains to place it.

Bowie fumbles with his cell phone on the nightstand next to the bed. Looking at the screen, he mumbles, "What in the hell?" Answering it, he questions, "What?"

I lift my head, grabbing my cell phone on the opposite side of the bed. It's four in the morning, only hours after we last dozed off. I feel sore in every delicious place possible as my mind runs back through last night's mindblowing events.

"Roger that. Yes, we could use an extra hand. Thank you." He ends the call, eyeing me bewildered. "That was the Amestoys, my closest neighbors."

"Isn't it a little early?" I ask, stretching.

"Yeah, and strange as fuck. Get dressed, Ji. We're about to be in that gunfight you've been jonesing for."

"Gunfight?"

"Yep, sounds like the Universe is ready to deliver on that chance for vengeance, too."

I jump out of bed, fumbling for my jeans, bra, holster, and shirt, not even messing with looking for my underwear. I check my gun's safety, making sure a round is chambered before I holster it, looking apprehensively at Bowie.

"The Amestoys absolutely hate my family. Been in the middle of a land war with them for generations. That aside, they just chased two white pickups and a black SUV off their property, filled with men with guns. Sounds like a mixture of church-goers and cartel members from their description. Moreau's cronies, maybe? They're headed for the cabin. We need to prepare."

"And the Amestoys?"

"To my surprise, they offered to provide backup firepower if I let them on my land, which I agreed to under the circumstances. Hope I don't regret it later," the cowboy says, hurrying into Wranglers and a button-down shirt. "Sounds like they're coming for the cabin. So, I figure we'll be off in the woods a distance, set a trap for them."

In the hallway, he opens a large safe, pulling out guns and ammo, loading my arms, and grabbing everything he can before locking it again. The man has a veritable arsenal.

"Come on," he nods towards the back slider. "We'll sneak out this way and wait. Shouldn't be long, considering where Fierce last saw them."

We sprint across the open lawn for the trees, tucking back into the thick vegetation and disappearing. Though Bowie brought his white cowboy hat, he removes it, hiding it behind some brush as we hunker down. He texts a group message on his cell phone. Then, he starts checking and loading firearms, preparing for a shootout.

I help, familiar with a variety of weapons thanks to my training over the past six months. Soon, we're loaded and ready to make our stand. Whatever that entails.

Tears fill my eyes as I look at Bowie, sick to my core that he's tangled up in all of this. If it weren't for me, he wouldn't be in the woods preparing for an ambush, outgunned and outnumbered.

I open my mouth to speak, but he cuts me off, leaning in for a kiss. "Don't you dare apologize to me, Hummingbird. You're the best fucking thing that's ever happened to me. You're my family now, something I always wanted … something that felt elusive until you saved me last night. No matter what happens, I will never regret my time with you. But I won't let you go, either. So, get used to being a part of something bigger than you or me. Because now that I've had a taste of you … of us, there's no going back for me. I hope you feel the same way."

"Yes, Bowie, with every part of my soul. You're my family and my home now, and I'll defend you to my last breath."

"Same, Hummingbird. But the trick is not letting it get that far," he whispers with a wink as the distant roar of engines makes us fall silent. Against the shell of my ear, he says, "You get your revenge here today. This is it, and then you never look back. Promise?"

I frown, unable to make that promise. Senator Moreau won't be in the ambush today. And I'm determined that man will pay for what he's done. No matter how long it takes, I will eventually get him.

Hurt flashes in Bowie's eyes. He still doesn't fully understand my compulsion for vengeance. Maybe because he thinks I'm choosing it over him. *Maybe I am.*

We wait silently as two white pickups and a dark SUV pull up to the cabin. They park haphazardly, men piling out and appraising Bowie's truck. The ragtag crew is a mixture of bearded, suit-wearing men like last night and inked gangster types, Senator Moreau's favorite mixture of associates, based on my research.

One, in particular, catches my eye, a short, stocky man with tattoos on his face and neck, their pattern unmistakable despite the grain of the closed-circuit TV where I first saw them.

His head is bald, and he's got the same goatee, the same build, the same way of carrying himself. He was captured on video surveillance at Lake Torrent's visitor center around the time Ae-cha supposedly drove into the lake.

My hands shake at the realization, my heart thudding behind my ribcage. Whatever happens today, that man is dead.

Bowie's eyes pan from mine to the man, and he raises an eyebrow. I lean into him, whispering almost inaudibly. "That man was at the lake the day my sister died."

He nods, his face hardening.

Another rail-thin man wearing a white tank top with sagging shorts and tattoos, pulls out a knife, slashing the tires of Bowie's truck. The cowboy's jaw tenses, his eyes darkening with rage.

If the neighbors hadn't called, Bowie and I would still be in bed asleep. No telling what would have happened to us with these men stalking around the property. Two skulk around the side of the house, carrying handguns and looking through windows as another two head up the stairs to the front door, axe in hand, peering through the massive windows.

The other two, including the man from the lake, cover the other side. One wears a backpack, and I can only imagine what's inside.

I raise my gun, watching them enter and leave my sights. I need the perfect shot. I have to ensure I kill the man who destroyed my family and ruined my life *if it's the last thing I do ...*

If it's the last thing I do. That's been my entire mindset for the previous six months, but as I glance at Bowie now, I realize everything has changed and shifted in the space of less than twenty-four hours.

Even more than revenge, I want a life with Bowie. I want a chance to start over, start a family, carry on my sister's memory, and ensure that what she died for won't remain in vain.

Bam. Bam. Bam. Gunfire breaks out from behind the house. I jump in my skin, but Bowie remains steady as a rock, assessing the scene critically.

"Amestoys," he whispers. "They're going to send those men running right to us."

"Are they shooting in our direction?"

Instead of answering, we both drop our heads to the ground as bullets whiz above us. Fortunately, the line of fire is a good three or so feet above our position. But we still feel the pinch of the action headed back in our direction.

"Steady," Bowie coaches. "We pick them off one by one. Like target practice at the shooting range."

I nod, pulse pounding and gulping for air. The men reappear, running through the backyard, straight for us, too pinned down by crossfire from the neighbors to reach their trucks.

My hand shakes as I raise my weapon, getting the man from the lake in my sights. *Steady, Ji. Steady.* At the same moment I pull the trigger, Bowie fires, and two men fall. Ae-cha's assassin, as far as I can tell, and the rail-thin man who slashed Bowie's tires.

Two more are down, taken out by the Amestoys. The last run at a breakneck pace. I train one in my sights and shoot. He spins around, grabbing his chest and falling to the ground. Bowie gets the other one, and I breathe a sigh of relief, pressed tightly to the ground.

A strange mixture of emotions grips me as I lie there, waiting for the ambush to end. Then, it hits me. I finally have what I've tirelessly sought.

Revenge.

Is it true that it's better served cold? I don't know, the distance having robbed me of the chance to let Ae-cha's killer know who I was and why he had to die.

But could I have delivered the same punishment at a closer range? Seeing the fear in his eyes? Hearing his voice and maybe even conversing with him? I doubt it.

How did it go down with Ae-cha? Did he taunt her? Did she fight back? Did she know what was coming?

"*Let it go, Sis. Live life for you and me.*" I hear my sister's voice almost as if whispered on the wind, traveling to me in ethereal tones, comforting and soothing me. Maybe she's right. Maybe it's time to let all of this go.

But how do you move on after revenge? After killing two men?

Eyeing Bowie, I have my answer. I would kill a thousand people to keep this man safe. Because he's mine, and I'm his. Forever.

How can I know this with total clarity despite only just meeting him? I doubt I'll ever be able to articulate it. No matter how long I live. But one thing's sure, I'll never let him go or squander this opportunity for another chance.

At life. At love. At a family.

The gorgeous cowboy turns towards me, raising a hand

carefully to stroke my cheek. "What are you thinking, Hummingbird?"

"Not thinking ... knowing to the depths of my soul. I love you, Bowie Reeves. With every part of my being. For all time."

He smiles warmly, eyes filling with emotion. "And I love you, Ji-su Park—now, until I draw my last breath, and *everything in between*. Because you're my soulmate. My twin flame. My world."

My heart overflows with love. More than I ever thought possible, and I can't help but feel Ae-cha looking down on us with a smile. Not because I avenged her death. Not even because I served up justice. But because her vibrant memory and heroic life will live on through me.

Bowie leans in, feathering his lips over mine and wrapping his arm around me, staying low to the ground, but conveying a world of need and longing through his soft lips and dark eyes.

He's my cowboy, now and forever. The man who brought me back to life, whom I choose to live for, rather than lead a shadow life of giving up, opting out, and running.

Sporadic gunfire gives way to an eerie silence as men appear from the treeline. Huge, robust, black-bearded men. Tall and handsome, muscular and rugged, and all wearing black berets. They look like something out of a Travel Channel documentary, holding rifles and surveying the scene.

"The Amestoys," Bowie whispers. "Friends," he calls in his loudest voice. "Don't shoot if we come out."

"D'accord," the largest man in the group hollers in deep-throated tones, and Bowie eyes me, shrugging.

"That's 'okay' in French," I say.

"Wait, you speak French?"

"Only what I remember from high school."

"Hope your memory's good," he says, raising his hands and standing up.

CHAPTER
TWELVE
BOWIE

I wave my white cowboy hat in the air as a sign of truce, counting all seven Amestoy brothers. I went to high school with some of them. Hell, I played on the same football team as Fierce Amestoy, the eldest.

Ji-su stands next to me, holding her hands up, too. "Why are they dressed like that?" she asks under her breath as she follows me forward.

"You mean the colorful scarves and berets? They're traditional Basque shepherds."

"And they normally hate your family, but they're helping you out today?" Her face betrays puzzlement.

"I can't wrap my head around it, either," I say as we close the distance. "Normally, it's us cowboys and them in gun or fist fights. Though we never shoot to kill ... just to piss off and make a point."

Fierce steps forward, and I nod.

I put my hat on and reach out to take his hand firmly. "Fierce Amestoy. If it weren't for you and your brothers, no telling what would have happened to my girl and me this morning."

The big man's face looks hard and intimidating. He nods toward Ji. "When did you get a woman, Bowie?"

"Last night." I reach out and tuck her under my arm. She feels good next to me like this, her curvy body fitting perfectly against my hard frame.

Fierce removes his beret, rubbing the back of his hand over his forehead. He looks like the provincial version of Henry Cavill with a beard. At least that's what all my sisters-in-law say.

In a deep, rich voice with a slight French accent, Fierce says to Ji, "Just so you know, it's not always like this around here. Usually quiet and nice. You'll have to come over for dinner. My wife, Felicity, would enjoy getting to know you, I think."

My jaw drops. Even more than saving each other's asses from gunmen, shared hospitality is unheard of between the Amestoys and the cowboys of Rough & Ready Ranch. In fact, the only person in my family who fraternizes with any of them is Rock, Fierce's tattoo artist. But that's still a working relationship, and we give Rock shit about it all the time.

"I suppose you could come, too," Fierce grumbles, eyeing me caustically.

"We haven't eaten together since high school, Fierce," I mumble, glaring back at him.

"Or spoken since the football team. You were a decent player, though your asshole brother, Christian, always had to rub it in everyone's face what a great quarterback he was."

I shrug. "That's Christian."

Fierce frowns, nodding toward one of the dead men. "We heard strange noises coming from the flocks this morning and ran out thinking it was coyotes or a bear.

Instead, we saw these dumb fucks driving through one of our fields, scaring the shit out of our sheep, trampling our fences. They made a royal mess we'll be cleaning up for days. Fils de pute!" He spits on the ground to make his point.

Continuing, he explains, "We chased them from our property, assuming they'd take one of the side roads back towards town. But instead, they exchanged gunfire with us and then retreated onto your property. Figured they were livestock rustlers of some sort. Thought the decent thing to do was let you know, especially if there was any chance that violence could bubble back onto my family's land."

In the distance, we hear the sounds of truck engines and the hum of a helicopter. Fierce looks up, and so do I.

"Is that Hawk?" the shepherd asks, his brothers congregating around him and lifting their eyes heavenward, shielding their faces with their hands.

"Looks like it. I texted Wolfe the first chance I had. Apparently, he called out the whole cavalry."

"You'll need it to clean up this mess," Fierce says, shaking his head. "Look, we've got to get back to our property and help the old men mend the fences these fuckers broke down while trespassing. Last thing we need are livestock deaths on top of all of this. But your brothers know where to find us when it's time for questioning. Call first, or we'll shoot them, too."

They turn to walk away, but I step forward, momentarily seized by a gratefulness I may regret later. Clamping my hand on Fierce's shoulder, I level my gaze on the man. "Thank you again. You likely saved two lives today. Ji-su and I weren't prepared for those sons-of-bitches."

"Ji-su?" Fierce says, turning and eyeing me curiously.

"Ji-su Park," I add.

"Nice to meet you. Hopefully, see you soon at the house. Again, call first to make sure one of my overexuberant relatives doesn't accidentally shoot you. A la prochaine."

"A la prochaine," Ji-su replies, drawing surprised looks from me and Fierce.

The big man laughs. "She knows French. Now that's a keeper. She will get along well with my wife." Eyeing me again, his face tightens with a challenge. "Maybe next time, tell your brothers and father not to be such assholes if a few of our herd end up on your property."

And with that, he and the other Basque shepherds stalk off into the trees where their horses wait, mounting quickly and riding off.

***

THREE HOURS LATER, we sit in Ormsby Security's headquarters in Ophir City at a large conference table surrounded by hired guns. My head still spins at the chaos of the afternoon. Though we shot in self-defense and the name of justice, I have trouble processing the loss of life and our roles in it.

Fortunately, there's no better clean-up crew than Wolfe and his men, which knots my stomach, wondering what other clandestine missions and activities they're involved in. It's on a need-to-know basis, and until today, I never really needed to know.

Ji-su spends hours relaying information and evidence she has on Senator Moreau and his ties to organized crime in the state. Wolfe crosses his thick, corded arms over his barrel chest, letting the woman's words and explanations wash over him.

"This is far from an exhaustive list," she finishes, biting her thick bottom lip. "But you get the idea."

"If you have even half of what you're telling me corroborated on those hard drives, then the good senator's about to swap places with Holden in prison. And we're going to bring this statewide corruption crashing down for good." My giant professional wrestling-looking brother with a perpetual crew cut and hazel eyes chuckles.

"I have it all, and now, so do you."

"About fucking time for Holden," I add, wanting to believe it. But I'll have to see it. After all, we've spent ten long years hoping for my brother's freedom.

Wolfe adds, "Please accept my condolences for your sister, Ae-cha. I can't imagine the pain you've experienced."

Ji nods sadly.

As they continue conversing, Ji-su is a wealth of knowledge. She cites countless documents from memory, even quoting the most damning passages. She discusses seemingly unrelated pieces of evidence captured on the drives, her mind a catalog, her memory photogenic, her words persuasive and precise.

She explains how it all pieces together, revealing a massive, incriminating picture of corruption so all-encompassing that we sit in silence. By the end, the picture that emerges is both overwhelming and undeniable, one that makes my stomach roil at the level of sophistication, organization, and moral decay it involves.

Wolfe shakes his head, leaning back in his chair, face straining to comprehend everything she testifies to. "This is unbelievable. The linkages Ae-cha's evidence and your research and legal work have highlighted between the senator's office and the cartels and church are mindboggling. They did this with such precision, with such organization. It's tough to fully grasp. And all to fuel drug and human trafficking in the region."

"It's a million if not a billion-dollar operation," she emphasizes. "Ae-cha collected so much working at the senator's office. She knew it was bad ... unbelievably bad. But I don't think she ever fully grasped where it was all leading or how it would tie things together. I've spent six months assembling the pieces of the puzzle, always on the run. But I could spend six years and still not be done. That's why I can't rest until this is finished. My only question is why the senator's office did such a poor job of covering this up in the first place. It's like they didn't even try."

"My guess," Wolfe says, face somber. "Is they assumed they'd never get caught. That nobody would take the time to figure it out. Or have the guts to go up against them. They didn't factor in heroes like you and your sister."

Ji-su nods, and I squeeze her hand beneath the table, so proud of her my chest aches. The woman's brilliant, gorgeous, sexy as fuck. I don't know what she's doing with me, but I'm going to enjoy every moment of our time together, showing her through every gesture, every action, all my words, and my life, that she's my everything. "They may not have factored her in, but they sure knew how to take her out. And they came close to getting me more than once, too."

"I'm sorry for all you've experienced, Ms. Park. But I'd like you to consider joining my team. Between your para-legal and research skills, the evidence you've already acquired, your expertise when it comes to the evidence your sister collected and you have continued collecting and organizing, and your understanding of the enemy, you would make a highly valuable member of our team. We can discuss pay and other details later. But promise me you'll at least think about it. We've got grunts for days on this team ... willing to get in the trenches and face down bullets. But we could use the cerebral and legal edges you can provide."

She nods, pressing her lips tightly together, face somber. "And I'm willing to face down bullets, too, if need be."

Anger surges inside me. "No way," I but into the conversation. "Over my dead body are you putting Ji in danger again. She needs protection, safety, anonymity. Not being in the thick of every dangerous operation you undertake."

"She needs to rebuild her life," Wolfe says, folding his hands atop the table and looking around at the assembled crew. "Every man seated here has had to rebuild his life in one way or another. Whether we're talking about Rutger and revamping his career after years being a sniper, McGregor and his battle with alcoholism, or Farzad and securing his legal refugee status from Afghanistan stateside. *This* is a team built from people who have risen from the ashes. We can help you do that, too, Ji-su."

I shake my head. "Nuh-uh. Not if it's going to involve her risking her life."

Ji smiles at me, intertwining her fingers with mine beneath the table. "We can talk about this more later, Lancelot—"

"Lancelot?" Wolfe and his Ranger buddies interrupt, faces incredulous. A howl rushes through the facility until they're running the backs of their hands over their eyes. The only one who doesn't laugh is Farzad, the reference clearly lost on him.

"What? It's one of my nicknames for him," Ji says, which doesn't help anything.

"Lancelot," McGregor repeats, doubling over with

laughter. "Sorry, ma'am, but he's no knight in shining armor."

"He is to me," she says, crossing her arms defiantly over her chest. I pull her into my arms, knowing full well there's nothing she can say to make my brother and his friends quit laughing.

"I know y'all got weird names with your women, too," I counter, shaking my head. "Honey boo boo, shit like that." Though I'm no fan of the teasing, I'm too blessed by the fact I have a woman to let it bother me. Besides, teasing is what these guys do.

Clearing my throat, I add, "I call Ji Hummingbird. You guys got a problem with that?"

They say nothing, so I point out their hypocrisy. "You have no problem with Hummingbird? But Lancelot's a no-go?"

"Hummingbird suits her," they all agree, faces earnest. "But Lancelot?" They guffaw some more. These fucking guys.

"What were you saying again, Ji?" I ask, trying to get our conversation back on track.

"Just that I want to consider this offer."

I shake my head. "But you already got enough revenge today, Ji. Let the past go."

"No," she answers, flashing eyes meeting mine. "What I got today was a taste of justice. But to avenge Ae-cha's death and to truly honor her memory and sacrifice, I have to follow the evidence all the way to Senator Moreau. Working with your brother could make this happen."

Wolfe nods emphatically.

Her words make my stomach knot. I furrow my forehead, desperate to protect her from the ugliness of the world.

Wolfe clears his throat. "You're right. We can help with that, Ji. That's precisely what we do and have been doing for a couple of years. Ae-cha's and your evidence is quite frankly the spark we've been looking for to set this whole state on fire. You deserve to help us do that."

I glare at my brother, tugging at the collar of my button-down shirt.

"With your help, of course," he adds, nodding at me.

Ji-su squeezes my hand. "I need to do this, Bowie. As a way to carve out a safe place for myself, for us to be together in Rough & Ready. I can't stay in hiding my whole life," she says resolutely. "And I can't let those who hurt my sister go unpunished. Not only because I need vengeance, but even more than that, I need to keep others from getting hurt, too."

I know she speaks the truth. I get it. But I need to protect and shield her more than I need to live. It's completely irrational. Yet, it's a truth I can't deny.

I concede quietly, "I know. I just want you to be safe."

She nods, eyes filled with tenderness. "They won't stop unless we stop them, Bowie. But we need to do this together, with the rest of your family."

"They brought the fight to our turf the moment they kidnapped Roxy," Wolfe reminds. "Now, together, we finish this."

Ji looks at me, puzzled.

I explain, "Roxy is another of our sisters-in-law, Hawk's woman. She was abducted a little over a year ago while driving home on the Three Nations Reservation after dark. Wolfe, Hawk, and the Ranger team rescued her and countless other human trafficking victims that night."

It was the first time we learned about the evil hiding beneath the surface of our idyllic mountain home. The wickedness propagated by a religious cult and aided by cartels. The abomination that reaches to the steps of the Senate, a scandal not even Ae-cha's murder could hide.

But the axe we have to grind with members of the House of the Seven Prophets, with Senator Moreau and his goons, goes far deeper than that. I grind out between clenched teeth. "The fight started long before that, Bro ... when they abused Axel. When they destroyed Holden's life. When they fucked up Zane and Birdie's future. *This* retribution has been a long, long time coming."

Wolfe adds, "Bowie, this bears repeating. My offer still stands for you to nix the fugitive recovery schtick for something less nomadic and more relationship-friendly. You and Ji would both be heartily welcomed to the team."

Rutger chimes in, "Yeah, that fugitive recovery bullshit's a helluva lot of work. And it's always taking you away from home. Bijou put her foot down hard. She can't stand having me gone all the time."

Bijou's the Creole nightclub singer he married a while back. Before moving to Rough & Ready Country, she had a regular gig in Nashville and New Orleans. Her voice is dark and silky like milk chocolate, something foremost in my mind because she performed in Paige and Ridge's wedding yesterday. It feels like lifetimes ago. One of these days, I need to take Ji-su to a Bijou show. After the dust clears a little.

Not only would I wager she'll love the performance, but like Fierce's woman Felicity, I could see Ji being friends with Bijou. She could fit in with this town, build a strong network of people who adore her. Create a family with me. Be embraced by my foster brothers and their women.

A familiar ache settles in my heart ... if only Holden could be here to enjoy this with us and Dee. But maybe some of the incriminating evidence Ae-cha collected against Senator Moreau can help him in the end. My brother needs to come home. I won't stop until I see that day, no matter what it takes.

My hummingbird eyes me hopefully, clearly intrigued by the idea of us both working for Wolfe. "I promise I'll consider the offer more seriously," I answer begrudgingly, knowing I might as well accept because I sure as hell can't fathom spending time away from Ji now that we're together. Funny how love works, changing priorities, rewriting habits, and needs on every level.

Ormsby Security. It could be a good move. The whole reason Wolfe started his business was to stay closer to his then-estranged wife, Izzie, and their two children, after years of working overseas as a Ranger and then a military contractor. It did the trick, reuniting him and Izzie and providing Wolfe with the stability to be the family man he always longed to be.

I should learn from his lessons and get ready now for the many babies Ji wants to have. The thought of a family, even as a distant hope, fills my heart with joy. I never thought I would feel this blessed, and it's all because of the woman who made a stand for me, even before I knew she existed.

The woman I'd burn down the fucking world for and break heads to protect. She makes me feral. She makes me violent. She makes me passionate in the most soul-stirring, love-filled ways, completely devoted to her and willing to do anything to make her feel safe, secure, and loved.

Wolfe crosses his arms over his barrel chest. "Revenge is one thing. Believe me, I've been there, too. But making a stand for what's right, carving out a safe place in your world, a zone of no retreat. That's what you did today, Ms.

Park. You started taking back your life, actively building and defending it instead of running and hiding."

Ji-su raises her chin defiantly, nodding. "No more running. No more hiding. No more playing dead."

I lean in, kissing her perfectly sculpted pink lips and wrapping my arm around her. "Instead, we hold our ground here together as a family, carving our life out of this land and creating a future. One that honors your sister's memory and sacrifice and helps us restore my brother Holden's freedom and honor."

"As a family. Together forever," she says tenderly, snuggling her head against my chest.

BONUS SCENE
JI-SU

ONE MONTH LATER

After walking the horses to cool them down and offering water and treats, Bowie helps me remove my saddle and bridle.

Then, he follows suit, showing me the basics for cleaning them.

"This looked a lot easier on *Yellowstone*," I mutter.

The gorgeous Black cowboy laughs. "That's because they never show basic shit like this on those Wild West television programs. It's all shootouts, cattle rustling, bar fights, and kissing. The dramatic stuff. Not real ranch life, which is nothing like what Hollywood depicts."

"Nope, they make it romantic and fantastical. Although I beg to differ about real ranch life being nothing like the movies and shows. After all, we do a lot of kissing."

"Not nearly enough," Bowie says unrepentantly, his gaze a slow simmer.

"Not nearly," I agree, shivers of longing running up and

down my spine. This is how every day goes with my cowboy—scintillating, seductive, temptation embodied.

"Not sure I can fit that bill, though," he murmurs, clenching his jaw and drawing my attention away from filthy thoughts back to our conversation.

"Fit what bill?" I scrunch my face.

"Of being romantic and fantastical," he clarifies, licking his lips sensually.

Yearning hums through me, centering in my lower core.

"I don't even know what you mean," I counter. "How can you talk like that when you're the cowboy who spoils me rotten?"

Bowie frowns. "And makes you clean horse sweat off leather."

"Who lets me clean horse sweat off leather," I correct, raising my chin determinedly. "So, I can call myself a cowgirl."

"The first time you rode this cowboy, you earned that honor, Hummingbird," he says, stepping closer.

I ignore his last comment and the shrinking distance between our flesh, body already aching and hot, cheeks glowing. "The same cowboy who won't even let me open my own door or a bottle of wine. Who insists on carrying me everywhere—"

"You feel good in my arms," he confesses. "Like I never want to let you go."

"And who likes keeping me very, very satisfied..." My pulse quickens as I watch his pupils dilate. He swallows loudly, his Adam's apple bobbing in his throat as he moves closer, inching towards me, anticipation building.

"You keep talking like that, Ji, and we won't get any of our stable chores done," he warns, nostrils flaring and eyes settling on my mouth.

"Oops," I say, not a hint of regret in my sultry voice.

Pulling me into his iron-hard grip, he asks, "You mean, making up for lost time?"

I nod, licking my lips. "If Belle and Fortune will be okay for a few minutes?" Belle's the dainty brown American Quarter Horse I rode, and Fortune, the gray dappled gelding Bowie prefers.

"More like a few hours." He growls. My body quakes at the masculine sound. "They'll be fine."

Thank God, because I don't think I can wait much longer to be claimed by my wild cowboy mountain man.

Tugging me closer, his voice softens. "I don't rightly know how I ever lived without you."

"Neither do I," I second with a naughty smile. "ALL of you."

"Mmm." He groans, pressing his hips firmly against my core so that his long shaft digs into my stomach.

"You know, I can think of much better places for that."

"Oh, yeah?" he pants, cheeks flushing. Grabbing me around the waist, he hauls me into his arms. My legs hungrily wrap around his waist and my arms around his neck.

"But what about the horses?" I tease, lips a hair's breadth from his. Electricity shuttles between us, searing and heavy. My pussy throbs, so close to his cock. I curse the fabric separating us. "Don't we need to check them for injuries and then wash and dry them?"

He nods, pride washing over his face. "There you go, Hummingbird. You already sound like a regular horse-woman." Bowie captures my mouth, claiming me ferociously.

"We should ... probably rub ... them down ... with liniment, too," I rasp between hungry kisses, gasping for air and speaking only when we reluctantly pull apart. "After all, we rode them hard today."

His twinkling eyes catch mine as another grin captures his face. "Not as hard as I'm going to ride you, Cowgirl."

I moan, pussy throbbing and head spinning.

His big, work-hardened hand slides between our bodies, fingers grinding over the crotch of my Wranglers. I strain towards him, desperate for friction.

"What do you have in mind, Lancelot?"

He chuckles at the silly nickname, cocking his head to the side so that our cowboy hat brims don't collide. Capturing my mouth, his tongue fervently mates with mine as my fast-paced whimpers and his chest-rumbling moans pepper the air.

"Well, the first time I met you, I handcuffed you. I still regret not doing more with you tied up."

"More? Like what?" I question breathlessly.

His eyes dart around the stable. "Instead of telling you, how about I show you?" he asks, voice dark and thick like audible molasses.

"And how do you plan on doing that?"

"I'm going to tie you up, and then I'm going to have my way with you. Every lovely, fucking, perfect inch of you."

"But I'm all sweaty from riding," I protest.

He furrows his brows. "You really think I'm going to let a little sweat get in the way? You don't know me very well then, Hummingbird."

"I knew you'd say that," I admit, playfully tipping his cowboy hat. He claims my mouth again, and my body melts like butter in a frying pan. My gray Stetson falls to the ground with a soft thud, and I couldn't care less.

Bowie lets me down slowly, reluctantly, the heat between our bodies heightened by my nipples dragging down his chest. As soon as my feet hit the stable floor, I bend to grab my hat and dash toward the exit, calling over my shoulder. "But first you have to catch me."

As if reading my mind, he grabs a nearby rope, sauntering in my direction. Whoosh! A rope drops over my waist, pinning my arms. An expert tug gently stops me, drawing me back to him. Pulling the lasso slowly toward him, my eyes meet his as I begrudgingly comply, inching in his direction. Our gazes lock, heat and anticipation steaming and smoking between them.

"Get over here, and take your man like a good girl."

My heart flutters in my chest, my cheeks burning. "Yes, Cowboy. Make me yours."

"You already are mine ... *forever*," he drawls low and dangerous as the rope vanishes between us.

LOVE AND REDEMPTION

AN EX-CON COWBOY
MOUNTAIN MAN / CURVY GIRL
SECOND CHANCE ROMANCE

TRIGGER WARNING

This book contains content/themes that may not be suitable for all readers, including discussion of human trafficking, physical violence, a deadly street fight, and gun violence.

Please read at your own discretion.

Holden steps off the bus, rough, focused, a force of nature caged too long.

He didn't want me to pick him up on the day of his release. Didn't want a big family party or show of solidarity. Didn't want a fuss, small-town hubbub.

A part of me gets it. Another part of me hears the echo of loss already written ... the inevitability of him leaving before he's even arrived.

Whatever his intent, silence and suspicion greet him.

He's not the man I remember. A dangerousness coils beneath his skin now, a weight in his every step, as if prison tattooed itself onto more than his flesh.

A decade ago, he walked with light ease ... still robust, still powerful. Now, each step feels like a risk, a battle against invisible chains.

I've read about it: post-incarceration syndrome. PICS, the experts call it. Symptoms neatly listed on a screen. But no article prepares you for the sight of it etched into someone you love. The rigidity, the wariness, the steps too heavy for a free man.

Am I surprised that out of everyone in this town—friends, family, foster brothers—Holden beelines straight for The Human Being and me, standing in front of it?

No. But nothing prepares me for the cold collision of reality and fantasy.

"Lila," he says, eyes narrowing, the corners of his mouth turning up.

Lila and lover boy. A verbal time capsule underscoring the years, the distance, the life that separates us.

I reach up, wrapping my arms around the mountain of a man. He drops his bag and freezes, as though he doesn't know what to do with his hands, his body. Hesitation keeps him stiff, tight.

It's been so long. *Maybe too long.*

My stomach knots.

"God," he whispers, finally melting around me, pulling me into his arms. "Need you," he murmurs, voice ragged, restraint dissolving, even though we're standing on Main Street.

But he doesn't smell like Holden. He smells like the penitentiary I visited for ten years. Like body searches and gruff guards, lack of privacy and the kind of yearning that gnaws people down to shadows.

He doesn't *feel* like Holden. He feels like a drowning man, clinging to anything to stay afloat.

"You should've let me pick you up." I straighten too quickly, brushing imaginary dust from my dress, trying to look natural in my stilted motions. Anger grips me. Not wild, passionate anger that blows arguments wide open and makes healing words possible, but the simmering kind that infects everything it touches.

His refusal for a ride, a celebration ... it feels like rejection. God help me if ten years of loyalty prove me the fool. I remind myself that there are no guarantees, only long-expired promises. Like the headlights of my father's truck when he drove away for the last time, abandoning a home, a family.

Instead of desperation, panic, what overwhelms me is need. Inky, devouring, infinite.

Passersby stop. Suspicious eyes glance our way. Reflected in the café's front window, we're locked together. My café. He's never seen this place. Never saw me become the woman worthy of owning it.

He presses a kiss to my temple, like he always used to.

Instead of melting into him, I step back awkwardly, throat tight and eyes stinging, wrecked, dazed.

He frowns. Disappointment flickering. But I can't pretend. Something warns me to protect the autonomy I've fought so hard for. To protect the me I was forced to become without him.

"Can't tell you how good it is to see you. My only anchor in a storm."

I lick my lips, pressing them together. His eyes tick down to my mouth. He knows what he wants. I want it, too. But reality feels different than any dream.

"How was your bus trip?" I ask, heart pounding, anger seething at the edges.

Anger at what? The lost years? The impossible role I'm supposed to play? Or maybe anger at him, for carrying a guarded energy he can't deny, and I can't ignore.

"Fine. Still mad I didn't let you pick me up?"

I bite my lip, hands knotting in front of me. "Not mad. You need to do what feels right. Whatever that may be."

My words come out colder than I intend. His eyes go wary.

"You waited ten years for me, Lila. Visited every chance

you could. Kept my heart beating, though I begged you to let me go." His brows furrow. "Can't ask any more from you."

His coldness mirrors mine; it stings. So does the sudden collision of timelines, proof that we are wildly out of sync.

"You look ... harder," I whisper, trying to be the woman he needs. "Time behind bars will do that, I guess."

Once, I could make excuses. Tell myself it was the stark prison lighting, the harsh uniform, the constraints of trauma, the new tattoos. Now, I can no longer ignore the differences. They feel like an unbridgeable gulf stretching between us. If I don't cross, I'll die. If I do, I'll lose myself ... everything I've worked so hard for.

And isn't that another kind of death?

He nods, simmering eyes full of unspoken things. Trauma. Secrets. The other life he lived.

Locals slow on the sidewalk. Snatches of conversation drift like poison arrows:

"Got out on probation."

"Dangerous."

"Special treatment ... sheriff's brother."

Holden's shoulders droop. The rebel of my youth, the boy who thumbed his nose at public opinion, looks beaten.

As a teen, I'd been bowled over by that rebellion and the man behind it. Now, that other time, that other place feels like a foreign country.

"It was self-defense," I snap at the gawkers. "Don't twist it."

My voice is caustic, my café customers glaring with pity, as though I'm delusional.

Holden shifts his weight, adjusts his old Stetson. His too-tight, tattered clothes echo the past. Memories swarm.

"Can't blame them for thinking the worst," he replies

drily, nodding toward the bus stop plastered with campaign posters of Moreau's smug face. "Senator now, though always a bastard. His son's grave in the ground, me rotting in a cell, and somehow he came out cleaner than ever."

"Yep," I whisper, resigned.

Anger simmers behind his eyes.

I press my fingers to my temple, aching for him to let go of the past ... break through the invisible wall. Claim me with a kiss, a demanding, desperate kiss.

Instead, he leans back on his heels. "Not sure how long I'll stay. Don't want to cause trouble. Especially for you."

Maybe he needs reassurance. But all I see is abandonment. Inevitability. The people I love most always leave.

I want to break into tears. Ugly cry. Beg him to stay. But I learned long ago, that never works.

Instead, I speak truth in a stilted voice, pulsing with unsatisfied yearning. "If you're trying to run ... you won't escape. Not from this. *Not from me.*"

He strips the hat off, dragging fingers through mahogany hair. "Was hoping you'd want me to stay."

"How could you ever question that?" I blurt, eyes on his.

A thin smile touches his lips. "There's that passion I'm looking for."

But his voice cracks, as if it's already slipping from his grasp.

"Still have them?" he asks.

"What?"

"My letters."

The plea in his tone undoes me. "Every one."

The sweet ones that dreamed of cabins and babies. The bone-tired ones, full of despair. The hopeless ones begging me to let him go.

His face darkens. He doesn't know what to do. Neither do I. So I fall back on habit. The café owner.

"Come inside for a drink."

"Yep," he croaks uneasily.

I wait for the old ritual. For him to open the door. He hesitates, puzzled, frozen. Finally, awkwardly, he leans forward, "Let me get that."

Inside, the café bustles—voices, clatter, lines. Everything designed to feel like home. For him, it's too much.

His chest heaves, eyes darting. Overwhelm etched in his face.

Conversations hush. All eyes rise to him. His name has lived too long in this town's gossip.

"What can I get you?" I ask.

He squints at the menu. "Thought you sold coffee, Lila. What's all this?"

There it is again. *Lila.* The girl I'm not anymore.

"Large coffee with cream," he says.

"A grande or venti?" Suzy, the barista asks, working hard not to stare. But her pixie-cut black hair, glittery purple eye shadow, and sparkling nose piercing all hum with salacious curiosity ... like everything and everyone in this room.

"The biggest, and ..." He pauses, eyes me with a wink. Then, a lopsided grin. Charm from another lifetime. "A caramel latte for your boss."

My chest aches. Once, that would have put an ear-to-ear grin on my face. Now it feels like he's reaching for the wrong version of me.

"Actually, I don't drink those anymore. Black coffee's fine."

My soft-spoken words land like a blow to the jaw. Holden steps back, confusion brewing. Suzy nods, sliding cups across. He fumbles with his wallet, jaw tense, time slamming into him.

"Come on," I urge, hand half-reaching before I stop.

He shakes his head. "I know you own this place, but I still want to pay. Care for you."

"It's on the house."

His face flushes. He slaps down a twenty. "It's necessary. I need to do something for you."

The bill sits there between us, stark and green, a paper wall I don't know how to cross. Not yet.

CHAPTER
TWO
HOLDEN

Lila's office. Everything about it screams *her*.

Splashy psychedelic posters. Framed vinyl—The Beatles, Led Zeppelin, Pink Floyd, Bowie, My Bloody Valentine, Depeche Mode.

I tap the glass over The Cure's *Disintegration*. Gave her that one. My angsty little love letter in album form. Same way I scrawled letters so jagged I wondered if she could even read half the words.

"My favorite," she says, dropping into the chair behind her cluttered desk. Notes everywhere, sketches, flyers, designs. Always planning. Always moving forward.

She's done well. Hell, better than I imagined. Meanwhile, I'm Rip Van Winkle, waking up after a hundred years, world forever changed. Bitterness seeps into the cracks of my bones.

I drink her in. Tension crackles like the second before a kiss, except now there's an ocean between us. The desk, her posture, her eyes.

My girl has outgrown me.

A storm of words clogs my throat. I should ask, talk,

bridge the gap. But all that re-entry crap I read rattles in my skull—pitfalls, mistakes, warnings. None of it helps. None of it stops this from unraveling.

Once, we sparked like live wires. Desire, need, fire. Now it's a chokehold. I can't breathe. Can't fix it. Hell, can't remember the last thing I fixed.

"The Cure. Lost count how many nights I lay there listening and thinking about you," I mutter, easing into the chair across from her.

Sadness flickers in her eyes. "Same." Soft. Wistful. Remembering.

"You've done good for yourself," I rasp. The words crack. Break me in half. She's too good for me now. Too good for the wreckage I drag behind me.

Scarlet hair, emerald eyes. The girl who ruined me first glance.

How the fuck do I let her go?

Her tie-dyed dress drapes to the floor, Victorian boots peeking out. Lace, frills, layers of necklaces glinting. Rings on every finger—*except the one that should still carry mine.*

Dammit.

Her eyes slice through me, peel me open. And then I see it. A thin silver chain at her throat. My ring, hanging fragile and defiant.

"You kept it," I rasp, eyes burning.

Her hand lifts, brushing the ring like instinct. Relief and grief twist in me, tearing me in half. I should make a clean break. Walk. But I need to crawl back inside her, back into what we were.

"I've worn it every day since you went away," she whispers.

"Saw it at visits." I swallow. "But you wore it on your finger ..."

"When I visited, yes. At work, it gets in the way."

The words land heavy. Just like me—gets in the way.

"You've got a good life here. No thanks to me."

"Why would you say it like that?" Anger rises sharp in her voice. Always did have a fire under the sweetness.

I cross my arms. Shrug like it doesn't gut me.

"Have you contacted your brothers or Wyatt yet? To let them know you're here?"

A fair question. Still cuts to the bone. My eyes narrow.

"You *are* going to see them, right?"

"How can you ask that?" My voice grinds low. I stare at the walnut desk like it matters more than the truth eating me alive. The world's too damn loud, too damn bright. I'd take my cell back over this.

"You wrote me letters for years. About that rift. Said it was your biggest regret, the one thing you had to fix—"

"Had to come here first," I cut in. It sounds weak even to me. But I needed her. Need her still.

"I can give you a ride to the ranch."

I shake my head. "Ridge and Paige are coming."

She nods, a storm of relief and disappointment in one small gesture.

"Dinner tonight?" I try, flashing the grin that used to wreck her. My panty-dropper.

Her pupils flare. Hunger flickers there, quick as lightning. Her hand trembles against the desk before she stills it. She may be angry. May not want me in her heart. But her body remembers.

"Won't your family want you tonight?"

"*You're* my family."

Her eyes snap to mine. My words hit.

"I'm sorry, Holden. I really am. But I have other plans tonight."

My chest burns. "That's what I get for not letting you pick me up." I try to joke, but it comes out all wrong.

She shakes her head. "It's not like that. I have a standing obligation—"

"On the first night your man's out of prison?" The words bite out sharper than I mean.

Her face hardens. She's not the girl I left behind. "I offered to throw you a party. Your family wanted it. Here. Or at the Silver Fork. But you insisted no fuss."

"Not necessary."

Her eyes flash. "Immediate family first. That's what you always wrote about. Healing things with Wyatt and your brothers. I shouldn't be there for that."

I want to tell her she's wrong. That I can't face any of it without her. But the words choke out. Don't want to sound weak.

"Maybe you're right," I mutter. Bitter.

"It seems like you already have your mind made up. Why?"

"How?"

"You stood outside talking about leaving. Now you sound like you might not even see your family."

"You've got it wrong."

"Do I? Or am I hearing what I'm afraid of?"

My eyes pin her. Savage. Trying. "I want you, Lila. Want what we lost."

Her eyes slide away. "I want it, too. But it's the past."

I shove my Stetson on, rising. "I never chose prison. Never chose to leave."

"I didn't mean—"

A knock at the door cuts her off. "Ridge and Paige are here," someone calls.

"Come in," she answers, cool as a queen.

357

Ridge barrels in, bear hugs me so hard my ribs creak. "Motherfucker." He hauls me clean off my feet. "How's it feel to be on the other side?"

Scary. Disjointed. Out of sync. I tell him what he wants to hear. "Good to be back."

"Damn right." Ridge grins, slapping my back. "Flynn and Bowie are itching to see you. Axel and Rock, too."

I wince. Never was a good influence on them.

Paige and Lila cling to each other.

"Christian? Logan?" I ask.

Ridge shrugs. "They'll come around."

"And Dad?" The word tears my throat raw.

"You two need to talk."

"Understatement of the year."

"He's older now. Weaker. Take it easy with him."

"Jerry. Want to see Jerry, too."

Delilah's face softens, beauty gutting me.

Ridge nods.

"And meet Bowie's girl, Ji-su. Can't believe that bachelor ever settled down. That any of you did."

Ridge glances at Paige, warmth in his eyes.

"Ji-su and Bowie really are perfect," she says. "Though it's hard, her still living in Ae-cha's shadow. After everything..."

I already know the story. Bowie filled me in. Ae-cha Park. Murdered for what she uncovered in Moreau's re-election office. Staged as a suicide. Only Ji-su knew the truth, and she has the evidence. Files tying him to cartels, cults, trafficking. Maybe his son, Gregory, too. Too ugly to fit in any obituary.

"Dee, you coming?" Ridge asks. Paige squeezes her hand.

"Not for this," the redhead says. "You need some time with Wyatt. Just you."

Her steady tone cuts me to the quick.

She adds, "And the work of a café owner is never done. You'll see me ... another time."

"But it's Holden's first day," Ridge protests.

"I promise I won't stay too far away," she says firmly. Her eyes lock on mine. Emerald fire. "You said it yourself— no fuss. Nothing special."

CHAPTER
THREE
DELILAH

I close the door behind Holden, Paige, and Ridge, leaning against the frame and breathing hard. My palm presses to my chest, as though I could steady the frantic thud of my heart.

The backs of my eyes sting as fantasy collides with awkward reality. His homecoming, imagined a thousand times, reduced to brittle words and wary looks.

I was as much to blame as him. We circled each other like strangers, sharp words thinly veiling wounds we weren't ready to show. Distance when every cell in my body longed to close it.

But his words still echo, a wall between us. *Not sure how long I'll stay. Don't want to cause trouble.*

That's the dark side of Holden—the side I once romanticized and can't excuse anymore. He could spend the rest of his life running, but he'll never outrun himself. Never find redemption.

A soft knock stirs me from my thoughts. Familiar. Gentle. Sophia.

I take a deep, cleansing breath, smoothing my dress like armor. "One second," I call, steeling my voice.

She beams up at me when I open the door, unruly curls spilling like ink around her heart-shaped, mocha face. Those dark eyes are far too knowing for sixteen. She's endured a hell I can barely fathom, yet here she stands, curious, resilient, mine to mentor if not to save.

"Hey, Pipsqueak. Aren't you a little early for our meeting?" I arch a brow.

She shrugs, breezing past me, beelining for the Boston fern by my desk. "You told me to hang out more. Soak up the entrepreneur life. Hope that's okay?" She sticks a finger into the dirt, grabs the slender waterer, and gives it a careful drink.

"Thank you," I say softly. She knows better than anyone how I love surrounding myself with plants, even if I can't keep them alive.

"Sure thing." She plops onto the chair Holden just left, her brow furrowing, her bottom lip caught between her teeth.

"Did you hear about the new lost media that was just found?" she asks, one of her favorite obsessions ... along with computers. But I guess that's all kids these days.

I shake my head.

"The *Backyardigans* pilot. People have spent years hunting it down."

And she's spent months talking about it, though it still goes over my head. "Very cool."

"Want to watch it together later?"

"Of course," I say, eyeing her. "What else is going on?"

Sophia shrugs. I take the chair next to her instead of retreating behind my desk, like a coward, as I did earlier with Holden.

She leans closer, conspiratorial. "You won't believe who my uncle and I saw leaving the café when we got here."

I brace myself, lips pressed together.

"Holden Boone," she whispers. "Uncle Jermaine said he went to school with him. And he said he's a murderer. Killed Senator Moreau's son."

My spine stiffens. "Your uncle doesn't have it quite right."

"He said Holden went to prison for years. That he's surprised Moreau didn't have him killed behind bars ..."

A chill snakes through me. Her uncle may be wrong about many things, but not about Moreau's hunger for vengeance. I've wondered countless times how far the senator would go. Even now, as scandal dogs him, he seems harder to kill than the truth itself.

Sophia presses on. "He said Holden should've never been let free. That the town isn't safe with him back."

"Your uncle's wrong," I counter, keeping my tone steady though heat prickles beneath my skin. My love for Holden has been broken, battered, questioned. But I will always defend him.

Her lips turn down.

"You'll learn," I say gently, "that more than one thing can be true at the same time. Yes, Holden killed a man. But it's also true that Holden was innocent."

Her jaw drops. "How can both be true?"

I pause, tongue heavy. "Holden was jumped by a group of men who beat him badly. He fought back. If he hadn't, he wouldn't be alive. One of them passed away from his injuries."

"So ... he defended himself, and someone died?"

"Yes. He fought to survive. That doesn't make him a murderer."

Her voice trembles. "So, like Holden was being bullied?"

"In a way." My heart twists with the unspoken truth. That he shouldn't have been there at all that night.

"Then is he dangerous? Like my uncle said?"

I shake my head. Holden has changed in every imaginable way, but dangerous to this town? Never. "The better word is *misunderstood*."

She rolls it around like it's foreign. "Misunderstood ..." She stares at her scuffed Vans. Suddenly, her gaze sharpens. "And how do you know so much about him? Did you go to school with him, too?"

"On and off. But he's older. Three years." I add gently, "If I remember right, Jermaine was the same year as Holden."

"The way you talk about him ... even how you say his name," she whispers. "It's different."

Heat creeps up my neck. I swallow. "Because Holden and I were in a relationship when everything happened." And in some ways, we never stopped being in one, though defining it is well past my current limit.

Her eyes widen. "Like boyfriend and girlfriend?"

I nod.

"But ... he has neck tattoos," she hisses, gesturing to her throat.

"Prison changes a person," I answer softly.

Her eyes grow misty. "You must've been so sad when they took him away."

Sad. Shattered. Grief-stricken. The memory wells in me like a wound that never closed. "My life changed that day. But not as much as his."

She studies me, thoughtful. "And how long has he been back?"

"This is his first day in Hollister."

Her mouth falls open. "And you're spending your time with me?" She looks torn between honored and horrified.

"Of course, I am. I wouldn't miss our sessions for the world."

She tilts her head back. "No offense, but shouldn't you be celebrating? Or ... on a date?"

Her voice holds a lighter echo of Ridge's earlier reproach.

"He has family matters to sort through tonight," I answer, voice steadier than my heart. "There'll be plenty of time for us later."

Her eyes don't quite believe me.

I clear my throat. "So, how's school?"

"Not great."

"Amy again?"

Her eyes gloss, and she sniffs.

Amy. The girl she always talks about. Though I can't sort out whether she's a bully or a bestie.

"Is she being mean to you again?"

She scrunches her face.

"Have you told a teacher? The counselor?"

She shakes her head. "So Amy thinks I'm a traitor on top of everything? No way."

I move closer, brushing her hair behind her ear. She looks seconds away from shattering.

"You deserve to feel safe at school. To be able to learn without cruelty and name-calling—"

She wipes her nose with the back of her hand. "It's not like that."

I hand her a tissue. She fiddles with it, eyes down.

"Then, what is it?"

"Nice. Mean. Her mood changes daily. Never know what to expect ... if she loves or hates me."

My heart breaks. "A fair-weather friend? That's tough. You deserve better."

"I don't want better," she whispers.

My heart cracks, old feelings from high school rushing back. Misunderstood. Bullied. Awkward. I was all those things ... except with Holden.

"Have you told your uncle?"

"Nothing to tell." She shakes her head. "He wants me to keep my distance. Auntie Josephine, too. Besides, they're already doing so much for me. Don't want to add extra stress."

I soften my voice. "Do you remember what I told you last time we talked about your aunt and uncle?"

She murmurs, "That they're family. That they're blessed to have me. That they're people I can count on."

I nod. "Exactly. Trust isn't easy for you, I know. But living a good life means learning to trust the right people."

Her eyes sharpen again. "Trust like with Holden? Even when everyone says he's a bad man?"

The words gut me. Guilt flares hot. My cheeks burn.

"Trust is earned, Sophia. Not blindly given." I've had those same words said to me before. At her age. In the context of Holden.

She nods slowly. "Yeah."

"Would you like me to come to your school? Speak with the staff about Amy?"

"No!" Her face pinches. "I'd rather crawl under a desk and die."

I frown. "Okay, but if she doesn't straighten up, keeps bothering you ... I want to know about it."

She nods, cheeks darkening.

I smile. "Now, how about your schoolwork? Are you keeping up?"

"Yes, in English we're reading *Romeo and Juliet*. It's so dreamy."

"My favorite Shakespeare play," I admit. "Though the ending—"

"No spoilers!" she interrupts.

I laugh. "Fair enough. But maybe keep this." I nudge the Kleenex box toward her with mock ceremony.

Her eyes sparkle. "Wait. You and Holden are like Romeo and Juliet."

The smile slips from my lips. "It felt like that once—tragic, dramatic, larger than life. But real love ... *real love has to survive more than poetry.*"

She leans back, swoony. "Still sounds romantic to me."

I don't argue. Some truths she'll have to learn for herself.

CHAPTER
FOUR
HOLDEN

I don't know what hits harder ... how little Rough & Ready Ranch has changed, or how everything in my life's been rearranged while I was gone. All those corny lines—can't step in the same river twice, the past's a foreign country—slam true right in the gut.

Getting out of Ridge's truck, I feel like I've aged a century. Paige and my brother clutch hands, climb the porch like they own it.

Ridge keeps looking back, like he thinks I'll bolt. Maybe he feels the battle raging inside ... between claiming my former life and woman or leaving it all behind. Trying to outrun my past and save everyone here a world of hurt.

Lila's voice replays in my head. *If you're trying to run ... you won't escape. Not from this. Not from me.* My hope lives in those last three words.

What do you do when the place you want most is ten years too late and stacked with a thousand broken promises?

The screen still screeches as we step inside. I stand in the front room, frozen in time. How Ruby Jean left it. Wyatt never redecorated after her. Turned the home into a museum.

It hits me low in the chest, achy. I'd do that for Lila. Maybe already have. Only not a home but a heart. My heart, an altar to us—the us I don't know how to get back.

Old wood. Polished leather. Floorboards creak under my boots like a goddamn metronome. Four walls that once kept me in now shove memories at me.

"Holden!" Bowie and Flynn slam into me, bear hugs, almost knock the wind out. Axel hangs back, shakes my hand like a man who means it. Maksim's gruff, but hugs longer than I expect. Rock hoists me up like I'm light as a pup. Christian and Logan keep it proper. Handshakes, clipped nods.

Others crowd in, but my attention's already pulled to the far side of the room. A portrait of my foster mom.

Then, Zane appears with Wyatt. Older. Frailer. Less sure than I've ever seen him. Prison robs you of confidence, sense of self, future. *So does life.*

"My boy," Wyatt says, voice raw. He grabs my face like I'm made of something precious. "You've been through so much."

I want to crack. Instead, I hold it together, dam near bursting.

"Make yourself at home. You'll always be welcome here."

I pull back, careful. He's unsteady and steady at once. "Thanks, Dad." I grumble it out. "I'll take you up on that offer."

Half my brothers look ready to square up. The other half nod like that's the plan. If anyone's got something to say, say it now.

Zane offers his hand like a line in the sand. "Not sure about you staying here with Dad."

"And why not?" I snap.

Christian gestures toward the table. "Let's talk."

We sit. My palm slides over the table, and my memory punches—Ruby Jean smiling, big ladles of stew, rosemary in the air. Wyatt insists I sit beside him and takes my hand. Least I can do. He stuck by me when I was a hurricane.

"Plainspoken," Christian starts. Blond, cold, all badge and lecture. "Welcome home. Glad to have you back." His eyes warm despite the polished demeanor. "But you've put this family through enough. Promise us, man to man, you'll keep to parole. Stay straight."

He still thinks I'm the twenty-one-year-old delinquent who went away. I lean back. "Staying straight didn't save me ten years ago."

He nods, grim-faced, an edge behind his eyes.

Logan clears his throat. "The past is the past. But now, time to get off on the right foot. That means keeping your parole. Getting a job. Sorting things with Dee."

They don't get what's going on with Lila and me. Neither do I. But that line—"sorting things with Dee"—lights something warm and stupid in me. Hope flares.

"And find a place of your own."

Wyatt shakes his head. "Holden will always have a place here—"

Logan cuts in. "But he's not the same man. He's made powerful enemies. We need precautions ... *just in case.*"

Christian adds the obvious. "Moreau's circling. He never forgave what happened to his son. Add to it Ji-su and Paige digging into his ties and corruption and Wolfe and his crew dropping trafficking rings like flies. Safe to say Hollister has a target painted on its back. The senator'll do whatever it takes to salvage his career and reputation. You're a prime target." He eyes me for emphasis.

Paige's face is firm. "We've been connecting dots, and we won't stop."

Ji adds steely-voiced, "Ae-cha died for what she found. And we're going to get it in front of the world, one way or the other."

We all hear it. We all know the game now.

Wyatt's done speaking. His word holds. Silence falls, thick, impenetrable. *Some family get-together.*

Bowie slices through the tension. "Alright, enough lectures. What do you want to do first?"

"Already did it." I say it like I'm done talking.

Eyebrows lift. "See Lila," I tell them. Quiet, because anything louder makes me look less in control.

They prod. I shut down. Not ready. Not yet.

Wolfe, the Army Ranger in the family, advises, "Wine her. Dine her. Start fresh." He forgets I never asked.

And start fresh? Sounds like surrender. Like giving up on what I've spent a decade holding on to. But I don't argue. There isn't a soul at this table who gets what living ten years in a box teaches a man.

"So what's the plan?" Logan asks again. He never shuts up.

"Stay for a bit. Get back on my feet." Short. Honest.

Rock offers a roof. "I can set you up."

"Appreciate it. Need work first, though."

"Handouts aren't for him," Christian says, steady like he's training a wild horse.

I grit my teeth. Challenge him with my gaze.

"Time to man up. Solve your own problems," he declares.

I scowl.

Maksim jumps in. "Everyone needs help sometimes."

Rock agrees.

Axel's voice is steel. "He's our brother."

A hand on my shoulder feels like a shield ... *and an unexpected attack.* I burst to my feet, nearly losing it. Ready to fight.

Axel flinches, stepping back. "Sorry, bro," he says.

I need air. I need Lila more. "I should go."

Maybe leave the ranch. Maybe quit the state. I don't know.

They ignore my words.

"No handouts but help. *That's* what family does," Bowie says, cutting Christian down with a look.

The room goes silent. Except for the sound of soup spoons clanging against stoneware.

Wolfe throws it at me, softly. "Not with Dee tonight? Going there later?"

God, I want to say yes. To be there with her. Instead, I mutter, "She's busy." My throat tightens.

"Probably with her mentee, Sophia," Paige says. It hits like cold water.

"A mentee?" I grimace, the word sour.

She chose some kid over me? It curdles in my gut. The girl doesn't deserve my jealousy. But envy doesn't know reason.

Paige nods. "Dee's done fantastic work with her. Poor thing grew up in an abusive home, ran away, ended up with a pimp. She's been through hell. And she looks up to Dee like no one else. Idolizes her, really. Having someone steady to admire means everything."

Of course, she does. Who wouldn't? Dee gives her time, her energy, her whole damn heart to everyone but me.

It stings. I picture Lila laughing with that kid, open,

warm. I choke on it. If she can love a stranger like that, I'll make her remember how to love me.

Envy eats me alive, irony close behind. Generosity, kindness, care. Those traits are why I love that scarlet-haired beauty. And the only explanation for why she's stuck with a loser like me so long.

I run a hand over my face. "She saves everyone but me," I mutter. "Maybe I don't deserve saving."

That's the truth I keep in my pocket.

CHAPTER
FIVE
HOLDEN

"You're up early," Zane says, sauntering into the kitchen.

I sit at the long table, hands wrapped around a steaming mug of coffee with cream.

My eyes tick to the microwave digital clock. Five a.m. "Not early. In the clink, days started at three-thirty."

"That's right." Zane pours coffee, sits across from me. "Kitchen duty."

My head flashes red sun and skull. A throat tattoo. A shiv. Blood spilling while someone laughed.

Last night's dream. Today's baggage. I try to shake it off. Don't need that memory with my morning coffee.

"Whoa, what's that look for?"

"Nothing." I look away.

"Do I smell muffins?"

"Blueberry. Eggs, bacon, and potatoes, too. Help yourself."

Zane whistles. "Sounds like a feast."

I shrug. Ten years cooking for men who'd stab you over burnt toast will teach you a thing or two.

Zane clears his throat. "Wanted to apologize."

"For what?" My brothers don't do apologies. Not him, not any of them. Inside, apologies mean weakness. Weakness gets you killed.

"Not visiting you more often."

"Figured you had your hands full becoming a PBR World Champ. Made me proud as hell, by the way."

"Really?" His eyes dart to mine, surprise etched in his expression. "Some of those after parties ... Bro, you would've loved them."

"The drugs and booze, maybe. The women? No, thanks."

"Only ever had eyes for Dee." His face softens. "So, what's going on with you two?"

I shrug. "What I should've expected."

"She's been loyal to you for a decade. Far as I can tell."

Loyal? Maybe to the outside world. Maybe even to my brothers. But I've seen the cracks up close. Terrified there's nothing left when she looks at me now.

"Don't know if that's better or worse."

"What do you mean?"

"I ruined her life," I spit too fast. Passion rising. "She deserved better. Still does." She carried more than just me back then. I can't forgive myself for the way it hollowed her. Or for how I refused to confront it.

"Believe me, I get it. How do you think it feels being married to a war hero? Birdie's got scars from her time as a combat nurse and the medals to prove it. Tough to live up to that."

"Pro bull rider's another kind of hero."

"Maybe. All I know is I'm too selfish to ever let her go. Even if she could do better."

"Too modest." I shake my head. "Unlike you, I've got a

rap sheet, PTSD, and a reputation worth dog shit. What's good about me?"

"Dee deserves what she wants, don't you think?"

"Lila." I say it like an oath.

Zane's brow shoots up.

"Lila. *She's* what's good about me."

He stands, surveys the food. Grabs a muffin, pulling back the paper wrapper like it's precious.

I rub my chest, right over my heart. "She deserves everything. I just don't know if I'm part of what she wants anymore."

"Sounds like you two need an honest conversation." He shoves half the muffin in his mouth, already going for another.

"That's what scares me."

He chases it with coffee. "Shouldn't. You're it for that girl. Always been."

God, I want to believe him. Want to believe all those letters weren't just a waste. I wrote her another this morning. Couldn't stop myself. Four words: *Still breathing. Still yours.*

Apologies don't erase years. Don't patch silence. But his words ease something twisted inside me.

Didn't sleep worth a damn last night. Tossed and turned. Coyotes howled, cattle lowed, the house groaned like it remembered me. Testing if I belonged.

But what kept me up was her. My Lila. I thought I'd wake tangled in her red hair. Instead, I'm in knots, while her warmth drifts across town toward some kid she mentors. Sophia.

"And as for your reputation," Zane says. "Everything will work out in time. Just gotta have faith."

"You heard Christian and Logan. Hell, you sounded like

you didn't trust me staying here, either." My words come sharp.

He waves it off. "That's just Christian being Christian. Logan being Logan. Don't take them serious. As for me? Yeah, I think you need your own place. You've always been rebellious as hell. Dad's roof won't sit right. And watching him get older? That wears you down."

"Never thought I'd see you back here either. Running the place."

He shakes his head. "Tougher than I ever imagined."

"Don't envy you."

"I'm not Dad. Looking back now, I don't know how he handled fifteen foster boys on top of everything else."

"And as a single dad."

"Tough act to follow." His voice drops, eyes wander.

"So, what's on deck for me today?"

"Weaning calves, feeding cows, mucking stalls, mending fences. Logan and Chris'll be out, too."

Guarding me, more like. Ranch feels like another prison.

"Can't tell you how many times I dreamed of being back here. Doing chores I used to hate. Guess we'll see if reality holds up."

Zane chuckles. "Yep. Got a full day's work waiting."

"Better get to it," I say, rising. "Mind if I drop a letter in the mailbox first?"

"Go ahead. I'm digging into the rest of this spread. You eat already?"

"Yeah." I shift my weight, pride flickering. "May not contribute much else. But I can cook."

"And shovel shit," he grins.

THE PALOMINO SHIFTS UNDER ME, strong and restless. Leather and sweat in my lungs. Freedom, finally, in the last place I expected. The ranch I once resented.

For the work it demanded from me. For how it challenged me to be a better man. This day's no different. But now, I'm ready to earn it.

Hours later, I'm chewed up and spit out by Rough & Ready. But it's good work. Honest. Fresh air, wide sky, sore hands. Purpose.

I mend fences until my fingers ache. Ride until muscles scream. Feels like home. Feels like maybe I belong again ... *for a moment.*

Then, the whispers start. Ranch hands bent over wire.

"Brother of the foreman. What'd you expect?"

"Still don't like it. He's a convicted murderer."

"Can't believe they'd trust Holden to stay with Wyatt."

They say *convicted murderer* like it's my full name. Digs under my skin worse than any blade.

I clear my throat loud enough to cut glass. They don't back down, not even a flicker of remorse.

I glare, the tension weighty as a roll of barbed wire.

Zane rides over, concern on his face. "Everything good?"

The hands look away, cowards now that he's here.

"Spectacular," I bite.

"I need you in the south field, checking fences. Running out of daylight."

Strange taking orders from Zane. But he respects me. I'll return it.

I nod.

Christian and Logan ride up.

"No need," Logan grumbles, "We'll go."

"No," I counter.

"We'll cover it," he says through clenched teeth.

"I've got it," I bark back.

Logan's mouth tightens. "Don't want mistakes. Enough eyes on us already."

"For God's sake, Logan!" Zane snaps. "What are you implying?"

Christian cuts in, sharp. "He's right to be cautious. Moreau's people are sniffing around. He knows how to hold a grudge."

Sounds noble. Perhaps even heroic. But really, they don't trust me.

Course, I could be wrong—too jaded, too guarded, too goddamned paranoid. Prison'll do that.

I circle back to earlier words. *A grudge?* My hands fist. Senator Moreau's not the only one who's sharpening the knife.

Gregory's face flashes unbidden. Shock in his eyes, the way he went down.

The politician lost a son that night. I lost my freedom, my girl, my family.

Even in this wide-open field, I'm not home. I'm caged. By suspicion. By the fact an innocent man can spend a decade in hell for refusing to die.

Release wasn't a favor. It came with conditions. With keeping quiet. Being grateful. Pretending justice was served.

Maybe it's time to rip the truth out of the dark. Awaken my grudge on Moreau. Blast light in the dark—like Paige, Ji, and Wolfe.

At the very least, wipe the smug look off Christian's face. Silence the mouthy ranchhands. Prove to Lila I'm still her man and all she'll ever need.

CHAPTER
SIX
DELILAH

Sophia perches on the stool behind the cash register, a new spiral notebook in her lap, hearts doodled in big, splashy strokes. She chats animatedly, renewed energy coursing through her.

It was a good day. More lost media mysteries to solve. Less mean Amy. *Romeo and Juliet*. God, I fear the fallout when she gets to the end.

"You do realize it's a tragedy, right?" I ask, trying to ease her into it.

Her eyes widen. "Tragedy? What does that mean?"

I can't imagine she's asking for a dictionary definition. More like stumbling over one of youth's seismic paradigm shifts. "It doesn't have a happy ending. Not even close."

Her brows furrow. "But it feels so romantic. Like fate. Like nothing can stop them."

My chest pinches. Fate doesn't always mean forever. "Sometimes that's the danger of it."

She bites her bottom lip. "Sounds too much like real life. I thought reading was supposed to be an escape."

"Sometimes," I murmur, eyes darting to the café door for the hundredth time today. I didn't hear from him last night. No call. No text. Not sure what I expected.

Each hour that ticks by convinces me of why I can't let my guard down. For all I know, he's already gone. The thought lances me, sharp behind my eyes.

I'll die if he leaves. At least, the most important part of me.

I should have told him that yesterday. Made my feelings clear. But that's the thing about the risk of real emotional pain. It locks shields in place, dries words on the tongue.

"More than escape, books should make you *feel* things. Sometimes ugly things."

Sophia scrunches her nose, dissatisfied. "Then, how are they any different than real life?"

The bell on the café door clangs, and my heart thuds. Again.

But this is different. The air thickens.

I feel him before I see him.

My world tilts when he strides through the door, uncertain yet driven. Huge and inked, muscles seething beneath the surface of a new black, button-down shirt and perfectly fit dark wash Wranglers. His eyes lock on mine beneath the shadow of his cream Stetson, and all that matters is the hunger. The need. The rawness of ten years lost.

The part of me I cobbled into existence after his incarceration trembles, certain it will shrivel to cinder in the heat of our reunion. But everything else knows it's inevitable. Like breathing.

"That's him," Sophia whispers, awe threading her voice.

I swallow loudly, uncertain of my ability to talk. But words still come. Protective ones. "Why don't you go upstairs, water the houseplants, work on your homework."

"But what about my S'mores Hot Cocoa?"

She's right. I've been spacey as an astronaut all day, thanks to the massive cowboy headed my way. "I'll have Suzy bring it up to you," I say, already unraveling.

Sophia jumps down, still sneaking looks at Holden as she disappears. Even Suzy's gaze lingers too long.

"Suzy?" my voice croaks. The barista blinks, caught staring.

Gravity freezes us in place. Only I can't tell who is orbiting whom. All I know is he and I, this moment, are as undeniable as the passage of time.

"One S'mores Hot Cocoa coming right up," she says quickly.

Whispers ripple through the café, mirroring Sophia and Suzy's curiosity. Only their interest comes from a more menacing place.

"Dangerous criminal."

"... death wish, tangling with Moreau ..."

"Convicted murderer."

One woman edges her chair farther away. A man sets down his mug with a loud clink.

Like they refuse to separate the past from the man.

I should care. But my whole world is the way he fills the café, every line of him too big, too raw, too mine.

Our eyes lock, and the room fades. All I hear is the endless beat of desire.

"Lila." He says it like a prayer. Maybe the unfamiliarity of the nickname softened its impact yesterday. But today, those two syllables cleave me wide open, raw and shivering.

"Here for coffee?" I manage, bottom lip trembling, echoed in my hands. His eyes scan me, noticing. His nostrils flare, and his pupils dilate.

"Here for *you*."

The café seems to inhale ... even mugs go quiet.

"Well, surely you want a drink, too," I suggest, floundering beneath the weight of his yearning. Carrying my own has been heavy enough. I can't bear a double load.

His Adam's apple bobs. "I'll take that, too. If that's what you want." His forehead furrows. Beneath the ink and scars, I see the boy I loved. Hurting. Needing me.

"Suzy will have to ring you up," I blurt. "I'm sorry ... there's something out back I forgot." I hurry down the hall, wiping at my cheeks.

The hammer of boots follows close behind. My heart jumps into my throat, apprehension colliding with anticipation.

The air of an autumnal evening kisses my face. I lean against the unyielding brick wall of the alley, shadowbound, burning alive.

He paces in front of me, hands fisting and unfisting. "Sorry," he mutters. "Need a smoke."

Five years I spent convincing him it was filthy. Five years before that sending him cigarettes behind bars. And now, God help me, I crave the familiar sin as much as he does.

He lights up, glow sparking against his rugged features. "Want to share?"

It would be so easy to refuse ... to prove I've changed, that I'm stronger. But refusing him feels like refusing myself. "Yes."

His cheeks darken as he extends his arm. Our fingertips brush. Flesh against flesh. Incandescent sparks. Igniting what neither of us is willing to admit. That we won't survive apart, though we no longer know how to be together.

The air sizzles, electric. I put the paper cylinder to my lips, inhale once, twice, handing it back slow enough to graze his skin again. Savor his warmth.

"I thought you gave up smoking," I whisper.

"Thought you did, too."

"I did."

"Same."

He pauses—shifts his weight, cocks his head. "But I figure it's the only way you'll let me taste those lips ..."

My voice catches in my throat.

"It's not enough, though," he growls, eyes darkening. "Not just the ghost of you. I need the *real* you."

He grinds the cigarette under his heel. Purpose fills the three strides that close the distance. Powerful arms cage me. A shadow of ash clings to his knuckles. I sense the faint tremor in his hands where they brace the wall by my head. He's as wrecked as I am.

What should feel like a trap is my salvation. He's not holding me in. He's keeping danger out—the prying eyes, the cruel glances, the hate-laced words, the awkwardness of a lifetime apart.

"Couldn't stay away, though I know I *should*." His voice scrapes raw. Up close, I see the thin silver line by his jaw, a scar I don't know. A story written in flesh that he refuses to share.

His gaze sizzles, head inching closer, hooded eyes settling on my mouth. One heated breath away.

Everything I want. Everything I thirst for. Everything I know will destroy the me that I've become.

"When have you ever done what you should?" I gasp, flattening my hands against his steel-hard chest. The boy is gone. A dangerous man stands in his place.

"Or you stayed out of trouble?" he grumbles, challenging me with scorching indigo eyes.

"Never," we speak in the same breath.

The answer hangs between us, fragile as glass, before shattering under the weight of his longing. He's on me—prayer and hunger in one rush—mouth crashing into mine, spark to tinder. Our kiss detonates, messy and brutal, teeth and tongues clashing until need swallows everything.

I drag him closer, fisting the front of his shirt, frantically unbuttoning it enough to slide fingers beneath, to feel the hot flesh I crave. He shudders at my touch, leaning into me, stealing my breath, tongue tangling with mine. The rhythm is primal, one I've missed for ten endless years. He tastes of smoke, satisfaction, and sin—the flavor of every dangerous thing I've ever craved.

Desperation and salty tears, held breaths are the cement. Because we can't break apart. We need each other too much to let go. Finally, when life forces us to pull away, gasping, he rests his forehead on mine, still sinking into me despite the necessary sliver of distance.

His rough, work-hardened hands come up, stroking my cheeks. "Lila." His mouth hovers, a storm about to break. I ache to drown in the downpour.

For a heartbeat, I think we might stop here, breathing each other in like air after submersion. That would be safer. Saner. But safety has never been what Holden and I do best.

His mouth claims me again. Chaotic, brutal, desperate. Souls clash, breath intertwines, passion ignites like dry timber.

Cold brick scrapes my back. His heat sears through my clothes. Hunger and lust and the taste of *him*. His tongue demands, devours. Hands possess, dropping to my waist, arching my hips towards his until his thumb grazes too close to my stomach, and I stiffen, protective.

He pulls back, gasping, eyes swirling with the unspoken.

But I'm not ready to let him go …

"Lover boy." Whispered through a veil of tears. Three syllables, another lifetime. My hands come up, palming his angular jawline, fingertips scratching over stubbly cheeks.

He chuckles low, raw. Starts to speak … then freezes.

We're not alone.

A shadow shifts. My stomach drops before I even see her face. In the same instant, I am both lover and guardian, and the clash nearly rips me apart.

Sophia stands wide-eyed, notebook clutched tight.

I gasp. "What are you doing out here?"

"Were you spying?" Holden growls.

She stammers, "No, I came looking for—" She stops. Sharp eyes flicker to me. "So which is it, Miss Dee? Cold as ice when you speak about him inside, or Juliet out here with your Romeo?"

Her voice is pointed, eyes wounded. My stomach twists. She's seen too much. Felt too much. And maybe she's right —maybe I am two-faced, preaching strength and boundaries inside while my heart betrays me in Holden's arms.

I clear my throat, pulse racing, head spinning. My body is alive in ways I haven't felt in so long, yearning shivering through me. Embarrassed by my lack of control.

"Go back inside, Pipsqueak," I say shakily. "Remember what I told you yesterday? That two things can be true even though they contradict?"

She bites her bottom lip, torn. "To me, it seems more like you want others to think one thing and Holden another." Dropping her shoulders, she retreats.

The door sighs shut behind her, and guilt nicks me. Fear follows fast. If she tells anyone what she saw, they might not let me mentor her anymore. Maybe not even let me *see* her again. It sours in my stomach.

Holden doesn't move, doesn't look away. His chest still heaves, his gaze pins me in place, like Sophia's words don't matter. Like the kiss already decided everything.

"I have to go after her," I excuse, ducking beneath his arm and beelining for the door, though every fiber in my being pleads for me to stay.

"That's it? One kiss, and you're out?"

I can feel the frustration in his voice. Softly but firmly, I counter, "No, but she saw us, Holden. She's confused. She needs me to be steady, not reckless."

"Reckless? That kiss felt like the only thing real in ten damn years."

I flinch, taking one step back towards him, torn to pieces. "It felt real to me, too. That's why I can't throw it in her face like it meant nothing. She looks to me for guidance ... I can't shatter that."

His jaw tightens, shame flickering beneath the frustration. "So she gets your time, your loyalty, while I get pushed into the shadows?"

"It isn't about choosing her over you. Don't mistake care for cowardice."

"Maybe the kid's onto something. Maybe you don't want others knowing about me ... about *us*."

"How can you say that?" I ask, voice simmering.

He shakes his head, lips pressed tightly together. But in the ache of his eyes, I see he doesn't believe me. And maybe ... maybe some part of me doesn't believe me either.

"All I know is she's a very traumatized sixteen-year-old,

and it's taken me nearly six months to gain her trust. To get her to open up to me. I can't undo that now."

"No worries," he mutters. "If I'm good at anything, it's waiting for you." He heads for the sunlight, me for the door.

I swallow the taste of him and step into fluorescent light, praying I haven't just betrayed them both.

CHAPTER
SEVEN
DELILAH

Sophia paces back and forth, her face hung low.

Guilt pricks. I step forward, sweeping my arm up to hug her. But she shrinks away.

"I don't get it," she says, shaking her head as fat water drops roll down her cheeks. "You made it sound like he's your past. A distant memory. But the way you were kissing ..."

"Pipsqueak—"

"Don't! I'm tired of people who say one thing and do another." She jerks away, wearing ruts into the office floor.

Her anger burns hot, but underneath, I hear the crackle of hurt. Of course, I know why. I've read her file. Abused again and again. Promises from teachers, social workers, counselors. All broken. Endlessly falling through the cracks ... until her uncle and aunt—new foster parents—and Rough & Ready Country. The same story. The story of me. The story of Holden.

Regret sears, though I did nothing wrong. But I can put myself back there ... into her sixteen-year-old shoes, when everything seemed monumental. I was only two years older when they took Holden from me … and so much more. I never got to—

I stop myself. Shaking my head to break the thought before it pierces me.

Still, despair hits me low in the gut. The empty ache of learning to live without a future. Swapping it for a half-life ten years too long. Stuck in the in-between.

His heat, his flavor linger on my lips. But his words chatter in my brain: *Not sure how long I'll stay. Don't want to cause trouble. Especially for you.*

They hollow me out. I tremble, uncertain how I'll move on if the narrative I've carefully built to stay afloat keeps springing leaks.

"You're a hypocrite, Miss Dee. Hiding Holden like Juliet hid Romeo. Only *you* don't have to."

"Sophia—"

"Afraid you'll lose some café customers?"

"Not at all," I bristle, fighting the urge to clap back.

"Then, why the hesitation? Why not claim him openly?"

I chuckle softly, shaking my head. "If only relationships were that easy." I used to think love could conquer anything. Maybe that's what kept me treading water all these years.

Her voice trembles. "I don't know what's worse. The way you're keeping him in the background or what'll happen if you get back together …"

"What do you mean?"

She swipes her hand over her face. "It'll be just like my mom. Never any time for me. A revolving door of boyfriends stealing her attention. Making me feel less-than."

I'm split in two. Holden's words still echo. Sophia's add

a bittersweet new layer. But there's nothing either-or about this situation.

"Sophia, that could never happen. I will make time for you. No matter what."

She eyes me warily, uncertain. I was her once. The outsider. The hippie girl ostracized. The daughter abandoned and estranged. By a father who left. By a mother who never wanted to be there.

"Holden and I have a lot to work out, Sophia. Ten years is a long time apart."

"But love is love. *No matter what*."

"I agree. And I will forever love Holden. No one and nothing will ever take that from me."

"Then, why were you kissing him in an alley instead of in front of the town?" She spits the word *alley* like a curse.

"Because everything about our relationship has played out in front of the whole world. Ever since his arrest."

For the first time, she doesn't look solely reproachful. Her brows knit, mulling over my words.

"You know," she says, gripping her notebook like a lifeline. "I've been doing a little digging. Some research into his case."

Her words floor me. She flops into the chair, motioning for me to sit. I perch on the edge, stomach roiling.

She opens the heart-decorated notebook, showing me messily scrawled notes. Newspaper articles taped to pages. Ten years ago alive again before my eyes. His surly mugshot. The crime scene. Evidence tossed aside. Public defenders bowing out. Nobody daring to stand against Senator Moreau.

"Where did you get these?"

"Googled the case and printed them out," she says proudly.

Silence settles between us as I struggle for the right words.

"But why are you doing this?" I whisper.

Her eyes flash. "Because I want to understand what you've been through. What happened with you two. *How* you were misunderstood."

There it is again. That word. Misunderstood. Dangerous beyond measure.

My fingers graze a black-and-white photo of Holden at twenty-one, glaring at the camera, face fierce, almost feral. I know how those warm lips tasted, how those indigo eyes burned, the way his smooth face felt beneath my palms.

How he said goodbye with every part of his body before doing the one thing he swore he never would ...

Surrender.

He said he did it for me, to spare me further trouble. I can see why as an adult. But at eighteen, it gutted me, betrayal at the exact moment I needed him most.

A page flips. Another photo. I spy myself in the corner. Somber, drained. Dead woman walking.

"There you are," she whispers.

The headline reads:

Romeo and Juliet at the Center of Plot to Kill Senator's Son

How wrong they had it.

"You didn't say before that you were suspected, too." She says, accusation cutting.

I exhale. "I helped hide him from the cops. So yes, I was initially charged, too."

"You hid him, like you're hiding him now?"

"It's not the same. I'm trying to sort everything out ... and protect him."

"But what's there to sort out? Clearly, he loves you, and

you love him." She points to a cutout of us as teens, hearts scribbled between.

"Too much to explain."

"And protect?" she arches an eyebrow.

"His heart. That's what needs protecting."

Her face softens.

"These articles only tell a tiny sliver of the story. They don't describe his infectious laugh. His wicked sense of humor, love of music ... his drive to protect those who needed it. The way his blue eyes glinted when he saw something he wanted ..." The promises made. The soul-searing passion. The vulnerabilities and secrets he shared only with me.

Prison took all of that from us ... forcing me to subsist on shadows of memory. Forcing him to become something he's not.

"The man you describe ... isn't who I saw today, Miss Dee."

"You're right," I admit, world-weary. Though sometimes, I catch glimmers.

"So, he's changed a lot, then?"

I nod. More than I can process.

She finally reaches out, pressing her hand over mine. "I'm sorry. Didn't mean to make you sad with this notebook."

I wipe my cheeks. "No, it's okay. I need to see this ... to remember where it all started." *With my lover boy.*

I glance at the photo of us—me at eighteen, him at twenty-one. The world could fall away. He was all I needed. And that's why fate took him.

Because the things and people I love most always go away.

Sophia leans forward, whisper-soft, and hugs me. Never has she been so vulnerable. I cherish it.

If things had gone differently. Is this what it would have felt like to have a daughter? Or son? I can't let myself linger here long. It will ruin me.

"Earlier, when I sat in the café doing my homework, I overheard people talking," she says. "Saying Moreau's men are tying up loose ends around Hollister. I wasn't sure what they meant. Then, I saw this. Buried on the back page."

She flips to another spot in her journal, finger tracing a small headline:

Local Moreau Whistleblower Missing

My gut tightens. Too neat. Too timed. My breath hitches. This isn't coincidence.

"Is this what they meant by loose ends?" she asks.

"I don't know."

I remember the man's name, the face from news clips. Vanished. My stomach twists cold. Threats too near. I can't lose more of what I love.

"You need to stop looking into this case," I warn. "And stay away from Moreau and his people. They're dangerous."

"The Weasel mentioned Moreau more than once," she adds, lip quivering. "I thought it was just name-dropping. But what if it was more?"

The Weasel. The man who pimped her out. My throat knots, rage flashing. If I could, I'd put him in the ground myself.

"He's under investigation. You need to let the authorities sort this out."

"But where have the authorities been all this time? These past ten years?"

I can't answer.

"They all ganged up on you and Holden. Like Montagues and Capulets. They should suffer."

She makes us sound so innocent. Like helpless victims.

But nothing is ever that simple. Especially when the "they" she speaks of remain shrouded in secrecy. "It's easy to talk retribution when you're not holding the blade."

"Don't you want to make Moreau pay? So you and Holden can be together forever?"

So simple. So naive. Like a Hallmark movie. My voice quivers. "Yes, more than anything. But nothing in life is that ... straightforward."

She eyes me skeptically.

"He said he might leave, Sophia. That he wasn't sure how long he'd stay."

"Because he wants *you* to make him stay."

The gravity of her words unseats me. My knees weaken, mouth going dry. Holden's implied it with roundabout words, sizzling glances. Yet, it takes her observation to lift the shroud of childhood wounds obscuring my vision.

"Maybe. But not all love stories have happy endings."

"Tell me about it. My stupid mother keeps chasing them down with every guy she lets in her pants." Her voice rises, anger biting.

"You shouldn't talk about her that way."

"And she shouldn't act that way."

I can't argue.

She worries her lip. "You know, that's how I got suckered in by the Weasel. *She* brought him home. *She* trusted him first."

My gut knots. "Do you want to talk about it?"

She checks the clock. "Oh shoot! Uncle Jermaine's here. Gotta go."

I hug her, holding longer than she expects. Relieved we've mended things. Rueful our conversation has to end here.

"See you tomorrow," she calls, notebook clutched like treasure.

Alone again, I unclasp the necklace, slipping Holden's ring onto my finger. Tears blur my vision.

Snippets of his letters call across time. I round my desk, opening a drawer and pulling one out. Never far from me or my thoughts.

Messy handwriting, messier thoughts. My fingers trace the ink. Desperation locked in each swoop and line: *Please, Lila, hold on for me. Hold on for us.*

I have held on, steel-gripped and grim-faced. Even when he begged me to let go. A game of chicken I sometimes felt like only I was playing.

A knock jolts me.

"Yes?" I cache the letter, closing the drawer.

Suzy breezes in with a stack of mail.

"Thanks," I murmur, shuffling through bills, flyers, coupons. I stop, frozen. Handwriting I'd know anywhere. Seen only moments ago.

The postmark is today. Too fresh, too close.

I tear it open. Four words sprawled in the center of the page:

Still breathing. Still yours.

The words blur in my vision but burn into my soul.

EIGHT

HOLDEN

I can't stop. Can't think. Nothing helps. Not smokes. Not booze, though I have half a mind to drown myself. Not drugs, though I still know where to get them, enough temptation to make my bones hum.

None of it touches the real addiction. Lila. *Always Lila.*

Even now, the memory of her—soft, warm curves under my rough palms—undoes me.

Her mouth parting. That breath I stole. Heat that burned me clean through.

She stiffened for a beat. Started to pull away. Then melted. Mine again. Ours. Forever.

Until that kid showed up. I catch myself mid-thought, shame hitting ... petty, jealous.

But you don't offer a starving man chewing gum.

Maybe I should get laid. Get it over with.

But Lila's the only woman I've ever had. When I think of love, romance, sex, all I see is her.

Need grates at me, clawing from the inside out. My hand's no help. What I need is inside of her. Only place I've ever felt safe. Beyond lust. Past drive. Deeper.

I pace the ranch house like a caged cat. Floorboards creak a mean rhythm.

Thought one taste would settle me. Maybe make goodbye possible.

Instead, it was crumbs to a hungry man. Stoked the fire. Emptied me out.

I don't know how I go on without her. Eyes stinging as my brothers drift in.

I drop my gaze. Hide the want.

Prison stripped everything—free will, agency, body, choice. Ground me to nothing. Only *she* got me through.

"No Holden dinner tonight?" Zane grins.

"I told you I'd be out," I snap.

His eyes narrow.

"Sorry," I grind out. "Rough day."

He nods. Hard face. "Just don't pull that on Dad. Understood?"

"Wouldn't." He's right. Still makes me feel like I don't belong, though. Like I've blown it again.

Zane steps in, hand lifting for my shoulder. I pull back. Don't want touch. I can barely handle anyone near me ... *except Lila.*

Ridge walks in, bringing the sunshine with him like always.

"No Paige tonight?" I ask, aiming for normal. He has no clue. *They* have no clue how much it steals from me.

"She, Ji, and Bowie are right behind me."

I nod. Jaw tight. Shoulders up. Another crowd. More noise. The unexpected.

Christian chimes in, eyeing me curiously, "Maksim's on dinner tonight. Antelope stew and homemade bread."

Good. Something else to think about.

My stomach growls, hollow as a busted drum. Hands shake like a junkie.

"Grab a bowl," Maksim calls from the kitchen, red apron on. He gets me. Doesn't do small talk. Doesn't expect civility. Lets me exist.

But the talkative brothers have my fists clenched. They make me want to bolt. I used to be one of them. Not now.

A retreat to my childhood bedroom won't shut out the noise, the normalcy. The things I fantasized about behind bars.

Maybe that's the worst part of doing time. Can't be what I was, though my brothers expect no less. *Maybe Lila does, too.*

Paige, Ji-su, and Bowie flood the front room. Volume spikes.

I grind my teeth to keep from covering my ears. Even the lights feel hostile.

Bowie aims for a bear hug. I put up my hands. "Not tonight, man. Need a break."

He doesn't flinch, face flashing with sympathy instead. He introduces Ji-su, the yin to his yang. I give a polite nod but keep my distance.

Bounty hunter. He gets ex-cons better than most. Christian does too … two sides of the same coin.

Christian expects the worst. Bowie demands the best. The outcome feels like blind luck. A random toss in the air … unless Lila comes back around. With her, I could be good. I will.

"Zane says work went well," Ridge says, sitting with his pretty brunette, Paige.

Zane nods, despite me snapping at him earlier. "Didn't miss a beat. Like the last ten years didn't matter."

The last part, I want to believe … that I could forget my

ugly past. That I could recapture what came before. *Only I can't.*

Cold sweats, prison dreams, twisting in sheets built for two. A lonely half of the only whole that ever mattered. That's all I am now.

Homecoming sharp as a twisted knife. More painful.

Unless Lila ....

Who am I kidding? I'd need to be a troubled sixteen-year-old girl to get her attention.

"Did you see Dee today?" Ridge asks, tearing at a thick slice of butter-drenched sourdough.

"Yeah."

"And?" His brow goes up.

I shake my head. Can't say it. Can't voice the need chewing me hollow.

His eyes narrow. "You're planning on staying in town, right? Working things out. Not just passing through?"

"Don't know yet," I mutter.

"You owe her more than that." He growls ... like he needs to shield her from me.

Bread down. Hands under the table. Fists tight. I run the re-entry coping playbook like a loop. Breathe. Just breathe.

All eyes are on me.

"I know," I say, short of air. Lights too bright. Room too loud.

I scrub my face. Inhale through the nose. Out through the mouth.

Axel reads me. He stands slow. "Come on." More command than ask. "Outside. Too hot in here."

Eyes track us. He doesn't care. I borrow his shrug.

Night air hits, and I could weep. To step outside whenever I want—no count, no permission—feels like a miracle.

Might sleep out here. Embrace freedom.

Axel doesn't try to touch me again. Doesn't expect anything. Just stands. Present.

He pulls out two cigarettes, handing one to me. Flames illuminate his face. He offers the lighter.

"Too much in there," he says after a drag. "I could barely sit still."

"Thanks," I say, throat thick.

He ignores the change in tone. Best kindness there is. Stares out over pasture. "Least I can do ... under the circumstances."

I shake my head. "I chose it. Let it go."

Stars pinwheel overhead. Stupid pretty. Makes my eyes water.

Ten years, and I thought I'd never see a night sky again. Didn't think I deserved to.

"Let's see," he says quietly. "You took my beating ... *nearly to death*. Gave me a fucking alibi so I didn't have to leave the ranch. Then, tossed ten years for me."

"Not how it went down," I grumble.

He turns, eyes darting to mine and then back to the Milky Way. "Exactly how it went down, though you *swore* me to silence."

I rub my chest. "I forced you. No choice."

He chuckles darkly. "Oh, I had a choice."

"A choice that would've wrecked me worse."

He looks at his boots, spits, "So you always said."

"Wrong place, wrong time, armed—that was bad enough. Add motive? Pre-meditation? I'd have been fucked."

Axel shakes his head. "But that's the thing, Holden. From where I stand, all I see is fuckage, and all I know is I had *everything* to do with it."

"Whatever." I'll die on this hill. "Sometimes life screws you no matter what you do. You know that better than anyone."

His shoulders slope towards the ground. "Yep."

We drag on our smokes. Quiet.

"I talked to a lawyer," he says. "You were right. About everything. But it doesn't make the guilt vanish. Doesn't make me feel any less shitty about everything. Especially with all that happened with you and Dee because of me."

"Not because of you. Because life's cruel. Nothing's for certain."

He nods. "You know I'm yours for anything. I owe you everything."

"Not keeping score."

"But what about you and Dee? You gonna try to work things out with her?"

"I *have* to," I grind out. "But don't know how."

"You should go see her. Spend some time alone. Discuss *everything* that happened. Air your secrets."

My breath shudders. "And how'd that go with you and your woman?"

"Aspen," he says, mouth tipping up. "She knows it all. My past, what happened as a child. You and me. And it didn't faze her ... didn't even make her blink. But keeping secrets almost killed it before it started."

"Some things are too damn painful to discuss—"

"Do it anyway. Bear each other's discomforts and shames, accept each other's darkest secrets. That's love."

"How'd you get so wise?"

"By doing every conceivable thing the wrong way."

I chuckle. "Think I've got you beat there."

"Not if you'd let me meet Gregory Moreau and his friends that night. Do the drug deal."

Teeth clamp on my lower lip. Guilt blooms. "Couldn't. It was set up. You were over your head, and they needed their asses kicked."

He nods toward the house. "I'll cover you. Go to Dee."

I start to protest. Can't. Smile hits me instead, hard as sunlight.

He tosses his keys. "Ranch house key's on there. I'll grab a ride with Ridge, use a company truck this week. And I'll tell Dad and Zane to lock up since you'll be ... elsewhere."

God, I wish.

I hesitate. Body coiled. Then it clicks.

Frustration becomes motion. Longing turns into aim. I stride fast towards his truck.

"Just promise me you'll be on your guard," he calls.

I turn, nodding and walking backward.

"Online rumors and whispers in town say someone's cleaning house for Moreau."

My body tenses, ready for a fight. "I promise," I grunt.

The keys bite crescents into my palm. His faith feels like a lifeline I didn't earn. I'll take it anyway.

Cold night air burns my lungs. Every muscle hums— her taste still on my lips, her name carved into my bones.

I can't stop now. Not after that kiss. Not after ten years of starving.

Axel's warning echoes as I yank open the door. *Loose ends. Moreau. Danger close to Hollister.*

For the first time in years, I've got something to lose.

And everything to fight for.

CHAPTER
NINE

HOLDEN

The big white truck growls to life under my hands, headlights cutting a pale path down the dirt road. Wheel slick against my palm, Axel's words a weight in my chest. *Loose ends. Moreau. Danger close.*

My parole officer's voice is in my head. Turn back. Stay in Rough & Ready. No trouble.

But safety, playing by the rules, will never get me Lila.

Every mile between us is a mistake—every second without her wasted.

The kiss branded me. I'll never scrape it off. And I don't want to.

Hollister's lights glow, faint in the distance, promising her. Promising trouble.

I can't decide which pulls me harder.

I park on Main Street, sauntering around the darkened café. "Closed" sign on the door. Around back, I *feel* her. Familiar energy, familiar music drawing me.

The Cure's *Lovesong* whispers down from the second-story deck. Caught red-handed ... thinking about me, too.

Sophia's bitter words from earlier wash back over me, her comparison of us to Romeo and Juliet. I have the balcony. Time to write a better ending.

The vine-covered wall is all purple blossoms and emerald leaves. I search for hand and footholds. Tracing them like hope up the terrace. The balcony beckons, verdant houseplants and soft, glowing light.

She appears above. A flash of scarlet and lavender satin. Necklaces jangle, rings shine. The Cure on her lips. God, her singing voice sucks. Bad as mine. I love it ... love every damned thing about her.

Now or never. I start up the wall. Cowboy boots don't cut it. But nothing could keep me away. Fires, earthquakes, tornadoes ... *nothing*.

My foot slips. Vine shakes. Her voice stops, head peeking over the balcony. Red locks curl towards me. I pause, hold my breath. Her emerald eyes narrow, peer into the night.

She gasps, voice catching in her throat. Hand slapping over her heart. One step back, breathing hard. Then, a tentative glimpse of her shiny curls. Green eyes glowing— wide-eyed, curious. Shock shifting into a warm smile.

Then, giggles, pure as rain, shimmering like a waterfall. Finally, the unguarded girl I remember. A weight lifts. I feel lighter. Like I could float to her.

"What are you doing, lover boy?"

The nickname punches into my heart. She remembers.

"You know." I concentrate, inches from the ledge and *her*. "What I did to get to you at your mom's house," I say thick-voiced.

Lila's bedroom. Deep kisses, free-roaming hands. Curiosity pricked, desire ignited. Where I lost myself and gained an obsession. A nickname, too. Neck heats, need throbbing.

I'm caged in the four walls of her heart. Have been too long to remember before. Try as I might, I can't outrun her ... *or us*.

Purple flower with a yellow center. I pluck it from the vine. Hold the stem between my teeth, straddle the parapet, and plant my feet.

She covers her mouth. Eyes fill with mirth, laughter spills between her fingers. She sighs, "You've lost your mind. We're not kids anymore."

I pull the flower from my mouth. "Got the bum knee to prove it," I mutter, leaning forward to rub the joint.

Her brows arch. "Are you okay?"

"Haven't been this okay since *before*." My voice drops. Its counterpoint the bittersweet behind her gaze.

I step forward. My hand comes up, tucking the large purple bloom behind her ear. Heart races at the silk of her hair, the smell of her lavender, patchouli, and love ... love simmering on her skin like a promise.

I press a kiss to her temple. Her body relaxes, remembering. Thank God.

"Didn't think I could stay away. Did you?"

Her cheeks flare pink. Jade doe eyes widen. Open, inviting. Everything I remember. "I wasn't sure after last night."

I frown. Last night. When I lost my nerve ... and shut her out.

"Or," she adds, voice trembling. "When you talked about leaving me." She pronounces it like an unforgivable sin ... the way she said *surrender* a decade ago. Acid on her tongue.

I shake my head. Pierced by the simmer beneath her

words. "Don't want to leave you. Never have. But I need you to want me, too."

"I thought you knew." She bites her bottom lip. "I can't exist without you."

"But you have. For ten years. Not just existed ... or survived. Thrived."

"I had to."

"I forced you to—"

"Not you. Fate." she interrupts.

"Still ruined your life." My voice cracks. "Probably should go."

"Ruined my life? Sounds like an excuse to make you feel less guilty about leaving me," she bites back.

"Don't want to go, Lila. Don't want to hurt you even more, though."

"*Nothing* hurts like you gone."

It's our truth. The unspoken weight we've carried too long. "Tell me what you want, then ... *anything*. It's yours."

A laughable statement from a broke ex-con. But Lila's never traded in most people's currency.

Her eyes radiate love. "Still breathing. Still yours. *That's* what I want."

My eyes sting, body taut. One last hesitation. Then, I pull her into me. Fast, firm. The way I breathe. Locking soft curves against firm planes. Everything worth it for this moment.

"Four words," I whisper. "Never stopped being true."

Her eyes pool and lashes flutter, voice thick. "I guess I always knew. But I wasn't sure." Her fingers trace my neck tattoos. Fire shivers down my spine. Her gaze drags over me. Finally seeing me. "You're so hard now. So different. The same and not."

"You're so independent. Polished. Like you don't need me. Like I'm a puzzle piece that no longer fits."

"I have never, not for one day, stopped needing you," she confesses. "Though it would have been so much easier. Less excruciating."

My mouth draws closer, eyes on her soft, pink lips. "To forget. Not remember. Would've been easier for me, too," I whisper, voice in danger of cracking. "That's why I did something I regret."

Her tear-rimmed eyes flash to my face. My hand drops to her stomach.

Lila gasps. Tries to pull away. "Don't."

Her voice cracks, fragile, like a cornered bird. But I can't let this stay buried anymore. I palm her stomach anyway, emotions spilling over with my tears. "You're trying to guard this from me. Have been for ten years, but it's my pain, too."

I pause, throat stinging, fighting for air. Haven't let myself think about this, process the loss. Years of emotion hit hard. Drag me under. Two warm trails streak my cheeks. Can't remember the last time I gave into the pain.

Her moist cheeks echo mine. The ache in her eyes matches the throb of my heart. First time we've spoken it ... mourned together. "Axel told me you were pregnant, though you didn't want me to know—"

"He did?" Alarm threads her voice.

"Told me when you lost—" I inhale sharp, fight for words. "I'm sorry. Didn't think it would hit me so hard." I look away.

Her hand finds my cheek. Coaxes me back into our moment.

"Could never let myself feel this pain behind bars—

losing our baby. Weakness, vulnerability would've gotten me killed. Or worse."

Her body shivers. "And I didn't want to tell you because you were already dealing with so much. How could I possibly ask you to bear more?"

"So, you bled for me, for our family, alone."

She crumples. Buries her face against my chest. "I'm so sorry. It was my fault. I was so stressed, so heartbroken. I didn't take care of—"

"Stop," I say. "Nothing you could've done differently."

"But—"

"*If* I had taken better care of you. Not gotten tangled up in Axel's mess ..."

"You'd have been mourning a dead brother."

I nod, dragged under the weight of destiny. *What if*. Too heavy to carry.

"It was a miscarriage. Nothing either of us could've done." Like justice, like our love, like our future together. And yet, here we are, both still standing.

We cling together in the half-light, silent but shaking, our bodies saying everything words can't. The world could end in this moment, and I wouldn't even notice. The ache is too big, the love bigger still.

"I wish it were different," she sobs. "Losing you was more than I could bear, Holden. But then, losing our baby ... It made me want to die ... I tried—"

"Know about that, too," I say softly.

She shakes her head, fighting another sob. "Axel was a terrible confidante."

"The worst. And the best. Couldn't bear the guilt of watching us come undone. Not after the role he played ... the secret we still carry."

She nods, recognition sparking. Before Axel confided in

Aspen, only Lila knew what happened that night. That I shouldn't have been there. Axel sworn to silence by me.

"Asked him to be there for you. Comfort and help you. Be a trusted friend when I couldn't. And tell me everything. A second lifeline apart from your letters and calls. So I knew about the ugly, messy version you hid beneath this sunshine." I stroke her soft jawline. "When I heard how you suffered. What you bore without me, it sawed me in two, Lila. Thought about dark things. That if I were man enough to end it, you'd move on."

Her hands come up. Thumbs graze over my cheeks. "We are so much alike."

"Making you live on standby destroyed me. It's why I begged you to move on. Why I tried to let go. But couldn't. Not if a sliver of a chance existed for us. The slightest hope of seeing you again, *tasting you one more time.*"

Her eyes search mine. Fire sparks through tears.

"It's why I came back to Hollister. Straight to your café and you. To say goodbye. Thought I could do it. But one look at you, and everything crumbled."

She draws in a shaky breath.

"Still, you deserve better than me. Always have."

Her pupils blow wide, ardent, swirling. "*I deserve what I want.*" Her words echo Zane's earlier. Like a neon sign from the Universe.

"And what is that, Lila?"

It's the question everything hangs on. Whether I stay or go. Whether I live or die. Too much pressure for one person to bear. Inevitable since the moment our paths first collided.

Main Street. Strawberry ponytails. Blueberry bubblegum. And freckled cheeks splashed petunia pink at first sight of me. The summer before we started school together.

Her hands grip my cheeks, smile spilling over into her eyes. "All I've ever wanted. *You*."

I bury my face in the crook of her neck, breathe her in, feather her cheeks with kisses.

For the first time in ten years, the pain doesn't feel bigger than the love.

This time, *I won't let go*.

CHAPTER
TEN

DELILAH

The scrape of gravel cuts through the haze of his kiss.

My breath catches. Holden's warmth is still pressed to me, but every nerve screams danger. *Is someone down there?* I mouth the words before I can stop myself.

He stiffens, the tenderness of a moment ago gone, replaced by a fierce protector. "Stay inside. Lock the doors."

I want to stop him. Beg him not to go. But prison carved steel into his bones, and I know better than to think I can hold him back.

I stand in the silence he leaves, heart battering, mind pinging between the memory of his tears on my skin and the terror of losing him all over again.

Rushing into my bedroom, I unlock the small safe where I keep a handgun. Its cold weight presses into my palm.

Flickers of controversy flash through my mind. Sophia's eavesdropping confession. The town on pins and needles since Holden's return. Whispers of Moreau's vindictiveness.

I need to know I can defend what's mine. Not let anyone take him from me again.

My hands still shake when he returns, clicking the lock behind him. I deposit the gun, closing the safe and slipping out into the hallway. Fearful of its presence violating his parole.

Everything feels like a threat that could steal him. My body seethes, desperate to make him mine. To hide him from the world.

He stands in the living room, shoulders filling the doorway, chest heaving, and braced for a fight. His eyes find mine, iron melting into something raw, though his hand lingers on the doorknob, his jaw tense.

"Street's empty," he mutters. But I don't hear relief in his voice. Just the same haunted edge I carry.

His words should quell me, disperse the electric warning sizzling up my spine. Instead, his gaze says he feels it, too. A wave about to break.

My heart trips. Ten years of longing stares back at me. Ten years of not knowing if we'd ever be able to touch again, ever do what comes so naturally to us—*exist for each other*.

In the alley, he broke first. This time I do.

Before he can speak, I cross the room and throw myself into him. For a heartbeat, I think I've lost my mind, reckless and wild, but waiting even one more second will break me. Need explodes. My lips crash into his, fingers fisting his shirt as if letting go might erase him.

He answers me the way we've been denied for too long—body to body, heartbeat to heartbeat—as if love is the only shield we've ever had against the dark.

Fabric rustles. A low, weighty moan. Heat floods, rough

palms scraping my skin. His mouth devours mine, mapping his way back to the place he's never left.

"You're my everything," he breathes. His arms are iron and mercy, his body cleaving to mine. He's under my skin, behind my ribs, the only rhythm I hear.

"I've carried you all this time," I gasp between velvet sweeps of his tongue. "Even far away, you were always with me."

His hands tangle in my hair, angling my head, deepening until breathing means him.

Desire knots in my throat. I starve for him, trembling from the soul outward, craving to belong to something bigger than I am alone.

My fingers fight his buttons. Hunger climbs. He palms my waist and hips, grinding me over his hard length. Heat sizzles, invisible smoke binding us.

"I've thought about this a thousand times," he murmurs against my ear. "Taking you rough, proving you're mine. My mouth between your thighs. Unraveling you with every part of me ..."

My head falls back as his hand slides beneath my lavender nightgown, slow, sure, climbing.

"But most of all—face to face, heart to heart. *Like the first time.*"

Memories wash over me. Of stilted breaths and whispered promises. Of inexperienced hands and learning together—how to awaken each other, how to push each other over the edge, how to make a promise with our flesh.

Leaning close, he adds in low tones, "You're the only woman I know how to make love to, Lila. The only one I've ever wanted."

Tears sting. I struggle to form words. His lips clamp to mine, erasing the need for speaking.

He walks me backward down the hall, pausing at each closed door like he's learning my life by touch. I catch his half-open shirt with one hand, pulling him with me. Twisting my bedroom doorknob and flicking the lights. His lips never leave mine.

Color swirls, lace, plants, a frame of us before fate stole him. It all blurs. For a moment, he hesitates at the picture, hand faltering as if it burns to see who we were. But his eyes return to me, hungry, and his hands shake as we reach the bed. Satin slides over my hips, not nearly fast enough. Need throbs, hollow and desperate to be filled.

I pull his shirt free and drink him in—inked and carved, muscle and tragedy. The boy I loved swallowed by the man he had to become.

My fingers trace the stories on his skin, pausing at the rough scar across his torso. The one I know about because the hospital and my tears made it real. *How many more marks do I not know?* The thought makes my chest ache.

"Condom?" he pants.

"No need," I whisper.

"You sure?" Care threads in the gravel of his voice, brow arching.

A condom is reasonable. It makes sense. No binding of our futures. No unexpected ties ...

But that's not what I want.

"I'm sure."

His smile grows. He knows what this means, what I'm saying about us and our future. Emotion thickens his voice. "I'm clean."

"Me, too." I back him to the edge of the bed as he pulls my nightgown over my head, lace sliding away like a secret. His mouth drops to my breasts, hot and greedy.

I gasp as his tongue teases, thumbs brushing hardened

peaks until fever pools low. He lies back and takes me with him. I straddle his hips, sliding slick heat over his hard ridge as he lifts his head and ravishes my nipples again.

Between gasps, I confess, "And I haven't been with anyone since you. It's only ever been you."

He swallows, pupils blown. "No one else could ever do," he whispers, knotted voice raw.

My answer is a kiss. Sizzling, aching ... taking and giving everything.

A tear slips from his lashes to the duvet. "I never thought this would happen, though I dreamed about it more times than I can count."

"It's happening," I whisper. "Now and forever."

He grips my waist, flipping us over and hovering above me with a braced arm. Gentle and decisive, putting me beneath him. A tug of play for dominance, neither of us wants to win.

He slides down my body, and anticipation strangles me.

"I thought you said—"

"I did." He growls. "But I need to taste you first. I'm so fucking hungry for your pussy."

A whimper catches, body dissolving as he bends and parts my legs. His movements are achingly slow and sensual. Fingers glide to the center of my ache and slip under the lace.

"So wet for me," he murmurs, reverent. He kisses over satin. My hips arch, begging his tongue. He inhales, shuddering. "Your smell. Your heat. God, I've missed you."

My legs hook over his massive shoulders. He meets my eyes through his lashes as a thick finger dips into me, and I come off the bed.

"This pussy has always been mine," he says.

"Only yours."

He pushes the lace aside and his mouth finds me—slow, sure, greedy. My heart hammers, knowing he's hungered for this as long as I have. Tongue circling, then lips sealing, a steady draw that makes my hips chase him. A teasing nip that steals my breath. My whole body quivers.

He chuckles, the sound rumbling against my core. "I'm going to come in my jeans."

"Should we—"

"No, Lila. I need to make you feel better than you ever have. I need to remind your body who I am."

My fingers knot in his short mahogany hair and press him closer. He swirls and sucks, humming low, vibration scattering through me, exquisite, excruciating.

"Yes," I cry, arching as his finger curls, lighting my sweet spot like a switch. No fumbling—only memory.

One, two, three pulls of his finger. I'm seconds from breaking. The world narrows to his demanding tongue.

My thighs tighten around his head. He adds a second digit, a delicious stretch. Tongue stroking, he refuses anything but surrender. I'm wrecked, quivering, beyond thought.

"Holden," I scream as he sucks me hard, slides in a third finger, moaning against me.

I gush across his face, walls spasming and sucking his fingers deeper. He goes feral, licking and lapping until I'm nothing but tremors. I melt—shaking, spent.

In one explosive move, he sheds denim and boxers, warm, hard planes pressing into me. My panties follow, flying across the room. One arm braces beside my head so he doesn't crush me. Wicked written all over his face.

But I'm no innocent, and I've waited far too long. I wrap my legs around his waist, impatient and needy. He lowers his forehead to mine, pausing, breathing the same air.

"Home," he says.

"Home," I echo. For a moment, the world stills, our chests lifting in sync, time suspended on a single word. The universe could end, and we'd still be here.

He grinds, small, precise shifts, and then his thick, slick length catches and slides inside. Slow, breath-stealing.

Every inch a revelation. He stills, lids squeezed shut, fighting for control.

Holden's soul radiates love when his gaze returns to my face. His hands cradle my cheeks, and he tucks a stray curl behind my ear, fingering the flower still in my hair. Time locks. Only us. Then, he moves, slow, authoritative, surrendering and leading with each long stroke.

From tip to base, he caresses me, letting me feel all of him. His hand curves my neck, thumb sweeping the vulnerable strip of flesh before his mouth follows. Feathering, worshipping, then, sucking, emblazoning me with his mark.

His other hand cups my breast, fingers teasing my swollen peak. I arch back, grinding against him. "I remember the first time you let me touch these," he mutters, boyish wonder flashing. I'm back in my second-story bedroom, warm fingers slipping beneath dainty lace to a breathless chorus of yeses.

"I've missed you," I pant, as his hips roll, retreat, claim.

"Being without you"—thrust, a slow pull—"gnawed me into"—deeper—"nothing."

He retreats and dips again, a slow and steady rhythm, every part centered on my pleasure.

Catching my waist, he draws my hips up towards him, adjusting the angle, driving and dragging over that spot again and again until language deserts me.

He's a storm building inside me, dark clouds expanding, electricity sizzling between layers of burgeoning gray.

I'm the thunder rolling closer, pulling him in with the same inevitability that kept us alive ... even apart. His pace quickens, breath roughening, muscles flexing under my hands.

"Oh, God," I cry, nails digging, as if he's the only thing rooting me against a hurricane.

"I want you to pull me under," he groans, driving deeper, harder ... need and prayer colliding.

I break over him, vision receding to black, then going starry. For a moment, it feels like drowning, like flying, like touching the edge of forever. I clutch him tight as he thrusts once more, buries himself to the hilt, and comes with me.

Heat floods deep. He rides the waves, groaning, shaking, splitting inside me after lifetimes apart.

I clutch his neck, unwilling to ever let go. He's mine. Nothing will separate us.

Shivers taper. Sweat cools. He strokes my jaw, eyes dark and heavy. "This is the only place I've ever felt safe. Home. Buried inside you."

"Souls touching," I whisper, the words from a hundred letters and two young hearts.

He nods, the corners of his mouth lifting as tears slip from my lashes. Somewhere below, a car door thunks. The night swallows it. Holden's thumb catches another tear, and for the first time in ten years, my exhale reaches the end of itself.

ELEVEN

DELILAH

I can't remember the last time I slept so little. Or woke up so alive.

It feels like a dream. Too good to be real.

Holden strokes a lazy hand through my scarlet hair, spreading it across the pillow like a crown.

"Burgundy silk. What I've dreamed of waking up to for a decade."

His arm anchors me, heavy and protective. His breath warms my temple. Every time he shifts, smoke and soap drift over me, the roughness and the softness in one man. This isn't a memory. He's really here.

His lips trail from my temple to my cheek, along my jaw, down my neck until I giggle into the pillow. It feels reckless to laugh in this new, fragile dawn, as if joy itself might shatter if I hold it too tightly.

"Thought you'd be tired of me after last night," I whisper, voice rough from heartfelt confessions and ecstatic cries.

"Not possible." He sucks at the hollow of my throat until I yelp and swat him. "Better wear a scarf today.

Haven't seen you look like this since your teens, when you swore to your mama you burned yourself with a curling iron."

I roll my eyes, smiling despite myself. "Always a bad boy. Always my greatest weakness. Not that she cared. Too busy with her own life."

"And me," he says, mouth curving against my skin. "Too busy with you."

"Let's keep it that way."

I tilt back towards him, a lazy invitation. He slides in slow, each stroke as easy as breath ... like the years between us were only a bad winter. He grips my hips, and time collapses.

Holden's groan rumbles against my spine, low and broken. We lost count last night. How many times desire overtook us, how many times the sheets cooled only to tangle again. Every sigh, every half-asleep moan rekindled the flame until dawn.

"You feel so fucking good. Heaven itself," he murmurs, hips rolling deeper.

"Yes, lover boy," I gasp, the nickname falling off my tongue like it never left. His thumb finds my clit, circling, coaxing, pulling me taut. "That's it ... oh God ... yes."

He knows my body like the tide knows the shore. His hand finds my breast. I arch into his tease.

His thrusts roughen. His voice raw. "Take me with you."

"Holden—" His name breaks from me as my body clenches and shatters in his arms. I'm quake and fire. He drives deep as heat floods me, and I melt, trembling, whole.

For long breaths, there's only panting, skin to skin, sweat cooling. Nothing but us in this decadent present.

Then, the clock's red digits intrude. Four-thirty a.m.

He'll have to leave soon. Back to the ranch. Back to the real world. My chest tightens.

I tug his hand to my lips, kissing each fingertip before sucking one playfully into my mouth. He groans, already thickening again.

"Call in sick," he mutters, grinding lazily. "Stay with me, Lila."

I turn to catch his earnest eyes and grin. "No one to call in sick to when you're the boss."

"Then don't work," he presses, forehead bumping mine.

"Not sure how I'll get anything done anyway," I admit, cheeks warming. "My mind will be stuck here ... on you."

"Welcome to my world." He brushes a curl from my face. "Since the kiss in the alley. Since I saw you on Main Street again ... scarlet hair, green eyes, pink cheeks. Just like the girl I fell in love with."

"And when did you fall in love with me?" I tease softly, needing the story again.

"Outside the Merc." He doesn't hesitate. "You were blowing blueberry bubbles. I rode past on my bike, and my heart did this weird thing."

"Yes?" I whisper, smiling.

He presses his hand to my chest. "Kathunk, kathunk. And I knew I was in trouble."

I laugh, shaking my head. "I couldn't have been more than eight. You were eleven. You still thought girls had cooties."

"I did," he grins. "But then, I started wondering if I might like your cooties. After that, it was one long snowball roll. Gaining momentum until your eighteenth birthday, when I could *finally* crash into you."

"*That* I'll never forget," I murmur, his heated gaze making me ache again.

"Never," he echoes, reverent.

I savor the silence. His warmth, his weight, the steady beat of his heart. But unease stirs beneath the sweetness ... the scrape of gravel outside, the shadow in his gaze, the knowledge our world isn't safe yet.

I bury my face in his chest and pray we can hold this sliver of peace before the storm finds us again.

Sophia looks like she hasn't slept, her eyes too bright, knuckles pale around her phone.

"What's up? That phone looks glued to your hand?"

She shakes her head. "Just ... online stuff."

"Like school drama?"

"Not that. Bigger." She bites her lip. "Trying to fix something. Make it right."

She's always been like this. Too curious, too relentless. In her, I find the teen I was and the man who never stopped fighting for me.

"You're going to have to explain that a little more ..."

The café door swings open. The room hushes. Holden steps in with a bouquet—violet roses and sunflowers as big as his hands. Suzy and Sophia gape. I can't stop grinning.

"Suzy, cover the register?" I ask. She nods, brows lifted.

Sophia blushes, whispering, "See? He's your Romeo."

"We're not done talking," I warn, patting her shoulder as I pull Holden back into my office. The moment the door clicks. Combustion ... mouths collide, hands roam, fabric rustles ...

Until a polite rap sounds on the office door.

We freeze.

"Miss Dee," Sophia calls. "May I come in and water the fern?"

Holden bristles, breath hot at my ear, "I wanted to do some watering of my own."

I swat his chest lightly. "Go upstairs." I hand him the flowers. "Put these in a vase. I'll be up soon."

"Don't make me wait too long." His scowl is pure sin.

"Never again." I straighten my skirt, checking my lip gloss.

"Your scarf," he says.

Another glance in the mirror. Strawberry kisses bloom at my throat. I guiltily rearrange the layers of necklaces and the scarf. "Next time, somewhere less visible, please."

"Yes, ma'am," he says cheekily.

I open the door. Sophia's eyes are wide, her brows knitted.

"I'll leave you ladies alone—" Holden starts.

"No, please." Sophia paces in, phone clutched tight. "I found something last night you both need to see."

Holden's gaze darts to me.

She pulls up a video and hands me her phone. Holden stands behind me. Grainy, low light. Two shapes. Voices. A third figure on the ground. Footfalls. Muffled curses. A sickening stomp.

"Where did you get this? And what is this?" I ask.

"I didn't film it," she blurts. "I hang out on lost-media threads, okay? People post old clips, weird stuff that vanishes. I post stuff, too. Like requests for lost media related to Hollister, Moreau, you and Holden. Most of what I've gotten back has been a snoozefest. But last night, this rando account—@no_signal—DM'd me, dropped a ten-second clip called 'Whistleblower Stomp.' As soon as I saved it, the message disappeared. Poof. Deleted."

Her eyes cut to Holden, then back to me. "It was a livestream, that's why it's shaky. The voice is masked, but —" she swallows hard, words tumbling faster—"you can hear someone say Moreau. Twice. And look—" She jabs the screen, "See that tattoo? It has to mean something. So I reposted it. Everywhere. Because if it spreads, they can't bury it, right?"

"What?" Holden roars.

Her shoulders stiffen, teenage bravado masking fear. "Yes, I posted it. If more people have it, it's safe. That's the point! If it's out there, whoever wants it gone can't just ... erase it."

"And what if whoever wants it gone comes after you?" His face hardens.

"Why would they? I didn't film it. I'm just keeping it alive."

"Exactly," he grunts.

Fear flickers in her eyes. "I didn't think—" She bites her lip, voice wobbling. "I didn't think they'd care about a kid."

"We need Wolfe," Holden murmurs, already deciding. "Maybe Christian, too."

"Who's Wolfe?"

"One of Holden's foster brothers," I say.

"Former Army Ranger," Holden adds. "Knows the Moreau case. Knows how to help little girls who go down the wrong rabbit holes, too."

"I'm not a little girl," she puffs, chin high.

"Well, you're not old enough for this," he says. "Not sure anyone is."

Alarm fills her eyes. "This is why I kept the analog notebook! So I wouldn't screw up online. But I was just scrolling and it spiraled—"

"Notebook?" Holden grimaces.

"Yes, notebook. Of you. Of Miss Dee. Of Senator Moreau. Just, like ... connecting dots nobody else sees."

His eyes dart to mine. "You know about this?"

"Kind of," I say. "Though I had no clue she'd take it this far."

Sophia paces a groove in the floor, phone clenched.

"Before you get more upset, let's see what Wolfe says," I urge.

An hour later, Wolfe watches the clip three times, jaw set. "If this really came from a livestream, the metadata's our lead. You still have it?"

Sophia nods, handing over her phone. Wolfe's thumbs fly. "Timestamp's embedded. File name's unusual — 'THEYALLFALLDOWN_0421_2.' Burner account, not scrubbed well. Amateurs."

Holden leans in. "So we can trace it."

"Maybe. It's a start," Wolfe says. "But why the DM? Why Sophia? All of this stinks to high heaven."

My stomach drops. Sophia sinks into the turquoise chair, fire flickering. For the first time, she looks small.

"There's more," she whispers, voice racing. "I'm getting death threats on Discord. Same forum. Not just comments —actual DMs. And my address, my school, they're out there."

Wolfe scrolls, face carved from stone. "Doxxed, too?" He stands, all decision. "We need to call your uncle. You've kicked a hornet's nest. The whole family may need protection until this blows over. You both, too." He glances at Holden and me.

"We can't tell my uncle," Sophia hisses.

"Why not?" Wolfe asks.

"Because then I'll be in too much trouble. And they'll send me away. Or get rid of me. And then what?"

Both men redden around the eyes. They've been here.

"Family sticks together," Wolfe says, firm as a vow. "It won't be different this time. But first, we protect you."

I reach for my phone, about to dial Jermaine's number, when a new text message catches my eye.

> Please tell me Sophia's with you

It's him.

> Safe and secure. What's wrong?

> Home invasion

> Place is a mess

> Not sure what they were looking for, but they trashed the house

> Especially Sophia's room

I gasp, covering my mouth with my hand.

Three pairs of eyes look up. Quickly, I read back his texts, voice trembling.

Wolfe commands, "Tell them to leave now. I want his cell. We'll give coordinate points for a safe house. Time for war mode."

TWELVE

HOLDEN

Wolfe turns his laptop around for all to see, jaw tight. Ji-su's hands shake as she rubs her face.

"Sol Rojo cartel tattoo," she mutters. "Same marks as the guy at the lake when Ae-cha died." Her black eyes burn.

The image glows on-screen. A jagged red sun curling around a skull, stamped across a throat. A mark you can't miss. A mark of belonging.

"Same as the surveillance footage from the lake. Same as the man who tried to ambush Bowie and me with his crew," Ji-su says, voice low and flat.

Bowie slides a hand to her back, steadying her.

Wolfe doesn't move. "That alone makes this real." The statement lands heavy in the room.

My chest tightens. "Seen that ink before," I say. Saw it close enough to taste rust on my tongue. A day in the yard, sun blazing, a face with that skull-sun grinning as he worked a shank. I carried the grin this past year, shaping how I read danger. This is not coincidence anymore. "Incident in the yard. Put me in the hospital. Small players with big mouths. Small players with big marks."

Lila's eyes round and pool. She knows what I'm talking about. Couldn't keep it from her, though I tried. Meddling prison officials and the hospital had my woman in tears.

Wolfe's eyes narrow. Rutger runs his hand over his stubbly cheeks. "Knew they tried to take you out. Never saw the connection."

"Me either," I frown. "I ran with—" I cut off, because naming that other world gives it life and space. Lila doesn't need to know about it. "Thought it was a dispute between ranks at the time. But this changes the frame."

Ji-su snaps her gaze up, vengeance bright. "All the more reason it's time for payback."

Her voice cuts. I get it. Anger sharpens everything, but my mind goes higher. Foot soldiers can bleed. They don't topple kings. "This only matters if it gets us to the top," I say, slow. "The one doing the trafficking, the drugs, the laundering, the campaign fraud. The architect behind the chaos." I don't have to say the name for everyone to hear it. Moreau hangs in the air like smoke.

"He's right," Bowie says. "You and Paige need to lock this down. Names, accounts, proof that climbs the ladder." This fight is personal. I see it blazing in his gaze.

Bowie adds, "That means staying here. Working with the team. Not trying to handle things alone."

Ji-su shrugs, avenging flames flickering behind her gaze as she scans a ledger. "Every trail runs into the same redacted block ... like a dead man's vault. We need someone with the master key." She levels her gaze on Wolfe.

He runs a hand over his buzzed hair. Teeth clenched. "Has to be another way."

Paige leans forward, brows furrowed, adding, "Every

ledger I dig into stops at the same point. Accounts go blank, shell corps vanish, everything reroutes into one dead address. Like it's locked behind a wall we don't have the key for."

Ridge mutters, "Moreau knows how to survive a scandal. We can pound him with whistleblowers, document trails till we're hoarse. But we *need* that missing piece."

The brunette shakes her head, frustration etched in her face. "There's already a grand jury file and a mile of witnesses, but he's slippery." She spits the last word like a curse. "He's built an empire on getting away."

"At least we shut down the House of the Seven Prophets," Axel says from the doorway, arms crossed. His voice is granite. Small victories, big cost.

"But it can't end there." Wolfe grunts. "If something's missing, we have to get to the bottom of it."

"It's not absence," Ji says darkly. "It's presence. Too clean. Like someone left a hole on purpose ..."

Like the informant DM'd Sophia ...

Across the room, the teen perches on the edge of the couch like a fuse about to blow, hands fidgeting in her lap. Safehouse rules—no personal devices, only secured laptops. She looks tortured without her phone. "Maybe we find the person who streamed that video," she says. "Figure out why they put it out. What else they know ... or want."

The room goes still.

Wolfe locks his fingers under his chin.

"Or it's bait," I mutter. "We don't know who's holding the other end." Sharp hook or saving grace?

Rutger, the Ranger sniper, spits, "Coming for us, setting traps on our turf, hurting our people? I'm done sitting quiet."

Wolfe's voice is steady, practiced. "We dig, but we do it

smart. I talked to Sophia's uncle and aunt. She stays in contact with the forum, but through us. Ghost accounts, rotating proxies, full disk encryption on every cache. If the uploader bites, it pings us first … a dead drop with fingerprint logging. One false move, and they get a sandbox, not a breadcrumb."

He looks at Sophia like she's a fragile grenade. "No posts without clearance."

She nods, eyes wide.

He names tools and threats with the calm of someone who's set up a hundred fences.

A laptop on the couch next to Sophia rings. Replacement for her mourned cell phone. Her stake in monitoring internet chatter. She leaps up and crosses to Lila, eyes bright. "Look." Her smile is too big for how raw she looks. She holds the screen like it's proof and salvation.

Lila eyes the laptop, breathless. "Hashtag trending..." She swallows. "#RememberHolden."

My eyes scan the results. A clip from a local reporter:

Holden Boone Framed? Hollister Divided

A stat pops: twelve thousand views in an hour. Under that, a legal fund started for my continued court battles … five grand in two hours.

Below that, a conspiracy account spinning it into a political hit job. The internet is chewing over my life and spitting it back louder.

My gut twists, and my chest burns. A private man long denied that common courtesy. Face plastered, life revealed. Discussed, berated, lauded. It's almost too much to bear.

Taking a deep breath, I ask Sophia, "You started this?"

She flushes. "Yes. I've been pushing your story … evidence they buried, the corruption. People are starting to listen." She looks proud and terrified all at once.

I feel violated. Public fodder.

Paige arches a brow. "Hasn't it hit your feeds yet? It's everywhere. A rallying cry."

Something in me uncoils—anger at being hailed and hatred at the attention. But there's an ember of something else, too. A warmth I haven't let myself feel in a decade. Strangers defending me?

Lila tangles her fingers with mine, steady and sure, eyes shining with a pride I don't deserve. For one long breath, the fight fades, and it's just her hand in mine. The only truth that's ever mattered. The only anchor I need.

I let my chest uncoil. Then, my fingers find the ridge of an old scar through my shirt. It's a small thing, a map I know by heart. I press it like a promise. Come what may, I'm ready.

And that's when I know if Moreau rains hell down on Hollister, I'll stand and take every bullet before I let him near my girl. We've already lost far too much at his hands.

Lila touches my arm, "They need to know the truth. What was done to you."

I squeeze her hand, voice low. "It means Moreau comes harder. Faster. He won't let this stand."

Wolfe nods. "It's inevitable. You, Paige, Ji-su, me, now Sophia ... we've all painted a big bullseye on Hollister. Time to defend our home."

"And take the fight to them," Ridge adds, arm wrapped fiercely around Paige.

"Like we've been doing. With Paige's investigation of the House of the Seven Prophets. Ji-su's data collection and analysis of Moreau's campaign finances and real estate deals. The cartel ties uncovered by Hawk and Roxy on Three Nations Reservation. Our human trafficking stings. We've got him right where we want him, which makes him dangerous ... like a cornered animal."

Ji-su's voice is a low growl. "He'll lash out." The map of her face hardens with the memory of loss.

I feel the room tilting toward a plan. "And we won't blink," I say. "We'll defend our community, then we'll take the fight to him." My words are clipped, determined ... words of a man with something worth fighting for.

Wolfe taps the laptop. "We'll set a controlled channel through Sophia. She can prod her lost-media contacts from our end. You good with that, little lady?"

The corners of her mouth turn up, face determined as she nods.

"But her safety—" I growl.

"We'll route her through three proxies, then air-gap the archive. If anyone pings it, they hit a false node." He looks at me like he's telling me how to hold a bomb.

I nod, jaw clenched. My eyes dart to Lila, stomach knotting at the thought of her in harm's way. Then, they find Sophia. Don't know the teen well. But if anything happened to her, I know Lila would be devastated. More than enough reason to guard her with my life.

Wolfe continues, "We'll hard-link what we find to financial trails—accounts, shell companies, anything that ties cartel movements to Moreau's real estate and campaign accounts." He names the scaffolding of the case like a surgeon mapping an incision.

Bowie adds, "We rig the café as bait if we have to. Wired, recorded, every angle covered. We don't pull the trigger unless we get what we need. A confession or incontrovertible evidence." He looks at me like he expects blood in the road and wants to be ready for it.

I nod once. The fight's moved from memory to plan. My

jaw unclenches a fraction. We'll make Moreau answer. We'll make his underlings and lackeys lead us straight to the center of the viper den.

"We'll be ready."

The vow echoes off the safehouse walls, swallowed by silence. On Wolfe's laptop, the tattooed throat glares back like a warning. On Sophia's, #RememberHolden scrolls faster and faster, a tide we can't control.

My gut knots. A final showdown with Moreau looming. Will the coward send more goons? Will he man up and meet face-to-face?

Memory hammers me. The last time I saw him. The ancient courthouse in Ophir City. Crowds gathered. Cameras flashing. Senator Moreau, the epitome of the mourning father. But if Gregory was his fixer ...

A tremor runs through me before I feel Lila's fingers lace with mine. Her touch steadies me, soft against the jagged edge inside.

"We'll be ready," she echoes. "He's not taking you from me again."

Her words slice through the fear, turning it into fire. I lift her hand to my lips, kiss her knuckles, and fix my eyes on Wolfe.

"We make our stand here. No more letting Moreau pull the puppet strings."

THIRTEEN

DELILAH

The Human Being is dark, a limp sign taped to the window: CAFÉ CLOSED UNTIL FURTHER NOTICE.

Videos of strangers chanting outside my door loop endlessly online. Faces twisted with anger, phones raised like weapons.

Someone dumps a bucket of mud on my stoop. Someone else posts my apartment door with the caption, "Guess who's hiding now?"

A live-streamer paces the sidewalk in new footage, breath visible in the cold, fingers trembling with the thrill of an audience. I feel like I'm watching my life from behind glass.

I can't go home. I can't even ask someone to water my plants without risking exposure. Everything I've worked so hard for—the little chipped espresso machine I saved for, the chalkboard menu I painted myself, the string of paper cranes hanging over the counter—blurs into a billboard of shame. Up in smoke.

The safehouse should feel like protection, but it's a coffin with Wi-Fi. Screens glow blue in every corner. Whispered strategies and clipped profanity thread through the room like a current. Somebody laughs too loud at a feed and then coughs, embarrassed. Every creak of the floor sets my nerves jangling.

Holden sits pressed against me, his palm anchoring mine. He smells of smoke and soap, steady and rough all at once. He's my lighthouse in the storm, yet always the epicenter of its fury. I knew the new me—the quieter, cautious me—would disappear in the flames when he came back. My stomach roils with regrets, and still I would do everything the same for this man. Even knowing how I've lost myself all over again.

Sophia's fingers fly across the keys of a safehouse laptop, chatting online as @starlingcurse. A new chat window blinks alive, and I lean in. I can't help myself. The screen feels like the town square, except the town is everywhere now.

@no_signal: *You've been watching. Monitoring the chatter.*

@starlingcurse: *And you've been filming where you shouldn't.*

@no_signal: *They all must fall.*

@starlingcurse: *Who's "they"?*

@no_signal: *You know.*

@starlingcurse: *That's boring. Need more.*

@no_signal: *He's coming for you.*

@starlingcurse: *Who?*

@no_signal: *Heard his name twice on the video.*

@starlingcurse: *How are you tied to him?*

@no_signal: *Close. Too close. Don't want to end up like Gregory.*

@starlingcurse: You said he was a fixer?

@no_signal: Chip off the old block.

@starlingcurse: Don't believe you. Easy to say a lot behind a screen.

@no_signal: Meet me. Then you'll believe.

@starlingcurse: What do I get from that?

@no_signal: A chance to do the right thing.

Then, user disconnected.

Sophia exhales hard, shoulders sagging. "Guess I'll repost the video." Her voice frays at the edges. She tries to sound light, perform with confidence, but her fingers hover over the keyboard like she's touching a hot plate.

Every upload vanishes almost instantly, but not before thousands watch. And each scrub only fuels the fire. Holden's name is everywhere. Hero. Fraud. Dangerous man. Wronged man. A million people with their million little verdicts.

The video of the beaten whistleblower raises questions. Has people wondering how many others Moreau has steamrolled, destroyed, murdered.

The teen grins as she waves toward the laptop. "Miss Dee, #RememberHolden is still trending … millions of people talking about it! And now #AeChaKnew, too."

The hashtag is a knife in Ji's chest, though her face stays serene.

Sophia taps at replies and shows me a comment where someone calls Holden a saint and another where someone compares him to a monster.

Her grin is too wide, her thumb trembling at the edge of the screen. I fight the urge to wrap her in my arms and take her out of all of this. But before I lean forward, formulate the right words, she moves to Ji.

The Korean beauty is a mask of calm, bittersweet

simmering beneath the surface, her deepest pain on display before the world.

The teen doesn't feel the weight. To her, it's a game. To me, it's the same mob that destroyed my youth, only bigger, louder, armed with hashtags instead of pitchforks.

I remember streetlights and shouting and a window that wouldn't stop rattling. I remember the smell of burnt coffee and the way a town can turn on you so fast it feels like betrayal by gravity.

And yet, here we are strategizing how to save Hollister …

Holden's jaw flexes, his hand squeezing mine. "If anyone touches you—" his voice drops, rough gravel, "They'll regret it for the rest of their lives."

My throat tightens. "Don't say that."

His thumb strokes slowly over my knuckles, gentling the steel in his words. "Say what? That I'll burn the world down before I let them near you?" His crooked smile almost undoes me, but then I see the worry behind it. The slight crease by his left eye, the way his thumb presses harder than it needs to.

Before I can answer, Paige's screen pings. Her face drains of color. The kind of whiteness that steals oxygen.

"They found him."

The room stills.

"Found who?" My stomach knots so tight I have to focus on my breathing to keep from doubling over.

She turns the laptop. A grainy photo fills the screen: the missing whistleblower. Likely the third man in the video. Face swollen, eyes glazed, body dumped behind a chain-link fence, one shoe missing.

The angle is horrible. Someone took it on a phone, shadowed and quick, and for the first time, the abstract horror becomes physical. The man I've read about in briefing notes and snippets, watched in pain on the video, now a cold thing you can almost smell through a pixel.

Sophia gasps.

I scold in hushed tones, "Don't look!" I want to obey my own words. But fascination, curiosity, horror grip me.

Somebody drops a cup. It shatters. My fingers register the ache of Holden's tightening grip. Heat surges up my throat, bile stinging. I taste metal, like when you bite the inside of your cheek on purpose to feel something real.

This isn't gossip. Not politics. This is murder.

Every cell in my body screams to run. To drag Sophia out of here, shove her into the car, and vanish before they mark her next. To beg Holden to disappear with me. Survive by hiding, like I've done before.

But that life hollowed me once already. The shell it gave me is quiet and empty. Survival isn't enough anymore. I refuse to be hollow again.

I straighten, voice shaking but clear. "Then we fight. Smart. Together. Because if we don't, he won't stop until it's us in the dirt."

The words leave a crater of silence, then fill the room like a challenge. Heads turn. Holden's gaze sears into me—pride and fury mingling tight as a fist. He presses a kiss against my temple, rough and reverent. "That's my girl," he breathes, so close I can feel the scrape of his stubble.

Standing, Holden pulls me down the dark hallway, away from the glow of screens and the drone of tense voices. The shadows swallow us whole. My back hits the wall, his body caging me in, heat radiating through his chest.

His mouth crashes against mine, rough and desperate, tasting of coffee and fury. His arms bracket me, unyielding, and for one dizzying second, the fear dripping from every corner of this safehouse evaporates. There is only us.

His hands roam down my hips, grip firm, claiming. My fingers fist the front of his shirt, dragging him closer, until there's no space left, no oxygen—just his breath, his heat, his pulse pounding into me.

"God, Dee," he rasps against my mouth, teeth grazing my lower lip. "Every second I'm not touching you feels like a war I'm losing."

My head tilts back, a moan escaping before I can stop it. His stubble scrapes my skin, delicious and raw. The weight of him pins me, yet I've never felt freer. I want him to tear the world away until there's only this hallway, this kiss, this storm of want.

I break for air, forehead pressed to his. "We can't—" The words shake. "Not here."

He breathes hard, jaw tight. "I know. But I needed to remind you you're mine. That no matter what happens out there—" His thumb brushes my cheek, tender after the roughness. "We burn together."

The voices grow louder, tugging us out of the shadows. Holden's body lingers against mine for one last heartbeat, then he steps back, sliding his armor on like a second skin. My lips are swollen, my pulse erratic, but when we reenter the safehouse's command room it's as if none of it happened.

Except it did. I taste him on my mouth, feel the imprint of his hands on my hips, every nerve still sparking. The room smells of leather, hay, sweat, gun oil. But under it all, I carry Holden's heat with me like a secret flame.

The others don't notice our absence, too focused on how the air shifts when the Amestoy brothers enter, Basque shepherds bristling opposite Rough & Ready cowboys.

Fierce clasps Sheriff Christian's hand. Old grudges linger between shepherds and cowboys. Maps spread, laptops glow, tension charges the air.

I stand taller, steadier, even as I slip back into the circle. Because of Holden's reminder in that dark hallway that I'm not just surviving this. I'm burning for it. Burning with him.

"Better we fight beside you than let this town rot," Fierce growls, French-tinged voice vibrating the room.

Christian scowls. "We don't need saving. But fine. Stay."

Wolfe cuts through the chest-beating, practical and cold as a scalpel. "Your women and kids safe?"

"Thought we'd send them to Rough & Ready." Fierce says. "Considering how tightly you've buttoned up your ranch." The half-smile that flickers across his face is meant to be teasing, but there's ice under the humor.

"Works for me," Wolfe growls. "Any objections?"

Holden's brothers shuffle uneasily, eyes flicking among themselves. Muscles flex, egos show, old grudges simmer just beneath the surface. A fragile alliance and a deadly quiet room.

"Just keep those fucking sheep off our pastures," Zane warns testily, eyes narrowing.

Fierce's jaw tightens. Tension crackles through the air.

Ridge cuts in, voice hard. "No objections. Safety of our families always comes first. We have to assume Moreau has eyes everywhere."

Ji's smile is sharp. "So do we. They think they're the hunters. They're wrong." There's a bite to her that makes me glad she's on our side.

The plan sprawls across laptops and notepads. Feed @no_signal information. Bait him into showing his hand. Offer him a false way out, and when he reaches for it ... spring the trap. It's dirty. It's surgical. It's exactly the kind of thing I'd have hated before, and now I'm oddly proud to be part of it. Either it leads to more information and a new ally, or it leads straight to Moreau.

Paige frowns at her scrolling feed, thumbs moving too quickly. "It's working. Internet chatter's clear. Someone wants Sophia and Dee ... to get to Holden. Bring maximum pain." Her voice is small, tight. She scrolls and points to a thread with coordinate drops and mentions of a fixer. "Someone is suggesting a meet tonight. Someone else joking about a ransom. All hidden behind the anonymity of the internet."

The illusion of safety cracks wide open like a door being kicked in.

Holden's mouth finds my ear, his whisper dark and sure. "Whoever they are ... they'll never touch you. Not her. Not you. Over my dead body."

"Please don't talk that way," I tell him, because words like that are promises that threaten like storm clouds.

Wolfe's voice is grim. "Got to be coming from Moreau ... his crew. He's a cornered animal. More dangerous than ever." He taps at a spreadsheet with a kind of brutal efficiency. "He *will* lash out. The only question is where and when."

"Need more evidence, better leads." Paige sighs, wary.

Fierce bares his teeth. "Why wait? Let's end him before he ends us." His hands are large and scarred, the kind of hands that braid ropes and take down bears that threaten the herd. Now, they close around the idea of a plan like a vise.

The Rangers, the brothers, the shepherds—all gathered, all ready. Somebody rolls out a map of Hollister and pins locations like pieces on a board. Ji marks potential choke points. Paige pulls up a live server trace. Ridge counts ammo with a careful, detached rhythm.

I stand in the center of it. No longer the woman who hides, minds her own business. But the woman who will choose where to stand and who to stand with. The storm isn't coming. It's already here, and for the first time in a long time, I don't want to run from it.

FOURTEEN

DELILAH

"Rutger, how's that facial recognition verification coming on the video and the photo?" Wolfe barks.

"Lining up, boss man. Think we've got our identities locked."

Sophia's eyes are dinner-plate wide, her face pale as she stares at the laptop assigned to her. I come up behind her, seeing she's still transfixed on the dead whistleblower.

"You need to stop looking at that, Pipsqueak. Maybe hang out with your aunt and uncle. Eat something. Take a nap."

Her eyes are glazed, her mocha skin washed out to ash. "I-I-I think I saw him die," she whispers. "At the end... after that loud crack, like a boot hitting the floor. He didn't move. Not at all."

I long to shield her from this nightmare, take away the fear shivering across her skin. But I'm helpless. She's already seen too much.

"Focus on something else for a bit, okay? You need a break. Clear your mind."

"How? We're locked in here like prisoners. No phone, no

friends, nothing. It's like being grounded forever, only worse."

"It's for your safety," I scold gently, resting my hand on her shoulder.

"Already put Uncle Jermaine and Auntie Jospehine through enough. Don't want to bother them."

"But you can't bother family," I interject.

She lets out a short, bitter laugh. "Depends on the family."

"Is there a problem here?" Holden asks, wrapping a possessive arm around my waist.

Sophia bites her bottom lip. "Nope. Just bored out of my mind." She wanders away, and Holden eyes me curiously.

"Bored in the middle of an undercover sting?" he asks, exasperated. "What do kids these days expect?"

"She wants her cell phone," I answer. "Going crazy without it."

His brows furrow. "But there are screens everywhere in this room."

The corners of my mouth turn down. "Not the right screen."

He nods, grim.

Across the room, Bowie comforts Ji, the fallout from #AeChaKnew finally settling in. I don't want to pry, so I look away, counting my blessings. That the man in my hashtag is still very much alive, though changed in so many ways.

My childhood friend turned teenage lover, then the source of all my pain and hope while behind bars. At least Holden and I share the security of existing in the same time, breathing the same air. Ji will never have that again with her sister.

Sophia curls up with another laptop, gasping. "They're

trending together now—#RememberHolden and #AeCha-Knew. It's blowing up. People are spinning wild theories, demanding justice, dragging Moreau's name into everything. It's like the internet's on fire!"

She says it like triumph, but my stomach knots. Holden shifts uneasily.

Christian rants and paces. "It's a damn media circus—"

Fierce cuts in. "Good. Now, Moreau can't hide."

I feel scrutinized, spied on, vulnerable beneath the public gaze. As if Holden's and my ruin is fueling a tsunami. Ji's bitter gaze echoes the sting, her hand clenching into a fist. Yet I also see quiet acceptance in her eyes, a kind of peace I don't yet know how to reach.

"Gotta go soon, bro," Christian's voice cuts in, tense.

Wolfe looks up. "Then, let's get to it. Everyone around the table."

Sophia stands back, biting her lip.

"You, too, little lady," Wolfe says, softening his tone and motioning toward an empty chair.

She beams like she's just been knighted, thrilled to be part of something bigger than herself.

"We have confirmation on the death of the whistle-blower, with Chris about to head back to the department to investigate," Wolfe says. "Body found in woods near the Gold and Fortune County borders. Any word on where the jurisdiction has landed?"

"Land survey crew's out there now. Shaping up to be a multi-county mess. Manhunt likely. I'll keep you posted."

"Now," Wolfe continues. "As for Sophia's work on the informant. We've got a meeting in the works. Question is where and when?"

Fierce growls. "Amestoy Ranch is yours. Secluded, quiet.

I know every chokehold, every ridge. We'd control the terrain."

Christian bristles. "Nope. No way. It should happen in Hollister or Ophir City. Keep jurisdiction clean."

They glare, the air thick with old grudges. Land wars, grazing rights.

"Physical location aside, we need to optimize our digital strategy," Ridge cuts in, ignoring them. "Use decoys, false chatter."

Wolfe nods toward Sophia. "Think you can help with that?"

"Of course!"

Fierce and Christian's voices rise again, sharp as knives. I can't take it. Infighting only means one thing … vulnerability. With an enemy like Moreau, any crack could be lethal.

"How about my café," I chime in, heart sinking even as I speak. "It's the most natural location to meet, especially if, as we suspect, the informant is using Sophia to get to Holden and me."

"No," Holden cuts in. "I don't want you anywhere near the danger."

"Everyone here is making sacrifices. I need to, too."

"Not at the expense of your safety. Not your café. Not your apartment."

Wolfe barks, "She has a point. The café makes sense. No informant's going to walk into a deserted town. We need normal. Life in Hollister going on as usual. Only eyes everywhere. Crowd control, too."

Holden shakes his head, fury simmering. I touch his arm, softening him. Lifting his chin, he growls, "Then I'll be there, too. In the fray. With Sophia and Lila."

"We'll do this together, like how we started it," I whisper.

Wolfe nods. "Dee, you're officially part of the team. Welcome."

Holden scowls, dragging me into his arms protectively. I melt into him, listening as Wolfe runs through the plan until questions give way to silence.

"Anything else?" Wolfe asks, face set in stone.

A heavy silence descends.

"If not, I better head to the department," Christian says. "Sort out jurisdiction on the body. Follow more leads into Sophia's home intrusion. Call me if you hear something new."

"Already sent files for corroboration," Wolfe replies.

Christian nods. "I'll have it back ASAP. Have to tread carefully. More eyes, more potential for leaks."

"I'm coming with you," Axel adds. "To check on Dad, our girls, and the kids. Make sure the Amestoys feel at home."

Fierce grins, savage though grateful.

"Stay frosty and keep your powder dry," Wolfe calls as they leave.

Holden pulls me by the hand, leading me upstairs. His grip is fierce, his face flushed with anger.

"I don't like it," he growls once we're behind a closed door.

"I promise I'll be careful."

He presses me against him, breathing in the scent of my hair. "I don't want you anywhere near this shit. You're my home. My sacred space. I can't risk danger touching you."

I step back, brow arched. "And I can't stay on the sidelines. We live together, we fight together. Whatever life demands, we do it together."

His face hardens.

I cup his cheeks. "You'll never win this fight with me. Not because you aren't my everything. But because I won't live hollow anymore. My café's already a mess, already covered in mud and graffiti. Let's make it matter."

His forehead rests on mine, hands gripping my waist. "You're stubborn."

"It's the redhead in me."

"It's the firebrand in you. Drives me crazy. Turns me on."

His lips find mine, fire and heat, tenderness and ache. I sigh, and he slides inside, tongue stroking away thought. Desire sparks, his hand slipping under my blouse, thumb teasing the underside of my breast. I moan, the sound swallowed by his kiss. It's desperate ... the melancholy kind when lovers taste doom in the distance.

He pulls back, panting. "I won't let anything happen to you. Ever."

"And I refuse to live apart ... ever again."

"Then we do this side by side," he whispers, fingering the promise ring.

"Miss Dee." Sophia's whisper cuts through the dark, her phone screen glowing against her worried face.

My stomach drops. "What is it?" I stir in bed next to Holden, and he groans, drawing me closer.

"I'm sorry," she blurts, voice trembling. "I screwed up."

"Hold that thought. Go wait in the hallway. I'll be right behind you."

I scramble into my purple, floral silk robe, padding out

into the hallway. Bright lights glare, and I shield my eyes until they adjust.

Sophia's face looks broken. My blood goes cold. "What did you do?"

"I ... I took my phone. I had to text Amy."

I blink. "The girl who gives you a hard time?"

Her smile flickers, nervous and shy. "More like the girl I can't stop thinking about. One second, she's all over me, the next, she acts like I'm a mistake. But tonight she texted me first. And I couldn't not answer."

"Oh, Pipsqueak." My heart aches. I know that look. I had it once, staring at Holden when the world told me he'd ruin me. Love makes fools of brave people.

"I just ... I miss her," Sophia says, eyes shiny. "And I wanted her to see I'm not some loser. So she wants me like I want her. Because I'm—" Her voice cracks. "Because I'm internet famous now."

"Internet famous?" My chest tightens. "Sophia ..."

She shrugs, trying for bravado but looking small. "My handle's everywhere. People are obsessed with the video. They're calling it, like, the holy grail of leaks."

I gasp.

"So I went back in ... just for a second. To screenshot stuff, show Amy the comments. And then—" Her breath hitches. "@no_signal DM'd me."

I take her phone, horror tightening my chest as I read:

@no_signal: There you are

@starlingcurse: And so?

@no_signal: Now or never ... where?

@starlingcurse: ???

@no_signal: Meeting tonight ... or not at all

@starlingcurse: The Human Being?

@no_signal: Breaking and entering?

@starlingcurse: Owner's like my mom. I have a key
@no_signal: 3 AM

Holden appears in the doorway, groggy-eyed and bare-chested in Wranglers. "What's going on?" I hand him Sophia's phone, and his eyes snap to life.

"Dammit, Sophia. You said you have a key to the café. That Lila's like a mother? Now, they know who you are, where you are, and how to find you."

"I think they always did ... Why else did they DM?"

"Maybe, but—"

"But that's what Wolfe said during the meeting. That Miss Dee's café would be the place to lure @no_signal."

Holden's chest rumbles with frustration, eyes simmering.

"I didn't think—" Sophia crumples, whispering, "I just wanted her to see me. Not ruin everything."

His eyes flick to mine, confused.

"I'll explain later," I say.

My head spins, eyes darting between the two people I care most about in this world. Sophia has collapsed all secrecy into one identifiable detail. I'm terrified we'll all pay for it.

Holden exhales hard, scrubbing a hand over his face. "Dammit, kid. You're smarter than this. You can't hand them your life like that."

Wolfe pops his head out of a room down the hallway. "What's up?"

"Take a look at this," Holden grumbles, heading toward him.

Boots thunder. Clipped commands. Texts fire as the house snaps awake.

Basque shepherds and cowboys load weapons. Rangers check gear. It's surreal. Generational grudges set aside, disparate groups working in affiliation.

"Never thought I'd live to see this," Wolfe says, coming up beside me. "How are you holding up?"

"Okay," I whisper. "But does it really have to be tonight?" I saw Sophia's text, but all of the commotion and hubbub still feels like overkill.

"Said tonight or never. One shot. Figure we better make the most of it."

"If this is Moreau's man. If they've been using Sophia to get to Holden and me ..." I shake my head, pressing my finger to my temple.

"Best guess?" Wolfe asks, raising an eyebrow. "They plan on abducting or killing Sophia."

The dangerous words rush through me like a bad dream. "But why kill her if the cat's already out of the bag? There's no way they can suppress that video now ... or stop what's started online."

"Yes, but they may want to use her as leverage to get to you or Holden." My stomach knots.

A tender kiss drops to my temple, and Holden slides his arm around my waist. Instead of the conflict I've seen in his face ever since arriving at the safehouse, he looks determined. "This is it. I can feel it in my bones. We draw Moreau out tonight."

I don't know if this will be a trap or a war. Only that tonight, everything changes.

FIFTEEN

The safehouse grinds with frenetic energy, each person a cog in the bigger plan. Boots tightened. Magazines loaded. Weapons holstered.

Wolfe sits at the head of the table, poring over the thrown-together op. He reads off names. People line up for assignments. To a mixture of Amestoys and Rough & Ready cowboys, he barks, "You guard the ranch and our families. This is ground zero. Any infractions, I hear immediately."

Grim nods all around.

"To the rest," he says, "Christian has Main Street covered, deputies concealed from sight. Choke points set, ready to block traffic if needed. Hawk's in the air with the bird."

"And Farzad?" Logan asks.

"Out of play. Flying in Hawk's stead at the hospital."

"The rest of us post at discreet spots to watch the café. Holden, Dee, and Sophia are wired. Rangers rush the place if it goes sideways. 'All clear' means you're good. If it isn't— say 'haywire,' hit the floor, and we take it from there."

Sophia's bottom lip trembles.

"Second thoughts?" Wolfe asks, and the hard edge softens.

"No, I just want to do this right. For Holden. For Ae-cha. For the whistleblower," she whispers, fierceness simmering beneath the fear.

"We're assuming the informant knows who you are," Wolfe adds. "Knows Dee owns The Human Being. Knows her tie to Holden. Otherwise, the initial DM makes no sense. So Holden and Dee stay with you the whole time."

"Will the informant have a gun?" she asks, eyes rounding.

"I'll pat them down," I say.

Wolfe continues, "Dee does what she does best. Serves coffee and listens. If anything's off—"

"Don't like this part," I grumble. "Lila or Sophia in harm's way."

"That's why they won't be," Wolfe fires back, looking past me to Jermaine and Josephine. "Just there to set the informant at ease. Without Sophia, my guess is they spook."

"It'll be okay. We'll be careful," Lila reassures, palm warm on my arm.

"No," I say, stepping in front of her. My body makes the point.

She steps around me anyway, stubborn to the bone, and takes her place at my side. Warmth spreads in my chest as frustration simmers.

A week ago, I was still the one getting searched. Tonight, I'm the one securing the scene. Funny how fast life flips.

"And what if the informant didn't contact me to get to Holden and Dee?" the kid asks.

"Unlikely," Wolfe says, eyes narrowing. "But if they're

real and clean, we figure out why they want you and how they can help us. They never said you had to come alone."

She nods, stony-faced.

Wolfe looks to her aunt and uncle. "Still good with everything?"

Jermaine hesitates. "Not completely. But if we don't find out who's contacting her and why, possibly why our house was sacked ... she's still in danger. We all are."

Jospehine ruffles her hair. "And knowing our Sophia, she won't stop until there's justice."

"I have three children," Wolfe reassures. "I won't take any unnecessary risks with Sophia. You have my word."

Sophia straightens, shoulders back. "I've got this."

Wolfe's frown gives nothing away.

Paige stands, eyeing the couple warmly. "Come with me. I'll set you up with comms as needed."

A reasonable enough request. An excuse to get them out of the room before the real briefing starts.

"Paige will push ambush points to all units," he says. "Once we roll, it's radio silence until everyone's set and targets are in sight. No cell phones. Walkies only when green-lit. Or you see something. You three stay on wire."

Ji steps forward, calm as stone. "No detail should be overlooked. Report everything. Even a gut feeling."

Ridge adds, "Stay sharp. Watch your six."

Bowie nods, pride and worry in his eyes. "Been a bounty hunter for years now. Seen a lot. But Moreau's guys? Unpredictable as hell. Keep your eyes peeled."

"Final questions?" Wolfe barks.

Silence.

"Ninety minutes to go-time. Move out."

A SHADOW STRING of SUVs wends down Four Eighty-Eight. Every mile towards Hollister tightens my throat a notch. Left hand on the wheel, right free, I find Lila's hand and squeeze—promise and anchor. Restless. Focused. Ready to put down anyone who lays a hand on my woman ... or the girl.

Sophia fidgets in the backseat, trying to act tough, whispering every few minutes to Lila. "What if they don't show? What if they do? What if there's more than one?"

Lila smiles, patient, unshakeable. "We won't be alone. Not even for a minute. We'll have Holden with us. And we'll be surrounded by combat-tested Rangers. The best."

Sophia knits her brows, unconvinced.

"Lila and I won't leave your side, Pipsqueak," I add before I catch myself.

She lets out a tense giggle.

I grimace. "Picking up nicknames from my girl."

"It's fine. I think you've earned it," she says.

"After tonight, it's tough stuff from now on," I grumble.

"Tough stuff," she repeats, mouth quirking.

Lila twists towards the backseat. Stretching an arm. Taking the girl's hand. "Always has been, if you ask me."

Sophia grins. "Earlier, I thought @starlingcurse was the coolest thing to be called. Internet famous and all. But I like 'tough stuff.' Might keep it."

The laughter thins as we roll past The Human Being. Boards. Spray paint. Slurs and prayers layered over each other. Lila's grip tightens. Color rises in her cheeks. She's trying not to react, but heat pours off her.

Ten years of building trashed. We drive past the block and park out of sight. Move quickly through the alley. Lila clutches the back-door key so hard I expect her palm to bleed.

For one heavy heartbeat, she just stands there, letting it hit. Echoes of her life in the quiet alley. The life I blew up by coming back.

"Sorry," I murmur at her ear, throat thick. "This is on me. For not saying goodbye when I should've."

Her eyes flash to mine, hot and sure. "Never. You're all I want. All I need."

Sophia slides between us, steals the keys, and grins. "Enough, Romeo and Juliet. We have a trap to set."

Lila's eyes dance. I swallow a laugh. Kid's got timing ... and guts.

I drop my mouth to Lila's ear. "We'll rebuild. Better than ever. I swear."

"We already are," she whispers, eyes shining. "No more talk of goodbyes. Promise?"

"Promise."

Inside, Lila takes back her café. Lights on. Broom in hand. Glass and grit in the dustpan. A draft snakes through the boards. The espresso machine hums to life, and the whir of the coffee grinder spins the air rich, velvety.

From a warped corner of the window, I watch our people fan out. Stealthy Rangers slide into position, Amestoys and cowboys settle into overwatch, rifles trained. Not enough time to pull boards, but enough gaps to see and be seen. I don't love it. Feels like a glass cage.

Sophia plants herself at a table away from the windows, sets up her laptop, and fingers the wire at her collar. She looks scared and steady at the same time. Makes me proud.

She reminds me of Lila as a teen. Strong, independent, able to carry the world the adults around her can't.

Lila draws shots, spilling them into two paper cups. Into a mug and saucer, she pours clouds of steamy milk. Mixes in ribbons of brown syrup with a long spoon. Then, adds a mountain of whipped cream sprinkled with curls of chocolate. She sets it in front of Sophia.

Haven't studied my woman in barista mode until now. It's sexy as hell. My mouth waters, mind grinding over the many ways I'd like to use that whipped cream and chocolate.

Sophia exclaims, "S'mores Hot Cocoa!"

"For luck," Lila says to the teen. She crosses to me and slides over a to-go cup. "To keep you on your toes."

I take a sip. "Perfect brew. Perfect amount of cream."

She nods, small smile, then brings her own cup to her lips.

"Black?" I ask.

"Still learning the new me, lover boy?" she teases, covering the tremor with flirt. "Black for me."

"Only subject I ace." I wink. Another detail to hold onto.

The clock crawls toward three. Tension tightens like a noose. Thick and quiet, full of breath and threat.

I itch to end this. To stake our ground and stop running. Tonight.

Sophia fidgets, fingers tap-tapping the table. Her face glows in the blue of the screen, lights dimmed to make scanning the scene outside easier on my eyes. I hear the soft patter of her scrolling.

"Not causing trouble, right?" I ask without looking.

She startles. "No, just scrolling the forums." A yawn she can't hide.

I return to watching Main Street. Looking for any signs of movement.

Empty. Waiting.

Sophia gasps. Lila and I spin.

"They just DM'd me," she whispers.

"And?" I ask.

She reads, "Knew you wouldn't come alone. Good."

Lila's eyes find mine.

Sophia shifts. "What does that mean?"

A black Lexus with dark tint slides by low and mean. Footfalls hammer the sidewalk ... heavy, deliberate.

Sophia squirms in her seat, face flushing. "Oh, my God, I can't do this."

Lila moves in, clamps her hand, forces a smile. "Yes, you can. You will. You've got this, tough stuff. I'm right here ... behind the counter."

Wolfe mapped every inch of this place. Telling us where to stand. Putting our eyes where he wants them. Me in shadow. Sophia and Lila front and center, like it's just another morning at the café.

Wolfe's voice crackles in my ear. "Eyes on."

The street goes still. The door handle jitters. Time stops.

A figure steps into the doorway, head-to-toe black. Balaclava. Eyes sweep the room. Calm, practiced.

"@starlingcurse," his deep voice rumbles, slight Hispanic accent. "Glad to see you could make it."

CHAPTER

SIXTEEN

HOLDEN

S ix foot three or four with dead black eyes and a muscular build. Voice deep, sharp. Athletic for a tech nerd. Too big, too light on his feet for an incel.

Shaved head under the mask at his neck. Hands smooth, skin tanned. No freckles or wrinkles. No wrinkles but every inch of skin tattooed. Prison. Cartel. A thousand counts of sin written on flesh.

"Brought along extras," he mutters, moving toward Sophia faster than I like.

I bristle. Step from the shadows. Jaw tight.

The man pauses, eyeing me, guarded. Steel-toed boots, chain to his wallet. Maximum pain promise buried in his stride.

Something familiar ... haunting. Like shivers on the scalp.

Lila clears her throat behind the counter, twisting her hands.

"Thought you might not come," Sophia says. Her voice cracks, but her chin juts high.

He stops mid-step. Rocks back on his heels. "You're young for this."

"Age doesn't matter." She says it steady. Tough. I catch the tremor under it, but the kid's steelier than most grown men I knew inside.

He shrugs, playing casual. But his eyes dart too quick. Measuring me. Measuring Lila. Mapping the room.

Wolfe and the crew are in my ear. Should calm me. Doesn't. If it comes down to it, I'm the only wall between this bastard and the two people I can't lose.

"Before you move another inch," I growl, crossing the floor. "Legs apart. Arms out."

My hands sweep him for steel. Boots. Waist. Pockets. Nothing.

Ironic as hell. Spent a decade spread-eagled on cold walls, waiting for strangers to paw me down. Gloves snapping. Barked orders. Hands lingering longer than they needed to. They stripped you of more than weapons. They stripped you of dignity.

Now I'm the one checking seams. No fan of the power. Unwilling to be carried backwards by memories too visceral to ignore.

"How's it feel?" he asks, like he's in my head.

"What?" I snap.

"Doing the patting for once?"

I growl, low and dangerous. The fucker's treading on dangerous ground. "Know a lot about an 'extra.'"

He chuckles. "Always do my research."

I straighten, rubbing my stubbled cheek. My gut twists. Guy's unarmed, but his energy? Loaded.

"First piece of lost media you ever posted, @starlingcurse?" he barks at Sophia.

A test.

Her scowl flickers. "First?" She hesitates, then snaps. "The abandoned Delicioso Market in San Jose."

He nods once. "And the last?"

I move closer.

Sophia's bottom lip quivers. "'Whistleblower Stomp.'"

"Why the trembling voice?" he taunts.

Her face wavers, but she juts her chin higher. "You think I'm scared? I've been through a living hell. Victimized, brutalized. Forced into modern-day slavery by one of my mom's trusted boyfriends." Her hands tremble on the table, but her eyes don't blink. "So don't test me like I'm weak."

Good girl. Brave as hell, even shaking. I file that away.

Her eyes narrow. "How'd you get the footage?"

"I was there. Eyewitness."

Her whole body stiffens. "Then why didn't you help him?"

He chuckles, low. "I'm here to expose Moreau. Not take a bullet."

Sophia shoots me a look. She doesn't buy it. Neither do I.

Something's off. I can't pin it. "For a guy gunning for Moreau, you don't sound scared."

"Could say the same for somebody already on his list," he mutters.

I bare my teeth. Step closer. "What's that mean?"

He tilts his head toward Sophia. "Your folks always this uptight?"

"They're family," she spits back, voice steady. "They've got my six."

"You sure about that?"

She nods emphatically.

His gaze drifts to Lila. "Like your second mom. Up at

461

three a.m., making you fancy drinks." His eyes flick to the mug on the counter. "Weird."

He looks at my girl again, and I'll put him through the window. Or his teeth down his goddamned throat ...

A flicker of realization.

I pause, shifting my weight. It hits me like a gut punch. He's not talking to us. He's feeding cues. Marking who's where.

"Not weird," I bark into the mic. "Haywire."

Sophia gasps. Lila stiffens.

Static rips the wire. Wolfe's voice skitters, gone. Comms jammed. Fuck.

My eyes go to Lila. Confusion etches her face. Realization, cold and hard in her eyes.

The guy keeps closing the gap on Sophia. Always closer.

"Want more lost media? Interviews, b-roll, stuff that'll bury Moreau and make you legendary?"

"Hold it," I snap, paranoia spiking. He didn't come alone. This is cover.

Sophia bites her lip, then blurts, "Sure. What's the catch?"

I plant myself between them. Ready to snap this motherfucker in two.

"Ditch the crew. Come with me," he says, voice tight.

Her brows pinch. "No way."

"Now, before it's too late."

I bare my teeth. "It already is too late. Back the fuck up."

Light slices the boards. Headlights crawling slow across Main. My breath locks.

I track every angle in the room—where Lila stands behind the counter, Sophia frozen at the table. Who I can shield first. How many I can drop before someone gets through. That one second of math heavier than the gun

Wolfe offered earlier, and I refused. Couldn't risk parole. Regret now ices my veins.

Then, the beams cut out, and the silence is worse than the light.

The informant smirks. Glances over his shoulder. "Right on time."

"It's an ambush!" I roar. "Down!"

The door slams wide. Boots flood in.

Pop. Pop. Pop.

Gunfire rips the night.

I hit the tile, cheek pressed to the cold floor, searching for possible weapons. Broom handle, glasses I can break. May not have a gun but still know how to destroy flesh.

Sparks crack off the walls. Bullets snapping wood and glass.

Sophia's under the table. Eyes wide, cheeks wet, hands clamped over her ears.

I belly-crawl toward her. Gut in knots.

The place swarms. Front and back. Rangers. Cowboys. Shepherds. Ink-faced killers. Clean-cut mercs.

And the man in black, cool as stone, pulling the strings.

Professional. Patient. Deadly calm.

My trigger finger itches. Got to make do without.

My pulse is a war drum. Bones and brawn ready to protect. Touch my girls, and I'll bury you first.

I've been in cages. I've stared down lifers with shanks.

But this? This is different.

Because this time it's not me on the line.

It's them. My girls.

And I'll paint this fucking café red before I let anyone touch them.

SEVENTEEN

DELILAH

Gunshot vibrations rattle through me. My mind flutters. Everything unfamiliar in the din. Lying flat, thoughtless, caught in a throat-grip of panic.

Hands trembling, livewire core, breath stuttering. Can't move. Can't breathe. Can't think.

Coffee grounds explode like ash—my life demolished in a heartbeat. Faster than I can recover … or form a plan.

Eyes scrutinize the haze. Sophia alone crouched beneath a table. My heart breaks. She was mine to protect. We promised her uncle and aunt.

I gasp. Air finally filling my lungs. Bullets whiz. Ding. Hitting walls. Ding. Splitting bright canvases in two. Ding. A silver hammer to my world.

This was my safe place, my life's work. Now, it's a war zone. A kill box.

A form flickers in the shadows. Large, stealthy, shielding Sophia with his body, moving like a predator.

But not to hunt. Not to kill. To save a life.

Holden and Sophia. My eyes water, body quakes. The

young girl's teenage recklessness surpasses my own. She's a hero ... if she survives.

Survival. The word bites on my tongue.

Holden and Sophia hit cover behind the big trash can, where customers once grabbed napkins.

Everything changed in a heartbeat. In the flash of gunpowder. A nightmare I need to wake up from.

Heat and sin. Flesh tangled in sheets. The dream that kept me moving for ten years.

Two realities collide, and I simmer in the devastation. Still gasping for breath. Still unable to move.

But Holden is the force of nature I saw step off the bus two days ago. No longer caged. Reigning down retribution with his fisted hands. His body taut and deadly. His gaze simmering and unbroken.

For vengeance? For satisfaction?

For one fraught moment, his eyes find me. No, for love.

He's brutal, terrifying, and efficient. Pride and fear coil in my chest. Desire tangles, dark and dangerous. Prison didn't break him. It sharpened him ... *for this moment.*

Zing. A stray bullet lodges in the wood next to me. Splinters flying. Heat on my cheek.

His eyes find me again. The look raw, wordless. *Don't die. Don't leave me.*

He fights towards me, wading through men. Tattooed and rough, others in business attire. Still others buttoned up like the Amish—from the dwindling ranks of The House of the Seven Prophets.

He can't reach me. Putting too much on the line in the process. I must move. Must fight to survive the way my man is. For me. For us. For the future taken before it ever started.

My hands come up beside me, feeling the contrast. Cold

floor, warm blood on my cheek. Scrambling to my knees, I move low to the ground, pushing towards the back of the café.

Boots hammer. Sharp commands with military precision fill the air. The Rangers. Finally.

Wide-eyed stares, tattooed skin seething, men fleeing in black and white suits. They never expected us to fight back. Tables turned. Men with guns, springing, pale-faced toward the back entrance.

Gunfire erupts from the back door. Frantic screams. Moreau's men are pinned inside. Searching, straining for another way out. Clawing at the boarded windows, slipping between the cracks and broken glass. Like rats finding their tunnels when light is shed on their dark nests.

I catch a black shape—the informant—moving slow, too calm to be accidental. This was planned. At least parts of it were.

It hits me in a nauseating wave. Shoot out at my café. Holden's battered fists. Alliances made in the dark between cowboys and shepherds. Sheriff's office and black ops.

It could all be spun ... spun into a firestorm that could devour Hollister whole. Spit it back out like ash.

All lost. All gone. The taste as bitter as the metallic warmth on my lips.

My body shudders. The café falls into a heavy, eerie silence — devastation draped across everything.

Smoke, glass destruction. The Human Being unrecognizable. Like my new life. In the wake of tragedy... more following so fast on its heels, I reel.

Would I do this all again for one man? Torch my whole world in a blaze of pain and heartache?

My gaze narrows, dragging over the scene, stomach

knotting, mind unwinding until I find Sophia and Holden. Still moving. Still safe.

I choke, emotion breaking over me like violence.

I crawl to them, fingers clawing the ground, unable to rise. Knees lock mid-shiver. In the center of the café, we unite. Sophia grips me fiercely, face pale, body shivering.

I can't make my arms work. All strength gone. A broken reed in a tornado.

Holden's at my side, face still seething with murderous rage. His eyes flash to my cheek. His hand comes up, fingertips brushing over blood.

His exhale is brutality. Eyes wild as a bull before the rodeo chute opens. Face twisting. "Lila, are you okay?" He says it like he breathes, gasping, shivering.

"Just ..." My voice falls like shattered glass in the space. No strength or breath behind it. I swallow hard, nodding. Trying to make him understand with my words, with my eyes that I'm okay. "Fine," I gasp.

But it's a lie. Everything about this is a lie. Surrounded by the shattered husk of my existence. Hollowed out to my very essence and the only thing that matters ...

Holden and Sophia.

Despite everything. Despite the risk and the consequences. My sun and moon. *All isn't lost.*

But everything else is ephemeral ... flammable. Maybe everything that needed to go to reach this point.

The muscle in Holden's jaw tenses, eyes still scanning the room. Body still taut for action. Brutal, without hesitation. Ready to stand, ready to die for what he protects.

I strain, using all my strength to place a hand over his. Grounding. Drawing him back.

His eyes smolder, red-rimmed.

All is not lost. I see it in his eyes. Feel it in how Sophia clutches me. But ...

We pull into the center. My hands shaking, Sophia clinging like she thinks I'll vanish. Blood drips onto her spotless, white BTS hoodie. More dries tight on my cheek.

She whimpers, breathing shallow.

"You're safe," I whisper, because words are everything I have. "I've got you."

Holden's jaw clenches, muscles wired. He touches my cheek, fingertips cold. His voice is a ragged thing. "Your cheek."

"Fine," I lie, and the lie tastes like cinder. We survive the night. But how long? The question opens a wound inside me.

CHAPTER
EIGHTEEN
HOLDEN

Cowboys. Shepherds. Rangers. They surround Lila and Sophia like mastiffs.

Protected. Safe. But I'm not done.

I squeeze Lila's hand too tight. Force a smile. "One more score. Stay here."

Wolfe's eyes catch mine. "The informant."

I nod. We head for the hallway to the alley. Lila's and my first post-prison kiss hangs suspended. An echo.

Muted gunfire rattles the door. Fight not finished.

Wolfe barks into the walkie. Waits. Crackling. Finally, "all clear."

We push through, ready to finish this.

Cold grease in the air. Dumpster rot. My breath a white knife in the dark.

The informant fills the alley. Muscles taut. Eyes feral. A cornered rattlesnake.

He spins at our footsteps. Snarl in his throat. "I go down. You go down, *Boone.*"

Lopez. The voice, the name gut me. Sick ache in my belly. Flashback in my veins. The shiv glinting in the yard.

Cold steel biting. Crowd roaring behind fences. The hollow thud of blade in flesh. The sadistic laugh.

He rips off the mask. The red sun tattoo coils alive, skull grinning. "Not about Moreau anymore. About you and me."

My fists clench. Neck cracks. No more cages.

Don't need words. Crave violence.

"First whiff of your blood in the yard got me. Addicted. Need to drain you this time," he taunts.

His movements are jerky. Like a livewire. Eyes blazing, teeth bared.

Speaking too much. Moving too fast. Mine to take down.

A growl builds in my chest. Raw, feral. The only sound he'll get from me.

Pacing, we circle each other.

Two bulls in a pit.

Sizing each other up. Looking for weakness. Any sign of vulnerability, impatience.

Teeth on edge. Tense as fuck. Breaths held.

Then, the flare of a nostril. A glint in his eyes. The rippling of muscle, like a loaded weapon.

Won't make the same mistake with him twice.

We charge. Flesh jarring flesh.

Rangers twitch for their weapons, but Wolfe lifts a hand. His face stone. This fight is mine.

Knuckles split flesh. His fist smashes my jaw. I stagger back, black fuzz crowding the edges of my sight. Almost drop. Almost.

No fucking way.

I lunge. Shoulder in his gut. Slam him into brick. Pain jolts down my spine, but rage keeps me upright.

He claws for his boot—steel flashes. I rip the blade free, send it skittering.

He yanks a gun; I torque his wrist till the joint pops, strip it, sling it across the concrete.

A Ranger scoops it. Out of play.

His eyes round. Fierce but with an edge of fear. The tattoo frowns. Less sure with the playing field evened.

No gun, no knife. Only fists. Only hate.

Gun in my hand means parole. Chains. Back inside.

So I fight bare. Bone on bone.

We trade blows. My ribs scream. His nose cracks under my swing. We're slipping in blood now, boots sliding. A prison-yard brawl without the bars.

His forearm clamps my throat. Headlock crushing. Breath strangled. I hear Lila's cry from the doorway. Sophia's whimper.

Not again. No more tears for my girl ...

I can't let them watch me fall.

Something tears loose inside me. White-hot. Survival. Not for me—for them.

I rip free. My hand locks on his throat. Slam him backward into the wall. The bricks tremble. His eyes go wide, panicked.

My fists rain down. Once. Twice. Over and over. Bone shatters. Skin splits.

No glory. No grace. Just demolition.

He claws at my face, but I don't stop. Not until his body slackens. The alley echoes with Wolfe's shout.

"Fuck!"

I freeze, chest heaving. Blood dripping from my fingers. The informant sprawls. Body sliding to the ground. Still.

Silence grips the atmosphere. All eyes on the body and movement that never comes.

Sheriff Christian steps up, voice flat. "Clean. Self-defense." His eyes sweep the witnesses. "That's the record."

"Old grudge," I add, doubling over and gripping my knees. Still heavy panting. "His, not mine. Came at me before." My hand goes to the scar on my torso. Searing pain remembered.

Wolfe's face is granite. Eyes narrow. "You heard the sheriff. You heard Holden." He eyes the gathered crew. Glare decisive. One account for all. "Armed, premeditated attack."

Cowboy hats tip. Shepherds nod. Rangers stand lock-step, faces grim, blank.

I straighten, staggering back, chest caving. Can't look at Lila. Hands red. Knuckles wrecked. A beast. A tyrant. She saw it.

Have I lost her?

Then, her cry—sharp, breaking me open—no. She rushes me. Arms tight around my neck. Her body pressed desperately against mine.

"You're alive," she gasps, clutching my face, gaze fierce. She can read the question in my eyes. The fear. The desperation.

I break. Press my forehead to hers. "I'm sorry." The words scrape like gravel. Never wanted her to witness this inky black. The darkness. The man prison ground me into.

Her fragranced body. Her soft flesh. Everything about her is too good for me. My grip loosens, feeling her slip through my fingers.

Christian's voice cuts in, grim. "Simple case of self-defense. Too many witnesses to bury it. He won't see a cell for this."

Maybe not. But I saw her face. Lila's eyes when I fought like an animal.

She knows what prison made me.

How can she love that?

"Not if Moreau has his way." I growl.

Lila stiffens in my arms.

Wolfe shrugs. "Wish this dumb fuck was alive," he says, circling the body. "Would've loved a chance to make him talk. Find out what he knows. How it all connects."

A whimper snaps the silence. Sophia edges forward, chin quivering.

"Miss Dee," she whispers. "Look."

Her hand points past me, to the body. The tattoo, glistening under blood.

"His neck ... it's not just ink."

Wolfe scowls. "What are you talking about?"

Sophia pulls out her phone, hands shaking. Snaps a picture. Pinches the image wide.

"It's a QR. See the alignment squares? Numbers in the rays. It'll scan."

I grimace, disbelieving.

Lila's face is a puzzle.

Rock, my tattoo artist brother, steps forward. His face betrays no skepticism. Only curiosity. He squats down, eyes narrowing at the swirls of red sun and skull.

A low, dark laugh follows. "Kid's right. Motherfucker tattooed a lock on his neck."

The alley stills. My pulse thunders.

Sophia looks up, vindication sparking through fear. "We can crack it. Whatever he was hiding ... it's still here. On him."

Lila pulls away. Steps forward and yanks the teen back, shielding her face against her chest. "No more looking. No more photos." Her voice is steel.

Sophia muffles against her. "But this could be the evidence."

Wolfe grimaces. "We'll let Ji and Paige run it. Hope we get lucky."

"QR and other encryption are getting more common in the tattoo world," Rock weighs in. "Kid's definitely onto something."

The corners of Sophia's mouth turn up. But the smile is hollow, tattered. She still doesn't get it. Not fully. The gravity, the situation. The death.

Too many hours spent peering at screens. Too many graphic videos and movies. She stares like it's still on a screen. Pixels, not blood.

"You got a future forensics tech here," Rock adds. "Steel stomach. No fear."

"Been through a lot," Sophia sighs. "Not my first dead body."

Rock's brow raises.

But Lila pulls her closer, smothering her curiosity and my brother's question.

"Clean up time," Wolfe barks. "Café and apartment secured. Bodies gathered and removed. No trace."

The Rangers scramble. Practiced efficiency. My gut tightens, first time seeing black ops at work.

Cowboys and shepherds hesitate. Shifting weight. Wolfe scowls, annoyed to direct. Nonetheless, the orders start.

Clear, precise. No detail overlooked.

His cold, military calculation exists in stark contrast to my brutality. Primal, animalistic, messy. Thankfully, final.

NINETEEN

DELILAH

The safehouse hums electric. Wolfe's team, Holden's brothers, Sophia, and I cluster around the glowing ice-blue screens.

Holden sits apart, face shadowed, head in his hands. Not brooding ... worse. A man simmering, bracing for chains. A man who knows the walls could slam shut again.

He hasn't said a word since the alley. Not about the fight. Not about the blood still drying on his knuckles.

I want to touch him, force him to look at me. But his silence feels like a cell door clanging shut. If I press, I might lose him entirely.

I ache for him. But a thrill buzzes in me, too. If Sophia and Rock are right, we might finally be holding the last piece.

The photo Sophia snapped of the informant's neck is now one of many from every angle. And the body's in the nearby compound morgue for safekeeping.

Wolfe and his team are top-notch professionals. No end to their expertise. Or their resources. But what they do with all of it? I've already seen more than I ever needed to.

Paige uploads it. Ji works in lockstep, decoding the QR swirls. A flash. The scan points to a server link, then a login portal.

The air shifts. Hope flickers.

Wolfe leans forward, voice low, reverent. "This is the nail. Let's hammer it."

Ji presses enter.

A red bar slices across the screen. Ominous text blooms: DATA PURGE IN PROGRESS. 60 SECONDS.

The screens bleed red. Files vanish in a cascade. Names, numbers, gone in a blink.

Ji's voice cracks. "Oh God, it's wiping itself!"

Paige scrambles, cursing, "Kill the link. Kill it!"

Wolfe slams his fist on the table, jaw set. "We're losing it."

My stomach drops. Tears sting. Rage boils. Always this. Every time we near victory, it dissolves. Holden lifts his head, face etched with defeat. A mirror of my own despair.

The room erupts—Wolfe barking orders, Ji's voice pinched, Paige's curses sharp. Fingers blur over keyboards. We're all suffocating at once.

Then, Sophia leans forward, steady where the rest of us shake. Her voice cuts clean. "Wait ... this isn't erasing. It's overwriting. Zero packets."

Paige snaps, "English, kid!"

Sophia chuckles, steady as stone. "Fake wipe. Seen it on leak forums. If we mirror the packets, we can blow them open before overwrite."

The room stares. Even Ji's wide-eyed.

"Translate," Wolfe barks.

"She means the data's not gone ... not yet," Ji mutters, awe creeping in.

Sophia shoves in beside her, fingers flying. *Packet sniffer.*

Mirror dump to secure drive. She narrates like a mantra, hands steady.

Everything's over my head. Maybe over the head of nearly everyone in this room.

The clicking of keys fills the air. Sophia's face is all focus.

Are we asking too much of her? Again? My chest tightens. Then Ji's expression shifts, lit with revelation.

"Yes!" she gasps, staring at Sophia as if seeing her for the first time. Then she grabs another keyboard.

Rutger dives in. "Rerouting power to keep the bandwidth steady."

Wolfe and Holden exchange a glance. My bruised warrior finally engaged, eyes sparking with something like hope.

The bar jerks forward in uneven lurches: 42% ... 47% ... 55%. Each jump is agony.

Server fans scream, the pitch so high it feels like the room itself might combust.

Ji mutters code. Paige taps commands on a second terminal. Sophia bites her lip but never slows her hands.

Holden stands next to me, squeezes my hand, his voice a rasp. "Come on, kid."

95% ... 98% ...

The screens flicker. Then, freeze.

Silence echoes the halls. Everyone holds their breath.

Ji gasps, "Wait. We've got fragments."

Paige leans in, eyes darting. "Not all. But maybe enough. Encrypted ledgers, payment trails ..." Her voice hitches. "Chat logs. Videos."

Ji exhales, shaky. "Maybe even video deposits of Moreau himself."

Wolfe's roar rattles the room. "Jackpot!" He grins for the

first time in forever, a wolfish flash that cracks his granite veneer.

Sophia leaps up, busting out a little happy dance. The girl beneath the steel peeks through.

And me? I laugh and cry at once, clutching Holden while the room buzzes like we've all come back from the dead.

Wolfe's big hand slams Holden's shoulder, eyes glinting wet. "A long time coming," he mutters, swiping at his face.

Holden doesn't cheer, just exhales, long and broken, like he's been holding his breath for ten years.

Paige turns to Holden's brother, Flynn. "Counselor? Want to do the honors?"

The black cowboy lawyer doesn't just step forward. He plants both hands on the table, shoulders rigid, eyes flicking down line after line. The man who fought every appeal, every uphill battle for his brother. For once, the law is on their side, and he knows it.

His face says it all. "Good God. This ... *this* is going to keep me up all night."

Jasmine, his wife and paralegal, peers over his shoulder. Brow arched. "Are you kidding me? This case will write itself."

Sophia beams. "Just goes to show you, zeroes aren't instant death," she giggles.

Wolfe grumbles, "Nice work, Pipsqueak."

"It's Tough Stuff, now." Holden ruffles her hair, pride flickering across his hard face.

I pull her close. "*That's* what real bravery looks like."

Jermaine and Josephine slip in, faces bewildered. "We heard cheering," he says. "Good news?"

"Your niece is a genius," Bowie grins.

"And due some ice cream," Wolfe adds, softer than usual.

Their eyes shine, but then Josephine stiffens, noticing the blood and dirt smeared on Sophia's hoodie. "What happened? Are you hurt?"

Sophia shrugs, grin toothy. "Nothing. Just doing my part to get out of this endless detention."

Her uncle's voice cuts. "Wait, you promised she'd be safe. Never in the thick of it." Face a storm, eyes flicking from Wolfe to me, accusation in both directions.

Guilt sours my stomach. "I'm sorry," I murmur.

Wolfe looks equally stricken. We asked too much, though we never meant to.

Sophia butts in. "I didn't just do this because it was supposed to be safe. Or for Miss Dee. Or Holden. I did it because justice needed to be served. Because you and Auntie should feel safe in your own home—"

"Our home," Josephine corrects warmly.

Sophia bites her lip, face contorting. "Thank you, Auntie. But please don't be mad at Wolfe or Miss Dee. I'm the one who caused all the trouble. Messed around on the wrong sites. Talked to the informant. Told him too much."

Jermaine and Josphine listen, faces ragged.

"Auntie, what's your number one rule?"

The lovely black woman pauses, pressing her lips together in thought.

"That if we make a mess, we clean it up," Sophia answers. "Well, I made a royal mess. So yeah, it took royal effort to clean it up."

She frowns, then lifts her chin. "But it had to be done."

My heart swells with pride. Accountability's been our focus for months. To see it bloom in her now nearly undoes me.

Holden nods, whispering, "She owned it ... like I had to own mine." Respect softens his eyes.

The tension uncoils. Laughter breaks loose, shaky but real. Relief rushes in like clean air through open windows.

Holden finally looks at me, gaze unbroken for a long moment. His Adam's Apple bobs in his throat. Like he has something to say. Instead, he slips away from the crowd, head down and shoulders hunched.

CHAPTER
TWENTY

HOLDEN

Cheers and celebration. I can barely crack a smile.
Fists like lead. Bright lights and flashes of pain.
Dark alley, brick slick with blood.

The violence. It hollowed me out. Has me questioning if I should be free.

Lopez deserved it. He touched my woman. Came for the kid.

A beatdown in the alley … too fucking good for him. But what does that make me?

A brute, busting heads, burying knuckles fist-deep.

Maybe prison changed me too much.

The room feels tight. Suffocating. Too much noise. Too many emotions.

Have to escape … clear my fucking mind. Shoulders drooped, I head for the stairwell.

Wolfe intercepts, hand on my shoulder. "This is the breakthrough we've been waiting for—"

"Believe it when I see it."

"It's enough to burn Moreau," he says.

God, I hope so.

The laughter. The lightheartedness. All too much.

I grumble, "Thanks, bro. For everything."

I escape into shadows. A part of me still longs for the four walls of my cell.

Never thought my prison would become my comfort. But it's everything I need.

Predictability. Schedule. Quiet.

Devil you know's better than the devil you don't. Couldn't feel more true.

Upstairs, I flip on the bathroom light like I'm turning up the sun. Tile so white it hurts. Mirror. Shower. Everything basic. More prison than refuge, but it's the only place I can breathe.

My hands are raw. My knuckles drum against the sink under hot water. Lip split. Eye swollen. The reflection is everything I can't walk away from: a man who knows how to break things and people.

I grimace, running water over busted knuckles. Splashing my face. I look like what I am. A no-good criminal.

Steam coils in the shower. I try to clear my mind. Pull myself the fuck together.

Lila's face. The horror and strain. She saw me. Guilt pounds me into the ground.

I scrub the memories. Run soapy fingers through my hair. Let the heat waterfall over strained muscles.

I wrap a white towel around my waist. Steam snaking out with me when I open the door to the bedroom.

Lila sits on the mattress. Same space where we tangled last night. Now, oceans apart. Again.

She washed her face after we came back. Her cheek still carries ugly welts where wood splintered.

Her eyes find me when I say, "Come on."

She follows me into the bathroom. Lets me fuss. Doesn't make it a thing. I care for her like I can fix the world. A warm cloth and a steady hand. I pluck splinters from her skin. Emblazon her little winces, slight hints of pain on my soul ... like vengeance.

I'd kill Lopez again. For hurting my girl.

Sandy freckles over ivory flesh. Round cheeks flushed. Carved lips, full and luscious ... my fucking obsession. And yet, I don't know what to say. Don't know how to cross the gulf mere inches between us.

"You touch me like I'm porcelain," she says. "Like I'll break."

"In the alley, you saw what these hands can do."

"I saw them save me," she answers. Quiet. Steady. "Save our future, too."

The room tightens. Everything I want. Everything I fear sits between us.

"Maybe I don't deserve this," I say, and the words are thinner than a blade.

"Don't say that," she whispers. Her hand finds my face. Cold. Real. Insistent.

I pull away, leaving the bathroom before she can respond, pacing in the bedroom. Body taut and agitated. Fears roiling. Desire smoldering. All about to break.

Her footsteps follow, eyes searching mine.

"Can't say I love you and do this to you," I murmur, heart dying. Words hollow. Pierced with pain.

"Do what?"

"Be the violence in your world."

"You can't say you love me and leave me," she gasps, voice trembling.

Her deepest fear. Abandonment. Thanks to her bastard father.

"Not leaving to leave. Leaving because I'm not good enough. Because maybe those punches I landed earlier will be the nails in my coffin." The words hang with dread. That I'll lose her. That I'll go back to prison. That fate fucking hates me. "Can't do that to you again."

"You speak like you already know the outcome. Like you're trying to put distance—"

"Trying to be realistic."

"Assuming the worst—"

"What else can we assume?" I ask, grief simmering. "It's always the same."

"You going away won't make anything easier."

"You so sure?" I ask. "Looks like your life is wreckage since my return."

"Not because of you."

"Because of what then? I'll go because I love you."

"Then, I'll hate you," she hisses, eyes darkening.

Her words slap me ... hard.

"Hate me?"

"Because I hate everything and everyone who tries to take you from me. This would be no different. And for what?"

"Chance at a normal, safe, peaceful life," I counter, voice raw. Feeling the weight of all I can't give her.

She steps closer, daring me. "I don't want safe. I want *real*. I want you."

Silence stretches, taut as barbed wire. My pulse hammers. Her lips part ... not in fear, but in challenge.

Something snaps.

I seize her face, mouths colliding. Brutal, consuming, like I'm starving. Like she's the only thing that will keep me alive. She moans into me. Hands clutch my shoulders, nails drag down my back. Begging me to take her.

Passion grips me. Primal, base. Like rutting animals. The pulse of life. I push her back until her spine hits the wall with a thud. The sound shudders through me. I freeze, every fear crashing down. That I've hurt her. Cracked her fragile exterior.

But she's no glass doll. Her arms grip my neck fiercely, locking her soft tits against my firm chest. My pecs brush her nipples. She whimpers, and I swallow the sound. Animalistic, driven, ready to shake the rafters.

My hands roam—hips, waist, throat. Fingers curl around her neck, thumb stroking over soft flesh. Eyes snapping to the marks I've left. Fingers gripping enough to possess, a necklace made of pure need.

Her breath hitches. Her eyes sear.

"Mine," I rasp against her lips.

She gasps, defiant and eager all at once. "Then, prove it."

That undoes me.

Mouths crash. Teeth clang. Lips collide, bleed. She yanks my hair, nails digging into my back. Counters, dark and dangerous, "All yours." Her hand snags my towel. It falls away.

I growl, swallowing her air. Breathing her in like it's the only oxygen left. I shove her skirt up, panties aside, and drive into her. We're nothing but collision. Wildfire.

"Ten years," I choke between kisses. "Ten fucking years robbed from us. "

"Now," she gasps, lips swollen, my blood on her mouth. "You have me."

Her words detonate inside me. I slam into her, frantic, half-mad to prove it. Her head knocks back against the wall, throat bared, and I mark her there. Teeth scraping, sucking hard enough to brand her.

She arches, crying out as I drive deeper, sliding rough and merciless. She clutches me tighter, fluttering and spasming, no fragile girl—my fierce, unbreakable woman.

She's smooth silk. So fucking wet. I drip with her arousal. She grips my neck, hips grinding me deeper.

When she fractures around me, shuddering, I go with her. Hard. Violent. Endless. I spill into her raw, and unrelenting until we're both wrecked, locked together against the wall.

My forehead drops to hers, sweat dripping. Her eyes are heavy, sated, burning with love. She grabs my hand from her throat, presses it over her pounding heart.

"Feel that? It's yours. Always."

"Always." A vow of flesh, blood, and bone.

My kisses slow, but they sink deeper. No longer just hunger but an oath.

"I can't lose you, Lila. Not now. Not ever. I'm too fucking selfish to let go."

Her hands cradle my face. Eyes fierce and tender. "Then don't. Stay. Build something with me. Burn the rest, but keep this."

My throat tightens, but I nod. Her lips brush mine again. Not frantic this time, but sealing a promise.

I shuffle toward the bed, and we collapse. Bodies tangled, breaths slowing together.

I stroke her face. Wipe my blood from her mouth. Caress her cheek like treasure. "If Moreau walks, I'll burn the world down myself."

She lifts her head, fierce as a thing reborn. "Then, let him come."

Such bravery. Words are good for that. But action. Action comes with consequences.

For the first time since before, I give in. Lay out my

cards. "I'm scared, Lila. Can't do this without you. Afraid I can't give you what you need."

"Everything I need is here," she whispers, feathering my face in slow, sensual kisses. "This moment. I refuse to think beyond *this* ..."

I nod.

Her eyes still search my face. "But I need you to say it, Holden. I have to hear the words."

"Say what?" I ask, voice raw.

"That you'll stay with me always. No matter what life throws at us."

"I'll stay." Comes out like resignation. But it's really fear. Fear I can't keep the promise, that I'll return to chains.

She cups my cheeks. Eyes flashing fierce. "I can't do this if you don't mean it. Or I'll live a whole life waiting for you to go. Waiting for that one thing that'll make you break ... that'll break us ... make you walk away." Her bottom lip trembles, a hidden undercurrent.

Her words hit me like a gut punch. Why she never told me about the baby. The miscarriage. Always. Since our first life together. She's expected me to go.

I pull her close. Breathe her in. Say the words with every part of me. To the bottom of my soul. "I'll never leave you. No matter what. Not now. Not ten years from now. Not twenty. You've got me till I'm cold in the ground."

Her inhale shudders. Eyes gleam. All she's ever needed. Me. Couldn't see it before.

"Forever," I swear, pressing her hard against me. "Mine and yours. Till my last breath."

"And beyond," she adds.

I grin. Can't help it. Kiss the tip of her nose.

Hippie girl.

Never really changed. Believing in things I'll never get.

The unseen, the felt-in-your-bones shit. "If there's a way," I grumble. "I'll find it. Be together then, too."

Now, she's happy. Now she snuggles tight under my chin. Face relaxing. Body melting. Nodding towards sleep.

My life. My breath. My air.

Could never leave her ... and survive. Despite the tough talk. The shields. She's always known this, too. But the words cement it.

We cling to each other. In and out of sleep. Bruised, fearful, unbreakable.

TWENTY-ONE

Calm. Determination. The safehouse feels different now. Not chaos or panic, but a mounting sense of accomplishment. Of building. Finding the right blocks, locking them in place, constructing Holden's defense, and our future.

All thanks to the QR code and the pieces of the puzzle it unlocked. Sophia is all grit and determination, her eyes alight with a new fire that goes beyond teen crushes and school drama. A lawyer or investigator in the making. A force to be reckoned with.

But it's so much more than that. As Wolfe provides a hushed update, as my eyes scan screens, hearing and seeing things I don't fully understand, one thing is clear. Moreau won't survive this.

His picture flashes across a web server. Language deriding, accusing. Hate spewing from comments. Legal figures, allies, friends, shrinking away. A man unseated, unmasked ... facing the world's ridicule.

Flynn and Jasmine sit together, eyes transfixed. Heads

nodding, smiles breaking out. Whispering and pointing to the screens as it all comes together.

Flynn's low voice cuts through. "Payment trails, offshore accounts, recordings. Not just compelling ... the shovel to bury him."

Wolfe's face is grim, more excitement peeking out with each revelation. "After all these years, he's cornered."

"And so is Gregory," Jasmine adds, excitement tinging her voice.

Gregory—the son Holden fought outside the bar so many years ago—was Moreau's fixer, on-the-ground muscle all along. The man whose death chained Holden to prison.

"Tell me more," I say, stepping closer.

"Like the informant said. Gregory handled the cartels and church associates. The dirty work. Part of that involved recruiting young men to deal in drugs and flesh. Axel was one of the easy marks, a good way to get to other brothers, to bring Rough & Ready Ranch to its knees. Destroy Wyatt's mission, even steal his land."

I knit my brows, trying to take it all in. "But I don't get it ..."

Jasmine shrugs. "Trouble with Axel, Rock, Maksim, other brothers following behind. Holden, too. Moreau underestimated Wyatt's impact on the boys. He thought he could drag them, like a ready-made squad of goons, into his dealings. Use them, trusted members of the community, to bring Hollister under his thumb. Blackmail them if they got out of line."

"Holden's sacrifice stopped all of that."

A shiver runs through me. Holden stiffens next to me, fingers squeezing mine like a lifeline.

To believe something more came from this. That his sacrifice wasn't in vain.

He needs this. I need it, too.

Flynn adds in, "I've been reading through recent texts with associates. Moreau never really gave up on the plan. He was looking into other ways to take down Rough & Ready, Amestoy Ranch, wipe Hollister off the map."

"Never." Holden growls.

"Never because of you," Flynn says, eyeing his brother proudly. "Now, with all Wolfe and the crew have done, Ji's work to expose the senator, he had a real ax to grind, his sights set on ending this place. Our way of life. Silencing you and Dee through Sophia, an unwitting pawn. A hostage who would lead you right to him. They underestimated her. Underestimated all of us. And when you took down Lopez," Flynn says, leveling his gaze on Holden. "It wasn't just revenge. It set off shockwaves in the underground. They lost an irreplaceable man ... and the killswitch burned into his skin. Now the cartels are turning coat on Moreau."

"And Sophia, everyone in this room, the Amestoys. Joint effort," Holden mutters.

"Maybe a joint effort. But not a joint sacrifice," Flynn urges.

Holden's eyes redden. He looks away. But not from me. Letting me feel his emotion, share in his grief and joy. This isn't just about bringing down a villain. It's about raising a hero.

He straightens, spine steel, chest broad and puffed out. Holding himself like the man he is, not the shadow they tried to make him.

Axel's face is torn. Mixed grief, shame, and admiration. He steps forward, clamping a hand gently on Holden's shoulder.

"Saved more than me, bro. You saved Wyatt's dream. The ranch. Our family. Maybe the whole town."

"Look at this!" Paige's voice cuts through. She projects a live feed on the screen. All eyes dart to it. News stations buzz with latest updates:

MOREAU WHISTLEBLOWERS EMERGE

EVIDENCE MOUNTING AGAINST CORRUPT SENATOR

HOLDEN BOONE SURVIVES ATTACK: WHAT WE KNOW SO FAR

LEADER OF SOL ROJO CARTEL DEAD, NOT MOURNED

I scan articles, words jumping out. *Sealed indictments. Cartel fractures. Domino effect.*

Holden pulls me close. He murmurs into my hair, "Not vengeance—justice, finally." The warmth in his voice is one I haven't heard since he came home. Hope, like something fragile and real, settles between us.

"You know what's next," Wolfe leads, eyeing Holden.

"What?"

"Perp walk in orange ..."

"And the snap of latex gloves," Holden says grimly.

Once a statement like that made me wince ... no matter the subject. Now it feels like justice, vindication. The closing of bars, not on the innocent, wrongly accused, but on the source of the evil.

Wolfe laughs. "Everyone's coming out of the wood-work. All of his associates, scrambling to survive the political fallout."

Flynn seconds, "All throwing him under the bus, trying to create political distance. They want him gone and forgotten."

"Still," Holden murmurs, voice simmering. "Even at its worst, he'll end up in white-collar prison. With all the perks. Spa day for rich criminals."

Flynn shakes his head, eyes steely. "Not sure I'd place my bet there. He's made enemies in high places. Whipped up too much public scrutiny to go down easy. Public won't sit well, knowing a human trafficker, one dealing in kids, gets off easy."

"Would love to see him in gen pop," Holden admits with a dark chuckle. "Wouldn't last long."

"You may get your wish," Ji chimes in. The first real hope I've heard in her voice in a long time.

"And we'll do everything in our power to make that happen," Jasmine says, her slight Hispanic accent emphasizing the passion of her words.

"What do you need from me?" Holden asks.

"Already got it. You made the ultimate sacrifice. Dee and Sophia, too," Wolfe says. "But I would like to talk later about a potential position for you. Here, working with the team."

He shrugs behind me. "More interested in cooking for Jerry or helping Zane on the ranch."

Wolfe's jaw tightens. "Thought you might say that. But my crew comes with perks: protection, resources ... Especially for someone with your fists."

A chill trickles down my spine. I know Wolfe means well, but iron strings always come attached. I don't want Holden pulled back into danger. He glances at me, as if asking permission—or warning.

"Got to discuss with the missus," he murmurs against my cheek. "Now, if you'll excuse us."

Holden pulls me down the hallway, leading upstairs to our bedroom.

"Not sure what to think, how to process everything," he says on the other side of the door. His shields are down. No longer trying to be stoic for me. Finally, sharing his heart again, his feelings, like we used to do.

"It's a lot to take in. Going from villain to hero," I answer, lips feathering over his face. I feel his body relax against my mouth. Tension fading with my touch.

"You know," he whispers darkly. "We keep having unprotected sex, you'll be a mama soon."

"Hope I already am," I confess, pressing his big palm to my belly.

"And me a daddy." Wonder tinges his voice, tears fill his eyes. "That'll tie us together forever. Something no one can take away."

"*Someone* who'll symbolize who we are. Who we were always meant to be *together* ..."

"Family."

"Worth sacrificing for. Worth dying for," I say, like a promise.

"Never leaving. Even when shit gets painful, beyond bearing," he murmurs, pulling me down onto the bed with him.

"I only got through the hell of prison because you refused to let go, Lila. Even when I begged you. Even when I tried to do it for you. Never thanked you for that the way I should. Still can't find the words. In my letters, when I called you my lifeline. It was literal. I would have died without you ... without your love."

"You don't need words," I say. "Touch is enough. It tells me everything."

His hand is gentle as it finds the buttons of my blouse, undoing them one by one as his mouth drops to my neck. Kissing, licking, claiming. But gently this time, like he's worshiping me.

My hands slide across his hard, muscular back. Feeling ridges and lines, flesh testimony of what he's endured. What he may never tell me about with words, but that I can feel and understand with my fingertips.

Each breath, each caress is an act of veneration. Breath rising with heat. Yet, stumbling over nothing. Not buttons on my shirt, not panties pushed to the side. A slow unwrapping, sensual meditation.

When he slides into me, face-to-face, hearts beating in sync, our souls meet in our gaze. Weighted, profound, a coming together ... despite everything.

His thrusts are tide and I the shore—pulling, yielding, locking him into place ... inside my heart.

I arch into him, desire prickling my skin, sheets tangled as he takes me to the edge. Again and again. Relentless, slow. A banquet after the firestorm pressed against the wall. I need both from him. The flames and slow swell, awakening to him with every part of my being.

His bruises line my hips, his love bites burgeoning on my neck. I feel my angry welts and claw marks on his back. A violent coming back together. Then, a soft afterglow. Where babies are made and futures bound. More real than vows beneath an arch. Though that will come, too. All of it, everything promised in his gentle caresses.

I bite his neck, scream into his flesh when I topple. Floating, falling, opening to him in every way. He follows behind as he's always done, waiting for me. That one breath of self-control before unraveling.

His love pools inside me. Our sweat seals the union. He presses his forehead to mine, tasting the quiet.

"Whatever comes tomorrow, tonight we're free," I whisper.

He breathes back, warm and steady. "Bound together—beyond time, beyond space."

I press my palm to his cheek and feel the promise there: flesh, blood, and an imperfect, sacred home we'll always return to.

EPILOGUE

DELILAH

SIX MONTHS LATER

Verdant pastures stretch off into the distance. Forests tower, indigo and purple mountains in the background. Still snow-covered, still waking from winter.

Calves with mothers. Birds singing and darting across the sky where puffy, white clouds hang soft as cotton against a periwinkle background.

Holden reaches across the console, tangling his fingers with mine, rubbing his thumb over my wedding band. Behind us in the extended cab of our truck, Sophia listens to music with her AirPods. Face relaxed, newfound confidence. No longer hiding from life. Fully embracing it and knowing, beyond knowing, that she won't settle for any less than the kind of love Holden and I have.

Someday, when her time comes.

Words break across the satellite radio, "Senator Moreau officially convicted today. Awaiting the judge's return and the prospect of multiple life sentences. No special treatment. No white-collar prison. The people demand no less. Discussion tonight of its implications on the ten o'clock news—"

Holden clicks the radio off.

I eye him. "I was listening to that."

"Sorry," he says with a lopsided grin. "But not today. He, Gregory, the cartels, none of them are allowed to bleed into this. Into *home*."

"You're right," I say, feeling the wisdom of his words. The way he never stops protecting me or our family.

"Moreau's name is ash now, blown from our lives. Can't touch us ever again." He smiles.

HOURS LATER, we sit at rows of long tables along the border between Amestoy and cowboy land. Once hotly contested. The center of unending feuds. Now, peaceful, idyllic, overlooking fields and forests stretching into eternity. Happy couples. Babies and children giggling and playing, making the celebration more than official. Making it light, happy, filled with new beginnings.

And sights I thought I'd never see. The Amestoys and Rough & Ready cowboys now breaking bread together regularly. Like real neighbors instead of hated rivals. A community pieced back together. Stronger, better than before.

Jerry Lee, Holden's longtime friend and owner of The Silver Fork, teases Wolfe, "Holden keeps making ribs like these, and I'll poach him from you."

Wolfe grumbles, "Not a chance."

The table erupts in laughter, Basque accents and cowboy drawls mingling like old friends.

Sophia's voice rises above the soft mumble. "And when are you going to offer me a job, Mr. Ormsby?" she asks, eyeing the Army Ranger. "Pretty sure I can figure out how to make office coffee ... besides cracking codes and taking down bad guys."

"First, you've got to start drinking it, Tough Stuff."

Sophia's aunt ruffles her hair, and her uncle throws a protective arm around her shoulders. "Your days of stings and decoding cyphers can wait *a little* ... until you graduate, go to college."

"But you'll always have a job with me when the time's right," Wolfe finishes with a wink.

"And what if I want to be you?" she quips, sassy smile. "Maybe I'll come for your job one day, too."

The big man and his crew laugh. "Finally, a retirement plan." He growls, squeezing his wife, Izzie's hand.

Jermaine and Josephine eye her with mixed admiration and pride. Hero in the making.

After dessert, as the crowd disperses, men play horse-shoes and petanque. Kids run around like busy bees. Women whisper about their latest romance reads and when the club will meet at my café again.

I take Holden's hand, leading him towards a tranquil cluster of aspens. White barked with black knots, splashy emerald leaves clattering together in the breeze.

"Didn't think I'd live to see peace," Holden whispers, wrapping his arms around me and nuzzling my cheek. "This feels good. Right. Worth everything."

"Our home always," I add, pressing a kiss against his stubbled jawline. "But some things change ..." Silently, I grab his hand, pressing his large, work-hardened palm to my stomach.

His breath catches in his throat, tears springing to his eyes.

"I told you when you came back. I still have every one of your letters. The passionate ones. The sad ones. The ones where you told me to let go. But my favorites are the ones about our cabin, our babies, our future together." I smile through the blur, heart spilling over with joy. "Soon, we'll bring those letters to life. We'll have more than just us."

"Thank God," he whispers like a devotion. Shielding me with his body, carving out a little space just for us and this intimate moment. "And now," he whispers, voice thick, "I'll spend the rest of my life proving those letters weren't just dreams."

My breath catches, a sob on my lips. He kisses it away.

"Never thought I'd belong outside four walls. But here ... with you ... I'm free. Building a family. More than I could've ever dreamed of."

"Forever," I whisper. I turn in his arms, staring out at the pastoral scenery, the harmonious afternoon. His hands cup my stomach, our future cradled between them.

In this moment, it all falls into place. Everything finally makes sense. The pain, the sacrifice, the loneliness. All for *this*.

Bars couldn't break us. Time couldn't erase us. And nothing will ever steal this from us again.

BONUS SCENE
HOLDEN

ONE YEAR LATER

The baby's breath comes soft and steady against my chest, warm as a coal banked for the night. His tiny fist curls into the fabric of my flannel like he's staking a claim. My son. Mine and Lila's. I'll never get over saying those words.

The cabin smells like woodsmoke and milk, like Lila's lavender lotion and the wood polish I used on the rocking chair earlier.

She's asleep upstairs, worn out but glowing in a way that makes my chest ache. She gave me a second chance at life. And this little one—our son, Laramie—made sure I'll never waste it.

A creak on the porch pulls my gaze up. The door swings open without a knock because Wyatt has never needed permission to walk into my life. He's older now, hair more silver than salt, but those blue eyes still cut right through me. He pauses in the doorway, the way he always does, like he's checking whether he belongs.

"Come in, Dad," I murmur, careful not to wake the baby.

His mouth twitches, but then he steps in, closing the cold out behind him. His boots stay on the mat like he knows Lila won't forgive him if he tracks snow into her cabin.

"Well, look at you," Wyatt says, voice rougher than gravel. "You finally figured out how to hold something gentle."

I glance down at the bundle in my arms. The kid stirs, sighs, then settles again. I rock him gently, my throat tight. "Didn't figure it out. He taught me."

Wyatt comes closer, his hand hovering like he's not sure he's allowed to touch. "May I?"

I pass the baby over, slower than I've ever done anything in my life. My palms feel empty the second Wyatt's arms take the weight, but then something else fills me. Watching the man who raised me—who saved me— cradle my son like he's the most sacred thing on earth ... it breaks me wide open.

Wyatt stares down at him, lips pressed tight. His eyes shine, though he won't let a tear fall.

"Well, I'll be darned," he whispers. "A redemption I can hold."

I clear my throat, but it doesn't help the burn. "Wanted you to be the first, besides us, to hold him."

He nods, rocking slow, just like he used to when I came to him broken and bleeding all those years ago. Only now he rocks my son, safe and new, born into a world I never thought I could give.

After a long moment, Wyatt lifts his gaze to mine. "You're a good man, Holden. Better than you believe. Don't forget it."

I swallow hard. "You made me one."

The old cowboy huffs, eyes shining again. "No, son. You did that yourself."

The fire snaps in the hearth, the baby sighs in his arms, and for the first time in my life I feel whole. Not just a man who clawed his way back from darkness—but a father, a husband, and a son who finally has a family worth every fight.

———

Love isn't done in Rough & Ready. Keep the fire burning with Catalina & Ambrose in *Bidding on the Fireman*—the first in my new Rough & Ready Firefighters series.

———

Or, if you're looking for more steamy, small-town romance box sets, start reading *Rough & Ready Country Christmas* now.

JOIN THE ENGRID EAVES COMMUNITY!

ALPHA-EMOTIONAL HEROES.

HEADSTRONG, CURVY GIRLS.

SAVAGE ROMANCE.

GIVEAWAYS. FREEBIES.

NEW RELEASES. LATEST NEWS.

Subscribe to my newsletter today to never miss out on a new steamy, small-town read.

SIGN UP FOR MY NEWSLETTER

ALSO BY ENGRID EAVES

ROUGH & READY COUNTRY

Love at First Blizzard - He's a reclusive mountain man who runs a husky rescue, but his world gets turned upside down by the curvy classical musician he saves from a freak March blizzard.

Love at First Campfire - She's a headstrong, curvy true crime reporter who's never needed anybody until a handsome search and rescue unit lead risks everything to save her.

Love at First Rescue - He's a small-town sheriff who plays by the rules until his sexy dispatcher changes up the game, initiating a rescue that sets long-time passions ablaze.

Love at Second Chance - She's the new home health nurse in Rough & Ready Country, but miles of history with the grumpy ranch foreman are in danger of reigniting, despite her best intentions.

Love at First Baby - He's a wildland firefighter who refuses to settle down for anyone until the curvy hometown sweetheart and an unexpected baby make him reconsider what and who he's living for.

Love and Forgiveness - She's a museum director trying to move on until her estranged husband's security company wins her facility's contract, resurrecting long-buried passions.

Love at First Relationship - Everything about Flynn's paralegal, Jasmine, is off-limits as his much younger, inexperienced employee. But a fake relationship proposal quickly blossoms into much more.

Love at First House - A marriage of convenience is the only way to help Turner's neighbor keep her family together. He tells himself it's a practical arrangement, but his heart has other plans.

Love at First Night - He's a helicopter pilot crushing on his best friend's little sister, Roxy. A cataclysmic night gives them a glimmer into a world of possibilities, but will love or heartbreak prevail?

Love at First Beat - Army cardiologist, Fletcher, excels at healing… But matters of the heart are another thing. Until he meets Drew, a romance writer, who specializes in happy endings.

Love at First Doubt - Kindergarten teacher, Effie, knows the town bad boy, Rock, is trouble. A tattoo artist and rockabilly musician, the cowboy's all wrong for the wholesome curvy girl. Or is he?

Love at First Wild - Ridge is a wild outdoorsman mountain man who goes viral with survival videos. Paige is a TV show producer determined to make him famous. But first, she has to tame him…

Love at First Secret - When Aspen and Axel meet on the Mountain Mates dating site, sparks flame and walls go up. Both hide secrets and lack trust, threatening to crush their blossoming feelings…

Love at First Revenge - When a paralegal and whistleblower hellbent on justice saves a rough-riding cowboy bounty hunter, worlds collide, hearts ignite, and vengeance finds a partner…

Love and Redemption - A decade apart hasn't cooled Holden's need for Delilah. She's his first love, his only, and he's back to claim her with the devotion he's carried every single day behind bars.

ROUGH & READY: COWBOYS AND MOUNTAIN MEN

Possessed by the Bounty Hunter - A six-figure bounty draws me back to my ex-fiancée and her mafia-linked Creole family. Soon, a centuries-old curse blurs the line between hunter and hunted.

Gifted to the Mountain Man - Farzad's first Christmas stateside is lonely until the woman he can't stop thinking about needs protection. As sparks fly, will his cabin and heart be big enough for two?

Mountain Man Santa - A blizzard leaves Jerry snowed in with his curvy server, Stacey. She may not be ready for commitment...or the secrets of his dark past. But naughty or nice, he won't stop until she's all his...

Hunted by the Mountain Man - Passions sizzle when an ex-military mountain man saves an innocent, curvy backpacker from unspeakable evil, in this high-stakes romantic suspense adventure!

ALPHA RIDGE CREEK MOUNTAIN MEN

Curves for the Mountain Man - Worlds collide, hearts ignite, and a rescue fraught with peril forces a wounded, ex-military, mountain man to envision a life beyond his reclusive existence...

The Mountain Man's Retribution - A nighttime escape sparks hot-blooded emotions, sizzling questions, and the drive for revenge...

Marked by the Mountain Man - A tattoo artist and mountain man's first look at his employee's younger sister becomes his last surrender ... if he can save her before time runs out.

Follow me on Amazon to explore the rest of my catalog, including cowboy and hockey romances!

ABOUT THE AUTHOR

ALPHA-EMOTIONAL HEROES.

HEADSTRONG, CURVY GIRLS.

SAVAGE ROMANCE.

Bestselling author Engrid Eaves writes steamy, fast-paced romances featuring gruff alpha male protectors and the headstrong, curvy girls they fall head over heels for.

Her heroes may have painful pasts, but they always find forever with their soulmates. Sexy, satisfying, heartfelt happily ever afters guaranteed!

If you'd like to stay in touch or get your next delicious cowboy mountain man, curvy girl romance fix (and who doesn't?), sign up for her newsletter: www.engrideaves.com.